Readers love
NICKI BENNETT AND ARIEL TACHNA

Out of Bounds

"This was such an excellent read…. Nicki Bennett and Ariel Tachna did a great job on this book."

—Gay Book Reviews

Stronghold

"In my opinion, *Stronghold* is by far the best love story in the All for Love series."

—The Novel Approach

"This is a wonderful series for people that enjoy historical romance."

—Alpha Book Club

All for One

"The story is well written with an interesting, complex plot and unique, new characters as well as five others from the first book in the series."

—Rainbow Book Reviews

By NICKI BENNETT

Always a Bridesmaid
Evan's Heaven
Flight
Home for Christmas
New Traditions

DREAMSPUN DESIRES
#10 – The Cattle Baron's Bogus Boyfriend
#58 – Bad to the Bone

With Ariel Tachna
Under the Skin

ALL FOR LOVE
Checkmate
All for One
Stronghold

HOT CARGO STORIES
Hot Cargo
Something About Harry

EXPLORING LIMITS
Exploring Limits

OUT AND ABOUT
Out of Bounds

Published by DREAMSPINNER PRESS
www.dreamspinnerpress.com

By ARIEL TACHNA

Published by DREAMSPINNER PRESS
www.dreamspinnerpress.com

EXPLORING LIMITS

NICKI BENNETT
ARIEL TACHNA

Published by

DREAMSPINNER PRESS

5032 Capital Circle SW, Suite 2, PMB# 279, Tallahassee, FL 32305-7886 USA
www.dreamspinnerpress.com

Exploring Limits
© 2019 Nicki Bennett and Ariel Tachna.

Cover Art
© 2019 Tiferet Design.
http://www.tiferetdesign.com/
Cover content is for illustrative purposes only and any person depicted on the cover is a model.

Trade Paperback ISBN: 978-1-64405-070-5
Digital ISBN: 978-1-64405-069-9
Library of Congress Control Number: 2018956390
Trade Paperback published March 2019
v. 1.0
Previously published individually as Exploring Limits, Stretching Limits, and Refining Limits by Dreamspinner Press, 2010.

Printed in the United States of America

This paper meets the requirements of
ANSI/NISO Z39.48-1992 (Permanence of Paper).

CHAPTER 1
SEDUCING JONATHAN

"THAT IS one fine hunk of man," Kit Webster commented, plopping down beside his costar, Devon Aldridge, on the grass of the *Camelot* set. "Too bad he's as straight as they come."

"Aye," Devon agreed, watching Jonathan Braedon, the American actor who played King Arthur, practicing sword moves, the heavy leather of the costume doing nothing to hide the hard planes of his body. "Though 'twould be a pure pleasure to introduce him to what he's missing."

"And I suppose you think you're the one to do it," Kit said. "You think you could convince him that he's been playing the wrong side of the field for, what, twenty years now?" Even as he scoffed, he had to admit the idea was tempting. Oh, the things he would do to Jonathan if only he were given permission!

Devon looked at Kit appraisingly. "Why not?" he drawled. Given the dearth of recent relationships Jonathan had confessed to him as they'd become friends, seducing him to the world of men might not be as difficult as it sounded. "He already likes me," he added, waggling his eyebrows. "And I can be very... persuasive."

"Hey!" Kit protested. "I saw him first. That's not fair!" Granted, he hadn't said anything about his attraction, but the moment he'd first seen Jonathan, he'd fallen in lust. In the intervening weeks, that lust had been joined by another, purer emotion as he'd discovered everything he could about the object of his fascination. Jonathan wasn't just an actor, although he was a damn fine one. He was an amateur photographer who would make a lot of professionals jealous, and an incredibly talented pianist and guitarist who wrote his own lyrics and melodies. Just yesterday, Kit had found out he also painted when he had spare time, although he hadn't seen any examples of it yet. Niall Clifton, the director of the BBC miniseries on King Arthur's court, had chosen well when he cast Jonathan as the once and future king. Despite the issue of his accent, the other actor had stepped into Arthur's shoes as if born to wear them.

"Well, what do you think would be fair?" Devon retorted. "Wrestle for him? Draw straws?" Any outcome that involved Kit being with Jonathan without him was completely unacceptable. Looking at Kit again, he was struck by a delicious idea. "We could always share him."

Share him.... That idea hadn't crossed Kit's mind. He left off staring at Jonathan long enough to look at Devon, trying to decide if his passion for the American could expand to include his fellow Englishman. He let his gaze wander over Devon's long, lean form, another picture of masculine perfection. He was pretty sure Devon and Jonathan were of an age, into their thirties but not pushing forty yet. He preferred his lovers that way, a good ten to fifteen years older than he was. All that glorious self-assurance and experience.... Every inch of Devon's body, at least the bits Kit had caught glimpses of as they changed into and out of costume in the trailer they shared, was hard muscle. A blond beard framed a square face, though Kit had seen enough publicity pictures of Devon out of character over the years to suspect the beard was an affectation for Lancelot's character. Either way, it drew attention to the line of his jaw and his high cheekbones and highlighted full lips Kit wouldn't say no to kissing. Yes, he could develop an interest in Devon too. "How do we do this?" Kit asked. "He's never shown the slightest sign of being interested in men."

Devon hid a smile at the smoldering look Kit gave him, letting his gaze return instead to Jonathan, who had stopped to lean on his sword and push the shaggy hair back from his eyes. *Oh, this will be a pleasure indeed*, he thought, already imagining removing the sweat-stained garments and running his hands over.... Reining in his thoughts with difficulty, he considered the best way to proceed.

"We're going for drinks once he's done. Why don't you join us?" Devon suggested. He was willing to play it by ear and see where the night would lead.

Kit nodded. "Where are you meeting?" If they were going to seduce Jonathan, he wanted to change clothes. He had just the outfit in mind: tight jeans, too-small T-shirt. If Jonathan was the least bit interested, it would definitely catch his eye.

"Going to tart yourself up?" Devon grinned. Kit was a bit younger than Devon's usual taste, but his slender frame and long limbs were certainly no hardship to look at, especially in the skintight and skin-baring outfits he favored when out of costume. "Nothing up to your usual standards, just our regular pub in town."

Kit scowled at Devon, both for the comment and for the boring choice of location. Then he reconsidered. The three of them snuggled into a booth.... There was potential in that situation. "Leave my clothing choices up to me," he suggested. "Shall I meet you there or at the trailer?"

Devon considered for a moment. "The trailer," he decided. "We can take one car, make it easier for all of us to wind up in the same place at the end of the evening." He winked at Kit. "And then we'll see just how... flexible... our king is."

"Shit, Devon," Kit said. "You keep it up with images like that and I'm not going to survive until the end of the evening. I'll be at the trailer in half an hour. Is that soon enough?"

"If I can convince the man of steel over there to call it a day," Devon agreed. "He'll need to shower, but that won't take him long." He clapped Kit on the shoulder, then pushed to his feet and headed over to where Jonathan showed every sign of being ready to continue for another few hours. Devon smiled to himself. He had high hopes of enjoying Jonathan's stamina in other, more pleasurable activities soon.

Kit stood as well, hurrying in the opposite direction. He would leave it to Devon to get Jonathan to the trailer and ready to go to the pub. He had his own preparations to make.

Movement in his peripheral vision made Jonathan turn in time to see Devon and Kit separating, Devon coming toward him and Kit disappearing to some unknown destination. With a sigh, Jonathan lowered the sword and waited to see what Devon had to say. As his friend walked closer, he felt an uncomfortable stirring in his lower body. *Damn,* he realized, *it's been so long, I'm even starting to find Devon attractive.* He looked up at Kit's retreating back. He wasn't even going there. Kit was too young for him. Period.

As he walked toward Jonathan, Devon watched a bead of sweat roll down the side of Jonathan's face, trickle through the scruffy beard, and continue down the tanned throat. A wave of desire rolled through him, mixed with something deeper. He'd felt an instant connection with Jonathan when they met, but until now he'd been convinced it was only friendship based on shared experiences that ranged from similar roles both on stage and in film to Jonathan's commiserating over Devon's ongoing divorce. Suddenly he was looking forward to sharing much more.

"Hey, Devon," Jonathan called in greeting. "Come to remind me of our date tonight?" As soon as the joking words were out of his mouth, he regretted them. He didn't want to put ideas in Devon's head. He was perfectly comfortable with them being friends. And the fluttering in his stomach was just something he'd eaten at lunch that hadn't agreed with him. Yes. Exactly.

"About ready to call it a day, mate?" Devon replied, clasping Jonathan's shoulder. "You've worn me out just watching you! Let's get ready to head to the pub—I convinced Percival to join us for once. Be good for him to hang with the real men for a change instead of always hanging out with the Orkney brothers."

Jonathan gulped. Drinks with Devon and Kit. Not a good idea in his current state. Oh well, nothing he could do about it now. "Sounds great," he said with forced joviality. "I'm ready to relax, that's for sure. Bert's sword exercises have about worn me out today."

"Well, get yourself cleaned up and we'll see what we can do about helping you relax," Devon promised, steering them back toward the trailer. The feel of the sweaty body next to him had already started the heat building in his groin. Waiting in the trailer while Jonathan showered, imagining the cool water flowing over his naked body, was going to make Devon horny as hell.

Jonathan let Devon guide him back to the trailer, wondering a little at Devon's sudden closeness. He wondered even more when he realized the effect it was having on him. He was going to have to get himself under control or he'd never survive an evening with both Devon and Kit, particularly if Kit was being his usual touchy-feely self.

"Kit's going to meet us back here in half an hour." Devon let his hand drop as they reached the door of the trailer. He stayed close enough to Jonathan that their bodies brushed together as they entered. With an innocent grin, he plopped onto the ragged couch and tried to will his growing arousal under control.

"I guess that means I need to shower," Jonathan said, relieved to have an excuse for a moment away from Devon's suddenly looming presence. He was tempted to use the cover of the water to jack off so he'd be rid of his nagging erection, but he wasn't sure the walls of the trailer were thick enough to block the noise, even with the water running. "I'll be back out in a few minutes."

Sharing a trailer with Jonathan meant Devon had plenty of opportunities to see the other man in various stages of dress and undress. While he'd always appreciated Jonathan's striking looks, he never thought he'd be able to appreciate them more personally—until now. Devon watched until the door to the shower closed behind Jonathan, now finding it hard to think of anything else.

In the shower, Jonathan rested his head against the cool tiles. He had no idea what had come over him today. Yes, he was horny, but that was his normal state. At home he had an impressionable young boy watching his every move. Here, when he left the set, he was a "movie star," but he refused to capitalize on that just to get laid. On set, the scarcity of women was overwhelming, leaving him with few choices there either. Maybe that was why he found himself eyeing his male costars more than usual. They were all he saw, day in and day out. This was ridiculous, though. He couldn't just go and proposition one of them. They needed to work together, for Christ's sake! He had never let himself act on an attraction to a costar. Especially when they were male.

As Devon knew it would, hearing Jonathan moving around in the shower led to a series of mental images that soon had his jeans uncomfortably tight. Closing his eyes for a moment, he stroked the growing hardness, imagining joining Jonathan in the cramped cubicle, their wet bodies sliding against each other…. He drew a deep breath and stood abruptly, pacing about as he brought himself under control. He didn't want to frighten Jonathan away, and it wouldn't be fair to Kit to start without him.

After finishing his shower, Jonathan dried off quickly and wrapped the towel around his waist, cursing inwardly at having left his clothes in the main part of the trailer. Now he had no choice but to walk back out to where Devon sat, with nothing more than a loose towel to hide his body's antics. Hoping Devon would be absorbed in something, he took a deep breath and made a beeline for his clothes.

Before Jonathan could even grab his boxers, the door to the trailer bounced open loudly and Kit breezed in, looking sinful in the tightest jeans and T-shirt Jonathan had seen him wear to date. "I'm here," he announced. "Let the fun begin!" Jonathan gulped, wondering just what kind of fun Kit had in mind.

Devon tried not to goggle at Kit's outfit—the lad's clothes were so tight they looked painted on. He thought regretfully that he could have changed into something nicer than his current jeans and sweater, but dressing up would only arouse Jonathan's suspicions, and that wasn't what he wanted to arouse.

Winking at Kit, he turned back to Jonathan and grinned. "Unless you're planning to go to the pub like that, mate, you'd better get dressed."

Devon's comment only served to underscore Jonathan's feeling of vulnerability at his near-nakedness. He grabbed his boxers and pulled them on under the towel, knowing it was ridiculous but unwilling to do otherwise. Turning his back on his friends, he pulled on jeans and a flannel shirt, comfortably safe clothes. They would give him the illusion that all was normal, even if his body was still going haywire at Kit's attire and Devon's raspy voice.

Kit smirked when Jonathan turned his back, taking a moment to ogle Jonathan's arse as he bent over to pull on his jeans before turning to meet Devon's eyes. Something had spooked Jonathan, that was for sure. Kit bounced across the trailer and threw his arm around Jonathan's shoulders. "Let's go. I'm thirsty."

"I'll drive," Devon offered, pushing at Jonathan's backside to urge them out the door, letting his hand linger just a bit longer than he normally would.

Jonathan coughed in surprise when he felt Devon's hand on his butt. They touched each other all the time, but it felt different somehow, just as Kit's clinging felt different. Telling himself to quit imagining things, he walked toward Devon's car.

Kit let Jonathan get in the front seat next to Devon, climbing in behind him on the passenger side. Forgoing his seat belt, he leaned forward and draped his arm over the back of the seat, trailing his hand down Jonathan's chest as he chattered happily about his day.

Devon watched Jonathan from the corner of his eye as he drove the short distance to the pub. Kit was never shy about hanging all over his friends, but tonight the attention seemed to be making Jonathan a bit uncomfortable. Hoping they were beginning to get to him, he let his arm brush casually against Jonathan's thigh as he shifted into Reverse to park the car.

It might have been an accident, a simple brush of arm against leg, but somehow it seemed… more to Jonathan. Almost deliberate. If Devon had been a woman, Jonathan would have said she was coming on to him, but Devon was his friend, not a potential lover. Wasn't he? And then there was Kit. Kit was always touchy-feely. It was part of his charm, but his hand was hanging perilously close to Jonathan's nipple. It couldn't be intentional. Could it?

Devon threw the gearshift into Park, repeating his contact with Jonathan's leg. Their king was looking decidedly unsettled. *In for a penny, in for a pound*, Devon thought, leaning over to unlock the passenger door and pressing against Jonathan as he did, his weight pushing Kit's arm firmly against Jonathan's chest. "Let's go. I need a drink in the worst way."

"You're not the only one," Jonathan muttered, scrambling out of the car, away from the disconcerting touches.

When they got inside, Kit offered to get the first round. That way, when he came to the booth, he would have a choice of where to sit—preferably as close to Jonathan as possible. "What are you having?"

"Black and tan," Devon requested, draping his arm around Jonathan's shoulders to steer him to a booth. He and Jonathan normally sat across from each other, but tonight he intended to sit as close as possible to his friend—soon, he hoped, his lover.

"Jameson," Jonathan croaked out as Devon's arm went around his shoulders.

Kit nodded and headed to the bar to get the drinks.

Devon slid next to Jonathan on the cracked leather banquette, sitting just a bit closer than he normally would. "You looked good today, Jon," he murmured huskily, pausing to let his gaze rake over Jonathan's lightly flushed features. "You're getting damn good with your sword."

Devon's presence at his side surprised Jonathan almost as much as his words. Not the compliment. That wasn't so unusual, but this particular one seemed double-edged to him, implying more than was said aloud. Again, Jonathan was left with the odd impression that Devon was coming on to him. He dismissed the thought. Devon had left the other side of the booth for Kit since everyone knew their Percival needed plenty of space to move in, and the comment was just a comment. It was only Jonathan's sex-starved brain that was adding depth to the words. "Thanks," he said simply, hoping Kit would hurry with the drinks so he'd have something to do with his hands.

Kit arrived with the drinks, taking in the picture they presented, the two handsome men squeezed into one side of the booth. He pouted a little at not being the one snuggled up to Jonathan's side, but he hadn't expected Jonathan to let Devon so close so quickly. Otherwise, Kit would have made Devon get the drinks so he could be the one next to Jonathan. That was all right. Devon would have to buy the next round, and that meant getting up. Kit would make his move then. He was surprised when Jonathan grabbed the whiskey and tossed it down. Usually he was a little more temperate. "Thirsty?" he asked teasingly, meeting Devon's gaze. Something had clearly happened while he was gone.

Devon hid a grin at Kit's thinly veiled displeasure at being denied the prime spot at Jonathan's side. *Age before beauty, lad*, he thought, even as he admired the lithe grace with which Kit slid into the opposite side of the booth. *Jonathan isn't the only attraction in this challenge*. He took a deep draught of his beer to cool his sudden flush of desire.

Kit settled into the booth, sprawling lazily to take up the entire space. He watched Devon's throat work as he swallowed his beer and then turned to meet Jonathan's eyes, even as he spoke to Devon. "You're looking a little flushed there, mate. Sitting too close to our king?"

"It is a knight's duty to serve at his monarch's pleasure," Devon answered, eyes twinkling.

"Well, Jonathan, how about it?" Kit challenged with a grin. "What's your pleasure?"

Jonathan gulped. This was getting way too deep for his comfort. "Another Jameson," he rasped.

"Your wish is my command," Devon promised, reaching up to squeeze Jonathan's shoulder. He left his hand there as he pushed up from the seat, knowing Kit would steal his spot as soon as he rose. "In all things, my king." He winked at Kit and headed toward the bar.

As soon as Devon vacated his spot, Kit bounced around the table and slid in next to Jonathan, pressing his hip and leg firmly against the other man's. "How does it feel having someone like Devon Aldridge at your beck and call?" he asked, laying his arm along the back of the bench so that he almost embraced Jonathan. "You know you're the envy of every woman under the age of forty on the British Isles, and probably a good number of the men too."

Jonathan's head was spinning. There was no way Kit's comment could be misunderstood. Kit was suggesting that Devon was interested in him. A denial sprang to his lips automatically but didn't see the light of day. An hour ago he would have said it was impossible, but now he was beginning to wonder.

"What, no glib answer?" Kit leaned forward so his body was almost flush with Jonathan's. "I thought you were the master of words."

Devon wasn't surprised to see Kit draped all over Jonathan when he returned to the booth. "Thought Percival was supposed to be chaste, mate?" He set their drinks on the table while sliding into the opposite bench, being sure to brush his legs against the other men's as he did so. "I didn't know you played both sides of the field, Jon. Or are you taking Niall's hints about some of Arthur's knights being more interested in each other than the ladies literally?"

Jonathan turned his head to meet Devon's emerald gaze. Again the words held so many levels. He closed his eyes for a second as he imagined the picture he and Kit must present, and he could see why Devon might draw that conclusion. He'd never played the other side of the field, as Devon put it, but it had always been out of caution, not out of disinterest. "No, I...." He looked helplessly back and forth between the two men.

Taking pity on Jonathan, Kit backed off just a little. "Nah, I was just taking the piss," he told Devon.

Still struggling with the situation and the feelings swirling inside him, Jonathan gulped his second shot of whiskey.

"You're drinking hard tonight, Jon," Devon observed, his gaze flickering lower for an instant before returning to his friend's face. Their actions were obviously having an effect on Jonathan, but he didn't want to make their next move in the noisy, crowded pub. "Why don't we take this back to my place? I have a great scotch I'd love you to try, and that way I can indulge m'self too."

"That sounds great," Kit chimed in. "You have room for both of us if we end up crashing. Say you'll come, Jon."

Overwhelmed and completely off-kilter, Jonathan nodded numbly. His mind was racing, reading sexual innuendos in everything his friends were saying. He had to be imagining it! If nothing else, maybe he could ask some questions at Devon's house that he couldn't ask in public. They'd laugh if he was wrong, but they all teased each other constantly—he could handle that. He knew they wouldn't carry tales.

"Let's do it, then." Devon drained his beer and rose to his feet. "C'mon, Percival, give the man room to get up." Watching Jonathan's face as Kit bounced out of the booth, he stretched out his hand and unwrapped Jonathan's from its grip on his empty glass. "C'mon, mate," he urged, dropping the teasing from his voice for a moment. "You'll enjoy it, I promise you."

A shiver ran through Jonathan at Devon's words, bereft of the teasing. *Enjoy it.* Yes, he might enjoy a glass of scotch, but there was so much promise in the words, the promise of other things to be enjoyed, other pleasures not yet sampled. He shook his head to clear it, sure the whiskey was making him hear subtleties where none existed. "I'm coming," he groused as he rose to his feet and followed Kit and Devon back to the car.

Not yet, but you will be, Kit thought as he headed back to the car. He was tempted to say it aloud but decided to wait until they were at Devon's, where it would be a little harder for Jonathan to escape. Instead, he draped his arm around Jonathan's waist as if to keep him steady on his feet.

Devon unlocked the car door and helped Kit slide Jonathan into the passenger seat, each of them letting their touches linger a fraction beyond need. He drove the short distance back to his house in silence, looking every so often to Jonathan's face, hoping their actions weren't frightening the other man off, relieved to see only confusion and something he hoped might even be a flicker of interest in his unguarded expression.

The short ride gave Jonathan a much-needed moment of reflection. He knew he might be misreading the situation, and if he was, he'd be embarrassed. But if he wasn't, he needed to decide how he felt about it. If Devon and Kit really were coming on to him, could he handle it? Did he want it? With his mind already soggy with whiskey, this was not the best time to be thinking, but this was the time he had. He might never get another chance if he passed this one up. He'd let an earlier opportunity with another costar slip through his fingers because of his son, knowing then he might not get another chance, but his son wasn't here now, and Kit and Devon were. Did he want this? He canted his eyes sideways, drinking in Devon's classic profile. He had only to close his eyes to conjure up Kit's impish face. Did he want this? His cock twitched at the idea. Did he want this? His body certainly did.

The car pulled into the driveway and Kit was out of his seat almost before it was in Park, opening Jonathan's door, reaching for his seat belt. "I'm not a child," Jonathan pointed out. "I can undo my own seat belt."

Kit took a small step back and waited. Jonathan stepped out of the car and right into Kit's waiting arms. "Let's go inside," he purred, his arms around Jonathan's waist.

Devon unlocked the front door and stepped aside to let Kit guide Jonathan through. He kicked it closed behind them, then moved to Jonathan's other side and threw his arm around Jonathan's shoulders to steer them into the small parlor. A single lamp burned dimly in one corner, but Devon made no move to turn on any other lights as he settled them onto the overstuffed couch. Meeting Kit's gaze over Jonathan's head, he was tempted to give in to the desire to pull him into his arms, but as unsettled as Jonathan was, he didn't think he was quite ready for that yet. "I'll go find that scotch," he said instead, rising to walk into the kitchen.

Kit snuggled up against Jonathan on the couch, resting against Jonathan's shoulder. He was tempted to kiss him, but that wouldn't be fair to Devon. They'd agreed to do this together. He settled for trailing his hand across Jonathan's chest. It seemed Jonathan wasn't the only one feeling his alcohol, though. The two shots of vodka impaired Kit's coordination just enough that he misjudged and brushed his fingers directly across Jonathan's nipple.

Jonathan jerked at the stimulating touch. "Kit?" he asked, turning to look into brown eyes dark with desire. "What's going on?"

Juggling the bottle of scotch and three glasses, Devon returned just in time to hear Jonathan's hesitant question. He didn't know what Kit had done to prompt it, but now that it was out in the open, it had to be answered. "If you have to ask, we obviously haven't been doing a very good job," he murmured, setting the drinks on the table and returning to his place at Jonathan's other side.

Jonathan chuckled, as much at the realization that he hadn't misinterpreted his friends' actions as at Devon's response. Maybe he could do this. Maybe he could finally let go of all his inhibitions and explore the side of himself he'd always suppressed. "Okay, maybe the better question would be why?"

"Have you looked in the mirror recently?" Kit asked in reply. "We'd have to be blind not to want you. And since we couldn't figure out a fair way to decide which one got to have a go at getting your attention, we decided to do it together."

"You've got my attention," Jonathan assured them. "What are you going to do with it?"

The challenge in Jonathan's voice might have been mostly bravado, but Devon wasn't about to let it go unanswered. "This." He reached up to frame Jonathan's face and turn it until he could reach the lips he'd wanted to taste all night. His first touch was gentle, tender, but as Jonathan moved beneath him, he gave in and kissed him hungrily, letting Jonathan taste his desire in return.

Despite his relative confidence that "this" was indeed what they had intended, Devon's kiss caught Jonathan off guard. It felt strange having a beard brush against his lips, but not unpleasant. Tentatively he returned the kiss, a reaction that met with great success as Devon's lips moved over his more forcefully. Jonathan could taste the beer Devon had drunk earlier, as he was sure Devon could taste whiskey on his tongue. When they finally broke apart, staring at each other carefully, Kit stole his attention.

"My turn," Kit said, turning Jonathan's head so he could kiss him as well. This kiss was as different from the first as the two men who had given them. Devon's kiss was hungry, almost demanding, whereas Kit's kiss was more cajoling, asking rather than taking. Both had enormous appeal.

When Kit released his mouth, Jonathan glanced uncertainly between them. "So you want to… share me?"

"Aye." Devon nodded, sliding around to sit on the table in front of Jonathan and holding his gaze. "If you'll have us. But what do *you* want?" He'd felt Jonathan's response in his kiss, could see the interest in his eyes, but he wanted, needed to hear him say it out loud before they went any further.

Jonathan tried to frame an answer but realized he had no reference points to draw on. "I don't even know what my choices are. I know I enjoy being with you, both of you. I know I'm turned on, by the innuendos at the bar, by the kisses we just shared, by the thought of learning more, but I don't know how much I'll be able to handle. Hell, an hour ago I was still telling myself I'd never sleep with a costar. And even when it wasn't another actor, I never dared act on my attraction to another man."

"Finally, something I have more experience with than you do," Kit joked before his face grew more serious. "This isn't rocket science, Jon. It's not all that different than sex with a woman. It's all about making your partner—or partners—feel good."

Devon cradled Jonathan's face in his palms, his eyes darkened with desire. "There are no rules here, nothing you have to 'handle.' We won't ask for more than you're comfortable with. We just want to give you, give each other, pleasure." He slid off the table to kneel before Jonathan and pull their foreheads together, their lips almost, but not quite, touching. "Will you let us do that, Jon? Let us show you how good it can be?"

"Please?" Kit added, leaning in so his head rested against theirs.

Jonathan nodded, letting the reassurances settle into his mind. These were his friends. He could trust them. And if it became too much, he could always ask them to stop. "As long as you remember that I have no idea what I'm doing."

"We'll take good care of you," Kit promised. "Won't we, Devon?"

"That we will," Devon agreed, closing the gap between them to claim Jonathan's lips again, letting his tongue trace across them this time, teasingly, enticingly. "Anytime it doesn't feel right, just say the word. Anything you want, tell us that too."

"I'll tell you either way." Jonathan let his tongue come out to dance with Devon's, then turned his head to kiss Kit as well.

Devon watched Jonathan kiss Kit, an idea forming as Kit arched closer. They hadn't had a chance to talk through the specifics of making this work—he realized with an internal laugh that neither of them had probably dared to hope for this result. He was also surprised to discover that watching the two of them kiss was almost as arousing as kissing Jonathan himself. When Kit broke away to kiss him every bit as enthusiastically, Devon knew this was going to be even better than he'd dreamed it could be. He pulled Jonathan back into the embrace, wrapping both his soon-to-be-lovers in his arms. "Let's take this upstairs," he suggested huskily.

Kit nodded enthusiastically. Making out was difficult enough on the couch with three. Making love would be nearly impossible, especially since they wanted to make this as good as possible for Jonathan. He wondered how the evening would play out, but he figured he could follow

Devon's lead well enough. After all, he was hardly inexperienced, unlike Jonathan. That thought was enough to send frissons of desire down Kit's back. He was pretty sure he'd never deflowered a virgin before.

Jonathan rose slowly to his feet. As strange as this should have felt, he wasn't uncomfortable. Nervous, yes, but not afraid. Kit and Devon had wrapped him in a warm cocoon of desire, and nothing bad could happen with them there. He smiled down at the other two men still sitting, one on the couch, one on the coffee table. "I'm ready when you are," he told them, realizing with a thrill that nothing had changed. He could still poke fun at them just as he always had.

Devon led them up the stairs to his bedroom, letting anticipation add to the growing intensity of his desire. As soon as the three of them were inside the darkened room, lit only by the moonlight filtering through the sheer curtains, he pulled Jonathan into his embrace, holding the back of his head with one hand as he began opening the buttons of his flannel shirt with the other.

Not wanting to be left out, Kit moved to stand behind Jonathan, pressing up against his back, rubbing lightly as he sought the buttons on Jonathan's jeans. He knew Jonathan was wearing boxers—he'd seen him put them on—so he wasn't worried about pushing him too fast. As soon as the pants were open, he let his hands slide over the thin fabric and then up across Jonathan's skin where Devon had opened his shirt.

Jonathan's head was spinning again, but not from whiskey this time. Devon's lips covered his. Devon's hands were undoing his shirt. That alone would have been enough to send his senses skittering, but then he felt Kit behind him, Kit's erection pushing against his ass as he began undoing his pants. And when someone's hands, Kit's, he thought, found the skin of his stomach and started caressing, he gave up trying to keep his sanity. It felt too good to think about anything else.

Devon pushed aside Jonathan's shirt, letting his palms slide over the lightly furred planes of his chest. He could feel Kit moving behind them, opening the button of Jonathan's jeans, adding his own caresses, could feel Jonathan beginning to tremble in response to the dual assault on his senses. Lowering his head, he kissed his way slowly down Jonathan's throat, sliding to his knees as he worked his way lower. When he reached Jonathan's waist, he pushed the jeans off Jonathan's hips, then reached to wrap his arms around Kit and pull him more firmly against Jonathan's back. At the same moment, he found a tightly furled nipple with his lips and nuzzled it to full hardness before worrying it gently with his teeth.

Jonathan threw his head back with a moan as Devon's mouth closed around his nipple, beard rubbing against his skin, as Kit's cock pressed more firmly against his ass. He tunneled his fingers through Devon's longish hair, encouraging him to suck harder on his aching flesh. Then he felt Kit's mouth on his neck, biting gently. He was about to remind Kit not to leave marks when the teeth moved lower, latching on to the curve of his shoulder below the line of his costume. His back arched with the sensual pain. "Harder," he pleaded, though he could not have said for which of them he intended his words.

At Jonathan's moan of "Harder," Devon's cock surged inside his slacks. He'd imagined Jonathan would be responsive but hadn't dreamed he might share his taste for a bit of rough. Moving to the other side of Jonathan's chest, he treated the other nipple to the same caress, biting down a little more firmly this time, careful not to go too far. There would be time to explore Jonathan's limits later; tonight they were just getting started. He tugged at the distended nipple gently, freeing a hand to slide the jeans the rest of the way down Jonathan's legs. As soon as they were out of the way, he moved up the lean thighs to cup the arousal that strained against Jonathan's boxers.

Kit's jaw tightened automatically at Jonathan's plea, hips jerking forward reflexively, grinding himself against the heat of Jonathan's arse. He could just imagine that heat closing around him, squeezing him tightly, making him come from the pure pleasure of it. He reached blindly for Jonathan's erection, his hands bumping into Devon's. He lifted his head from Jonathan's shoulder and peered down at Devon for a moment. "Get naked," he suggested. "I've got Jon."

I've got Jon. The words echoed in Jonathan's head as Devon thrust against him, kissed him, kissed Kit. He was amazed at how freeing it felt to know someone else had him, that he didn't have to be the one in charge as he'd always felt he had to be with his lovers. He wondered whether that was always a dynamic of gay sex or whether it was these two men who made it so. He leaned back into Kit's arms, relishing the continued caresses and love bites as they watched Devon undress. Jonathan couldn't have said what made it so fascinating now. He'd seen Devon get in and out of costume so many times that it should have been nothing special. Except this time Devon was undressing for him. And, Jonathan realized as the boxers fell, he was fully erect. Jonathan couldn't tear his eyes away. He knew what an erection looked like—he dealt with his own often enough—but this was not his. This one was for him. Because of him. And another one was pressing firmly against his backside.

The way Devon's cock was throbbing painfully against his zipper, he didn't need to be told twice. Rising to his feet, he pressed against Jonathan momentarily, molding their bodies together, letting Jonathan feel the firmness of his arousal. He found Jonathan's mouth again, his tongue seeking inside this time, thrusting firmly as he ground their cocks together, groaning his pleasure against Jonathan's lips. Breaking away, he reached over Jon's shoulder to pull Kit forward and kiss him with equal fervor, if less body contact. Panting slightly, he backed away and quickly tore off his clothes, letting them fall to the floor with a sigh of relief as his cock was freed from the stranglehold of his boxers.

He prowled over to the bed, sprawling on his back as Kit continued to fondle and nip at their lover. Devon watched them from the bed with hooded eyes. He'd seen both men nearly naked almost daily as they dressed and undressed in their trailer, but he'd never allowed himself to look at them this way, never allowed himself to see them as lovers. Jonathan was lean and well muscled, his chest and limbs dusted with an enticing coating of soft hair that Devon longed to feel rubbing against his own. Kit was more slender, almost thin, the smoothness of his warm olive skin equally inviting.

"C'mere, you two," he invited, pushing up onto his elbows and spreading his legs to stroke lightly over his rigid erection.

Devon's invitation galvanized Kit. He ceased his playing and efficiently stripped Jonathan of what little remained of his clothes. After giving him a push that made him drop onto the bed, he dealt with his own clothes posthaste and followed, intent on experiencing all the delights now gracing Devon's bed. The two bodies lured him in, acres of hard male flesh waiting to be explored, worshipped, devoured. God, he loved a mature man. And now he had two of them to relish—and to relish him. Today was his lucky day.

Pushed off-balance by Kit's shove and his own roiling emotions, Jonathan knelt on the foot of the mattress and crawled forward, pausing hesitantly when he reached Devon, uncertain what to do next.

Seeing Jonathan's hesitation, Kit crawled onto the bed behind him and pressed his body the length of Jonathan's spine, pushing Jonathan toward Devon, onto Devon.

Devon grunted softly as Jonathan's weight fell onto him, held down by Kit's pressure against his back. "I've got him," he assured Kit, spreading his legs to settle Jonathan between them as Kit rolled to the side. Running his hands up Jonathan's back, he kissed him again deeply while he slid one hand lower to cup the lean buttocks. Pressing downward, he swallowed Jonathan's moan as their cocks slid together for the first time without even a barrier of cloth between them. Jonathan stirred against him, the friction of their slick erections rubbing together making him moan into the kiss himself. As wonderful as this felt, though, it wasn't how Devon wanted them to find their first release. He pulled out of the kiss, resting their foreheads together as he fought to steady his control. "Tell me what you want," he urged, realizing Jonathan might not know what to ask for but feeling he should offer him the choice.

"I... I don't even know where to start," Jonathan replied as he ground against Devon's hard body. He only knew how good he felt and that he didn't want the feeling to end anytime soon. "You'll have to show me."

Kit thought that sounded like a fine idea, but the glint in Devon's eyes made him suspect the other man had a plan. He could wait to see what it was before making his own suggestions if necessary.

"There are lots of ways for men to make love," Devon told Jonathan, grasping his hips to hold them still. "Cock to cock like this is one of them, but as good as it feels, it's not the way I want you to come the first time." He turned Jonathan in his arms to face Kit, positioning himself against his back, his cock just brushing the crease of Jonathan's arse. He hadn't asked Kit about his preferences, but he didn't think Kit would have any complaints. "In time we can explore all of them, but tonight we'll start with the basics. You're going to make love to Kit," he whispered against Jonathan's ear, "and then I'm going to make love to you."

Devon's words sent fresh shivers through Jonathan. "Yes," he said slowly. "Yes, I want that." He looked at Kit. "If it's all right with you."

All right? Kit thought it sounded like heaven. "I think I can deal with that." He rolled onto his stomach, offering himself to the two older men. "Help yourself."

Devon touched Kit on the shoulder, coaxing him to roll back to face them. "It might be easier for Jonathan the first time face-to-face," he suggested, running his hands through Kit's tangle of dark unruly curls. "And that way I get to enjoy watching you too." Guiding Jonathan through bringing Kit pleasure would only add to his own arousal. "Show him how to get started, Kit," Devon urged. "I'll get what we need."

Kit grinned and reached for Jonathan's hand, guiding it to his erection. "Just do whatever you usually do to yourself," he instructed. "It'll feel good to me too."

Jonathan looked down at his hand curled around Kit's cock. It didn't feel all that different from handling his own, except for the angle. Tentatively at first, he stroked the silky flesh.

"It's okay, Jon. You can use a firmer touch. You won't hurt me," Kit assured him.

Devon slipped back behind Jonathan on the bed, taking a loose hold of the lean hips to brush his cock again over the crease of Jonathan's buttocks. Lowering his head, he ran his tongue across the line of Jonathan's collarbone and bit down on the fleshy part of his shoulder, sucking at the reddened flesh as Jonathan groaned in pleasure.

Jonathan was just getting used to having another man's cock in his hand when he felt Devon rub up against him. His hips jerked when Devon's erection brushed his backside. That was a reaction he was going to have to unlearn, he realized. Taking a deep breath, he made himself push back against Devon instead, trying to get used to the feeling and get rid of the strictures that said he should avoid such contact. When Devon's lips closed over the same spot Kit had sucked earlier, Jonathan bucked in reaction, grinding his ass back against Devon instinctively.

Making a sound of distinct displeasure at Jonathan's inattention, Kit dropped his hand to Jonathan's cock and wrapped his fingers around its solid girth. He stroked upward, seeking the sensitive tip, thumb teasing across the bundle of nerves and the weeping slit, wringing another cry from Jonathan. Smiling, Kit leaned closer and whispered in Jonathan's ear. "Which do you like better? My hand on your cock or Devon's cock up against your arse?"

Jonathan gasped. "Both." He might have said more, or tried to, but Kit's lips stole the breath from his lungs as they captured his mouth once again.

"You like this, do you?" Devon growled, spreading Jonathan's cheeks to rub his cock directly against the tender flesh between them. "Like the way my cock feels, nudging up against you, leaking for you? Starting to wonder what it would feel like to have me buried inside you, moving… stroking… thrusting?" He rocked against Jonathan in a slow, gentle motion, sliding back and forth along his crease, baptizing it with the creamy fluid leaking from his tip.

Jonathan broke the kiss with Kit, gasping for breath as he tried to formulate an answer to Devon's questions. He finally decided "Yes!" was a sufficient response.

Devon leaned over Jonathan's shoulder to catch his mouth, nipping at his lips, already swollen from Kit's kisses. "You're going to want it even more," he promised between sharp, loving bites. After coating a long finger with lube, he slipped it alongside his cock, adding to the moisture coating Jonathan's crack, teasing around the puckered opening that clenched beneath his fingertip. "You're going to want it so badly you're going to beg for it. And you're going to make Kit feel the same way."

"Tell me how," Jonathan pleaded, clenching his hand around Kit's cock. "Tell me what to do."

"Keep doing that!" Kit replied, thrusting into Jonathan's suddenly tight fist. He knew Devon's words were intended to inflame Jonathan's senses, but the images they evoked were having the same effect on Kit's. He lowered his head to Jonathan's chest and nipped at the pale pink nubs, wanting to drive Jonathan as crazy as his touch was driving him.

"Give me one of your hands," Devon ordered, then squeezed a healthy dollop of lube onto Jonathan's trembling fingers. He guided their joined hands back to Kit's arse, starting Jonathan in the same slow gliding movement his other hand was still tracing down Jonathan's crease. "Like that," he coaxed, taking his hand away and adding more lube to his other fingertips. "You have to stretch him, make him open enough to take you." Both Kit and Jonathan groaned at his words, making Devon's own cock tighten and jump in response. "Now whatever I do to you, you do to Kit," he told Jonathan, circling his tight opening with the tip of one finger.

Kit settled himself on his back again, legs spread, releasing Jonathan's nipple to give him complete access to his body. He clenched the sheets in his fists as he set himself to endure what would surely be an erotic torture session. Devon would be as thorough with Jonathan as he knew how, and that meant that Jonathan would be thorough with him. Not that he was complaining, of course. He just didn't need the same preparation Jonathan would need. As horny as he was, he didn't need *any* preparation, but that didn't seem to be an option.

Jonathan rubbed the slippery gel between his fingertips, learning the texture before he moved to copy Devon's motions. One finger circled Kit's entrance, round and round and round, teasing but not penetrating. Damn, but he wanted that finger to penetrate. Feeling precocious, he pressed against the tight ring until the tip of his finger slid in, up to the first knuckle. He smiled when he heard Kit's hiss of pleasure. He was obviously doing it right.

Hearing Kit's indrawn breath, Devon guessed that Jonathan had jumped ahead in the lesson. He smacked Jonathan's backside playfully, hard enough to tease but not to hurt. At the same time, he slid his own finger into Jonathan's tight channel, stopping when he felt it clench down around him. "You're not going to be a backseat driver, are you?" he groused, wiggling the finger just enough to ensure he had the other man's attention. "Because we can turn this car around right now."

Jonathan flinched reflexively when Devon swatted him, but it hadn't hurt. It didn't even sting. It just…. He didn't know what it did, and he didn't have time to think about it, not with Devon's finger suddenly invading his body. "No, don't stop," he begged. "I'll do what you tell me. Just don't stop now."

Jonathan's words made Devon's breath catch in his chest. Even though he'd told Jonathan it would happen, hearing the pleading note in his voice, his agreeing to do anything Devon told him, was arousing as all fuck. He slowly pressed his finger deeper into Jonathan's heat, until his fist rested against the firm cheeks. "Go as deep as you can," he instructed hoarsely, matching his own actions to his words. "Move around. Slide in and out until he can take you easily."

Jonathan did as Devon instructed, probing Kit's ass gently at first, until Kit started to squirm against his finger. "Right there!" Kit blurted out as Jonathan touched a protruding knob in the otherwise smooth walls. "Oh shit! Do that again."

Jonathan figured that since Kit had asked, it wouldn't get him in too much trouble with Devon. He pulsed his finger against the piece of flesh, thrilled when Kit's hips pushed down on him, fucking himself against Jonathan's hand.

"You're a quick learner, aren't you?" Devon chuckled, recognizing that Jonathan must have found Kit's sweet spot. "Bet you were always reading ahead in school." He searched for and found Jonathan's corresponding bundle of nerves. "*That* is your prostate," he informed Jonathan, "and it feels bloody brilliant when you do *this*." He rubbed against it in slow but firm circles until Jonathan was arching back against him.

Jonathan tried to imitate Devon's caresses against Kit's prostate, but his concentration was shot all to hell by Devon's fingers. Still, Kit was moaning beneath his touch, so he couldn't be doing too badly.

"Damn it, Devon, don't take all bloody night," Kit cried, already so close to the edge from Jonathan's fingers that he had no idea how he'd wait for the cock he so desperately wanted. "Get us ready so he can fuck me already."

"You're not always going to be this demanding, are you?" Devon asked Kit. "You're not getting fucked until Jonathan's good and ready, so just deal with it." He guessed Kit didn't need nearly as much preparation as Jonathan, and he was going to be damn sure Jonathan was as ready for his first time as Devon could make him. He added a second finger slowly and twisted them inside the tight passage. "Tell me how it feels?" he asked, needing to know that Jonathan was still okay.

Devon wanted him to talk? "Full," Jonathan forced himself to say. "Good." Single words were all he could manage. He hoped that was enough for Devon because coherency was beyond him as he felt his body being filled, stretched for the first time.

It took a moment, and Kit mewling in protest, for Jonathan to remember to reciprocate the caress, to do to Kit what Devon was doing to him. Carefully he slid his finger out of the hot sheath and reinserted two, twisting them a little, slowly penetrating again. Or it would have been slowly if Kit hadn't pushed up against his hand, forcing his fingers in as deeply as they would go.

"More," Kit told Jonathan, though he was sure Jonathan wouldn't listen.

Convinced by Jonathan's words—or rather by his near incoherency—that he wasn't in pain, Devon added a third finger. When he was able to slide them in and out without resistance, he began to stretch them apart, hitting Jonathan's prostate just often enough to keep him constantly on edge as he widened the channel enough to accept him.

Jonathan pressed back into each thrust, unconsciously seeking more. "That's right," Devon encouraged him, "fuck yourself on my fingers. Does it feel good? Do you want more? Do you want to feel my cock inside you, filling you like this?"

The question itself was almost more than Jonathan could bear. "Yes!" he cried again, trying to emulate Devon's care on Kit and knowing he had to be failing miserably. "Please. Fuck! Devon!"

"That's right, Jon," Kit panted from beneath him. "Stretch me wide open. I can't wait to feel you inside me."

Devon could have kissed Kit for his words, but he didn't want to break Jonathan's concentration. "You're doing fine," he praised, judging that Jonathan was nearly as ready as he could make him. Only one thing remained to ensure he was fully relaxed. Devon reached beside him, tore open a condom, and rolled it over Jonathan's leaking cock. Devon wished they could forgo the protection, but of course they needed to be sure they all were safe. Maybe, if they stayed together, all got tested.... Devon shook his head, refusing to let himself think that far ahead. He warmed a handful of lube in his palm and slicked it liberally over the condom. Kit probably didn't need so much lubrication, but this was about teaching and reassuring Jonathan. Devon savored the feel of the thick cock sliding inside his fist for a few more strokes, until Jonathan was moaning steadily. With a final twist against Jonathan's prostate, he slipped his fingers from Jonathan's arse and pushed him gently forward. "Now you know what Kit feels like," he prompted Jonathan. "Give him what he wants."

"How?" Jonathan started to ask, but Kit's hands were on him, guiding Jonathan between his legs, lining his cock up with the hole he'd so recently been playing with.

"Just take your time," Kit said. "Slide in slow and easy."

Jonathan pushed against the resisting muscle, hesitating when he didn't immediately slip inside.

"Just a little harder," Kit encouraged. "I can't wait to have you inside me."

Jonathan gulped and pressed harder, the tip of his cock finally penetrating the guardian muscle. Kit hissed, but there was no sign of pain on Kit's face. Jonathan closed his eyes for a moment and savored the sensation of the clenching ring around the tip of his erection and the incredible heat, even through the condom.

Devon had never thought of himself as a voyeur, but watching Kit guide Jonathan to his entrance, seeing the tip of Jonathan's cock push slowly inside, most of all watching the expressions on both their faces, was even more erotic than he'd imagined. He could almost feel it himself as Jonathan slowly slid deeper, drawing a gasping moan from Kit. He fisted his own erection gently, deciding that Jonathan was a natural at this.

Jonathan felt like a natural. As soon as he was inside Kit, he knew this was right. It felt too frigging fantastic to be anything else. Despite the stretching he had done, Kit was tight, tighter than any woman Jonathan had ever made love to, and so responsive, whimpering and moaning, writhing and thrashing beneath Jonathan in obvious ecstasy. Even knowing Devon was right there, watching, wasn't a deterrent but a turn-on.

Jonathan's slow, deep thrusts were driving Kit wild. Jonathan didn't need any help finding his prostate. His cock dragged across it with every stroke, much to Kit's delight. He looked beyond Jonathan's shoulders and met Devon's eyes. He had no idea if Devon bottomed, but if he did, Kit would highly recommend Jonathan as a top, and this was his first time. Kit could only begin to imagine what a little experience would do.

The low moans and groans wrung from his two lovers' throats were making it hard for Devon to maintain his own control. He wanted to kiss one of them, both of them, wanted to feel their moans vibrating against his mouth. He wanted to lick at the sheen of sweat that glazed Jonathan's back, nip at the tendons standing out in Kit's throat as he strained to take Jonathan farther inside. He wanted to be buried inside Jonathan himself, feeling the hot, tight contractions around him, wanted to make Jonathan claw at the sheets the way Kit was....

Jonathan wanted to drag this out, for Kit's pleasure if not for his own, but there was little chance of that happening now, not given how long it had been since he'd last had sex, not given how hot and tight Kit's body was, not given how aroused he was knowing Devon was right there, watching, waiting, wanting. He thrust faster, his body striving for release.

Beneath him, Kit's moans deepened. "Fuck! Jonathan, need—" A particularly well-placed thrust stole Kit's breath, and the words died in his throat.

Devon hoped he wasn't being selfish, but Kit was surely ready, and the sooner he came the sooner Devon could make love to Jonathan himself. "Touch him, Jon," he instructed hoarsely. "Touch his cock, fist it. He's almost there, take him." He drew a shuddering breath as the first touch of Jonathan's hand dragged a wailing cry from Kit. "That's right, feel it. Make Kit feel it. Make him come."

Emboldened by Kit's cry, Jonathan tightened his grip and moved his fist in time with his hips. He needed to come, needed it desperately, but he had never been a selfish lover. Kit had to come first. "Are… you… close?" he gasped out, his hips and hand moving ever faster.

Kit tried to answer, but his release caught him by surprise, turning his words into a long, loud keen of passion, his body bowing upward as ecstasy coursed through him.

The sensation of Kit's sheath convulsing around him sent Jonathan over the edge as well. His rhythm stuttered as he pounded into Kit's willing body, his seed spurting out of him. He collapsed on top of Kit, breathing raggedly, hoping he wasn't crushing his lover but unable to move to check.

"Ah fuck," Devon groaned, squeezing his cock tightly to fight back his own need to come. Watching the two of them bring each other to release had him throbbingly, achingly hard. He took a few short, panting breaths to steady himself before crawling closer to his two sated lovers, letting himself run a palm up Jonathan's sweat-soaked back and down Kit's trembling shoulder as he gave them time to recover.

The sound of Devon's voice and the touch of his hand were enough to bring Jonathan back to himself. Holding the condom, he withdrew slowly and flopped to Kit's side. He knew he should tie off the condom and get rid of it, but he wasn't quite to the point of practicalities yet. Instead he turned his head, his mouth seeking Kit's.

Kit felt the hand on his shoulder as Jonathan withdrew, knew it had to be Devon's, but Jonathan nuzzling his cheek demanded more immediate attention. He tilted his head into the kiss, a gentle, loving one this time. At least Kit hoped it was a loving one. It certainly felt that way to him. He leaned back with a sigh when Jonathan broke the kiss to dispose of the condom. "What's next?" Kit asked.

Devon rolled Jonathan onto his side and gave in to his own need to kiss him, his teeth and tongue plundering Jonathan's mouth until they were both breathing heavily again. "Now I make love to you," he answered, tipping the other man's head up to capture his sea-dark gaze. "If that's still what you want."

Jonathan might have paused, might have reconsidered if Devon had said anything else, but having the choice, knowing he could back out if he truly wanted to, gave him the confidence to reply, "I still want."

"Good," Devon growled softly, "because I still want too." He pressed one last hard kiss against Jonathan's parted lips before turning his still-sated partner in his arms. "Let me show you another way to make love," he murmured throatily, fighting a fierce need to rock into the firm arse in front of him, knowing he couldn't stop himself from coming if he did. He had no idea what Jonathan's recovery time was, but he wasn't going to come without bringing his partner with him, and that meant reining back his own desire while he reignited Jonathan's.

Giving in to the temptation that had lured him ever since Jonathan crawled into his bed, Devon ran his tongue across Jonathan's sweat-damp back, loving the salty taste of him. Biting kisses down the bones of his spine, he combed through the tawny curls on Jonathan's chest to find his peaked nipples. He played long fingers over the pebbled nubs as his mouth reached the base of Jonathan's spine. In the dim light, he could barely make out the outlines of a tattoo. He traced over it with his tongue and then bit down, sucking just hard enough to leave a mark.

Jonathan arched into Devon's mouth, loving the feeling of teeth against his skin, the sensation heightened by the brush of Devon's beard. He always tried to be a considerate lover, but he occasionally wanted a little aggression with his sex, something his female partners didn't always understand. It appeared that wouldn't be a problem with Devon. To his surprise, he could feel his arousal stirring again. For all that he wanted what Devon was offering, he hadn't expected his desire to reawaken quite so quickly.

Feeling Jonathan push up against his mouth, Devon clenched his teeth a bit harder, thrilled at his responsiveness. Sliding lower, he cupped Jonathan's pale cheeks as he soothed the skin he'd just bruised. Parting the twin globes, he ran the flat of his tongue down the musky crease, holding Jonathan's hips firmly as he traced up and down again and again.

Jonathan trembled beneath the onslaught of Devon's tongue. Never in his wildest dreams had he imagined someone putting his tongue there, but it felt fucking incredible. He tried to tell Devon that, but no words came out, only a strangled groan of pleasure. Hoping he wasn't committing a breach of etiquette, he pushed back into the wandering tongue.

When Jonathan groaned, Devon let the tip of his tongue pierce the tight muscle that trembled beneath it. Jonathan bucked wildly, pushing Devon farther inside the velvety heat he was soon going to bury his cock deep within. But first he was going coax more of those deliciously needy sounds from Jonathan's throat, make him so open, so ready he'd barely feel the burn of being penetrated for the first time. He pulled Jonathan closer, thrusting deeper with his tongue.

Jonathan jerked when Devon's tongue breached him, the intimacy enough to have him hard and aching again. He could feel his body opening, stretching, as Devon penetrated him, and suddenly it wasn't enough. "Please, Devon," he begged. "Fuck me already!"

The ache in Devon's groin was building, his pulse pounding in his bollocks as Jonathan writhed beneath his mouth. He could no longer stop his own hips from rocking in time with the quickening thrusts of his tongue. When Jonathan finally pleaded with him to fuck him, he knew they were both more than ready. He scrabbled for the condom he'd left at his side, pulling away from Jonathan just long enough to tear open the package and roll the latex over his leaking shaft. He slathered it liberally with lube, the touch of his own hand almost more than he could bear. Swallowing hard, he wrapped himself around Jonathan's back, molding their bodies together and reaching up to turn Jonathan's mouth to his. "Taste yourself," he whispered before easing his tongue between the panting lips to seek its mate. "Taste how delicious it is to love you."

Jonathan gave his mouth willingly when Devon asked for it, surprised and aroused by the dark, musky flavor on Devon's tongue. He rocked back against Devon's erection, wanting it inside him, wanting to know what it would feel like, what he had made Kit feel.

Rubbing just the tip of his cock along the crease he'd so generously wet with his saliva, Devon stopped when it nudged the well-moistened hole. He pulsed against it with quick juts of his hips, not trying to push inside yet. "Tell me you want this," he rasped, the tip just breaching the opening as he curled his arms around Jonathan's heaving chest. "Tell me you're ready to feel me inside you."

Jonathan did not even hesitate. "Now," he urged when Devon's erection pressed against him. "I want you now."

With a gasp of indrawn breath, Devon pressed slowly forward, feeling the friction as the passageway stretched to accept him. "Oh fuck, Jon," he groaned, easing back gently, then sliding in deeper than before. "Feels so fuckin' good…. Is it good?" He caught Jonathan's mouth, needing to slide his tongue against his lover's in the same slow tempo as his hips.

Jonathan tried to reply, tried to tell Devon how amazing it felt, how liberating it was to give up control, to be the one to accept, how complete he felt with Devon's cock filling him as he had never been filled before. He wanted to say those things, but words deserted him. All he could do was suck Devon's tongue eagerly into his mouth and thrust back against the invading erection.

Hand on his own cock, Kit whimpered as he watched the two men. He could see the effort it was costing Devon to go slowly, see the expression of wonder on Jonathan's face as he was breached for the first time. He wanted to be a part of it, but he hesitated to intrude. Once Devon had shown Jonathan what to do with Kit, he had left them alone to make love. It seemed the least Kit could do to return the favor now. He could not, though, suppress the sound that escaped him when their lips met and clung, bodies straining together.

Devon wanted to go slowly. He wanted to make this first time last forever, make it something neither of them would ever forget. But Jonathan was so tight, so hot, his muscles squeezing so hard around the unaccustomed fullness, that Devon didn't know how much longer his control would last. With an unsteady hand, he bent Jonathan's upper leg toward his chest, letting his cock slide precious millimeters deeper and changing the angle to rub harder against Jonathan's prostate. Jonathan shuddered, filling him with an overwhelming sense of pride and power to be giving him this much pleasure. Holding the lean hips close with one hand, he tweaked at a sweat-slick nipple with the other, consciously avoiding the cock that leaked steadily against Jonathan's stomach. "You're close, aren't you?" he panted, licking at the cords of Jonathan's neck. "Can you come like this, Jon? Come from feeling me inside you?" He snapped his hips, rocking in a series of short jabs as he fought to hold back his own climax.

Jonathan was nearly delirious with desire, all the sensations swirling together into one overpowering rush: Devon's fingers on his nipple, pinching lightly; Devon's cock inside him, dragging across his prostate; Devon's voice in his ear, whispering inciting words. He moaned as his sweet spot was repeatedly struck. "I… I don't know," he rasped in reply to Devon's question.

"One day you will," Devon promised hoarsely, the need to find his own release becoming almost overpowering. He glanced toward Kit watching them with wide brown eyes, stroking his own resurgent erection. "Help him."

"How?" Kit asked, wanting to give Devon the choice, though he knew what his own preference would be. He wanted to close his lips around the steadily leaking erection and suck it dry.

"Suck him," Devon growled, biting back the words as he fought to last a few moments longer.

Kit did not need telling twice. He bent his head and closed his mouth around the tip of Jonathan's cock, swirling his tongue in the slit and then over the bundle of nerves at the base of the mushroomed head.

Jonathan threw his head back against Devon's shoulder with a shout when moist heat surrounded the tip of his cock. He thrust forward into Kit's mouth and then rocked back onto Devon's erection. His groan of pleasure echoed through the room as Kit took him all the way in and Devon drove deep inside him.

Jonathan's cry shattered the last remnant of Devon's control. Crushing Jonathan's hips to his, he rocked fiercely as the flood of pleasure raged through his body, biting into the curve of Jonathan's shoulder.

The dual pleasure of Kit's mouth and Devon's cock were enough to send Jonathan's passion spiraling out of control again. He tried to speak, to warn Kit, but his release left him before the words could.

When the salty fluid flooded Kit's mouth, he increased his suction, hoping to draw out Jonathan's orgasm as long as possible. Finally he released the softening shaft, licking carefully along it and around the base, little kitten licks designed to catch every last drop. When he was satisfied, he looked up into the faces of his sated lovers with a smile.

"So," he drawled when Jonathan opened his eyes again, "which did you prefer? Top or bottom?"

"You mean I have to choose, Kit-Kat?" Jonathan replied lazily, the nickname seeming apt given the way Kit had lapped up his cream. "I rather enjoyed things just the way they were."

"Then we'll have to change things up a bit next time." Devon grinned, slipping out of Jonathan carefully before tying off the condom and tossing it toward the bin. Leaning forward, he claimed a deep kiss from each of the two men sharing his bed. He could get used to this very quickly. "There are lots of other things we can show you, if you're still interested?"

Kit's breath caught in his throat at Devon's question. He was almost certain what Jonathan's reply would be, but he couldn't stop himself from adding his own encouragement. He slid up Jonathan's body, rubbing at every point of contact until he could reach Jonathan's lips. "Just think," he murmured. "Lancelot and Percival at your beck and call. What could be better? We'll teach you things you can't even begin to imagine."

"I think you'll find I'm a quick study," Jonathan replied, claiming a kiss of his own from both his lovers. "Count me in."

CHAPTER 2
LOVE BITES

NOW THAT the makeup girls were gone, Jonathan pulled off his surcoat and slumped down in his chair in their trailer, pleased to finally have a few minutes to himself. He had been too busy since his night with Devon and Kit to really think about it and what it meant.

That he had enjoyed it was not in doubt. That he wanted them again, likewise, was not a question he needed to ask. He did wonder, though, how this would work. They were three very different men, surely with different tastes and needs. He knew, and he was sure Devon did as well, that relationships were hard work.

The word brought Jonathan up short. Was that what they were building? A relationship? Was that what he wanted? The sound of the door opening broke into his thoughts. He turned his head and smiled when he met Devon's eyes.

Devon rolled his head, stretching his aching neck muscles as he entered the trailer. "This damn armor gets heavier every day," he grumbled to Jonathan, who was pulling off his sweaty tunic and the linen shirt beneath from his chair in front of the makeup mirrors.

Devon's gaze was drawn to the livid purple mark discoloring Jonathan's left shoulder, evidence of their first passionate night together. At least Devon hoped it was only the first of many such nights, but seeing the bruise they'd left on Jonathan's body, he wondered if the other man was having second thoughts. Kneeling beside the chair and wrapping his arms around Jonathan's chest, Devon dropped a gentle kiss on the abused flesh.

"Is this still sore?" he asked quietly. "I didn't realize we'd been quite this rough on you."

The touch of Devon's lips on his shoulder again, on the mark his lovers had left, sent shivers down Jonathan's back.

"I don't remember complaining," he observed a little hoarsely. "In fact, if memory serves, I rather enjoyed it."

The husky rasp of Jonathan's voice and the tremble that ran through him at the touch of Devon's mouth made Devon's cock stir in response.

"Then we'll have to see about giving you something else to enjoy soon," he suggested, holding Jonathan's head still for a short, hard kiss.

The door slammed open again and Kit stormed in, frowning. He threw his bag on the chair in disgust and stomped toward the makeup chair. Before he reached it, though, he caught sight of Jonathan and Devon and realized they'd been kissing. His bad mood evaporated at the thought.

"Starting without me?" he teased. "I really must protest."

Damn, but he's one fine-looking piece of arse, Devon thought, remembering how arousing it had been to watch Jonathan make love to Kit for the first time.

"Don't protest. Just come join us," he invited. "Plenty to go around for everyone."

Jonathan stretched out his hand, silently seconding Devon's invitation. Deciding he deserved a little pleasure after the shit day he'd had, Kit crossed the trailer to join them, insinuating himself onto Jonathan's lap. The bruise on his shoulder caught his eye as he settled himself.

"Did I do that?" he asked, aghast.

"I think we both made our mark on the king," Devon objected, surprised at the twinge he felt at Kit's words. Of course it wasn't jealousy, just guilt at having taken his taste for a bit of roughness a little too far.

Jonathan shook his head. "Would you both stop apologizing for something that I *wanted*? Feeling your teeth on me, feeling you mark me, was one hell of a turn-on!"

"Really?" Devon's cock twitched again at the words, remembering that Jonathan *had* seemed to want it just as rough as he did. He leaned forward to press his lips to the bruise again and closed his teeth over it, just hard enough to be felt. "What else turns you on, Jonathan?"

Jonathan's moan was his answer, the sensation of Devon's teeth enough to leave him struggling for words.

Kit watched the scene play out, a little uncomfortable with the turn it had taken. He had never seen the allure of pain during sex. A love bite, maybe, but the bruise on Jonathan's shoulder was more than just a hickey. And now Devon seemed determined to add to it, at Jonathan's behest. Kit held back, watching, waiting to see what would transpire.

Jonathan's moan set the match to the fuse of Devon's own response. Raising his head, he pulled Jonathan toward him, crushing their mouths together in a clash of teeth and tongues.

"Fuck, Jon," he groaned. "What you do to me."

"It's mutual," Jonathan ground out, glancing over at the door. "Is that locked?"

Kit shook his head, rising from Jonathan's lap to secure the door. When he turned back to face his lovers, the sight that met his eyes had him groaning in anticipation. Jonathan had risen from his seat and was shedding what remained of his costume. Kit met Jonathan's gaze and smiled. He was all for getting naked together again.

Devon stood and tugged feverishly at his costume, fighting to pull Lancelot's heavy chain mail over his head. "Shite," he swore as his arm caught in the links, pulling the other side of the metal garment tight against his chest. "Gimme a hand here, somebody, before I strangle in this fuckin' thing."

Laughing, Kit started across the trailer, intending to extricate Devon from the trap of his own making. Before he could get there, though, Jonathan was at Devon's side, fixing Kit with a hot stare.

"Get undressed," Jonathan growled. "I'll help Devon."

Kit did as he suggested, the sight of Jonathan's nude body already affecting him. He pulled his own tunic off and shed the tight leggings, his eyes never leaving the two other men as Devon's golden skin was slowly revealed.

Jonathan's hands seemed to burn into Devon's skin as he pulled the mail tunic from his chest. As soon as the offending garment was pulled over his head, Devon tossed it heedlessly to the floor, his attention claimed by the expanse of lightly furred flesh in front of him.

"Jon," he groaned, pulling the other man toward him and latching his teeth lightly around a pale pink nipple.

"I'm not fragile," Jonathan scolded gently, sliding his hands into Devon's longish hair. "You don't have to hold back." He wanted Devon's teeth, Kit's teeth, on his body, biting, bruising his skin. He wanted them to mark him, and he wanted to mark them in return.

In response to Jonathan's words, Devon bit down harder, sucking the flesh deeper into his mouth and pulling back to stretch it away from

Jonathan's chest. He twisted his head from side to side, worrying the nub more roughly, unable to hold back a low moan of arousal.

Kit winced and almost protested when he saw how hard Devon bit at Jonathan's chest. The words died in his throat at the look of sheer ecstasy on Jonathan's face. Such a look could only come from pleasure, though Kit himself could not see the appeal.

With a deep growl, Jonathan grabbed Devon's hips and rubbed himself against them, letting him feel his arousal. As wonderful as that felt, though, something was missing. Turning his head, he looked for Kit, stretching out his hand.

Still uncomfortable, but also unable to deny his desire to be with them, Kit swallowed his unease and stepped forward to take Jonathan's hand.

When Jonathan rubbed his hard length against the throbbing cock beneath Devon's leggings, Devon threw back his head in pleasure. He ran a thumb over the swollen nipple he'd just released, aching to feel Jonathan apply the same suction to his own chest. He reached blindly for the shaggy head, pulling it toward him as he arched forward.

"Please, Jon," he panted, "God, please, bite me."

Jonathan winked at Kit before bending his head to Devon's chest and doing just as he requested, fastening his lips over a pert pink nipple, pulling and sucking on it, tongue and teeth stimulating the sensitive flesh.

"Ahhhh, more," Devon groaned, his hands tightening in response to the fierce ecstasy of Jonathan's mouth on his skin. "Harder, feels so fuckin' good, harder."

The words went straight to Jonathan's groin, but at the same time, he realized Kit still had not joined in. "Help me with him?" he asked Kit.

Kit nodded wordlessly. Devon was obviously deriving great pleasure from Jonathan's love bites, regardless of how brutal it seemed to him. And they were supposed to be doing this together. He didn't want to back out now, not when he finally had the right to touch Jonathan— and Devon, of course—so he swallowed his reservations and reached for Devon's leggings. Maybe he could get involved another way.

Between the exquisite torment of Jonathan's mouth and the feel of Kit's hands sliding off his leggings, Devon was quickly losing the shreds of his self-control. As soon as Kit pulled away the last of his clothing, Devon drew him in, capturing his mouth in a deep, rough kiss. He slid a hand down the smooth flesh of Kit's abdomen, searching lower, closing it around the long, erect cock as he bit at the delicious lips.

The roughness of the kiss took Kit aback at first, though he should probably have expected it, given the way his lovers had gone at each other. He started to pull away, but Devon held him fast, keeping him engaged in the kiss.

Jonathan grinned and guided them toward the bedroom at the back of the trailer. They had all crashed there at various times in the course of filming. Now they were going to crash there together. He lowered his head to the curve of Devon's shoulder and bit down fiercely, sucking to raise a bruise to match the one that still marked his own skin.

"Fuck yeah," Devon panted, lifting his mouth from Kit's as he fell back onto the bed, Jonathan's weight landing on top of him, teeth still fastened to his shoulder. "Do it," he growled, wrapping his legs around Jonathan's lean hips and grinding against him, even as he reached out to pull Kit back toward them. "Mark me."

Jonathan didn't hesitate to do as he was told, digging his teeth into Devon's skin, drawing blood toward the surface. Devon bucked as Jonathan bit deeper, his groin tightening at the dual onslaught of his lover's cock and the ferocity of his mouth.

As Devon tossed his head against the bedding, he saw Kit still standing hesitantly at the side of the bed. Reaching out, he tugged him closer, urging him next to them on the tumbled sheets.

"You too," he pleaded, twisting his hand into the brown curls. "Want to have both your marks on me."

Kit froze for a second, but Devon's grip was implacable. Slowly, not sure how he felt about this turn of events, Kit lowered his head to Devon's chest, settling his lips on the muscle just above Devon's nipple. He sucked on the skin, nibbling at it lightly.

Releasing Devon's shoulder, Jonathan rocked back on his heels to watch as Kit left his own mark. "Harder," he encouraged Kit. "You won't leave much of a mark that way."

Devon whined as Jonathan pulled away from him, already missing the sting of his mouth. He pulled tighter at Kit's head, holding it firmly against his chest.

"Use your teeth," Devon urged again, groping about with his other hand until he brushed against Jonathan's thighs, desperately needing the connection with both his lovers. He closed his fist around the rigid shaft and squeezed tightly, starting an up-and-down motion that matched the rocking of his hips. "Want to feel you... need to feel you both."

Devon's urgency was catching, and Kit gave in to it, letting his teeth connect finally with Devon's skin. He had no idea how much would be too much, so he started slowly, nipping more than biting. Devon's hand tightening around his skull encouraged him, and he applied more pressure, letting the moan of pleasure egg him on.

Devon's hand on his cock sent paroxysms of desire through Jonathan, his words only adding to them. Jonathan had no real idea yet where Devon's sensitive spots were, but he knew his own and figured Devon's couldn't be that much different. Hoping he was right, he lowered his head to Devon's belly, near his hip, and bit down hard before soothing the spot with his tongue. He glanced upward, waiting anxiously for Devon's reaction.

Devon was losing the ability to form words as Kit increased his pressure on his chest and Jonathan bit fiercely at his abdomen. He wanted to tell them both how good it felt, how wildly arousing it was, but all he could do was arch upward and speed his strokes on Jonathan's cock, hoping they'd realize how close he was.

Kit pulled back and looked down at Devon, his lover's face a rictus of ecstasy, his body tensing. He knew those signs, though he hadn't been in a position to see them the first time the three of them were together.

Lowering his head again, Kit slid his lips down Devon's body, aiming for the copiously leaking erection. Stopping to steal a kiss from Jonathan, Kit worked his way down until he teased around the head of Devon's cock.

Devon cried out as Kit's lips skated over the head of his erection. He thrust upward, trying to force his way deeper into the warm, seductive heat. He was so damn close, but he wanted to take Jonathan with him, wanted to feel the sweet pain of his lover's teeth as they both came. He tightened his fist around Jonathan's cock, gasping for enough breath to speak.

"Please, Jon," he panted, even as he searched for Kit's head with his other hand, "God, more, please."

Kit had no idea who the second plea was addressed to, but he had no problem with fulfilling it. He relaxed his throat and slid down on Devon's erection, taking it all the way into his mouth, bobbing his head up and down, sucking strongly.

The increased friction of Devon's hand on his arousal nearly pushed Jonathan over the edge. He shifted to give the other man better access, his teeth returning to the spot he had so recently teased, biting down hard as he neared his climax.

Between Kit deep-throating his cock and Jonathan's vicious love bite, Devon didn't stand a chance of holding back any longer. He sobbed in ecstasy as his release tore through him, emptying himself in pulse after pulse down Kit's throat. He lost the rhythm of his strokes on Jonathan's erection, his hand squeezing convulsively as he shuddered in pleasure, but it was enough to take Jonathan over the top with him, coating his fingers with thick creamy fluid.

Jonathan collapsed on the bed next to Devon, breathing hard as the aftershocks of his orgasm rocked through him. He stared almost blindly at the sight that met his eyes, Kit still teasing at Devon's cock, his kittenish tongue lapping at the head to clean it. Kit had done the same thing to him the last time they were together, but Jonathan had been so strung out he'd barely been able to appreciate the sensation. Now, watching Kit and Devon, he knew he wanted to feel it again, and soon.

When Devon's orgasm eased, Kit had pulled back, cleaning his lover tenderly and thoroughly, aware of Jonathan's eyes on him and not above putting on a little show. After all, Kit still needed to get off, and he had no interest in his own hand. That meant getting one or the other of his lovers sufficiently interested again.

Devon's lids fluttered open as the shuddering waves of his climax finally began to wane. The first sight that met his eyes was Kit, lapping at his softening member with a self-satisfied smile on his face.

Devon ruffled the tousled dark hair with a saucy wink and turned his gaze to Jonathan, collapsed bonelessly next to him on the sheets. Pushing up on one elbow, he captured his somewhat unfocused stare, raising the other hand still covered with Jonathan's seed to his lips. He licked at the cooling liquid, savoring the salty taste; then he traced over the livid mark Jonathan had left on his stomach with the damp fingertips.

"That was so bloody good, Jon," he husked, cutting his eyes back toward their partner. "But I think we still need to take care of Kit."

CHAPTER 3
CROSSED WIRES

JONATHAN RETURNED Devon's smile and turned his attention to Kit, nipping lightly at his lips. He was developing a definite fondness for that particular taste, and now there was something new to it, a flavor Jonathan imagined must be Devon.

Kit responded instantly to the kiss, incredibly turned on by having watched his lovers together. And now their attention was focused on him. He could deal with being the center of that attention. Eagerly he returned Jonathan's kiss, waiting for Devon to join them.

Still feeling the pleasant aftereffects of an incredibly powerful orgasm, Devon pushed up on his elbows and gazed down at the two men responsible. His lovers were lost in a passionate kiss, and watching Jonathan plunder Kit's mouth made him hunger for a taste himself. He slid free of the bodies quickly entangling above him, crawled to Kit's side, and ran his tongue over as much olive skin as he could reach.

Kit shivered as he felt Devon's tongue on his back, licking in long, smooth strokes over his skin, his scar from his scoliosis surgery, his spine. He purred through the kiss, trying to express his pleasure without losing contact with Jonathan.

The taste of Kit's skin was different than Jonathan's somehow, in a way Devon couldn't quite define to himself. Spicier, maybe? Different enough that he was sure he'd be able to tell them apart in the dark, just by their taste. Trying to pin down the elusive flavor, he slid his open mouth across Kit's back, following the tempting curve at the top of his buttocks. When he reached a jutting hip bone, he bit down, sucking a mouthful of skin between his teeth to savor more of the intriguing taste.

Kit tensed momentarily before relaxing against Devon's mouth. The caress was still gentle, for all that it was more potent than his tongue alone. Kit's senses were pulled in two directions, wanting to pay attention to both Devon's explorations and the attention Jonathan was lavishing on him. He moaned softly and parted his lips more, urging Jonathan to deepen the kiss.

Jonathan complied eagerly, thrusting his tongue into Kit's mouth, chasing down every trace of Devon's flavor, reveling in Kit's responsiveness. He shifted enough that their bodies lined up, Kit's hard cock brushing against his reawakening one.

Kit moaned into Jonathan's mouth, squirming sinuously against him, trying to increase the contact and the friction between them. His senses were already overloaded from giving Devon a blow job, and this was additional stimulation he wasn't really sure he needed. What he needed, wanted, was one of his lovers inside him. Telling them that, though, wasn't an option with Jonathan's tongue so far down his throat he could hardly breathe. Not that he was complaining.

The undulation of Kit's hips as he arched into Jonathan and the sounds of pleasure muffled by their kiss made Devon hunger to give Kit even more to moan about. He bit down harder on the angular hip bone, sucking more skin into his mouth, while his other hand followed along the curve of Kit's arse to tease at the crease in rhythm with Kit's rocking movements.

Kit jerked at the suddenly rougher touch, his moan of protest as lost in Jonathan's mouth as his moan of pleasure had been. He tried to wiggle away from Devon's mouth, but the hand on his arse held him in place. He thrashed a little harder and succeeded in turning sideways, freeing his skin from Devon's teeth.

Jonathan swallowed the second moan, thrilled beyond words that they could bring Kit such pleasure. He regretted the loss of contact when Kit moved away from him, but he adjusted quickly, bringing his hand up to hold Kit in place as he continued to plunder Kit's mouth. He let his body settle to Kit's side, giving Devon uninhibited access to the rest of their lover's body.

Devon felt Kit pull away and increased the pressure of his hand against the tight backside, letting the caress linger around the puckered opening. At the same time, he dropped a kiss to the mark he'd left on the reddened hip and licked his way up the juncture of leg and torso until he reached the cloud of tight curls at the base of Kit's shaft. Inhaling the scent of Kit's need, he nuzzled into the thicket, tugging at hairs and delicate skin with his teeth.

Kit relaxed a little when the touch of Devon's mouth gentled, nuzzling around his shaft. Between that and the feeling of Devon's hand teasing along his crack, he again found himself lost in desire. He let one arm come up and encircle Jonathan's back, fingers tunneling into the shaggy hair, returning the kiss with more ardor as his nervousness over Devon's roughness passed.

Devon felt Kit lose some of his tension and began to press the tip of one finger against him, enough to tease but not to penetrate. He'd need to get the lube before he began that, and that would mean moving, and right now he was enjoying what he was doing too much. In fact, there was only one thing that could tempt him to change positions, and the sounds coming from both Kit and Jonathan as they lost themselves in their kiss reminded him of what it was. He gave a final nip to the patch of skin he'd been nuzzling, letting his teeth dig in for a moment, then turned and crawled his way up Kit's torso. Bending over his lovers' heads, he ran his tongue across the jointure of their mouths, insinuating himself into the kiss.

Kit pushed back against Devon's teasing finger, knowing they wouldn't make much progress without lube, but even that stimulation felt amazing. He started suddenly when he felt Devon's teeth so near his cock, but they were soon gone again, and Devon's tongue was teasing the seam where his lips met Jonathan's.

Jonathan eased up on the kiss to allow Devon to join in the fun. After a moment of dueling, he ceded Kit's mouth to Devon and wandered downward, seeking Kit's nipples, wanting a taste of his skin as he had already tasted Devon's.

Devon held back a sound of disappointment when Jonathan pulled out of the kiss—having both his lovers' tastes in his mouth, both their tongues tangling with his, was fiercely arousing. But he and Jonathan had found release once already, while their partner beneath him was still unfulfilled. Determined to do something about that, Devon delved deeper into Kit's mouth, grinding their lips together as he continued to rub his fingers against Kit's hole.

Jonathan nibbled gently, at first, on Kit's dusky nipples, but the gentle caress wasn't enough, wasn't an expression of the fierceness of desire he felt for both his lovers. He bit down hard, pulling at Kit's flesh as he had so recently pulled at Devon's.

Kit jerked when Jonathan bit him roughly, his cry of protest lost in Devon's mouth. He tried to pull away, but he was caught between his lovers with no place to go. He reached for Jonathan's shoulder to pull him away, but his tight grip seemed to have no effect.

Feeling Kit's reaction to Jonathan's ardor, Devon swallowed his cry. He loved Kit's responsiveness, loved knowing that he and Jonathan could bring him to the same peak of need he had brought Devon to moments before. Twisting to give Jonathan greater access to the lithe body writhing between them, Devon caught Kit's hands and held them down, sucking the wriggling tongue into his mouth as he deepened the kiss even further.

Jonathan heard the muffled sound and smiled to himself. He loved knowing he could lavish that much pleasure on Kit. Feeling Devon shift to give him better access, he reached for Kit's other nipple, pinching at the tight peak, twisting it a little as he continued to bite and pull on the nub between his teeth.

Panic welled up in Kit along with the pain from Jonathan's bites when Devon pinned his arms. Did they not understand that it hurt, that he wanted them to stop?

Jonathan lifted his head and let his eyes wander down the length of Kit's body. The deeper pigment of a birthmark that graced the young man's lower belly drew his gaze and raised a desire to taste. Lowering his head again, he let his lips wander over the colored skin before biting down, adding his own mark to the one already there.

Kit groaned when Jonathan's teeth bit into the outline of his birthmark. *Damn it, that fucking hurt!* He pulled futilely against Devon's grasp, unable to break the bigger man's grip on his arms.

As Kit's moans increased, despite his seeming to struggle against their actions, Devon smiled. *So their Percival liked to play hard to get, did he?* He could go along with that. Devon let his teeth rake over Kit's questing tongue before catching it with a firm clench of his jaws. At the same time, he leaned forward to pin the slender shoulders beneath his, dragging his chest roughly across the nipples Jonathan had pinched and bitten to distention.

Jonathan released Kit's skin and slid lower still. He was getting such an enthusiastic response that he thought he'd see if Kit was as sensitive as Devon where his hip joined his thigh. He caught the smooth flesh between his teeth and sucked on it before worrying it with his teeth.

Kit's groans changed to whimpers as Devon bit his tongue and Jonathan bit his thigh. He had to make them understand that he wasn't enjoying this, but he couldn't get his mouth or his hands free to get their attention. With almost a sob, he resigned himself to enduring until Devon released either his lips or his wrists.

Jonathan's actions were coaxing such a strong reaction from Kit that Devon decided to drive him over the top. Releasing Kit's mouth with a final hard nip, he slid down to capture one of the tantalizingly swollen nipples between his teeth, suckling and twisting to wring as much sensation as possible from the sensitive flesh. *Let's see how you like that, lover*, Devon thought smugly.

"Stop, damn it! Let me go!" Kit shouted as Devon's teeth dug into his nipple. "It fucking hurts!"

Devon and Jonathan both recoiled, mouths agape, to stare at Kit. They glanced quickly at each other and then back to Kit, who struggled to blink back tears. For a moment they were both silent. Then they both started speaking, words tumbling over each other.

"Oh God, Kit, I'm sorry. I'm so damn sorry, I thought you were enjoying it or I'd never—you have to know that, I'd never—"

"Bloody hell, Kit, I didn't know, I thought you were playing, and you tried to tell me, didn't you, and I wouldn't let you? Fuck me, I'm such a bloody fuckin' idiot—"

Released from Devon's grip, Kit sat up and stared at them in disbelief. They hadn't understood he was protesting? He almost scoffed, but the genuine distress on their faces and in their voices convinced him that they were sincere. Gingerly he rubbed his palm over his throbbing nipple, bruised from both their bites, trying to decide what to say. He could get up, tell them to go to hell and leave them to each other and all the roughness they desired. It was an option. *Yeah, right. Like I'd leave them after all the trouble we went through to get Jonathan here with us.* Or he could see if they could figure out a way to keep this from happening again.

When Kit didn't respond, Jonathan panicked. He'd only just discovered what Kit and Devon could make him feel, and more importantly, what he was coming to feel for them—and his ignorance had ruined things already. "I fucked this up completely, didn't I?" he rasped, running his hands through his hair in frustration. "I don't know what the fuck I'm doing, but if I can't even tell when the man I—I'm loving doesn't like what I'm doing, I'd better go back to fucking celibacy."

Devon didn't know whether to respond to Kit or to Jonathan first. *Some bloody brilliant idea this had turned out to be, hadn't it?* He'd managed to fuck up plenty of relationships in his life, but this was the first time he'd fucked up two at the same time. And if he couldn't tell by now when a partner was unwilling…. "This is all my fault," he muttered hoarsely. "I'm the one who suggested this in the first place, and I'm the one who—" He broke off, looking regretfully at both his lovers— former lovers now—and shook his head. "I'm the one who turned things rough."

Kit sighed. They both seemed so sure that their relationship was damaged beyond repair, but he was less certain. "Do you want it to be fucked up?" he asked them both. "Because it isn't unless you want it to be. I mean, maybe I don't like it rough as much as you two do, but that doesn't mean we don't have any tastes in common. And maybe… maybe if I knew it was coming, if I could tell you when to stop…." He wondered if they really wanted him to stay or if they were just looking for an excuse to get rid of him.

Jonathan looked up, almost afraid to hope. "You'd do that?" he asked unsteadily. "You'd be willing to give me—"

"Us," Devon interrupted urgently, holding Jonathan's gaze with an imploring stare.

Jonathan nodded and squeezed Devon's shoulder before turning back to Kit. "Give *us* another chance, after the way we treated you?"

Kit smiled, a little shyly, amazed that everything suddenly seemed to revolve around his whim. "You didn't know I didn't like it, right? I mean, you didn't set out to hurt me. So it was an accident." He shrugged. "Accidents happen."

"Some people think a little pain adds to the pleasure," Devon admitted, "but never if the feeling isn't mutual." Fuck it, what would it take for him to learn that lesson? "I—We know you don't like it now," he promised, "and we won't make that mistake again." He glanced at Jonathan, who nodded vehemently in agreement, then back to Kit. It was a pure gift that Kit was so forgiving, even open to the possibility of learning to appreciate their tastes. "There are ways to make sure of that, if you're serious about wanting to learn. And I would love to teach you."

He included both his lovers in his twisted grin. "But right now, there's something else I think Jonathan and I both want to show you."

"What is that?" Kit asked.

"How sorry we are," Jonathan answered, knowing he spoke for Devon as well.

"And how good we can make you feel," Devon added. "If you'll let us."

Kit grinned. "I'd be a fool to pass up an offer like that."

Devon reached forward gently, conscious of keeping his touch tender and unthreatening. "Lie back, then," he urged, coaxing Kit's shoulders onto the pillow. "Lie back and let us take care of every place we hurt you."

Kit reclined back against the pillows, opening himself again to his lovers' touch. If he was honest, a little trepidation remained, but he remembered vividly how careful Devon had been with Jonathan their first time together, and he held tightly to that memory now.

Devon could sense Kit's hesitation and again gave silent thanks for his trust. But before he could repay that debt, he had another reparation to make. Turning to Jonathan, he pulled him into his embrace and kissed him, a slow, lingering apology. "I'm sorry I hurt you too," he murmured, resting their foreheads together.

"I wanted it as much as you did, Devon," Jonathan protested.

"But I shouldn't have let it get out of control the way it did," Devon objected. "Not without being sure Kit wanted it, and not without setting some ground rules first. I don't ever want you to doubt yourself that way. You didn't do anything wrong but follow my lead, and I think you should trust yourself instead. Your instincts are probably better than mine." He grinned again, almost giddy with relief that he hadn't managed to chase either of his lovers away. "You can tell me when I'm being an arse, you know. Never let it stop you before this."

Jonathan couldn't help but laugh. He rubbed his forehead against Devon's and then pulled back with a final kiss. "I can't think of anyone else I'd want to teach me," he replied, "but right now we can't keep our Kit-Kat waiting."

Kit waited, mostly patiently, as Jonathan and Devon talked. *Trust.* That seemed to be the crux of the matter, and something they would have to work at building. Right now, though, he wanted their hands and lips back on him, gently this time. "That's right," he teased. "Don't keep your Kit-Kat waiting."

Devon winked at Jonathan. "I think I'm going to have to find another way to keep him quiet," he groused, bending forward to smooth his lips over Kit's temptingly pouted ones, this time with exquisite tenderness. He brushed back and forth slowly, letting his mouth soothe the swelling his earlier harshness had raised.

Jonathan hesitated for only a moment, grateful that he hadn't forfeited the right to touch Kit forever with his earlier treatment. Vowing never again to make assumptions about his partners' feelings, he reached forward to caress his lovers' cheeks and let his hand glide slowly down Kit's chest to the marks he had raised with his teeth. He ghosted his fingertips over each mark, as if he could erase them with the tenderness of his touch.

Kit quickly discovered that his lips were sensitive like never before, Devon's beard tickling his skin, tantalizing him with the light contact. He purred against Devon's lips, a sound of unmistakable pleasure this time. He tilted his head into Jonathan's fleeting touch before returning his attention back to Devon's teasing mouth.

When Jonathan's fingers trailed down his chest and over the tender spots left by his teeth, Kit sighed at the sense of being cherished that washed over him, with their gentleness and care. It really had just been a misunderstanding. They couldn't possibly touch him with such care now if they didn't mean it.

Devon smiled against Kit's lips at the purr of pleasure—there was no way it could be mistaken for anything else this time. As tempted as he was to deepen the kiss, he kept the contact light and undemanding, finding the gentle pressure surprisingly arousing. He tamped back his own response—this time he was concentrating only on Kit's pleasure. He sought out Kit's hands, not to hold them down this time but to entwine their fingers in a loving clasp.

Kit squeezed Devon's hands gently, conveying his appreciation and, he hoped, his desire.

Hearing Kit's sigh at his touch gave Jonathan the confidence to replace his fingers with his tongue, lapping at each trace of teeth, each bruise, kissing them with soft, moist lips. "I'm so sorry, Kit," he whispered against the damaged flesh. "So very sorry."

Kit's heart clenched. It moved him beyond words to hear the broken sound of Jonathan's voice as he soothed each sore spot with lips and tongue and beard. He pulled one hand free of Devon's loose grasp so he could thread his fingers into Jonathan's hair, hoping the touch would assure his lover of his enjoyment.

Devon hesitated when Kit pulled his hand away. Had he been holding him too tightly? He leaned back in concern to check Kit's face, but a blissful expression suffused his features. Seeing that Kit had only freed his hand to stroke Jonathan's hair, he relaxed and returned his attention to Kit's lips, using his tongue to gently trace their fullness.

Jonathan slid farther down Kit's torso, pressing a gentle kiss to the edges of his birthmark, soothing the angry bruise on his jutting hip bone, laving the crease between hip and thigh he'd bitten so fiercely. Each mark reminded him again how insensitive he'd been to Kit's discomfort. He'd never treated a female lover that inconsiderately—why should being with another man be any different? He still had so much to learn; he only hoped he'd never make another mistake like this one, a mistake that had nearly cost him the two men who were coming to mean so much to him.

Kit sighed. Their caresses felt incredible, but he needed more now, because he needed to come. "Jonathan," he murmured, breaking away from Devon's mouth. When Jonathan looked up, Kit reached for his hand and squeezed it. "Touch me," he requested, guiding Jonathan's hand to his crease, "like you did the last time."

Jonathan hesitated. "Are you sure? I don't have anything to use on my fingers, and the last thing I want to do is hurt you again."

Touched by Jonathan's concern, Kit considered for a moment, mentally ransacking the trailer for something they could use as lube. "Get the stuff the girls use to make you look sweaty," he said, inspiration striking.

Jonathan chuckled at the appropriateness of using the makeup girls' special spray—which was composed primarily of lube—for its original purpose. "Okay, but you realize if Carol or Stacy find out about this, we'll never hear the end of it." He padded out to the main part of the trailer and began opening drawers and cabinets in search of the slippery substance.

Kit chuckled but didn't reply to Jonathan's comment. He was right, of course, but if they were careful and cleaned up after themselves, the girls wouldn't find out. In the meantime, he had another lover at hand, who was far too tentative now for Kit's tastes. Smiling up at Devon, he ran a hand over his cock. "You could return the favor," he suggested slyly.

Knowing that Kit still trusted him that much made Devon determined to return every bit of the pleasure Kit had given him. "Thought you'd never ask," he replied cheekily to hide the surge of emotion he felt at the thought. Twisting around, he dropped a tender kiss on each of the nipples he'd mistreated before raising the long, slender cock to his lips. A few drops of precome shimmered on the smooth tip, and he caught them with the edge of his tongue, savoring the taste.

Kit groaned at the incredible feeling of Devon's lips on his erection. He'd known it would feel good, but he wasn't prepared for just how good. "Fuck, Devon!" he gasped. "Feels... amazing!"

Emboldened by Kit's response, Devon let his lips slide down the head of the sleek shaft, spreading the slit with his tongue and squeezing gently to coax out more of the creamy fluid. He used his lips to slide the loose skin up and down, taking a little more of the length into his mouth with each gliding motion. The scent of Kit's arousal, the taste filling his mouth, the little moans of pleasure he was causing were nearly as intense as being on the receiving end himself.

Jonathan hurried back to the bed, the bottle he'd been searching for in his hand, and stopped short on the threshold to appreciate the vision before him. Kit was spread out on the bed, clutching at the sheets. Devon bent over his cock, mouth sliding up and down as Kit arched up to meet it, moaning in pleasure. Judging by the expression on Devon's face as he watched Kit, he was enjoying it as much as Kit was. Jonathan remembered how incredible Kit's mouth had felt on him when Devon was making love to him. What would it feel like to give that kind of pleasure to one, or both, of his lovers in return?

As incredible as Devon's mouth felt on his cock, there was something missing. Forcing open eyelids that had fallen shut in bliss, Kit looked around for Jonathan, finding him hovering in the doorway. Rolling sideways a little to offer his arse to his lover, he smiled as invitingly as he knew how.

Kit's smile banished the last vestige of hesitancy or uncertainty as Jonathan knelt beside him, squeezed a generous spray of lube onto his fingers, and rubbed them together to coat them thoroughly. He tried to remember Devon's instructions, stroking gently between Kit's cheeks and around the puckered opening, coating it with the moisture from his fingers.

Eagerly, Kit pushed back against Jonathan's tentative caress. He wanted those fingers inside him again, rubbing over his prostate, driving him wild. He was so close to release, from going down on Devon earlier and from Devon's lips on his cock now. "Hurry," he pleaded. "Inside me."

Devon growled at the tone in Kit's voice as he pleaded with Jonathan. Kit was close; he could tell by the way he was rocking back and forth, torn between thrusting into Devon's mouth or pushing back against Jonathan's fingers. Trying to tip the scales in his direction, Devon increased the suction of his lips, taking Kit deeper into his mouth until the dark patch of curls at the base of Kit's cock tickled his nose. He rubbed his tongue over the smooth head as he rocked up and down, humming his own pleasure at the feel of Kit fucking his mouth.

Jonathan couldn't resist the plea in Kit's voice. Sliding the tip of one finger into the inviting heat, he watched his lover's face for any sign of discomfort. Seeing nothing but enjoyment and desire, he pushed farther inside, searching for the node of nerves he'd discovered that first night, the one that made Kit do... *that*!

That was arching in ecstasy and letting loose a sharp cry of pleasure. Remembering, though, the miscommunications of earlier, Kit hastened to add "More!" while rocking back and forth between Jonathan's hand and Devon's mouth. His body was racked with a surfeit of sensation, and he knew it would only take a little more before he came. He wanted to fight it, to hold off and enjoy being the center of attention for as long as possible, but his body had other ideas. This would not be the last time, he reminded himself as his climax built deep inside him. Their adventure was just beginning.

Kit's body arching in pleasure pushed him even deeper into Devon's hungry mouth. Anxious to drive him over the edge so he could taste him fully, Devon stretched a hand to Kit's backside, where Jonathan had, as he suspected, used more than enough lube to spare Kit any further discomfort. Looking up to wink at Jonathan, Devon slid his own blunt finger into the slick channel next to Jonathan's, moving in counterpoint to his gentle motions.

Kit howled when Devon's finger joined Jonathan's inside him, moving in opposition so one or the other was constantly brushing his prostate. That was more stimulation than his control could bear. With a hoarse shout, he let go, spilling liberally into Devon's mouth, his body clenching tightly around both intruding fingers.

Devon eagerly savored the salty taste of Kit's release. Remembering how carefully Kit had seen to him after his own climax, he continued the gentle suction on Kit's cock until the last twitches ceased, then lapped at the emptied bollocks just in case any drops had escaped him. Letting Kit's now-relaxed member slide from his lips at last, he raised his head to survey Kit with a hint of the same self-satisfied grin Kit had bestowed on him.

Jonathan tensed momentarily at Kit's howl when Devon's finger breached him, then relaxed, relieved by the expression of pure bliss that transformed the handsome face. After Kit arched up and then shuddered with the intensity of his climax, Jonathan gently slid his finger free and gathered their lover into a loose embrace. "We didn't hurt you, did we?" he asked, pretty sure of the answer but determined not to take anything for granted a second time.

Kit turned toward Jonathan. Lightly, he caught the other man's lips with his. "No, you didn't hurt me. It felt incredible." He trailed his fingers down Jonathan's body to the straining erection before glancing over at Devon's matching arousal. "Although it looks like you two are hurting a little."

Sliding up the relaxed body between them, Devon pressed a kiss to Kit's lips before leaning over him to take Jonathan's mouth with his own. "Oh, I'm sure we can find some way to deal with it," he answered. "Feel up to another lesson, Jon?"

"Always." Jonathan pulled Devon's head back to kiss him in return. He couldn't imagine what could feel better than the sensations he'd already experienced, but he was certainly willing to find out.

"Can I make a suggestion?" Kit interjected.

"Something in particular you'd like to watch?" Devon asked with a grin.

Kit shook his head with a Cheshire-cat smile. "No, something in particular I'd like to try."

"The resilience of youth." Jonathan laughed.

"I knew he was going to be demanding," Devon agreed. "What exactly do you have in mind?"

Kit's smile widened. "A Kit-Kat sandwich."

CHAPTER 4
SAFETY FIRST

JONATHAN GRINNED at Kit's words. The image they conjured was vivid and undeniably attractive. Devon sinking into Kit as Kit sank into him. His eyes fluttered shut as he remembered what it felt like to have Devon moving inside him. Surely that sensation would be even more intense with both of them moving, with the strength of them both thrusting into him. "I'm game," he said with a leer for both his lovers.

Devon let his eyes roam appreciatively over both the men in bed with him—Kit reclined on his back in sated languor, already beginning to stir again in anticipation; Jonathan pushed up on one elbow opposite him, still hard from the stimulation of bringing Kit to orgasm moments before. As much as he'd been aroused himself by sucking Kit off, as much as he wanted to just take what both his partners were offering, he knew they needed to talk before things went any further.

Taking a breath to calm himself, he placed a restraining hand on each of his lovers' shoulders. "I don't want to throw a spanner in the works, but I think we need to set a few ground rules first," he said quietly. "We just saw what can happen when all of us aren't on the same page. We need to make sure something like that never happens again."

Kit frowned, his body aching to sink into Jonathan's tight heat. The only conversation that interested him was the one to decide who was going where in their sandwich, but he had to acknowledge that Devon was right. After all, he knew firsthand just how wrong things could go without some guidelines. "What do you have in mind?" he asked slowly, reminding himself that this was just a delay, not a cancellation of their plans.

Devon's words sent a chill down Jonathan's back, a reminder of how close they had come to ruining their nascent relationship. He tamped down on his desire and waited to see how Devon would answer Kit's question.

"First of all, I'm not sure how much experience you've had with men, Kit, and Jonathan's just starting out. We know already that Jon and I like things a little rougher than you do. There's nothing wrong with that, mind you," Devon was quick to add, hoping his words didn't sound like criticism.

"I've been around the block a time or two," Kit acknowledged, not really wanting to talk about his past lovers. They were all former lovers for a reason. Hopefully, though, he had learned from his mistakes. "You're not likely to shock me with anything common. But you're right that I've never gotten into anything really… kinky. Never had the chance, I guess."

Jonathan chuckled. "What constitutes kink?" he asked. "Until a few days ago, being with one man, much less two, would have fallen under that heading for me."

"Good point," Devon agreed, leaning in to claim Jonathan's lips in a firm but tender kiss. "Right now, my kissing you is no longer kinky, yeah? But what if I said I wanted to blindfold you, tie you to the bed, and fuck you with my tongue until you come? How would that make you feel?"

Jonathan just moaned. The idea of being helpless at Devon's mercy, or Kit's, of having them moving over him and in him, sent fresh desire through him. His cock twitched against his belly. Kit, though, laughed and said, "The only part of that I might consider at all kinky is having my hands tied. The rest? Bring it on! I love being rimmed."

Devon grinned at Kit in return. "I'll have to keep that in mind! So what would you consider kinky, sunshine?"

Kit thought for a minute. "Anything involving deliberate pain," he said finally. "And maybe anything that really required making myself a sub. Not a bottom, but a sub. Does that make sense? That's not to say I'd refuse outright. Just that I'd like a choice, a way out if it got to be too much." Even as he spoke, he wondered if it would be too much, if he could obey Devon's commands, or Jonathan's, subjugating himself to their will. He'd always resisted the idea, but now he wondered if it wouldn't be liberating in a way.

Having already aroused himself thinking about rimming a bound and blindfolded Jonathan, the image of Kit kneeling before him in submission sent a bolt of pure lust twisting through Devon's guts. *Later*, he told himself firmly. *It's far too soon for anything like that.*

"We're all still feeling our way," he agreed, with a wry grin at the unintended pun. Unable to resist the desire his words engendered to at least touch his partners, he seductively slid his hands down each man's chest, enjoying the contrast of smooth flesh and lightly furred skin beneath his fingertips. The answering quivers from both his lovers made him long to abandon the conversation for more pleasurable pursuits, but he knew how important this was to their future together. "Even if we tell each other now what we like and don't like, you might not know until we're in the middle of something that you're not enjoying it. We all have to be able to tell each other if there's something you don't want to do."

"Did you have something in mind?" Jonathan asked, seeing the sense in what Devon was saying.

"I think we should each have a safeword," Devon suggested, watching carefully for each man's reaction.

"Isn't that pretty hard-core?" Kit asked immediately, quailing at the thought of some of the descriptions he had read and heard of debasement and abuse in the BDSM scene. His stomach roiled a little at the thought that Devon might be expecting something like that. That was not what Kit had signed up for when he agreed to this relationship. "Do we really need to go there? I mean, why can't we just say 'stop' if we don't like something?"

"You tried to tell us to stop earlier, didn't you?" Devon reminded him ruefully. "And I thought you were just playing. With a safeword or an agreed-upon gesture that means stop, no matter what's happening, if it gets too intense, everything stops. No questions, no judgment, no shame attached."

"What's yours?" Jonathan asked, familiar enough with the concept to buy into it, even if he had never been involved in that sort of play. He still wasn't sure he wanted to be involved in anything extreme, but then he imagined some people—Kit, even—would consider the biting he had so enjoyed to be extreme. "I see the logic in what you're saying, but I have no idea what to use."

Devon released a breath he hadn't realized he'd been holding when neither Kit nor Jonathan seemed overly shocked at his suggestion. A part of him had been afraid at least one of them might just reject it outright. "It should be something you'd never normally say during sex. Mine's 'Devils.'"

"Manchester United?" Kit asked, laughing. "You really are obsessed with footie, aren't you?" As he spoke, he ran his hand over the team name tattooed in red on Devon's shoulder. Even that simple touch was enough to have his fingers tingling again. The chemistry between them amazed him. His attraction to Jonathan wasn't new. He'd known that would be explosive, but the attraction to Devon was new enough still to surprise him in its intensity.

"Yeah, you know what they say about Man U fans—cut us and we bleed red," Devon answered, leaning into Kit's touch. He swallowed back the memory that conjured. This was to ensure things never went that far.

Kit shivered. "Cutting? Definitely not my thing!"

Devon silently agreed and slid his fingers down to trace gently over Kit's bruised birthmark. "So, what's yours, then, hmmn?"

Kit blushed a little and then scolded himself silently. "I like to watch and be watched," he said softly. "I like knowing that what I'm doing or what's being done to me is turning on someone else, someone outside." An image of wanking in front of Devon and Jonathan flashed into his head. He wondered how long they'd be able to watch before they joined him. Not long, he suspected, if their dealings so far were any indication.

"Watching you and Jonathan together was one of the fucking hottest things I've ever seen," Devon admitted, hardening further just at the memory. "But I meant, what's your safeword?"

Kit was sure his cheeks were burning now. "Um…. Frodo," he said finally. "That's my dog's name," he added quickly, not wanting them to wonder why he would choose the name as his safeword. "Not everyone's as sports-mad as you are."

"So I could use Steelers, then?" A curl of arousal warmed Jonathan's belly at Kit's original admission. He could all too easily imagine how much more of a turn-on it would be to actually watch Kit touching himself, bringing himself to climax. Swallowing hard, he forced his attention back to Devon and away from that seductive imagery.

Devon smiled at Kit's flush of embarrassment and Jonathan's obvious interest, promising himself they'd give Kit a chance to enjoy his preference very soon. "Okay, then: Devils, Frodo, Steelers. Any time we hear one of those words, we'll stop whatever it is we're doing."

"Is there anything else we need to talk about before we get back to that Kit sandwich?" Kit teased lightly, knowing their discussion was important, but also aroused by the conversation and in need of release.

"Getting impatient, are you?" Devon chuckled. "That's something else I'll have to remember about you! But we should talk about where it's okay to play, and what's off-limits," he added in a more serious tone.

"On set," Jonathan said immediately. "Our games can't interfere with our work. Too much is riding on this for us to fuck it up because our minds are elsewhere."

"You're right about filming being important," Kit interjected, "but that doesn't mean we can't ever play on set. It depends on what the game is and what's going on. I'm not saying everything would be okay, but it could be fun to see what we could get away with now and then."

"So if I were to put you in a cock ring all day to teach you some patience, you'd be okay with that?" Devon asked. "Just think how hard you'd be, how badly you'd need to get off by the end of shooting, how good it would feel when we finally took it off and made you come."

Kit moaned at the thought. "You wouldn't," he said, almost pleading.

"Only if you wanted us to," Devon agreed, running a finger over the head of Kit's lengthening erection. He gathered the droplets of fluid from its tip onto his fingers and brought them to his lips, flicking his tongue out for a taste before extending them in offering to Jonathan. "Wouldn't the thought of coming home to that help get you through a long day's shooting, Jon?"

Jonathan sucked on the offered fingers, tasting Kit's essence on the outstretched digits. "I see your point," he agreed, imagining slipping away from set, peeling away one costume or another to steal a kiss or a caress, hidden by the trees or a fold of the land. "So how do we know when it's okay to play and when it's not?"

The images flashing through Devon's mind were so erotic, he was finding it hard to concentrate on the conversation when he was getting so hard in other places. "We'd all have to agree ahead of time," he said slowly. "And it has to be discreet. We can't do anything that would disrupt filming—we owe Niall that much."

"So if I want to put that cock ring you mentioned on Kit, I just have to be sure both of you agree with it first?" Jonathan asked, his own cock swelling at the thought.

"What's with wanting to put me in a cock ring?" Kit protested, though he couldn't deny the rush of hot blood to his erection at the thought of being bound that way.

"Don't worry, while you're in the cock ring, Jonathan will be wearing a butt plug to be sure he's as ready as you are," Devon responded, returning to squeezing the base of Kit's straining shaft, then lingering to stroke in a gentler caress.

"And what will you be wearing," Jonathan asked softly, steel underlying his voice, "to get you ready for us?"

The unexpectedly dominant tone in Jonathan's raspy voice sent a thrill along Devon's already sensitized nerve endings. "What would you like me to be wearing?" he answered huskily.

"I have a string of anal beads we could stick up his arse," Kit suggested, his hips hitching upward at Devon's caress and his breath catching at the idea of his lovers stretched and waiting for him. "That would have him hot for us."

"I'm bloody hot for you right now," Devon growled, deciding the conversation had gone on long enough. It was time for action. Looking up at Jonathan, he smiled lasciviously. "Wasn't someone saying something about a sandwich?"

Jonathan grinned and lay back on the bed, spreading his legs for Kit to settle between them. "About time," he teased.

Devon raised an eyebrow at Jonathan's unspoken assumption. "Don't make yourself too comfortable there, Jon," he murmured, glancing back at Kit. "I'm looking forward to getting some cream filling myself."

Kit had been poised to move on top of Jonathan, but Devon's words stopped him cold. "You? But... I mean, I'm not complaining, but I thought...." He wasn't sure what he wanted to say or why he thought Devon wouldn't be willing to bottom. Devon was just so... *dominant*.

"You thought I'd always want to top?" Devon smiled. "Why would I want to limit my pleasure that way? You'll find I enjoy all sorts of things you might not expect, and right now what I want is to feel that long cock of yours buried so far in my arse that I can feel it in my throat."

When Devon put it that way, it made perfect sense. Kit leaned over to kiss him, tongue thrusting into Devon's mouth in imitation of what was to come. "With pleasure," he husked when he pulled away finally. "If the king will get off his lazy butt and give you the bed, that is."

Jonathan scrambled off the bed, standing a little awkwardly beside it, despite being completely turned on by the thought of making love to Kit and to Devon through Kit. "I'll show you lazy," he threatened with a mock scowl.

"Just make sure we have plenty of that lube concoction the makeup girls put together," Devon requested. "I think we've all had enough rough play for tonight." He reached out to pull Kit back to him, sucking on his tongue hungrily until they finally broke to draw a much-needed breath. "Tell me how you want me."

"On your back," Kit replied hoarsely. "I want to see your face." He reached for the bottle Jonathan had brought in earlier, making sure it was full. "Yeah, there's plenty here," he assured Devon before throwing a grin over his shoulder at Jonathan. "Although you might have some explaining to do when Stacy and Carol see how empty it'll be tomorrow."

"I'll have explaining to do?" Jonathan grinned as he thought about why the bottle would be so depleted come morning. "You two use this trailer too."

"But it's *your* lube," Devon retorted, rolling onto his back and spreading his legs wide. He reached down to stroke his erection lazily as he regarded his two lovers with unveiled anticipation. "I'm ready whenever you are."

The sight of Devon's hand on his own shaft was too much for Kit. He jumped on the bed next to Devon and pulled his hand aside, replacing it with his own. With the other hand he pumped the bottle of lube, coating his fingers so he could prepare Devon. He looked back at Jonathan, still standing by the bed.

"Go on." Jonathan gestured, his hand around his own cock, eager to watch what he had thus far only felt. "Get settled, and then I'll join you."

"If you're sure." Kit hesitated, not wanting Jonathan to be left out.

"I'm sure," Jonathan promised with a tender smile. "You'll be the filling in our sandwich before long."

Jonathan's words, together with Kit's hand on his cock, fanned the urgency Devon felt to be fucked good and hard. "C'mon, Kit," he urged, bending his knees to open himself further. "Want to feel you inside me, fucking me, so I can feel Jon fucking you."

"How long's it been?" Kit asked. "How gentle do I need to be?" He knew Devon liked it rough, but he wasn't about to put Devon in a position to safeword for a simple fuck.

"Too bloody long," Devon admitted, "but you don't have to worry about that. I can take whatever you can give me, sunshine."

Kit ignored the nickname and the boast. He would take his time and make sure Devon was ready. He trailed slick fingers from Devon's knee, down the inside of his thigh, to the crease of his buttocks, teasing lightly across the puckered skin before dancing away to play up the other thigh and back down.

Devon growled in his throat and caught Kit's wandering hand, moving it back to where he needed it to be. "Don't tease, Kit," he warned, canting his hips to press into his touch. "Do it. I need you inside me, now." He pulled Kit back into a demanding kiss.

Kit gave in to Devon's order, sliding one finger inside his lover's sheath, searching the walls for Devon's prostate. He let Devon plunder his mouth unimpeded, though he would chide him for his impatience when he had the opportunity.

Feeling the desire to be part of the beautiful tableau before him, Jonathan lowered one knee to the bed, moving his hands to touch wherever they could: the curve of Kit's shoulder, the outside of Devon's knee, the dark hair that waved to Kit's chin, the scruffy beard that covered Devon's cheek. It didn't matter that they weren't erogenous zones. He simply wanted to touch, to prove to himself that this was real.

Feeling Jonathan's tentative touch on his cheek, Devon tore his mouth away from Kit's and turned to the other man, raising a hand to beckon him nearer. "Kiss me, Jon," he invited, needing to restore the connection with both his lovers.

Jonathan lowered himself to the bed next to Devon, insinuating his face next to his lovers', his lips catching the edge of Devon's even as he reached for Kit's head, keeping him there as well, so all three mouths met in a clash of teeth and tongues and needy moans.

Deciding Devon was probably ready, and if not would be sufficiently distracted by their kiss, Kit added a second finger next to the first, scissoring them slightly to stretch the tight entrance. He gave himself over completely to the kiss, the meeting of mouths the perfect symbol of what he wanted: the three of them together.

Devon arched against Kit's hand, the fleeting brushes against his prostate not nearly enough to satisfy him. "More," he groaned against the hungry mouths that crushed against his.

"Sounds like I'm not the only one who needs to learn patience," Kit joked, raising his head. "Should I go find that cock ring?" Even as he teased Devon, he gave him what he wanted, pressing down firmly against his prostate, massaging it with intent strokes.

"Fuck the ring; just gimme yer cock," Devon gasped as Kit's fingers pressed hard enough to make him see stars. He wrapped his hands around Kit's slim hips, pulling him closer until their groins brushed together, rocking to try to increase the tantalizing contact.

"Give him what he wants," Jonathan whispered in Kit's ear. "So I can give you what you want."

Kit shivered. With a nod to Jonathan, he shifted enough to align his erection with Devon's entrance. He pushed gently and felt the exquisite heat close around the head of his cock. It felt incredible… too incredible. With a muffled curse, he pulled back, panting.

"Kit, damn it, stop teasing!" Devon roared as he felt the penetration he craved, only to have it immediately withdrawn.

"I'm not teasing," Kit snapped. "I don't have a condom. I wasn't planning on this when I left the house this morning."

"Shite," Devon swore. "Bloody fucking shite! I don't have any with me either." He groaned in frustration. "Looks like we're all going to have to wait for this sandwich."

"I have some," Jonathan said softly, a pale blush staining his cheeks. "I… hoped this would happen again, and I got some in case we were at my place. They're still in my bag."

Despite the urgency of the moment, Devon couldn't help but laugh. "That's our king, always prepared," he gasped. "What are you waiting for? Go get them!"

Blushing harder, at the compliment and at the fact that he needed to be told, Jonathan hurried into the other room and fumbled in the knapsack he carried with him everywhere. He grabbed the box of condoms and came back into the bedroom. "Here," he said, tossing the box on the bed.

Kit laughed, looking at the jumbo-size box. "Eager much?" Even as he teased Jonathan, though, he was tearing into the box to pull out a foil packet. He rolled it down his cock, hissing as the touch of his hand pushed him closer to orgasm.

"None of that," Devon insisted, reaching to pull Kit back toward him. "Stop playing with that thing and put it back where it belongs."

Kit hastened to obey, needing to be inside Devon as badly as Devon seemed to need him. He settled back against the other man's body, realigning his cock and sliding inside the tightly clinging heat, not stopping this time until he hit bottom. As wonderful as it felt to be inside Devon, it couldn't compare to the taste he had gotten without the condom. "Like that?" he asked Devon, rocking his hips gently.

"Fuck yeah," Devon groaned, bucking against the gentle motions of Kit's hips. He glanced back at Jonathan, who was watching them with wide eyes and a hungry look. "Your turn, Jon," he invited, his voice breaking as Kit's cock slid against his sweet spot.

Jonathan smiled and lowered his head to the small of Kit's back, trailing his lips across the silky skin. He closed his hands around the firm cheeks presented for his delectation, separating them gently to reveal the pink rosette. Remembering what Kit had said, he took a deep breath and leaned in to kiss the puckered skin, just his lips first, then his tongue, brushing across Kit's entrance, savoring the pungent taste.

Kit's hips jerked when he felt Jonathan's tongue on him, burying him deeper within Devon. He moaned in delight and pushed back, hoping Jonathan would open him that way, not that he needed much preparation after the fingerfucking they'd given him earlier.

Jonathan drew back a little, not quite done with his explorations. He flattened out on the bed so he could reach lower, laving Kit's sac and the base of his shaft before teasing around Devon's entrance as well.

Devon moaned at the feeling of Jonathan lapping against his stretched opening while Kit thrust deeper inside him. "Oh, bloody hell, Jon, yeah," he gasped as the seeking tongue continued its explorations. Some day he was going to feel both his lovers buried inside him, he promised himself. But right now, the configuration Kit had asked for would be just as sweet.

"Shit, Jon!" Kit shouted, struggling to keep himself under control. "Get inside me now, or you're gonna miss out!"

Disappointed at being stopped so soon, Jonathan nevertheless did as Kit asked, sheathing himself in a condom and covering it with lube. "Are you stretched enough?" he asked, testing Kit's hole with his fingers.

As much as he needed to feel Kit moving inside him, Devon held him still, denying both of them any further stimulation until Jonathan could join them. "Fuck him, Jon," he entreated, fighting his own need to thrust against the heat filling him. "Fuck him so I can feel you fucking me too."

With Devon's words urging him on and with nothing from Kit stopping him, Jonathan sank slowly inside Kit for the second time, no less amazed at the incredible tightness and heat of his lover's body welcoming him in. Experimentally, he thrust, wanting to see how it would work with the three of them together this way.

Feeling Jonathan inside him had Kit moaning in delight. He timed his movements to Jonathan's, withdrawing from Devon as Jonathan pulled back and then driving in as Jonathan filled him. The sensation was as incredible as he had imagined, filling and being filled, surrounded on both sides by hard bodies. He trembled as he tried to hold back his climax just a little longer.

Kit's shiver as Jonathan pushed into him was as arousing as Devon had known it would be. He reached around to clutch Jonathan's buttocks, rocking upward to pull them closer as he thrust in time with the flex of Jonathan's hips. His cock leaked against Kit's abdomen as each rocking motion drove him closer to losing control.

Jonathan's thrusts increased in depth and speed, taking Kit with him, driving him harder and faster into Devon. The tight sheath around his cock and the repeated stimulation of his prostate was quickly more than Kit could handle. Despite his best attempts to wait for his lovers, his release tore through him, his passage contracting around Jonathan's arousal as his hips stuttered against Devon.

Jonathan gasped when Kit's release hit, the spasms making his guardian muscle contract rhythmically, milking Jonathan's aching cock. With a shout he drove into Kit frantically, repeatedly, as his own orgasm hit, the force of his thrusts pushing Kit into Devon.

Jonathan's frenzied thrusts provided the final friction Devon needed. Wrapping his legs around Jonathan's hips and rocking fiercely, he threw back his head and groaned deeply as his climax tore through him, his cock pulsing between their sweat-slickened bodies.

Jonathan rolled to the side as he collapsed, not wanting to crush Devon beneath his weight on top of Kit's. They lay there panting for several long minutes, coming down from the sensual high.

"You know," Kit said in a deceptively casual voice when he felt somewhat in control again, "if we got tested, we wouldn't have to worry about condoms anymore. Just think how much better it would feel without the latex in the way."

"Sounds good to me," Devon agreed. "I don't want to have to go through coitus interruptus like that again because someone forgot the supplies."

"Or because it's a spur-of-the-moment decision," Jonathan added. "It's been so long since I've last been with anybody, and then it was a woman, that I'm almost certainly clean, but I'll get tested again. I don't want to take any chances with either of you."

Devon felt a warm glow at Jonathan's words. "Of course, that implies that once we're tested, none of us has unprotected sex with anyone else," he felt compelled to add, even though he knew that wouldn't be an issue for him. With these two in his bed, he'd never need to look anywhere else.

"I'm not planning on having any sex with anybody else," Kit declared. "So unless somebody else is, I think we'll be okay on that count."

"Me either," Jonathan replied. "I'm too old to play those games."

"I didn't think it would be a problem, but I don't want to take anything for granted anymore," Devon said. "I've learned my lesson. You both mean too much to me to risk that."

A thought struck Jonathan. "Until then, we can still play, right? I mean, we'll have to keep using condoms, but we can still be together, can't we?"

"As much as I want the two of you, we'd better stock up on condoms." Devon laughed. "In fact, maybe we should go shopping after we get tested. We need to stop using up the makeup girls' lube, or we'll be outed before we know what hit us."

"Why wait until we're tested?" Kit asked. "Why not go tomorrow? We could pick up some toys too."

Jonathan smiled at the thought. He had the perfect thing in mind. Now all he had to do was slip away long enough to pull it off.

Devon grinned in anticipation. He couldn't wait to see what "toys" appealed to his two lovers. "As soon as we finish filming tomorrow, then. I know just the place."

Chapter 5
Good Vibrations

JONATHAN SIGHED and rubbed at the stiff muscles in his neck as he followed Devon back to their trailer. Today's scenes were primarily interplay between Arthur and Lancelot, and the glint in Devon's vibrant green eyes as they traded lines and sparred to prove Lancelot's skills had been enough to keep Jonathan in a constant state of semiarousal all day. He let his eyes drift over Devon's strong torso and shapely backside, smiling at the thought of watching—or better yet, helping—Devon work his way out of his elaborate costume.

"Bollocks, I'm wiped," Devon complained as they climbed the steps. "I thought Niall was never going to find a take he liked of that last scene in the practice yard." He grinned over his shoulder, holding the door to let Jonathan precede him. "After you, my king." He appreciated yet again how damned sexy the man looked, even—or especially—disheveled and sweaty. The dust raised by the afternoon's swordplay limned his straight hair, making Devon itch to brush his fingers through the shoulder-length strands. Blue eyes met his with an arch expression, as if reading his thoughts. Devon couldn't resist a giving a firm squeeze to the king's cheeks beneath their tight leggings as Jonathan entered before him. "I could stand a pint or two to unwind. What about you?"

"No," Kit exclaimed, bouncing across the room from where he'd been waiting on the couch to wrap an arm around each of his lovers. "No pints 'til after we go shopping! I've been wound up all day thinking about it." He pressed a kiss to each sweaty, bearded face. "Come on!" he insisted. "I'll make it worth your while!"

As tired as he was, Devon couldn't resist the pleading note in Kit's voice. He chuckled to himself as he realized how quickly it had become important to him to give Kit what he wanted. That didn't mean he had to make it easy for him, though. He rubbed a hand over Kit's head, ruffling the wavy dark hair. "Oh really? And what exactly can you offer that is worth the while of the two doughtiest knights of the

Round Table?" he teased. "What do you think, Jon? What should we make him do for us?"

"Whatever you want," Kit replied without thinking. His cheeks burned when he realized what he'd said and exactly what that might entail.

The semiarousal beneath Jonathan's leggings tightened into a full-fledged hard-on at Devon's question and Kit's uninhibited answer. A host of erotic possibilities flashed across his mind: Kit undressing them, Kit kneeling before them, Kit bound to the bed…. "Why don't we think about it while we head to the store?" he suggested. "We may find something there to help us decide."

Kit's blush deepened as he imagined all the toys that might give his lovers ideas. Dildos, cock rings, restraints… they'd have him trussed up and fucked six ways to Sunday. "Hurry," he moaned.

"I suppose that means you aren't going to let us shower first?" Devon asked, though he was sure he knew the answer. Jonathan was already pulling off his costume, and Kit was all but vibrating with excitement.

"Not unless you're inviting me to join you." Kit's mind filled with images of his lovers in the shower, wet muscled bodies sliding sinuously together. He wanted to go shopping, but that was an image he was going to revisit with them as soon as possible.

"You'll just have to deal with our manly aromas, then," Devon retorted, stripping his tunic over his head and watching appreciatively as Kit shimmied a pair of tight-fitting jeans over his firm arse. He quickly kicked off his leggings and pulled on his own jeans and a clean shirt. "Grab your wallets and let's go toy shopping, mates."

KIT LOOKED around the shop, simply named Adult Shoppe, with wide eyes. He'd thought he was fairly worldly, but he could feel his horizons broadening as his gaze lingered on the variety of toys and other devices that filled the shelves. He grimaced at the sight of the rather large collection of floggers and paddles and the wide variety of restraints. "This is… interesting," he said softly to Devon.

Knowing Kit's objections to anything involving the deliberate infliction of pain, Devon took him by the shoulders and gently turned him toward a large display case containing every size, shape, and color of dildo imaginable. "Don't worry, lad, we're not in the market for anything from that side of the aisle." *Not yet, anyway*, he added silently. *Not without a lot more talking first.*

Jonathan gave a last considering look at a pair of soft suede restraints before turning to follow his lovers. Something told him that the reason Devon was so willing to steer Kit to less... restrictive toys was that he had no need to make that type of purchase. The thought was more arousing than he would have imagined only a few days earlier. His new lovers were teaching him more about his own desires than merely that they extended to both sexes, a fact he'd long acknowledged but never dared act on.

With a sigh of relief, Kit let Devon guide him toward the kinds of toys they had come to buy. He picked up a bright purple dildo and looked at it appraisingly. "Nah." He put it back down. "Too small. I wouldn't even feel it compared to you two."

"Flattery will get you flat on your back with my cock up your arse if you keep that up." Devon laughed, handing Kit a model at least half again as long and twice as thick. "Is this more what you had in mind?"

Instinctively, Kit glanced around the shop, both making sure no one was near enough to hear their conversation and checking to see if there was a private room where he could take Devon up on his offer. The answer to both seemed to be no. He took the fake cock from Devon, measured it playfully with his hands, and said, "That's about right, I think, although...." He looked speculatively at Devon's groin and then at Jonathan's.

Jonathan chuckled. "Maybe, if you put both of ours together." He flushed as he realized the other way his words could be interpreted.

Devon's cock, already stirring from his teasing conversation with Kit, hardened at the image Jonathan's words painted in his mind. Judging by the red tinge on Jonathan's cheeks, he'd just realized exactly what he'd said. "That might be more than you're ready for," he answered, "but it's definitely something *I'm* looking forward to."

Jonathan bit back a moan of pleasure at the thought of what Devon was offering—it had been incredible enough to slide into Kit's tight channel, but to think of feeling Kit's cock against his own as they both slid into Devon had him so rigid it almost hurt. "Fuck, Devon," he whispered, "don't say things like that where I can't even kiss you!"

Kit's eyes bugged out. "Is that even possible?" he asked softly. Even as he spoke, he couldn't help imagining what it would feel like to slide inside Devon next to Jonathan. The thought alone had him hard as rock. He could only imagine what the reality would do to him.

"Oh, it's possible," Devon purred. "But unless we can find someplace where all three of us can get naked very soon, I suggest we stop talking and get what we came here for."

Kit looked down at the dildo in his hand, turning it over and realizing it vibrated. "I want to get this too," he said, almost defensively.

Devon grinned at the look on Jonathan's face as he realized Kit was serious. "Want to pick one out for yourself, Jon?" he offered, gesturing toward the display.

"I think the one we have is big enough to share," Jonathan retorted, determined to stop reacting like a schoolboy to everything Devon said. "Let's find the lube. Carol was already giving me funny looks when she got me ready after lunch."

"The lube is up front," Kit interjected, eager to get home and try out his new toy, preferably with the help of his lovers. "I saw it when we came in."

"What's your pleasure?" Devon asked as they examined the shelves full of choices. "We'll need to get some plain lube to replace the makeup girls' supply, but after that, anything you like."

Jonathan shook his head at the variety of flavors available. "Kiwi strawberry? Chocolate-covered cherry? Licorice stick? Cookies 'n' cream?"

Kit considered the possibilities. "Chocolate-covered cherry sounds interesting, not that any of us have a cherry left, but licorice? Not my flavor!" He looked around a little more. "Vanilla bean sounds good. Then again, none of us are very vanilla from what I can tell."

"And you'll have reason enough to be glad we're not," Devon promised, picking out several pocket-sized tubes in addition to the larger bottles they'd selected. "Learned from our king that we should always be prepared," he added with a grin.

Jonathan merely smiled, his attention caught by a display behind the next counter. Glancing at his two companions, he casually edged his way closer, an idea that had teased him earlier quickly formulating into a plan.

Kit looked at the selection in their hands. "I think that's everything. Shall we pay?"

"Eager, youngling?" Devon chuckled, though his cock had jumped at the sultry promise in Kit's voice. "Are you sure you don't want to look at any other toys as long as we're here?"

Kit skimmed over the other merchandise the shop offered: butt plugs, ball gags, erotic costumes of every style imaginable. "No," he finally answered. "We can always come back if we find there's something we need. We'll eventually need more lube anyway. We can look again then." He grinned. "I don't need anything to spice up my sex life anyway. I have the two of you."

"Jon?" Devon asked, noticing the other man had walked away from them slightly. "Anything else you're interested in?"

"No, I'm good," Jonathan answered quickly, heading toward the checkout.

Kit bounced on the balls of his feet while the clerk rang up their purchases. He dutifully pulled out his wallet and contributed his share, wanting nothing more than for them to get somewhere private. "Whose house are we going to?" he asked as soon as they had paid and were heading outside.

"You're welcome to come back to my place," Jonathan invited, hesitating as they walked toward the car. "But I just remembered I left the condoms in the trailer. I'd better get some more." Without waiting for the others to reply, he turned hastily and reentered the store.

Kit frowned at Jonathan's retreating back. "We could have gone to your place or mine," he commented to Devon. "There are condoms there."

"Let him be, lad." Devon smiled. "This is all new to him, remember. You can't blame him for being a little anxious about wanting to do things 'right.'" He unlocked the car and slid behind the wheel as Kit climbed into the passenger seat.

"I suppose that's true," Kit agreed, remembering how hesitant Jonathan had been their first night together. "I'm just used to him being more... I don't even know the word. He does realize whatever he wants will be fine with us, doesn't he? That *we* wanted him badly enough to pursue him, and that we're not going to change our minds if something is a little awkward?"

"I rather like seeing our king thrown a little off-balance," Devon admitted. "But you know how much of a perfectionist he is. We may need to help him relax a bit, show him that he gives us pleasure just by being himself."

Kit grinned. "That'll be a real hardship." His mind whirled with all the ways they might show Jonathan how much they liked him just the way he was. They'd tie him down so he had to just lie there and accept their attentions as they kissed and caressed every inch of his beautiful body, whispering words of love and praise, until Jonathan had no choice but to realize that he didn't have to change for them.

Jonathan hurried out of the shop and into the back seat of Devon's car, placing the bag he carried on the floor at his feet. "Okay, all set," he announced. "We've got enough condoms to keep even Kit-Kat satisfied for the night."

Kit glanced over his shoulder at the bag in Jonathan's hand. "Either that's a really big bag or there are enough condoms there to hold me for a month. And after that, hopefully we won't need them anymore."

"We'll have to be sure to use them all up before then," Devon challenged as he pulled away from the curb, the thought of getting tested and not having to worry about condoms making him even more eager. "After all, we wouldn't want them to go to waste."

That comment elicited twin groans from his lovers as they considered the suggestion. "Drive faster," Kit urged.

JONATHAN GAVE a quick glance around as he unlocked the door to his bungalow. "Sorry for the mess," he apologized. "I really wasn't planning on guests dropping by." He headed toward the bedroom, still clutching the bag with his purchases. "Help yourself to beer from the fridge. I'm just going to put some fresh sheets on the bed."

Kit looked at Devon. This had really gone quite far enough. Shaking his head, he followed Jonathan into the bedroom and wrapped his arms around his lover. "You don't have to be perfect. This doesn't have to be perfect. We want you just the way you are, mess and all," he assured Jonathan, nuzzling his neck.

Jonathan groaned as Kit's lips teased at the sensitive skin at the back of his neck. Dropping the bag to the floor, he turned in Kit's arms and captured the tempting lips in a hard kiss.

"Oi!" Devon shouted from the living room. "It's gotten too quiet in there. You two had better not be starting without me! Get out here and drink your beers, mates!"

Kit ignored the shout for a moment, leaning into Jonathan's embrace, parting his lips and offering his mouth completely. He knew they would have to separate, to go back and join Devon, but he wanted to linger a moment longer.

He could lose himself in Kit's kiss, but Jonathan had spent the entire day thinking about undressing Devon, about touching him intimately. He lifted his head and nudged Kit toward the living room. "We're coming, Devon."

"Not without me, you aren't!" Devon roared.

Kit clung to Jonathan tightly but allowed himself to be moved back into the living room. The sight that met him made him reconsider the desire to stay in the bedroom.

Devon sprawled across the sofa, his shirt unbuttoned and pulled from his slacks, the gap revealing a hard chest coated in soft golden hair. One hand was wrapped around a cold beer, the other skimming over the hard bulge tenting the front of his jeans.

As soon as Jonathan entered the living room, the desire he'd struggled against all day flared back to instant life. "God, Devon," he rasped, pulling Kit with him onto the couch. "I've wanted to do that to you all day. It was all I could do to keep from dragging you behind a tapestry and jumping you."

"You weren't the only one," Devon admitted, his breath catching as Jonathan slid his hands beneath the open sides of his shirt. "There's something about that sweaty king that makes me so bloody hard—must be all that spray-on lube."

Kit grinned. "No, it's the way his arse looks in those leggings he runs around in." He reached over and caressed said arse lasciviously. "Although it looks even better with nothing covering it."

"Why don't you work on that while I take care of the rest of him?" Devon suggested, pulling Jonathan's shirt over his head to nuzzle at the already-hard nipples revealed.

Since Jonathan was busy trying to push Devon's shirt off his shoulders at the same time, this resulted in a few moments of tangled confusion. Kit watched with a grin as the two men wrestled each other's tops off before dropping them both to the floor.

As soon as their shirts hit the floor, Kit hurried to reach for the button and zip of Jonathan's jeans and to strip them down his legs. As he did, he leaned forward and nipped at the muscled cheeks, knowing Jonathan would appreciate the little bites.

The nip of Kit's teeth on his ass made Jonathan jerk forward, forcing his erection to grind against Devon's hard groin. "Fuck, Kit," Jonathan growled, "I have to ride a horse tomorrow, in case you've forgotten."

"Does that mean I can't fuck you either?" Kit asked, pressing his cloth-covered erection against Jonathan's naked backside.

Devon pulled Jonathan's hips back down to his, bucking upward to increase the contact between them. "You, strip," he ordered, leveling a finger at Kit as he wriggled his own jeans down and off. "Anyway, I thought you wanted to play with your new toy."

Kit pouted playfully and stripped off his own shirt. "I thought you two were my new toys." He pulled down his jeans and boxers so he stood completely naked beside the couch.

Jonathan reached forward to run a hand down Kit's smooth flank. As good as it had felt to have his costar pressed against his back, he'd been imagining Kit pleasuring himself—or pleasuring *him*—with the dildo ever since he'd seen it in the shop.

Devon spread his legs to let Jonathan settle between them and cupped his hands around the king's firm cheeks. "We are, and you can play with us anytime," he agreed with a leer, "but I seem to remember you offering to make it worth our while to go shopping right away."

Kit grinned, going to the bag and pulling out their new toy. Flipping the switch to make sure it worked, he walked back over to them, knelt on the couch, and ran the buzzing toy down the seam of Jonathan's arse.

Jonathan flinched again at the unexpected sensation. This time, though, there was nothing between his cock and Devon's as they slid together, making both of them groan.

Kit grinned and slid the toy lower, so it teased over Jonathan's bollocks.

Jonathan rocked harder against Devon as the vibrations shuddered through him. "Fuck, Kit, stop, too much."

Devon wrapped his legs around Jonathan's and ran a soothing hand down his back. He was enjoying the feel of Jonathan lying atop him too much to want the other man to come so soon. "I thought you said you liked being watched," he purred to Kit. "Why don't you show us what you like to do to yourself, sunshine?"

Jonathan didn't think he could get any harder, but the image Devon's words conjured sent a shiver of pure heat racing through him. "God, yes," he rasped to Kit. "Would you do that? Let us see you that way, pleasing yourself?"

Any hesitation Kit might have been feeling evaporated from the heat in Jonathan's voice. "You want a show, do you? Where shall I sit?" he asked them, wanting to give them the best show possible.

"Right there. Lean back and spread your legs wide so we get a good view," Devon directed, pulling Jonathan closer so they could both see their young lover clearly.

Kit nodded and leaned back against the opposite arm of the couch. He dug in the sack for one of the tubes of lube they'd bought and flipped the cap open, then set it on the floor within easy reach. Closing his eyes for a moment, he trailed his hand down his chest, stopping to tease at one nipple, then the other, before opening his eyes and meeting his lovers' gazes. This was for them, to titillate and tantalize them, perhaps even tempt them to do more than just watch.

Leaving one hand cupped around Jonathan's arse, Devon slid the other between their bodies until he found Jonathan's nipples, teasing them with the same caresses Kit had just given himself.

"Fuck, Devon," Jonathan moaned, arching his back to encourage a firmer touch. Not taking his eyes from the delectable sight in front of them, he lowered his head to Devon's, joining their mouths in a slow, wet kiss.

Seeing Devon imitate his caress, seeing Jonathan focused so completely on him despite the kiss, Kit grew bolder, moving his hand down to curl around his own erection as he reached for the lube on the floor, coated his fingers, and began to stretch himself.

Devon deepened the kiss, his tongue sliding in to tangle against Jonathan's as their legs tangled on the narrow couch. He brushed his hand lightly down the crease of Jonathan's arse, not penetrating, but echoing Kit's actions.

Kit moaned as Devon mimicked him. He plunged his fingers inside himself, suddenly eager to feel the vibrator. He had picked a big one, though, and he didn't want to hurt himself by rushing. Jonathan wasn't the only one who had to ride a horse tomorrow.

Kit's moan and the still-new touch of Devon's fingers against his opening wrenched an answering groan from deep in Jonathan's chest. He turned his head just enough to drag his lips across Devon's stubbled cheek. "Is this turning you on as much as it is me?" he husked raggedly against Devon's ear.

"Can't you tell?" Devon growled, canting his hips to drag his stone-hard length against Jonathan's abdomen. He pinched at the tight nubs on Jonathan's chest, wishing he had some of the lube himself to ease his fingers inside his lover.

Deciding he was stretched enough, Kit coated the dildo and played the tip around his opening. His eyes closed as he hissed in delight at the thrill the vibrations sent up his spine. He deliberately teased himself with the toy, dragging it along the length of his leaking cock and down over his sac. Hoping they would add to his lovers' arousal, he didn't even try to hide his sounds of pleasure.

Kit's wanton noises made Devon's cock throb and his bollocks tighten with desire. He worked his hand lower between his body and Jonathan's, mirroring the way Kit slid the vibrator over his shaft, gathering the fluid that leaked from Jonathan's cock to lubricate his fingers.

Jonathan's breath hissed as Devon slid his fingers over his cock, and he couldn't prevent himself from arching into the touch. He threaded a hand into Devon's hair and bit at the cords at the side of his neck, lightly enough to not leave a mark but firmly enough to feel Devon stir beneath him in response.

Between the dildo's vibration and watching his lovers, Kit's arousal built quickly, and he struggled for control. He'd wanted to put on a show for them, and instead they were drawing him in. Determined to rebalance the scales, Kit spread his legs wider and drew his knees up to his chest, opening himself completely to their gazes. As seductively as he knew how, he breached himself with the vibrator, rocking the dildo deeper and deeper inside him.

Devon wrenched his attention from the growing need to simply push into Jonathan and find their release together, returning it to the erotic vision before them instead. The sight of Kit's face contorting with pleasure as he slid the vibrator inside himself only increased the tension growing inside him.

"Let us hear you, Kit," he rasped, his fingers finding their way back to the crease between Jonathan's cheeks. "Tell us what you're feeling."

"Full," Kit groaned. "Stretched and tight, and fit to burst." He closed his eyes. "I'm imagining it's you inside me, either one of you, filling me, the other one stroking my cock, trying to get me off. You make me feel so good, so sexy. With your hands on me, your cock inside me, I feel like the most desirable man alive. How else could I have convinced both of you to touch me?" He opened his eyes and released his cock and the dildo, still buried inside him. "Touch me."

Jonathan was already reaching toward Kit when Devon captured his hand, trapping it between them. "No," he reminded Kit. "You're supposed to bring yourself off, remember?"

Kit whined in protest. "I want your hands on me."

"Devon," Jonathan pleaded, pulling against the restraining grasp, "let me...."

Devon silenced him with a hard kiss that left both of them breathing unevenly. "No," he insisted. "He told us he'd do anything we wanted. Don't you want this, Jonathan? Don't you want to watch him make himself come? You want us to watch you, don't you, Kit?"

Kit remembered his impetuous words in the trailer. Devon was right. He had promised. So be it. If he wasn't going to have their hands on him, he'd just have to give them such a show that they'd wish they'd been involved. Grinning in anticipation, he shifted so he was lying flatter against the edge of the couch. Stretching one leg out, he let his foot run up the back of Jonathan's leg as he began to shunt the dildo back and forth inside himself. They were beautiful lying there together, his two lovers, Jonathan's back mostly to him as he lay almost fully on top of Devon. As Kit moved the dildo faster, he slid his foot between Jonathan's legs and farther up so he could nudge his toes gently against two sets of tight bollocks. After all, no one had said he couldn't touch them.

"Kit...." Jonathan groaned at the feel of Kit's toes pressing against him, pushing him into Devon's matching hardness.

Kit wriggled his toes. "More?" he asked, his voice husky with mounting desire. The vibrator hit his prostate, tearing a moan from him. "Not gonna last much longer." His eyes rolled back in his head as the stimulation continued.

Devon teased his fingers over Jonathan's opening as he nuzzled his lover's stubbled cheek. "He's beautiful this way, isn't he?" he whispered hoarsely, sliding a fingertip inside as Kit sighed in pleasure and winning an answering moan from Jonathan. "You can almost feel him squeezing around you, hot and slick and tight, can't you?" Jonathan clenched around his probing finger, intensifying Devon's need to claim either or both of these two incredible men. "Come for us, sunshine," he urged Kit. "Let us see you."

The words, the idea that Jonathan and Devon were watching him fuck himself with the toy, were enough finally to send Kit over the edge. With a hoarse shout, he climaxed, his come shooting out and coating his stomach. He collapsed limply against the arm of the couch, too spent even to turn off the vibrator and pull it out.

Jonathan turned his head blindly, his eyes locked on Kit as he sought Devon's mouth, plunging his tongue deep inside as Devon stroked him and Kit writhed and groaned his way to climax.

Watching Kit come as Jonathan ground against him and kissed him fiercely nearly cost Devon his own control. He eased his hand from Jonathan's backside and held him still, gentling the kiss until they both lay panting in the aftermath of Kit's orgasm.

Finally Jonathan levered himself up enough to reach over to Kit and slide the vibrator from him. "You okay, Kit?" he asked, running a hand over Kit's still-trembling abdomen.

Kit forced himself to focus through the haze of satiated bliss. "Yeah," he said softly. "That was… really fucking hot, touching myself, knowing you were watching. I… I haven't come that hard from my own hand since I was a kid."

"It was fuckin' hot watching it, too, lad," Devon admitted, wrapping one arm around Jonathan and reaching for Kit with the other. "You pay your debts in style, I have to admit."

Kit snuggled up close to his lovers. "What do I get in return?"

"I think we owe him something in return," Jonathan conceded, hoping whatever their lover asked for would let him relieve the aching need that twisted inside him.

"What do you have in mind?" Devon asked warily.

Kit grinned and took one of their hands in each of his, bringing each man's hand to his own cock. "Now it's my turn to watch you."

CHAPTER 6
COMING ATTRACTIONS

JONATHAN GROANED; he was so aroused that even the touch of his own hand was almost too much. "As hot as it was watching you and necking with Devon, that's not going to take long," he admitted.

"Necking?" Devon complained, though he agreed with Jonathan's sentiments completely. "Is that what you call it? What is this, high school? Next you'll be suggesting we do a circle jerk."

"Maybe we should make this a little more interesting," Kit teased, "a little less high school. How about this? Whichever one of you lasts longer gets a reward."

"He *is* suggesting a circle jerk." Jonathan chuckled. "Though back in high school, the goal was to see who could come the fastest."

"And where's the fun in that?" Devon agreed. "Longer is *definitely* better, don't you agree, Kit?"

"Oh, definitely." Kit nodded. He waited to see if they would ask what the reward would be or if they would simply accept that he would give the winner one. Grinning, he slid a hand over each of their cocks. "I'm waiting for my show."

"What's the reward?" Devon willed himself to concentrate on something other than how good Kit's hand felt on his cock.

"And are there any ground rules?" Jonathan asked, thinking that the husky growl in Devon's voice when he was aroused was possibly the sexiest thing he'd ever heard.

"I'm the reward," Kit replied with a cocky grin. "Whoever lasts longer gets me, in whatever position he wants. As for ground rules, the only one I can think of is that you can only touch yourself."

"Right, then." Devon slid away from Jonathan's tempting presence to give himself a bit more space to work in. "Watch and learn from an expert, lad," he added cheekily, letting his hand slide with teasing lightness over the length of his thickening cock.

Jonathan snorted at Devon's comment. "I can't imagine you have to worry about taking care of yourself very often." Leaning back against the sofa cushions, he raised his hands to his own chest, letting them ghost over his pecs, just grazing nipples already hardened from Devon's earlier attentions.

Kit smirked. He should have known his lovers would get into the competitive spirit. That suited him just fine. He got to enjoy watching them. And maybe even helping a little, if they'd let him. Testing the waters, he reached over and tweaked a nipple on each broad chest.

Jonathan purred as Kit's fingers closed around a nipple. Closing his eyes, Jonathan brushed his thumb back and forth over the other sensitive peak. The muscles in his abdomen contracted and his cock leapt against his stomach as the friction hardened his nipples even further. Biting his bottom lip, he rolled the tip between his thumb and forefinger, a low rumble building in his chest.

Devon yelped in surprise at Kit's touch. He'd been so busy staring at the vision of Jonathan's hands running over his lightly furred chest that he hadn't paid attention to what their younger lover was doing. "I thought it was against the rules to touch."

"I said you two couldn't touch each other," Kit reminded Devon. "I never said anything about me. But in the interest of fairness, I promise to do the same things to both of you, at the same time. Unless, of course, you don't think you can handle it."

"Isn't the whole purpose of this game to show you how we handle it?" Devon countered. Between Kit's touch and his own, though, the heat within himself swelled too quickly. He'd never be able to outlast Jonathan at this rate, especially since Jonathan hadn't even started touching his cock yet. Breathing deeply, Devon slid his hands off his shaft and down the inside of his thighs, trailing lightly up the delicate skin, tangling into the blond curls that surrounded the base of his erection.

Kit tweaked both nipples again. "Do you really want me to stop?" he asked Devon with a low purr.

"Fuck no," Devon growled, flicking his tongue out to wet his lips as he skated his fingers over the loose skin of his bollocks and Kit tweaked at his chest. "Feels too fuckin' good to stop."

Since Kit was taking excellent care of one side of his chest, Jonathan let that hand move down his torso, gliding lightly up and down his abdomen, feeling the muscles clench beneath his fingertips. He slipped beneath his gently bobbing erection, catching his breath when the back of his hand brushed against the smooth, hot flesh.

Kit tracked his lovers' progress, watching as they touched themselves, noting what they seemed to like. He wanted to know exactly how to pleasure them when the time came.

As he rolled his bollocks gently within his palm, Devon risked another look at Jonathan. Fuck, the man was pure seduction, his eyes closed, his mouth open slightly to release short, panting breaths as he pulled at a nipple with one hand and teased the underside of his cock with the back of the other. Devon moaned as he involuntarily clenched around his tightening sac, making his cock swell and jump.

The short moan surprised Jonathan into opening his eyes. "Damn, Devon, you're so fucking sexy like that," he rasped. Devon's large, capable hand was curled around his own balls, squeezing them as his body quivered and the thick column of his cock bobbed against his stomach, a gleaming pearl of precome leaking from its tip.

"You're both too damn sexy," Kit replied, glancing down at his own reawakening erection. "I just came. I haven't touched myself at all, and I'm already half-hard again."

Jonathan's voice—the one Devon was beginning to think of as his "prelude to a fuck" voice—and Kit's admission were more than Devon's cock could resist. Throbbing against his belly, it demanded to be taken in hand. He slid the loose skin back from the tip, coaxing more fluid to slick down its length, letting his hand glide more easily.

Kit licked his lips, the sight of Devon's hand moving over his own cock enough to have his mouth watering for a taste. He didn't lean down—that would have more than just bent the rules—but he promised himself that sometime soon, he'd indulge that particular desire.

Kit's words—thinking of his young lover hardening against him, underneath him, inside him—made Jonathan's gut tighten and his cock surge. The teasing brush of the back of his hand was no longer enough. He wrapped a loose fist around the base of his cock, not moving yet, just feeling the blood pulse beneath his hand.

Settling into a familiar rhythm, Devon stroked himself slowly, watching Kit's expressive face as his gaze flickered between him and Jonathan. When Kit's tongue slipped out to wet his lips again, Devon's breath caught, imagining what it would feel like to slide into the moist depths of Kit's mouth, to have that tongue tasting him.

Jonathan flexed his hips, pulling his shaft through his circling fingers and then pushing forward again in a rocking motion that let him skim easily over the silky skin. He'd found his pleasure often enough this way since his arrival in England, and now at last he could let himself fantasize without guilt about the two men on either side of him, knowing he only had to ask to make those fantasies a reality.

"Do you have any idea how fucking sexy you two are?" Kit asked them, leaning back on the arm of the couch and clenching his fist in the cushion to stop from touching himself. He wanted that pleasure to come from one of them. "You're both so hot when all you're doing is standing around waiting for the next take. But now, naked, pleasuring yourselves… you're the hottest things I've ever seen. I can't wait to watch you come. I can just imagine you, your stomachs coated with come, all wet and sticky." He let his voice trail off, his words arousing himself as much as he hoped they would arouse his lovers.

"Shite, Kit," Devon moaned, the words painting such a vivid image in his mind that a dribble of precome leaked from the swollen head of his cock. He glanced at Jonathan, wondering if he was affected the same way, and immediately wished he hadn't. Jonathan was a picture of wanton abandon, his hips arching as he fucked his fist, his other hand tracing over the line of hair that led down his abdomen.

Jonathan threw his head back as the sensation built within him, knowing he needed to rein in his response or Kit's words would become reality all too soon. Stroking his abdomen soothingly, he murmured softly under his breath, concentrating on the words to gain some control over the steadily spiraling heat inside.

Dragging his attention from Jonathan's delectable body, Devon focused on his lover's face. Jonathan's eyes were closed, his sandy hair brushing his shoulders as he tossed his head, his lips moving silently, almost as if he were whispering to himself. "What… what's that yer saying, Jon?" Devon gasped, finding it harder to draw a steady breath as his control became more tenuous.

Kit concentrated for a moment, so lost to the seduction of Jonathan's voice that the words weren't immediately recognizable. When he realized the strangeness was due to more than Jon's husky cadence, he couldn't hold back an amused chuckle. "Sounds like Middle English," he told Devon. "He's reciting a poem."

"*Morte... Arthure*," Jonathan confirmed between increasingly panting breaths. "One of the... earliest.... English verse... romances. Learned... part of it... to prep for... the role...."

"Who were the romances between?" Kit teased. "Niall certainly seems to have his doubts where Arthur's affections truly lay."

Devon couldn't hold back a crack of laughter, despite his desperately building need to come. "Bloody... method actor," he rasped, no longer able to keep his hand from moving more quickly over his leaking shaft. "Only you would... think about... shite like that... while yer... wankin'...." The final word trailed off into a deep moan as a wave of heat flared through him, his bollocks filling and tightening. "Fuck," he groaned. "Close... too bloody close."

Jonathan heard the need in Devon's voice and, knowing he couldn't hold out much longer himself, decided to see if he could push the other man over the edge. "Let it go, Devon," he urged, his voice sounding hoarse and harsh in his ears. "Let us see you. Let us watch you come."

The deep, seductive huskiness of Jonathan's voice coaxing him to come was more than Devon could endure. With a low cry, he closed his hand around his cock as it twitched and emptied, coating his belly with thick creamy fluid.

Kit pounced as soon as he saw Devon start to come, wanting the taste he'd fantasized about earlier. He lapped eagerly at the sticky mess, cleaning Devon thoroughly.

"Oh hell, Devon, yeah," Jonathan groaned, his lover's moans of pleasure overcoming the last of his control. He couldn't stop rocking as his release washed over him, his fist smearing the pulses of come over his softening length through wave after wave of aftershocks.

The sight of Jonathan coming was enough to have Kit shivering with desire. Jonathan had won the bet and the right to claim Kit this time around, but first, Kit would have to reawaken Jonathan's desire... and his cock. Perhaps it was time to introduce a different sort of game into their relationship.

Adopting the accent he used on set, he looked at Jonathan from beneath lowered lashes and murmured seductively, "What is this, m'lord Arthur? Have you been dreaming about your lady off in Camelot? Or could it be someone closer to hand who occupies your mind?"

CHAPTER 7
ACTING UP

JONATHAN COULDN'T suppress a shiver of desire as Kit addressed him in Percival's voice, the more formal accent and cadence conjuring the younger knight's presence despite the absence of costume or weaponry. He'd already started entering Arthur's headspace when he'd struggled to hold back his orgasm, and the innuendo in Kit's—Percival's—words was enough for him slip back into character.

Kit saw Arthur come into Jonathan's eyes, but he didn't speak. Seeing that he was going to have to take the initiative, Kit slid closer to his king. He might have been a young knight, but he was not averse to taking the lead. "My lord?" he repeated, placing his hand boldly on the king's bare thigh. "You remain silent. Have I misread the glances you cast my way? I have been biding my time, hoping to find my chance to swear my fealty to you privately as I have already done publicly."

Jonathan's cock twitched at the warmth of Kit's palm against his intimate flesh, causing Kit to tighten his fingers into a firmer grip. Swallowing hard, Jonathan summoned Arthur's regal tone, grateful his voice didn't quiver the way his insides were. "It is my place to observe all the knights, especially the newest, to be sure they demonstrate skills and behavior worthy of a knight of the Round Table. That you have been named to that number speaks of the regard you have earned." He raised his chin, meeting Kit's gaze with the king's mien. "What have you to offer beyond that all knights swear when they join our company?"

"Only my admittedly humble person," Kit replied meekly, though his hand slid daringly higher on Jonathan's leg until another centimeter would put it against his cock, "but I would swear that to Your Majesty's service as well, if you would have me."

Niall would certainly not recognize his chaste Percival in Kit's openly bold actions and the innuendo in his last phrase, though Jonathan wasn't about to call him on breaking character. Not when he'd spent more than one night since filming started fantasizing about pulling Kit into his arms, about kissing him, tasting him—even before Kit and Devon had seduced him. And now Kit was offering to make the fantasy a reality.

"Yes," Jonathan admitted, leaning forward to close the gap between them. "Yes, I would have you...." His mouth closed over the knight's tempting lips.

Kit returned the kiss eagerly, ceding his mouth to Jonathan as completely as he knew how. Their tongues met and tangled, sliding wetly over each other as a moan escaped Kit's throat. Perhaps he could suggest to Niall that Percival should dispense with some of his modesty in order to gain what both he and the king desired. It had certainly worked to get Kit what he wanted: Jonathan beginning to move beneath him.

Devon slid quietly to the other arm of the couch, as it was obvious his two lovers had forgotten his presence for the moment. He smiled, the ease with which the two had fallen into the role-play not really surprising him. He'd seen the almost electrical connection that leapt between the two on set together. Their characters seemed to have recognized the attraction between them long before the actors had.

Jonathan gave himself over completely to the kiss, to the slick glide of tongues over lips and teeth, the soft moans as they explored each other's mouths. He cradled his partner's head, threading his fingers into the long, silky hair, the part of his mind still retaining a bit of clarity grateful they'd been able to forgo wearing wigs; the rest merely thrilled at the sensual slip of soft strands against his skin.

"How would you have me, my liege?" Kit rasped when he broke their kiss. "I am but a young knight with little experience in the art of love. You must teach me how to please you lest in my ignorance I do something distasteful to you."

"Loving is not like battle, where the goal is to dispatch your opponent with all speed." Jonathan let a bit of humor color his voice, leaving one hand threaded in Kit's hair, moving the other slowly down his lean back. "For the moment it is enough to hold you thus, to kiss you...." He slid his lips down the inviting column of Kit's throat, lingering where the pulse beat at the curve of his shoulder. "To learn your person, as you will learn mine."

"Truly, my lord?" Kit moved at Jonathan's urging so their bodies aligned. The touch of Jonathan's lips to his throat caused a hitch in his breath. "Surely you will not be satisfied for long with such innocent contact."

"Surely a lusty young man such as yourself has not reached Camelot wholly untouched," Jonathan retorted, fighting to keep the smile from his voice as he tangled his legs with Kit's. Their bodies molded together perfectly, and he was curious to see what Kit might do next. "Pray show me what you have learned, that I may judge in what ways best to further your education."

"My lord!" Kit protested, rearing back as if shocked, letting the motion rock their groins together. "I was raised alone by my mother until I traveled here to Camelot. Before I met you, I never dreamed of letting another man touch me." He dropped his eyes, as if in shame. "Now I can think of nothing else." If the first part was a blatant lie to stay in character, the second part was nothing but the truth.

Jonathan slid the hand from Kit's hair to lift his chin, thumb playing over the smooth skin. The admission warmed him as much as he suspected it would have gratified the monarch he was portraying. "But surely you have touched a maid?" He bit his lip at the almost imperceptible shake of Kit's head. Kit even managed a hint of a blush. *Chaste knight, my ass*, Jonathan thought, memories of Kit pleasuring himself with the vibrator still heating his blood. "Even so, you must at times have touched yourself. Show me how you bring yourself pleasure."

Kit's gaze flew to Jonathan's in surprise, but he forced his voice to stay level. "What maid, my liege?" he asked. "My mother was the only other person I knew. And she would have beaten me silly for something as lewd as touching myself, but if my king orders it, I will do my best to comply." He rolled to the side, wedging himself between Jonathan and the back of the couch, his hand hovering hesitantly over his slowly reawakening erection.

"Nay, I give no orders in love. Here, we are equals—or, at least, I claim only the superiority of experience," Jonathan insisted, catching Kit's hand. "If it goes against the grain too much to touch yourself, then practice on me instead." He brought the captive hand to his chest, drawing a hissing breath as Kit's arm inadvertently brushed a bruise on his side, his arousal swelling at both the touch and the memory of the pleasure he had received from Kit's and Devon's mouths. That thought reminded him of their other lover, and he glanced up to find Devon's eyes locked on them.

Watching Jonathan and Kit melt into each other's arms had already started Devon hardening again. He smiled at Jonathan and adjusted his position on the arm of the couch, letting his hand drift down to smooth over his abdomen, not yet touching himself. For now, he was getting enough pleasure out of just watching the two play at discovering each other.

Jonathan had filmed enough love scenes that he'd long since lost any discomfort at being watched, but feeling Devon's eyes on them was surprisingly arousing. He forced himself back into Arthur's mind-set with an effort. "Explore as you will. There is no part of myself I would deny to you."

Kit wanted to grin like a kid in a candy shop, but he subsumed that into Percival's shy smile. He trailed his hand down Jonathan's side with a tenderness that welled from his heart, not his loins. "You would grant me the time," he verified, "to learn every inch of your travel-weary body, soothing the ravages of our quest." His fingers found one of the bruises left from his and Devon's teeth the day before, circling it tenderly as if to heal the purpled flesh. "You are perfection, my liege," he added, resisting the urge to press a kiss to the marks.

"I am but a man, like yourself," Jonathan assured him, the reaction of his body to even the tentative touch proof of his assertion. He raised his head to take Kit's mouth again, sliding an arm around his back, pressing their chests closer together as they continued to explore with lips and tongues. "Touch me," he invited in Arthur's voice, though Kit's kisses were making it increasingly difficult to stay in character. "Learn my body, as I plan to learn yours."

That was a request Kit was eager to fulfill. He pulled back from their embrace enough to shift his weight to one elbow, leaving his other hand free to explore Jonathan's body. They had done this before, but not as thoroughly as Kit would have liked. Now was his chance. Jonathan had just offered him free rein, and he was going to take advantage of it. He dropped one more kiss on Jonathan's lips before turning his attention to the lanky, muscular body fully on display in front of him. He took in the whole picture before narrowing his focus, starting with Jonathan's chest. He would work down from there. He lifted his free hand to the solid expanse of bone and muscle and began to explore, tracing the lines of sinew, learning their strength and testing their sensitivity. He attempted to keep his touch light, perhaps even hesitant as Percival's should have been, but that was a lost cause. If Jonathan questioned it, he would simply tell the other man that Percival had lusted after the monarch for too long to restrain himself now that he had permission.

Jonathan drew a rough breath as Kit's hand moved tentatively over his chest. It was still so new, so incredibly arousing to feel his friend's—his lover's—touch. He ached to reach for Kit in return, to conduct his own slow, heady exploration of muscle and skin, but he forced himself to lie still beneath the tantalizing touch, only the shakiness of his breathing hinting at the effect it was having on him.

Kit slid his fingers down to Jonathan's nipples, circling one, then the other. He lifted his fingers to his mouth to wet them before returning them to Jonathan's chest, then bent his head and blew on the moistened skin, watching with rapt attention as the nubs tightened. He toyed with the stiff flesh for a moment before looking up to meet Jonathan's eyes. "You are so responsive," he husked. "I had no idea it could be like this."

Feeling Kit's fingers, his saliva, his breath on his nipples left Jonathan trembling. "I have dreamed of your touch for so long," he admitted, "but even in my dreams, I had not imagined it could feel like this."

Kit desperately wanted the words to be true, but he knew they were just part of the role-playing. Jonathan had not shown any signs of acting on his attraction to men before he and Devon had seduced him. He only hoped Jonathan never regretted it. "How long?" he asked. "How long have you dreamed of me, Arthur?"

Although Arthur's voice had spoken the words, Jonathan realized they were true for him as well. He'd tried to convince himself it was only the connection between their characters that sparked his interest, but he admitted now that a part of him had always longed to give in to this fierce attraction for the beautiful young man beside him. "From the first moment I saw you," he confessed, imbuing his voice with all the conviction he could. Kit might dismiss it as merely part of the role-play, but Jonathan was speaking truth. "How could anyone be unmoved by such perfection?"

Perfection. There were days Kit hated that word. He'd worked hard to establish himself for more than just his looks, and he knew how very far from perfect he was. He just hoped Jonathan never saw it, or Devon, either. He let none of that show on his face, though. "No more perfect than any other knight, and much less than many," he replied, amazed at the effort Jonathan was putting into his character even here, offscreen and away from any audience. He hoped one day to have as much skill.

Although he had promised himself to let Kit set the pace in deference to Percival's so-called innocence, Jonathan saw the flicker of disbelief in

Kit's eyes and couldn't stop himself from reaching up to capture his lover's chin. It suddenly became very important that Kit understand that these were not just words. "It was not only your physical beauty," he insisted. "Your friendship, your courage, the way your presence shines like the sun—these are the things that draw me to you." He brushed the back of his fingers down the long curve of the knight's throat. "That make me—" Jonathan stopped suddenly, the words he had been about to say dying on his lips. *Love you*, he'd been about to say. He was beginning to think that might be true too, but it was certainly too soon to admit it, not when Kit—or Devon, for that matter—had not hinted at wanting anything more than physical pleasure from their relationship. "That make me desire you," he finished unsteadily.

Quiet on his end of the couch, Devon narrowed his eyes at the note in Jonathan's voice. He'd watched his lovers fall deeper into their roles, feeling a little envious of the pleasure they were giving each other, but knowing he could join them anytime he wanted and they wouldn't object. But this—the emotion in Jonathan's voice, his hesitation before admitting to his desire—made Devon wonder. Jonathan was an amazing actor, but either he was truly losing himself in this role or something deeper was going on than perhaps even the two of them realized.

Jonathan's words appeased Kit's fears somewhat. At least he knew that Jonathan saw more than just his body. "The desire is mutual," he assured his lover, though he knew his own feelings went much deeper than simple desire. "From the moment I laid eyes on you. Now that we have admitted it, perhaps you will do more than simply admire me from afar?"

"I want to do more," Jonathan agreed, though for now he would concentrate on only the physical side of his desires. Pushing up on one elbow, he followed the path his fingers had just traced with his lips. "So much more," he murmured between slow, moist kisses down Kit's throat. "I want to touch you... to taste you."

Kit sank back against the sofa, letting Jonathan rise over him. "Whatever you want," he murmured huskily, the desire to feel Jonathan's hands and lips on him again swamping him. "Do whatever you want."

Granted permission to indulge himself, Jonathan slid his hands down the smooth expanse of Kit's chest and lower, stopping when they grasped Percival's slim hips. His mouth followed a meandering trail, lingering at particularly enticing spots—the swell of Kit's Adam's apple, the hollow just below his left shoulder. Jonathan ghosted his lips over a large dusky nipple, teasing until the nub pebbled. "So sweet," he whispered around it, then tongued the hardening peak. "So sweet." He let his teeth tug, ever so gently, sucking at the moistened flesh.

Kit gasped as pure pleasure darted through him. He loved having his nipples sucked, and Jonathan seemed determined to lavish them with attention. Catching his lover's name just before it escaped his lips, Kit forced Arthur's name out instead. He tangled his fingers in Jonathan's hair, arching to urge Jonathan to increase the suction.

The catch in Kit's voice before he gasped Arthur's name made Jonathan smile. He'd have to see what else he could do to break the knight's concentration. Letting the hardened nipple slide from his lips, he kissed a leisurely path to the other side of the smooth chest. Lifting a hand to tug at the swollen flesh he had just released, he repeated his attentions on the other nipple. When it was as thoroughly pleasured as the first, he slid lower, tracing his tongue over ribs and waist, following the faint line of hair that led down the firm abdomen. Kit's cock was hard against his stomach, the tip already glistening with pearly moisture. Jonathan couldn't resist lapping up the creamy essence. "Delicious," he breathed, closing his lips over the rounded tip.

Kit moaned again, the wordless sound escaping him with a long, drawn-out breath. His hips hitched upward of their own accord, his body no longer his to control. "Take me," he pleaded, struggling to keep his voice in character. The one corner of his mind that still functioned rationally pointed out that this was perhaps his only chance to speak what was in his heart, since neither of his lovers had spoken of anything beyond the physical pleasure of the moment. "All that I am is yours."

Kit's words sent a thrill of need spiraling through Jonathan—a need to claim his lover completely, more than just physically. He took Kit deeper into his mouth, stroking his palms over the sleek flanks to slip between his cheeks. Kit was already open from using the vibrator, and Jonathan slid a still-moistened finger inside, adding a second and easing them in and out until Kit was rocking against his hand.

Shivering with desire, Kit gave himself over to Jonathan's care, caught between his mouth and his fingers. His body twitched restlessly, trying to move so as to maximize his pleasure, but not knowing which way to go. "Please," he begged, needing Jonathan inside him. His voice lost what little remained of Percival's tone as his desire swamped his ability to stay in character. "Make love to me."

Jonathan groaned as Kit—not Percival—pleaded with him to make love to him. Not to take him—to love him. Pushing up on both hands, he knelt between Kit's spread legs. Inwardly cursing the necessity, he paused for a moment to reach for a condom, quickly smoothing it over himself, thinking eagerly of the day when they would no longer need to consider this distraction. He bent his head to claim his lover's lips in a slow, deep kiss as he positioned himself to slide inside, just as slowly, just as deeply. "Mine," he whispered hoarsely, rocking his hips in short, gentle motions, no longer caring whether Kit heard Arthur or Jonathan. "Mine."

Kit gasped with the pleasure of being filled and whimpered with the joy of being claimed. "Yes," he whispered in reply, leaving it up to Jonathan to interpret the word. He pushed up against Jonathan's thrusts, wanting to feel the connection as fully as possible.

Devon had been growing steadily more aroused as he watched his two lovers struggle to remain within the boundaries of the role-play. Something was happening here, something he'd think about more when he wasn't so damn hard—but right now, he needed to remind his partners that there was a third member of their quest.

Grasping his thickening shaft, he moved to stand beside the couch, looking down at the two self-absorbed lovers. Falling into his Lancelot voice, he murmured silkily, "So one knight is not enough for you, Arthur? You must need bed every one you see?"

Kit opened his eyes quickly, seeing Devon standing there and hearing the accusation in Lancelot's voice. Forcing himself to become Percival again for the moment, he glared at the intruding knight but held his silence. Percival would never overstep his bounds by challenging Lancelot without far more assurance than Arthur had currently given him. That didn't stop him from rocking his hips into Jonathan's again, though, making sure his lover did not lose interest in the proceedings.

Jonathan could not hold back a low moan when Kit's movement caused his cock to slide even deeper inside him. He saw Devon's eyes widen at the sound and Devon's cock twitch in its nest of golden curls. "Jealous, Lancelot?" he rasped, a wicked smile playing on his lips. "Do not think I have not noticed you watching him with lust in your eyes."

"His eyes follow you as well, my liege," Kit amended, "when he thinks you are not watching." He glanced at Jonathan before looking back up at Devon. For all that he had spoken words of challenge, what he wanted was Devon there, in all the same ways he wanted Jonathan. His heart, he was discovering, had enough room for both men. He managed to keep Percival's voice in place, but the tone had softened considerably, a reflection of his own emotions.

"You have but to ask if you wish to join us, Lancelot," Jonathan offered, hoping Kit would not mind. "If Percival will not be scandalized."

Devon slowly knelt beside the couch, reaching his hand out to slide over Jonathan's sweat-slickened back. "I would join you," he admitted, an unexpected tremor in his voice. He realized that he was not only speaking of physical need, though that was the most urgent right now. He wanted to join with these two, to bind them to him, in every way possible. "What say you, Percival?"

"Who better to teach me the arts of love than the two most powerful knights of the realm?" Kit husked in Percival's voice, knowing he'd totally ruined his image as a model of chastity, but he didn't really care when the alternative was having both his lovers with him.

Turning his head to meet Devon's hungry gaze, Jonathan unlocked a hand from Kit's hip and grasped a handful of tousled blond hair. His quickly spiraling desire readily expanded to include both his lovers, giving him a surprising sense of power. Pulling Devon's head forward, he seized his lips in a hard kiss.

Kit's groin tightened further as he watched his two lovers kiss. He knew himself well enough to fear that he wouldn't last until Devon joined them if he didn't get Jonathan to pull back, at least for the moment. His hands on Jonathan's hips, though, had no effect whatsoever.

Jonathan felt Kit push at him, but it felt too good to be buried inside his heat. He wasn't ready to leave it just yet. Breaking the kiss with Devon, he turned his head to smile at the young knight. "I know what you wish," he answered. "But if I have learned anything in my path to becoming king, it is patience."

He slid his hand from Devon's hair down the strong column of his throat, feeling the quiver that ran through his frame. "And what of you, Lancelot? What would you have of us?" he asked, brushing his fingers over a furled pink nipple.

Devon held back a bubble of laughter at Jonathan's response. So his king was in a playful mood, was he? Two could play at that game. "That is a good start," he answered, gliding his hand lower down Jonathan's back, drifting over the taut cheeks.

"And what would be a good continuation?" Kit purred, unable to decide where to place his hand. He knew where he wanted to put it, but he would see if Devon had a preference first.

Devon turned his head to seal his lips to Kit's, kissing him deeply, urging the dark head closer. He slid his hand from Jonathan's arse lower still to cup around his bollocks.

Jonathan gasped when Devon's palm closed around his balls, making his cock jump inside Kit's constricting heat. With a low growl, he pulled Devon's head away from Kit's and ground his lips against Devon's, teeth and tongues clashing as they each fought to dominate the kiss.

Kit might have protested the loss of the kiss if it weren't for the sudden push of Jonathan's cock inside him. He couldn't see what Devon had done, but it had certainly met with Jonathan's approval. Determined to get in on the act, he shifted so he could reach both shaggy heads, pulling their faces close enough to join the kiss, his tongue snaking out to tangle with theirs.

Devon opened his mouth wider, sucking in a panting breath as he tried to taste both his lovers at once, lips and tongue flicking back and forth between their eager mouths. Feeling both their lips on him at the same time was so arousing that he needed more of it. Inching closer, he pushed both heads downward, throwing his own head back to gulp in a lungful of air.

Jonathan knew what Devon was asking for. Lowering his head, he closed his lips around the nipple his fingers had been teasing at, dragging his tongue roughly over the hardened tip. He caught Kit's eyes and dipped his head slightly, hoping Kit would get the message.

Catching on, Kit slid his lips lower and latched on to Devon's other nipple, sucking hard, the way he knew his lover liked. Just because it was not his own preference didn't mean he wouldn't indulge Devon's. Out of the corner of his eye, he saw Jonathan lavishing attention on the other nipple. The sight gave him an idea. Pulling back from Devon's chest, he suggested, "Stand up, Lancelot," hoping Jonathan would catch on to what he had in mind.

A flare of heat raced through Devon at the erotic promise in Kit's voice. Asking Kit to join him in seducing Jonathan was definitely one of the best ideas he'd ever had, Devon decided as he rose slowly to his feet.

Staring down at the still-joined couple below him, who were once again kissing, he raised a hand to each man's cheek, cupping them tenderly even as he turned their heads to face him.

Jonathan stole a quick kiss from Kit, tempted to linger but just as tempted by what he knew Kit had in mind. Tearing his lips away from the ones that ravished his so softly, he reached for Devon, urging him to step closer so that his groin was within reach of their hungry mouths. When their Lancelot stood where he wanted, Jonathan licked down one side of Devon's cock. "Help me pleasure him, Percival," he urged.

"It will be my pleasure," Kit assured them both, licking his own path up the other side of Devon's shaft. He swirled his tongue around the tip, capturing the drops of clear fluid that had leaked from it, and following an irregular course back down to the base, shivering whenever his tongue brushed against Jonathan's.

Having both his lovers' mouths teasing his cock was a such a fierce pleasure that Devon knew he wasn't going to be able to stay in control for long. He wove a hand into each man's hair, as much to keep himself standing upright as to urge them on. "By our Lady," he gasped, managing somehow to stay in character, "you will undo me...."

Kit lifted his head long enough to reply, "Perhaps that is our intention." Then he returned his attention to the hard shaft that bobbed invitingly in front of his face. At the same time, he twitched his hips, hoping to encourage Jonathan to begin moving again.

Jonathan was certainly not resistant to that idea. He angled his hips forward, starting a slow rocking motion that stirred him gently inside Kit. The delicious friction, combined with his first taste of Devon filling his mouth, was quickly bringing him close to his own limits. "Perhaps," he agreed, speaking around increasingly wet laps over Devon's straining cock. "Though perhaps Lancelot... would prefer... not to be... inside your mouth... when I make you come." He caught Kit's head and pulled it closer to his, joining their lips around Devon's cock.

Jonathan's words sent fresh lust spiraling through Kit. He returned the kiss eagerly, tonguing Devon's erection as he sought Jonathan's lips. He wanted to come, wanted to feel Jonathan come in his arse, Devon in his mouth. He moaned at the thought.

Watching Jonathan and Kit kiss with his cock between their lips, their tongues sliding over his slick skin, was the most arousing sight Devon had ever seen. When Kit's moan vibrated around him, he thrust forward involuntarily, and fuck if that didn't feel so good that he had to do it again, and again. "Close," he groaned, fisting his lovers' hair as he rocked against their mouths. "Close... so close... so good."

The taste he'd already gotten of Devon was enough to whet Kit's appetite for more. He lifted a hand to cup Devon's arse, encouraging him to thrust again as he sucked harder on the firm flesh.

Jonathan opened his lips wider around Devon's thick shaft, trying to catch Kit's elusive tongue, each thrust and moan bringing him closer to his own peak. He circled a hand to cup Devon's ass, brushing over Kit's doing the same, before sliding it lower to squeeze gently at Devon's full sac.

The feel of two mouths sliding over his rigid cock, two tongues dueling around him, was turning Devon's insides to pure molten heat. When Jonathan's hand closed around his bollocks, Devon erupted, crying out as his come pulsed over his lovers' joined mouths.

Still holding Devon as his cock jerked against their lips, Jonathan lapped up as much of the creamy fluid as he could reach, savoring the salty taste and the knowledge that he had helped bring Devon to this state. Letting the softening shaft slip from between his lips, he leaned forward to clean the drops that spattered Kit's face, hungrily seeking his mouth once again.

Kit swallowed rapidly as Devon's release hit his mouth and face. The sight of Jonathan cleaning first Devon's shaft and then reaching for Kit's own face had him moaning again. He surrendered his mouth completely when Jonathan claimed it, tasting their other lover on Jonathan's tongue.

Devon slumped back to his knees, panting raggedly as he slowly came down from the adrenaline high of his release. Jonathan and Kit were kissing again, and he felt such a surge of emotion for each of them that reached for their hands, needing to ground himself with the continued contact.

Kit squeezed Devon's hand in acknowledgment and welcome when he felt the other man's grip, but his attention now was firmly fixed on his own climax, hovering just out of reach. It wouldn't take much. If Jonathan would just hit his prostate one more.... Before he could finish the thought, the cock stirring within him found his trigger and he went off, his release shooting out of him to soak their stomachs.

Jonathan felt Devon searching for his hand, and he threaded their fingers together blindly, unable to pull his mouth away from the shared taste of his come on Kit's lips. White heat pooled inside him and flared behind his closed eyelids as he rocked into Kit. He gave in to his own climax, moaning into Kit's mouth as he filled the condom with his hot essence.

When his breathing slowed, finally, Kit looked at his two lovers. "Damn!" he exhaled softly. "I can't remember the last time I had to work so hard to stay in character. That's definitely not an exercise we did at Guildhall."

"I'm just glad no one made any jokes about Devon using his Lance-a-lot." Jonathan grinned, slipping from Kit and easing off the condom until he could dispose of it. "I would have lost it then and there."

Devon stood and arched his back to stretch the stiff muscles. "At least you two got to lie down," he groused good-naturedly. "I was on my feet again, and after standing around all day, I am definitely looking forward to getting horizontal as soon as possible." He tugged at the hands that were still entwined with his. "C'mon, lovers, let's go to bed."

"Getting old, Lance?" Kit teased as he squirmed out from under Jonathan and stood, then turned back to Jonathan. "My liege, shall we put the old man to bed?"

"I'll show you old," Devon growled, swatting at the alluring backside. "We still have a lot of condoms to use up, after all."

CHAPTER 8
MATCHING RINGS

DEVON SLUMPED a little lower in his makeup chair, trying to find a more comfortable position as Stacy combed the tangles out of his hair and styled it into Lancelot's knightly locks. Jonathan had taken his pleas for "more" last night seriously, and he had some definite teeth-shaped bruises on his bum to prove it. Smiling to himself at the memory, he glanced across the trailer at his lover, who seemed to be sitting rather gingerly himself. And Kit was nowhere to be seen yet—he wondered if they'd finally managed to wear the young 'un out. Lord knows they'd given it their best try!

Kit could barely contain his excitement as he breezed toward the trailer. His test results had been waiting for him when he went by his place this morning. Negative. If Jonathan and Devon had gotten theirs, too, then they could finally dispense with condoms. And not a moment too soon. It got harder and harder each time the three of them were together to force himself to don the rubber sheath. He wanted to know what it felt like to sink bare inside them, to feel their skin sinking inside him. Shivering with anticipation, he opened the door and walked inside, giving Stacy an enthusiastic kiss on the cheek before doing the same to Devon and then to Jonathan.

As soon as Stacy left to get more spray gel—muttering under her breath as she went about how much they seemed to be going through—Kit turned to his two lovers. "Negative," he announced proudly.

Jonathan couldn't help but grin at the excitement in Kit's voice. "Me too," he said softly, the quiet tone not disguising his own pleasure at the news. "I picked up the message when I stopped home this morning. I didn't want to say anything until the two of you had heard too."

Both men turned to look at Devon expectantly. "You hardly gave me a chance to check me mail last night, did you?" he grumbled good-naturedly. "Kit had my pants off before I had the door halfway shut! And I didn't think to look before we left this morning." He frowned, hating the thought that he'd have to wait through a long day of filming before he could find out his results. He was sure he was negative, but the confirmation would finally let all three of them enjoy each other without the aggravation of condoms.

"Check your voicemail," Kit suggested, hiding his disappointment. "I had a message on my cell along with the letter in my box. Maybe they did the same for you."

Devon had just dug his cell phone out of his duffel bag when Stacy returned to the trailer. Taking advantage of her teasing lecture to Kit about being late, he punched up his voicemail. He couldn't hold back a whoop of excitement when he heard the message.

"Yes!" he crowed, pumping his fist and smiling broadly at Jonathan and Kit before realizing Stacy had turned to stare at his reaction. He flushed and dropped the phone back into his bag. "Man U won," he muttered sheepishly, meeting Jonathan's laughing eyes in the mirror.

Kit's disappointment faded the moment he heard Devon's reaction. He couldn't stop the smile that split his face despite Stacy's lecture. "I'll do better," he promised her, trying to sound repentant. All he could think of, though, was the box of condoms that was going in the trash the moment the three of them were alone again.

The thrill of anticipation that ran through Jonathan at knowing tonight they could finally dispense with condoms was too delicious not to savor. And he had the perfect way to share that anticipation with his lovers. As soon as Stacy had finished arranging Percival's dark locks and left the trailer, wishing them a good day's filming, he pulled a small bag out of his knapsack and spun around in his chair, facing the other two men.

"To commemorate this momentous occasion, I have something for each of us," he said formally, hoping he didn't sound as nervous as he felt. This had seemed like a good idea at the time, but now he wondered if Devon and Kit would think so. "I saw these at the shop the day we bought the lube, and I thought… well, I thought it would be nice if we had matching rings." He held out his hand to reveal three shining silver bands, each etched with a knotted Celtic design, resting on his palm.

"Cock rings?" Devon snorted with laughter, as much at Kit's bewildered expression as at Jonathan's action. "You realize you bought us matching cock rings?"

"I know what they are," Jonathan protested, stalking toward the laughing blond. "I'm not *that* innocent." He straddled the makeup chair, settling onto Devon's lap and leaning forward to rock their groins together. As he'd expected, he wasn't the only one already hard. "Tell me you aren't going to spend the whole day thinking about how it will feel tonight," he rasped. "This will make it so much better. You can think all you want, and it will just make you that much more ready for when we finally get home."

A bolt of lust went through Kit when he realized what Jonathan had bought, the comments leaving him hard and aching and stifling a moan. He walked over to his lovers, a hand going to the back of each of their necks. "I think we're corrupting you," he teased, nuzzling Jonathan's throat.

"And I'm loving every minute of it," Jonathan agreed, turning his head to meet Kit's lips in a lingering kiss, then pivoting back to claim the same pleasure from Devon. "I can't wait to get both of you home tonight so we can be together with nothing between us. But until then, I think we should all put these on."

Devon hated having to rein in Jonathan's enthusiasm, but he was clearly the most experienced of the group—even if he wasn't always proud of how he'd gained that experience. "These are the most beautiful rings I've seen—and I've seen quite a few—but they aren't the safest." Forestalling Kit's protest, Devon held up his ring, running a finger around the inside circumference. "First of all, they definitely aren't one-size-fits-all. More importantly"—he worked three fingers inside and spread them against the unyielding metal—"they don't give. Which is fine if you're only going to be wearing one for a few minutes, and you know you're going to come at the end of it." Kit still looked unconvinced, but he could see comprehension dawning on Jonathan's face. "If you wore this all day, even assuming it was the right size for you, I can guarantee after a few hours it would be painful. And if you had to take it off—say, to use the loo—well, it might be close to impossible unless you wanked first."

"I thought you could still piss even with a ring like that on," Kit said, eyes fixed on the beautiful silver work, his cock hard at the thought of being confined for the day.

"Probably easier when you're not hard as a rock," Jonathan said with regret. "Which I can guarantee I would be all day long around the two of you."

"I knew someone who bruised himself badly wearing that kind of ring." A dark shadow fell over Devon's expression before he pushed the memory aside. "Not to denigrate your gift, Jon, but I have something else we could use instead." Standing, he reached into the closet for the jeans he'd worn before changing into his costume. "These will have the same effect, but they'll be more comfortable to wear and easier to remove at need." He handed them each a narrow band of soft black leather with a snap closure at one end and an adjustable cinch at the other.

"And why, dear Lancelot," Kit drawled, taking the band and examining it carefully, "do you have a set of cock rings in your jeans pocket?"

"Because we talked about playing on set, of course," Devon answered in the same casual tone. "I notice you didn't question why Jonathan had them with him."

"I should probably take these back, then." Jonathan reached for Kit's ring, but Kit pulled it back out of his reach.

"No," Kit insisted, looking for a safe place to put the ring. "They might not be the right kind to wear very often, or at all, but they're beautiful. If you don't mind, I'd rather keep it. I can add it to the keepsakes on my key chain. No one but us will ever notice it's there, but I'll have the memory of it with me always. And Jon told us why he brought them today."

"You've enough on that key chain already that it's a wonder you don't walk leaning to one side. But I'd like to keep mine too," Devon added in all seriousness. "It really is lovely, as is the thought behind it. Thank you for that, Jonathan."

"You're welcome." Jonathan smiled. "I have to admit I'd hate to think of trying to take these back. The clerk had enough to say when I bought them in the first place."

"Oh really?" Kit teased, slipping his into the pocket of his backpack. He'd put it on his key ring later. "Like what?"

Jonathan flushed slightly. "He said he admired my ambition if I thought I could handle both of you. If I brought them back, he'd probably think you turned me down."

"No fear of that," Devon asserted with a grin.

"Never!" Kit promised, returning to Jonathan's side and kissing him hard. "No way in hell I'd turn you down. But someone's going to come knocking soon if we're not on set. So how do we do this?"

"I think you should put them on us, Jonathan," Devon said. "After all, they were your idea."

"With pleasure," Jonathan growled, sliding off Devon's lap to kneel on the cool floor of the trailer. He reached up to untie the strings of Lancelot's costume, freeing the long, thick cock he was hungering for. Leaning forward, he slid his mouth over the engorged column, slicking it thoroughly with his saliva. When Devon moaned appreciatively, he pulled back, easing the soft leather strap over the head and down until it nestled against the riot of golden curls at its base. "Tell me when it's tight enough," he asked, gently tugging on the free end through the rings of the cinch.

The pressure of the strap around his erection was not an unfamiliar feeling to Devon, but he struggled against an impulse to pull Jonathan's head down again, to thrust up into that delicious mouth. "There. This is going to be a bloody long day," he muttered, trying to remind himself of the benefits they'd reap tonight by enduring the day's frustrations.

Kit moaned at the sight of Jonathan's mouth on Devon's cock and then at the sight of the ring fastened snugly around the base of the thick shaft. He reached for the laces on his breeches. "My turn," he said in a breathless whisper.

"Let me," Jonathan insisted, covering Kit's hands with his own. He dropped a quick kiss onto each hand and then reached beneath them to expose Kit's slender shaft, so different than Devon's but every bit as addictive. With a hum of pleasure, he spiraled his tongue from base to tip, wetting the column until it gleamed. He slid the leather ring down the slippery length, closing his mouth over the smooth head to lap up the moisture beading from its tip, before settling back on his haunches to adjust the fit until Kit moaned his approval. "Look at the two of you," he marveled, appreciating the unique beauty of both his lovers, their hard cocks encircled by the leather straps resting in beds of light and dark curls.

Kit shivered with delight, the constriction an exquisite agony. His erection swelled at the sensation. The thought that he would spend the day in this state was enough to have his knees trembling. "What about you?" he asked.

Jonathan had already risen to his feet and was reaching for the laces that held his leggings together when Devon leaned forward—hissing a bit at the constriction caused by his movement—and swatted his hands away. "Ye can't put on yer own cock ring," he complained, taking the third band from Jonathan's hand.

"Absolutely not," Kit agreed, dropping to his knees. "We'll put it on you. After all, this is a gift for all of us to enjoy, right?"

"I'm sure we'll enjoy taking them off more than putting them on," Jonathan said with a wide grin. "But by all means, make yourself useful." He looked down at the two men kneeling before him, feeling lust and something deeper, something so strong he had to joke to mask his emotions. "I'm sure I'll never have both of you on your knees for me like this again!"

Kit chuckled. "All you have to do is ask." He leaned forward to moisten Jonathan's cock. Jonathan could interpret that as he wished.

Devon reached below Kit's chin to cradle Jonathan's bollocks. "I wouldn't be sure of that," he murmured huskily, squeezing gently as Kit let the saliva-coated shaft slide from his mouth. After fitting the strap over the tip of Jonathan's cock, Devon used his lips to push it down the swollen shaft as far as it would go. He sucked lightly as he slid his mouth back upward, releasing the head from his lips with a pop. "As your finest knight, I might want to demonstrate my fealty to you on a regular basis." He sat back on his heels with a smile. "Especially when it tastes that good."

When Devon lifted his head, Kit reached for the strap on the cock ring, not quite elbowing Devon aside as he carefully adjusted the constriction. He couldn't resist bestowing another wet lick on the throbbing flesh as he fitted the cock ring to meticulous—but hopefully not painful—tightness.

Jonathan bit back a moan at the feel of first Kit's mouth, and then Devon's, closing over his erection. His blood pounded behind the ring's constriction, a constant reminder of how much he wanted these two men. He offered a hand to both of them, pulling them to their feet and giving them each a quick kiss. "We'd better get dressed before Carol or Stacy come back to get something and realize where all the lube is disappearing to," he said reluctantly.

Kit frowned in displeasure, but he knew Jonathan was right. He glanced at the clock. "We're due on set in a few minutes anyway." His arousal was not subsiding at all, and it wouldn't, he knew. "This is gonna be one hell of a long day."

Devon reached forward to tuck Kit back inside his snug leggings, sneaking a final squeeze of the bulge beneath them. "Percival is packing a concealed weapon today." He smirked at Jonathan as he adjusted his own breeches.

Kit eyed the bulge in Devon's trousers that disappeared beneath his long tunic. "So's Lancelot," he retorted. "The only difference is that Percival's man enough not to hide it."

"I'm not sure Niall would think that's a good thing, however much we appreciate it," Jonathan said, tucking himself up carefully, the weight of his breeches stimulating his already-hard cock. Just walking like this was going to be arousing as hell. Only knowing that Devon and Kit were enduring the same erotic torment was going to let him make it through the day.

Devon clasped Jonathan and Kit by the shoulders and then let his hands caress his lovers' backs, lingering over their buttocks. "Another day, another dollar," he said in a credible version of the American accent Jonathan had carefully shed as Arthur. Jonathan grinned at him over his shoulder, and Devon gave them an encouraging nudge forward. Admiring the view as they started out of the trailer, he adjusted himself again, trying vainly to find a comfortable position for his cock before following them out the door.

When they got to the set, Niall was already talking to Bevan Campbell and Fraser Reid, the actors who played Gawain and the Green Knight, setting the scene for the knight's arrival at Camelot. Kit hid a sigh of relief. The scene called for a lot of close-ups of Gawain and the Green Knight, with just the occasional wider shot of the whole Round Table. If all went well, the three of them would be able to mill about or even slip from the crowd, partially hidden from the others' sight, while Bevan and Fraser went through the scene until Niall was satisfied. And as long as they were quiet, there was nothing to stop them from getting in a few gropes under the cover of the darkness.

Giving silent thanks that it was Gawain and not Arthur who would be confronting the Green Knight, Jonathan leaned against the wall of the Great Hall set while the director lined up the scene, trying not to squirm. He was quite sure that Arthur wouldn't squirm, even if it felt like he had a second sword sheathed inside his leggings.

Devon hid a smile as he watched Jonathan lean, attempting to seem nonchalant, against the fake stone of the castle set. His king was definitely feeling the effect of the ring. Ambling over slowly enough to minimize the friction against his own hidden arousal, he slipped past Jonathan to take up a position next to him, letting his hip brush against the front of the king's state robes as he did so.

Jonathan inhaled sharply as Devon rubbed against him, his cock throbbing against the firm pressure around its base. Leaning over, he turned his head to make it look to any observer as if he were murmuring something to the Breton knight. Knowing the darkness shielded them from view, he slid his tongue sensuously around Devon's ear before closing his teeth over its tip. "Bastard," he growled quietly.

Seeing his lovers enjoying each other's company, Kit sauntered over, knowing his tunic would hide nothing if he got too much more aroused. He would just have to stand so that only they could see it. He flanked Jonathan so the king was once again sandwiched between him and Devon. "Doing all right?" he purred.

Pressed close between his two lovers, Jonathan realized he had the perfect opportunity for some teasing of his own. Inconspicuously, he moved his hands behind Percival and Lancelot, sliding underneath their tunics. Letting his fingers follow the contours of their backsides, he skimmed tantalizingly down each man's crease.

It was Devon's turn to hide a gasp when Jonathan's fingers began playing along his arse and teasing against his crack. Reaching behind him as unobtrusively as he could, he grasped Jonathan's hand, trying to push it away, but Jonathan was surprisingly strong—and persistent. "Bloody tease," Devon hissed, his cock straining at the arousing touch.

Kit suppressed a yelp when Jonathan squeezed his arse. He pulled back in surprise, his boot catching on one of the fake paving stones on the floor. He kept himself from falling, but not without making more noise than was acceptable on a film set.

"Cut!" Niall called, annoyance clear in his voice. "What's going on, Kit?"

Hoping the dimness of the twilight set hid his blush, Kit tried to frame a reply. "Sorry, Niall. I tripped on the edge of one of the floor stones and lost my balance, but I'm good now. It won't happen again."

Jonathan dropped his hands, trying not to flush at Niall's reproof. "Sorry," he whispered, quietly enough that no one but Kit and Devon could hear. "We can't do anything that's going to disrupt filming."

Devon nodded in agreement but couldn't help grinning at his partners. "True, but we'll be breaking for lunch soon," he murmured. "I'd say the three of us need to practice our lines. Don't you agree?"

Kit nodded. "Somewhere private," he added. "Where no one will break our concentration."

"We could go back to the trailer," Jonathan suggested. "And lock the door."

"Sounds perfect to me," Kit replied immediately. "Devon?"

"You have no idea what you're asking for, do you?" Devon grinned. "We'll see how long an untried knight can hold out against the king and his champion."

"Not long at all if past experience is any guide," Kit replied. "Of course, I don't remember the king and his champion being much more successful at resisting the knight."

"I don't plan on trying to resist either of you," Jonathan admitted softly. "I just need to be able to touch you. To kiss you." He trailed off; just saying the words was making the aching need even stronger.

Devon reached over to squeeze Jonathan's hand, not trying to arouse with his touch this time, and was relieved when Jonathan squeezed back quickly before dropping his hand to his side. Lunch couldn't get here soon enough to suit him.

Niall announced the midday break a few minutes later, much to the relief of all three of them. One by one they slipped away, each pleading a different excuse to return to their trailer. They had called enough attention to themselves, however accidentally, that morning. They didn't need more attention now. The lunch hour passed far too quickly amid the kisses and caresses that were all they dared in costume, knowing they would have to return to the set for afternoon filming. The tap on the door found them reluctantly ready to return to work. Fortunately, the afternoon scenes required more of their attention, diverting some of their focus from their throbbing erections.

JONATHAN KICKED off his shoes the instant he walked into his house, stretching to try to work the stiffness out of his back. No amount of stretching, though, was going to help the stiffness farther down. "I didn't think this afternoon was ever going to end," he complained, closing the door behind Devon and Kit.

Kit embraced him, sliding his hands to Jonathan's lower back and massaging gently. He knew all too well the way back pain could ruin the mood for anything more... athletic. And since Kit definitely wanted relief for pain of a different kind, he did his best to ease Jonathan's aches. "It's over now," Kit purred. "Now we get to the fun part."

Despite the gentleness of Kit's touch, Jonathan was already straining almost painfully against the zipper of his jeans. He'd managed to control his arousal enough to finish the afternoon's filming professionally and drive home without causing an accident. Just the touch of Kit's hands, though, even if he wasn't consciously trying to entice, had him as hard as he was when they'd first put on the rings. Struggling to regain his control, he stepped away from Kit with a smile and headed into the kitchen to retrieve the bottle of champagne he'd kept chilling in the refrigerator since the afternoon they'd all gone to be tested.

"Would you grab a couple of glasses, Devon?" he asked, working open the wire cage over the cork. "I thought we should celebrate getting rid of the condoms."

Devon had been drinking at Jonathan's enough times to know where to find the wineglasses. Stretching into the cabinet to reach them had never been quite this much of a challenge, though. He was tempted to simply strip off to relieve the ache, but Jonathan had obviously gone to some effort to make the evening special. Devon had some ideas of his own in that regard, but a glass or two of bubbly first wouldn't hurt any of them. "Fill us up, my king," he agreed, handing Jonathan the glasses.

Kit was vibrating with arousal, but he promised himself he would stay in control at least as long as his lovers did. He might be younger than they were, but he was no green kid. He could savor the joys of anticipation too. He took the champagne flute Jonathan offered him and waited until the other two had glasses as well. He lifted his and smiled. "Here's to us," he said, clinking his glass against theirs.

"And only us," Jonathan agreed, draining his glass. "Speaking of which...." He headed into the bedroom, his two lovers following him, removed the nearly empty box of condoms from the bedside drawer, and slam-dunked them into the wastebasket.

Kit couldn't suppress a cheer at seeing their remaining condoms go to waste. He was more than ready to do without them.

"And good riddance," Devon agreed, topping off their glasses with the bottle he'd carried into the bedroom. "Tonight's a special night. I'd like to make it even more special, if the two of you agree."

"What did you have in mind?" Kit asked, fresh shivers of desire running down his back. Devon was endlessly inventive, and they had benefited more than once from following his lead.

Jonathan watched both his lovers speculatively. Devon had a look in his eyes that was almost predatory, while Kit was practically vibrating with eagerness—both of which Jonathan was finding sexy as hell. "Whatever it is, I hope it involves us getting naked and out of these rings as quickly as possible," he interjected, moving his free hand to the top button of his jeans.

"You're half right," Devon responded, finishing his wine and setting the empty glass and bottle aside. He turned toward Jonathan, lowering his voice as he slowly opened the fastening of their king's faded jeans. "We should definitely get naked. But I think we should leave on the rings as long as we can."

"Bloody hell!" Kit swore. "Are you trying to kill us?" Seeing that Devon was getting Jonathan naked, though, Kit set his glass down and went to help. The sooner they were all undressed, the sooner they could do something about the damn rings.

"Leave it on?" Jonathan nearly snorted in disbelief. "All I've been thinking about all afternoon was coming home and getting it off!" He smiled wryly as he realized what he'd just said. "Well, you know what I mean! Why would you possibly want to leave them on, Devon?" His voice trailed off to a low, throaty growl as, between them, Devon and Kit slid his jeans down his thighs and sandwiched him between their equally hard bodies.

"Because," Devon purred, flexing his hips in illustration as he began unbuttoning the other man's shirt. "If we take them off now, this will all be over in a few minutes. If we leave them on, we can"—he slid his fingers under the plaid flannel to hunt for Jonathan's pink nipples—"enjoy each other much, much longer."

Kit drew the shirt off Jonathan's shoulders and reached around to burrow his hands between his lovers. He pressed against Jonathan's back, rubbing his erection over Jonathan's arse. "Can you wait?" he asked. "Can you let us show you how much we…." He couldn't say *love you*. They hadn't talked about love. It wasn't supposed to have any part in their equation. "We appreciate your gifts," he finished lamely.

"My gifts?" Jonathan gasped, finding it increasingly difficult to concentrate as Devon's thumbs rasped over his nipples and two denim-clad cocks rubbed against him. "Oh, you mean the rings? Even though we couldn't use them?"

That wasn't exactly what Kit had meant, or at least not all he meant, but he made a sound of agreement because the last thing he wanted was to spoil the evening with unwanted declarations.

Devon chuckled and let one hand trail down Jonathan's toned abdomen to circle the straining column of his erection. "Yeah, but these gifts are pretty damn impressive too," he added, squeezing gently.

"Fuck, Devon," Jonathan growled, his cock jumping at the caress, "if you're going to manhandle me, the least you can do is get naked yourself first." *So I can do a little grabbing of my own.* He needed to touch Devon almost as much as he needed more of his touch.

"Brilliant idea." Devon met Kit's gaze over Jonathan's shoulder. "No wonder Merlin recognized him as the future king, eh, sunshine?" He held Kit's eyes as he quickly stripped off his own clothes, wondering if Kit remembered the discussion they'd had the afternoon Jonathan must have bought the rings. "Why don't we show him how much we appreciate him just the way he is?"

"I can do that," Kit replied, nodding at Devon from behind Jonathan's back. "What do you say, my liege? Do you think you can handle what we dish out?"

The momentary respite while his two lovers hurried to remove their own clothes let Jonathan regain a little of his control. Deciding he'd been passive long enough, he pivoted to reach for Kit, pulling him forward to fit their naked bodies together. "You're not going to be any better off than I am, Kit-Kat," he countered, leaning down to kiss him as he cupped Kit's delectable ass and ground their torsos together.

Kit didn't care about being better off as long as Jonathan's hands were on his body, Jonathan's lips covering his. He rubbed against him provocatively, hoping to encourage more attention.

Dropping the last of his clothing to the floor, Devon watched Jonathan and Kit fondle each other with increasing intensity. He climbed onto Jonathan's bed and leaned back against the headboard, his legs stretched out and his cock rigid with delicious anticipation.

"Right, you two," he called finally, beckoning them to join him. "C'mere, Jon," he invited, drawing the king down to straddle his hips. "Kneel up." He reached one hand to cup Jonathan's heavy sac as he leaned forward enough to run his tongue over the engorged head of his cock.

"Fuck, Devon!" Jonathan repeated as Devon swirled his tongue around the head of his cock. By now he'd normally have been leaking precome, but the ring's constriction prevented all but a few drops from escaping.

"Maybe later," Devon promised before sucking the length of Jonathan's cock into his mouth. He loved the taste of sweat and musk on his tongue, the little motions Jonathan made with his hips as he tried to keep from thrusting into Devon's mouth, loved the hungry sounds he was coaxing from his lover.

Wanting in on the fun, Kit climbed onto the bed and crouched near Devon's feet, angling his head so he could slide his tongue along Jonathan's crack. He had wanted to do this to Jonathan for a while, but they always seemed to end up doing something else. Tonight he refused to be sidetracked. He was going to get a taste of Jonathan's arse.

Jonathan leaned forward to brace himself against the headboard, moaning as his lovers' mouths teased at him from front and back. He wanted to touch them, to kiss them in return, but it was all he could do to hold himself erect as the sensuous assault went on and on. Without the ring, he knew he'd have come already. He trembled as the tightness in his belly grew stronger. "Oh God," he gasped. "Oh God, Kit, Devon…."

Kit took Jonathan's words as an invitation and prodded at Jonathan's entrance, thrusting inside as deeply as he could. He heard the desperation in Jonathan's voice and wanted to add to it, wanted to show Jonathan without words how he felt.

Devon increased the suction on Jonathan's cock, reaching up to flick at his nipples. He could tell from the increasingly ragged gasps and moans that Jonathan was close—or would be, if the pressure of the cock ring wasn't holding him back. He rolled Jonathan's swollen sac gently in his other palm as he relaxed his throat to swallow as much as he could of Jonathan's length.

The thrusts of Kit's tongue pushed Jonathan forward, deeper into Devon's mouth, until the base of his cock was pressed firmly against Devon's lips. His balls tightened, throbbing almost painfully as the sensations built and built, beyond anything he'd felt before. When Devon took him deep into his throat, Jonathan's entire body stiffened, and he cried out wordlessly, spasms of pleasure wracking him. He groaned and trembled through a climax as powerful as any he'd ever felt, but the sensation didn't lessen, his cock didn't soften, his balls remained rock-hard with unreleased seed. "Stop," he pleaded as the tremors went on and on. "Can't... too much."

Regretfully, Kit gave Jonathan's pucker one last, loving lick before pulling back. The pause was only temporary, after all. If Jonathan had truly wanted them to stop, he would have used his safeword. Kit's own body was demanding attention now, driven to the edge by the dark flavor of Jonathan's body and the wanton sounds that fell from his lips. Leaning over to the nightstand, he grabbed the lube, coating his fingers. "Let me know when you're ready for more," he told Jonathan, kissing his neck softly.

"More?" Jonathan moaned, tangling a hand into Devon's hair and pulling him away from his oversensitized cock. "Oh fuck, Devon, stop," he implored, pulling his head up and kissing him roughly, passionately.

"More," Kit repeated, though he was not sure Jonathan heard him. He slid his lips up to Jonathan's ear. "I want to fuck you."

As overstimulated as he already felt, Jonathan's cock twitched at the need he heard in Kit's voice, at the taste of his own sweat in Devon's mouth. It was too much, and yet it wasn't enough.

Giving in to the insistent demands of his own need, Devon broke away from Jonathan's kiss and slid down from the headboard. Grasping his lover's shoulders, he pulled Jonathan with him until he was positioned over Devon's cock. "Suck me," he urged, arching up toward his mouth. "Suck me, and let Kit fuck you."

"Yes," Jonathan moaned, his lover's pleas and his own unsatisfied need more than he could withstand. Leaning forward, he lapped at as much of Devon's cock as he could reach. "Oh fuck, yes," he agreed, sucking Devon into his mouth, trying to return as much pleasure as Devon had given him.

Kit took Jonathan's words as an invitation, sliding his slick fingers into Jonathan's crack, seeking the hidden flesh he had so recently anointed with his tongue. He wanted to take his time, but while the cock ring held back his orgasm, it didn't give him patience, and his erection was growing steadily more demanding. It was all he could do to start with one finger, but even that finger wasn't as gentle as he knew he should have been.

Jonathan groaned around Devon's thick shaft when Kit's finger breached him. Clenching involuntarily around the invading digit, he thrust backward, forcing it deeper inside, craving the fullness, the burn, the release that was still denied him.

Devon tossed his head against the crumpled bedsheets, fighting the impulse to thrust into the hot suction of Jonathan's mouth. The hunger that had been building all day flared into white-hot pleasure as his lover's tongue circled him, flicking over the vein that throbbed against the constriction of the cock ring. "Yesss," he hissed, unable to stop his hips from rocking upward. "Take it, Jon, take all of it, ahh fuck…."

Feeling Jonathan thrust back against his hand, Kit added a second finger, scissoring them urgently, wanting to sink into Jonathan's heat. *Now*. He knew what Jonathan's tightness felt like through a barrier of latex, but he wanted that feeling on his bare skin. Hoping he'd prepared Jonathan enough, he coated his erection with lube and pushed inside, groaning at the mind-blowing sensation. He was almost grateful for the cock ring. He would certainly have come on the spot without it.

"Oh God. Kit," Jonathan groaned, letting Devon slide from his mouth and arching his back to take his lover as deeply inside him as he could. The heat, the friction of Kit's silky skin against the walls of his channel, was so much better than anything he'd felt before. "More," he pleaded, pushing back wantonly into Kit's hips. Bending down, he swallowed Devon's length again, craving the feel of being filled by both his lovers.

Kit obliged immediately, thrusting steadily, deeply, into Jonathan's willing passage. Over Jonathan's shoulder, he could see Devon's face, see the approaching ecstasy written there. "Finish him off," he urged Jonathan. "I want you inside him when we come. I want us to all come together."

Watching Jonathan writhing above him as Kit thrust into him, Devon couldn't continue to resist the demands of his own need. As Jonathan's mouth closed around him again, he drove his fingers deep into Jonathan's sandy-brown hair, pumping his hips in short, shallow strokes, riding the ecstasy long past the point he would have come without the ring. When Kit urged Jonathan to finish him, to take him, he was more than ready. "Do it, Jon," he agreed, sliding forward and spreading his legs wide in invitation.

Jonathan fumbled for the lube with fingers made clumsy with need and desire. He sucked in an unsteady breath, forcing himself to enter Devon with gentle fingers. No matter how loudly his body screamed at him for release, he had to be sure Devon was as ready as he was. "Open up for me, babe," he rasped to his golden-haired lover, twisting his fingers as he stroked Devon's saliva-slick cock with his other hand. "Open up so I can love you."

"Ready," Devon panted as Jonathan's blunt fingers brushed over his prostate, sending tendrils of fire racing up his spine. "Now, Jon, take off the fucking ring and fuck me."

"Let me," Kit interjected. He reached between the two men and undid the snap on Jonathan's cock ring. When he had tossed it aside, he positioned Jonathan's erection at Devon's entrance. "Now you can fuck him properly."

His cock free at last from the ring's constriction, Jonathan surged against the sweaty crease of Devon's ass. Gritting his teeth against the imperative need to come, he pushed into Devon's heat, sheathing himself to the root in a single stroke. Holding himself as still as he could with Kit still buried inside him, he reached forward to unsnap the ring from Devon's cock. "Now," he grated, pulling rhythmically at Devon's shaft, rocking back against Kit and thrusting deeper into Devon with each stroke. "Now," he groaned. "Coming—come with me."

"Wait for me, damn it," Kit swore, pulling back enough to snap the cock ring off roughly. All he cared about was getting back inside Jonathan and getting a reprieve from the daylong arousal. With a sigh of relief, he sank back inside Jonathan, thrusting a little deeper, a little harder than before now that the artificial restraint on his passion was gone.

Devon groaned in relief when Jonathan unfastened the ring from his aching cock, but once its restriction was gone, nothing was going to stop the spiraling waves of pleasure from crashing over him. Jonathan couldn't have thrust into him more than twice, dragging his hand over the throbbing head of his erection, when Devon exploded, spurting what felt like a never-ending stream of come between their heaving bodies.

The raw power of Kit thrusting into him, and the unbearably tight heat of Devon clenching around his naked cock as he climaxed, shredded the last of Jonathan's control. Crying out in ecstasy, he pumped his hips erratically, filling Devon with his release.

Kit fought his orgasm as long as he could, wanting to savor this moment of communion, but he couldn't resist the sounds of his lovers' cries of ecstasy or the overwhelming sensation of Jonathan's channel contracting around his bare cock. Giving in to his passion, he let his climax tear through him, his seed coating Jonathan's passage.

Kit collapsed forward onto Jonathan's back, knowing his weight combined with Jonathan's had to be crushing Devon, but he was floating on the incredible rush of the long-delayed orgasm, too blissed-out to focus on anything beyond the immediate glow of satiation.

Eventually, though, he made himself roll to one side so Jonathan could move as well. Staring toward the ceiling through unseeing eyes, he murmured, "I had no idea I could feel anything that intense."

"Guess the rings were a pretty good idea after all," Jonathan agreed. He probably had a ridiculous grin on his face, but he was still too high on the euphoria of their lovemaking to care.

Devon levered up on one elbow to look at both his well-satisfied lovers. "You seemed to enjoy that." He grinned at the understatement. "Would you be open to trying a few other things you might not have considered before? If I could assure you they'd be just as intense?"

"What did you have in mind?" Kit asked, not rejecting the idea but not sure he was comfortable with it either.

"Toys," Devon said, watching to see if Jonathan shared Kit's uneasiness. "We've got a long weekend break coming up. If you're interested, I could bring over some toys, let you see if there's anything you'd like to"—his voice took on the low, purring tone that Jonathan was learning to love—"play with."

Kit relaxed. After all, what was his vibrator but a toy? He nodded with more enthusiasm.

Jonathan would have sworn he was completely sated, but at Devon's words, his cock stirred back to life. "I'd say we're interested," he agreed, glancing at Kit for confirmation. "But if we're going to... play... we should probably find someplace a bit more private. I don't particularly want a troupe of knights interrupting us again," he added, remembering the close call they'd had earlier in the week when some of their castmates had decided to pay an unannounced visit to his house.

"I know a little place on the beach that will be perfect," Devon said, his mind already racing with possibilities. "You two be ready to leave as soon as we finish filming. I'll pack the toy box."

CHAPTER 9
BLACK MOOD

DEVON OPENED the door to his closet and ran his hand along the hangers, trying to decide what to pack for the weekend. Who was he kidding? He was trying to work up the nerve to pull out his leathers. For reasons he'd never fully explored, he kept them with him, just as he did his toys, even when he wasn't in a relationship that needed them. He wondered now what that said about him.

It was far too early in his relationship with Jonathan and Kit for that dynamic. In fact, he wasn't sure if they'd ever be ready for it. Or that he was ready to go there again himself. Surprisingly enough, it was Jonathan who'd shown signs of interest, though Devon didn't think he would be satisfied as a sub for long. Jonathan reminded Devon of himself when he'd first been brought into the BDSM scene. *That* thought would lead him in a direction he didn't want to go, and he forced it aside. Kit, now, had stated more than once his aversion to intentional pain, his unease at the idea of submission. Remembering the distress he and Jonathan had caused Kit once already sent a stab of guilt lancing through him. He couldn't risk that again, *wouldn't* risk anything that might threaten what was building between the three of them.

Devon hesitated to put a name to their relationship, not when they hadn't talked about anything more than the present. Sure, they'd gotten tested and gotten rid of the condoms—that memory brought a rakish smile back to his face—but that was more about the practicalities of now than it was about making long-term promises. While they were together, they'd be faithful, would protect each other by those choices, but they hadn't talked about beyond filming. It was easy to forget, in the middle of such a long shoot, that it would end eventually, but Devon had been on enough sets, enough shoots, to know the illusion was just that.

His thoughts turned back to one film in particular and the aftermath of its ending—*No*. No, he refused to relive it again or give it any more power over him. He wouldn't repeat his past mistakes, especially when it actually meant something this time. Pushing hangers aside roughly, he reached to the back of the closet and pulled out the supple black leather garments. Maybe it was time to associate them with more pleasant memories.

His hands shook as he stripped out of his jeans and sweater and replaced them with the soft leather. The last time he had worn them still haunted him, still colored so much of his perceptions about dominance, about submission. He was no longer that man, though. He had learned the true meaning of giving and taking since then, but not in that context. *Things are different this time*, he reminded himself. *This time, I can control what happens*. He glanced back at the toy box he had packed earlier, knowing what he had included and what he had deliberately left out. Restraints, yes. Whips, no. Not when Kit had said he didn't want pain.

His skin prickled with goose bumps, each tiny individual hair standing upright as he smoothed the butter-soft leather over it. He reached for the fastenings of the trousers and realized just how badly he was trembling.

"Bloody hell!" he cursed, drawing a deep breath. *You can do this. You can control this.* Knowing it was probably a mistake but needing something to numb the remembrance, he reached up to the closet shelf for the bottle of scotch he kept there. Not bothering with niceties like a glass, he unscrewed the cap and took a long pull, letting the fiery liquor burn down his throat.

Fortified with liquid courage, he tied the laces quickly, before he could think any more, stuffed the bottle back in the closet, grabbed his gym bag with the toy box and some toiletries in it, and all but ran out the door. Anything to get away from the memories.

SHIFTING THE car into gear, Jonathan checked the mirrors before driving off the ferry ramp and through the crowded traffic of the Calais docks. The cottage Devon had rented was only a few hours' drive down the coast, according to his GPS. Kit had lobbied for taking the train from London, pointing out that it was much faster and that once they got through the Channel Tunnel they could transfer from the Eurostar to a TGV that would get them to their destination more quickly, his leer making it perfectly clear how he hoped to take advantage of the extra time that would afford them. Devon, somewhat surprisingly, had argued for taking the ferry instead, claiming (rightly, as it turned out) that the view sailing from the White Cliffs of Dover wasn't to be missed. Jonathan didn't have a preference either way, but when it turned out that the seaside village where they would be staying was too small for train service, it made more sense to take his car than to rent another when they landed in France.

Once he was safely on the road, Jonathan couldn't help but glance in the mirror again, this time to check the view of the back seat. He lingered appreciatively on the image of Devon's long, lean body encased in tight black leather. He was going to have to watch his speed on the way to the cottage. The anticipation was already tempting him to break the rules.

When Devon had shown up at his house that morning, Jonathan's first thought had been to jump him right then, and if Kit's drooling was any indication, he had felt the same way. The leather clung to every bulge, every plane of Devon's body, outlining, highlighting, and drawing attention to his incredible physique. Jonathan wanted to run his fingers over every last inch.

He might have done it too, except Devon had seemed distracted somehow. He would almost have said uncomfortable if it were anyone but Devon. Oh, he had smiled and laughed at Kit's exaggerated leering and cheeky comments, but something in his eyes didn't match the rest of his expression. Maybe he was just tired; it had been a grueling week of filming, and they all needed to unwind. Jonathan hoped that was all it was. He'd just have to be sure to lavish enough pleasure on Devon to banish that look from his eyes.

And if that wasn't all it was, if, heaven forbid, something else was wrong, he'd coax and cajole until Devon told them what it was, and then he'd make sure they made it better. He had no idea what he and Kit could do to help if it was something wrong at home, something to do with Devon's pending divorce, but at the very least, they'd make sure Devon knew he wasn't alone.

Thinking about all the things he could do to show Devon how much he meant to him was making Jonathan's jeans uncomfortably tight. He glanced in the mirror again at the triangle of golden skin showing through the opening of the leather jacket. He'd start by slowly peeling the jacket open, tasting every inch of flesh as he revealed it and worshipping the tight pink nipples until Devon was begging for more.

Then he'd slip the jacket down Devon's shoulders, trapping his arms in the sleeves, and lick all the lines of his six-pack, tracing every muscle. If Devon asked nicely, maybe, just maybe, he'd take the jacket the rest of the way off so Devon had his hands free to return the pleasure. Then again, the idea of Devon at his mercy was incredibly tempting.

With his arms trapped, Devon wouldn't be able to stop Jonathan from loosening the ties of the leather pants, catching the fine golden hairs in his teeth and tugging at them, just hard enough that Devon would feel the skin of his abdomen pull taut. He'd push the leather aside to bare the other man's hip bones and trace them with his tongue, dipping just a little lower each time, breathing in the heady scent of Devon's arousal as he teased his way closer to it.

Jonathan glanced in the mirror again, his sensual daydream faltering at the reflection of Devon's brooding expression as he stared blankly out the window. Something was definitely wrong. Devon had been Jonathan's friend before he was his lover, but even when he was fighting through problems with his estranged wife, Jonathan hadn't seen Devon look this distressed. He wondered if he should say anything now, or if it would be better to wait until they got to the cottage and he could focus on Devon completely. He glanced over to the passenger seat at Kit, wondering if he'd also noticed Devon's behavior.

Kit had taken the front seat next to Jonathan when they left on their trip for one very simple reason: if he sat in the back seat with Devon, he wouldn't have made it to their destination before molesting the man. Kit had been called sex on legs more than once, usually with a bit of teasing thrown in, but he knew, as surely as he knew his own name, that he had never looked as good as Devon did in the skin-hugging leather pants and tight leather jacket.

The only concern he had at this point, besides getting to the cottage as quickly as possible, was the frown he saw on Devon's face anytime he thought the other two weren't watching. Kit had seen a lot of different expressions on Devon's face, both when he was acting and when he was not, but this one was new; more introspective, more—Kit hated to use the word—desolate. And that worried him almost as much as the leather aroused him. Whatever was going on in Devon's head, it wasn't good, and that didn't bode well for their vacation. Kit hid a frown of his own. As soon as they got to the cottage, they were going to get to the bottom of this so they could all relax and enjoy the time off.

Devon realized he'd been staring out the window for almost an hour and couldn't describe the scenery they'd passed if his life depended on it. He also realized that both his companions were unusually quiet. Not that Jonathan was one for small talk, but it was unlike Kit not to have something to chatter about. Hoping he hadn't infected them with his own black mood, Devon tried again to shake off the unwanted memories. "How much longer 'til we get there, Jon?"

"If you start asking if we're there yet, I'll turn this car around right now," Jonathan answered, relieved to see Devon pull out of his private world, and determined to lighten the mood. "The village is just ahead, and it should be easy to find the cottage since it's right on the beach."

"And not a moment too soon." Kit turned to look at Devon. In a deliberate effort to bring a smile to his lover's face, he added, "I'm so worked up just thinking about you in those leathers, mate, that I could just about come sitting here!"

"You'll come when I let you," Devon snapped without thinking, realizing what he'd done an instant later when two sets of eyes widened in shock at his commanding tone. "Bloody hell," he groaned, dropping his head into his hands.

Making a final turn as the GPS announced they had reached their destination, Jonathan pulled into the driveway of the cottage and killed the engine. "Devon?" he demanded, turning anxiously in his seat. "What's wrong? Let us help you, whatever it is."

The words Kit wanted to say froze in his throat. He wanted to assure Devon that he loved him, that whatever the problem was, it wouldn't touch Kit's emotions, but he had no idea if the sentiment would be welcomed. Instead, he added his plea to Jonathan's. "We're here for you, Devon. You know that, right?"

The tightness in Devon's chest eased a little at the concern evident in Jonathan's voice and Kit's words. He was not with Robert this time. They cared for him, maybe as much as he was growing to care for them. And he owed them an explanation for his behavior.

"I've been a right bastard all morning, haven't I?" he muttered. "Let's go inside, and I'll try to explain."

Kit opened the door and climbed out of the car, stopping at the boot to grab his bag. On impulse, he grabbed the other two as well. The sooner they got inside, the sooner they could deal with whatever was bothering Devon.

As soon as Devon unlocked the door and it closed behind them, Kit dropped the bags and took Devon's face in his hands. He stared intently into the troubled green eyes for a few moments before deliberately closing his mouth over his lover's and kissing him thoroughly. When he pulled back, he smiled. "When you're ready to talk, we're ready to listen."

Jonathan wrapped his arms around Devon, pulling him back gently into his embrace and kissing the strip of golden skin above the collar of the black leather jacket. "There's nothing you can say that will change the way we feel about you," he added, knowing that for himself, at least, those feelings had grown far deeper than mere physical attraction.

For a moment Devon let himself be soothed by the kisses, drawing strength from the two men who had already given so much to him. He turned his head to meet Jonathan's lips, opening himself to the warm, moist kiss.

"Trust us, Devon," Jonathan urged. "You don't always have to be the strong one."

"Tell us what's wrong," Kit encouraged. He took a step forward so Devon was caught between his body and Jonathan. He stretched up to join his mouth to the two already connected, bringing the three of them together in this, as he wanted them to be together in all things.

Bracketed securely between his two lovers, Devon realized he no longer felt angry or guilty or fearful. He felt safe. He felt... loved. Raising a hand to cup each man's cheek, he drew back and smiled ruefully. "Let's sit down, yeah? And I'll try to explain."

Kit drew back enough so they could move to the couch, but he had no intention of moving any farther away from Devon than that. Whatever was on Devon's mind, it was clearly bothering him, and Kit wanted to be close enough to provide physical comfort along with whatever words he needed to say.

Once they were seated on the overstuffed sofa, Devon glanced at the men on either side of him, wondering how much he should tell them. Enough to explain his uneasiness, certainly, but there were some things he wasn't ready to share, things they didn't need to hear. "This isn't the first time I've been... involved... during filming," he began, knowing there was no comparison between then and now.

The bleak expression in Devon's eyes tore at Jonathan's heart. He was shocked at how much he wanted to find the person responsible for putting that expression there and make them pay for hurting Devon. He ran a hand down the collar of Devon's jacket, tracing the transition from cool leather to warm golden flesh. "Does this—does the leather have something to do with that involvement?"

Devon nodded grimly. "It was nothing like this. It started as just sex, but he—" Devon stopped, unable to force himself to choke out the name. "The… other bloke… he—we…." He trailed off as the memories ensnared him.

Kit didn't want to ask, didn't want to know, but something told him they needed to. "What did he do, Devon?" he pressed. "You need to tell us so we don't accidentally set you off."

"It was BDSM, wasn't it?" Jonathan asked gently. He might have no experience with that type of relationship himself, but he was widely read enough to recognize the indicators. "He abused you."

Kit didn't need to hear Devon's confirmation. The anguish on his face was all the confirmation he needed. "Fucker," he muttered under his breath, anger filling him at the thought of anyone hurting his lover.

"I was willing," Devon admitted. "Eager, even, in the beginning. I wanted to give in to him, to let him teach me, control me. But then he decided that my being a sub wasn't enough. I don't know why. Maybe he just got bored. Maybe he got off on watching me dominate someone else. But I started to feel uncomfortable. I didn't like the person I was becoming." He stared at his hands, scrubbing at the knuckles, his voice cracking. "Every time, he demanded more, from both of us, before he'd let us… before he'd… and I—I couldn't stand to look at myself in the fucking mirror anymore, you know?"

Kit didn't know. He didn't know at all, but he couldn't get past the image of Devon's shattered self-esteem. "That's not who you are," he said softly. "You've never been that way with us. I refuse to believe you've just been pretending. You wouldn't have been so upset over the misunderstanding we had if you were that man."

"I thought I'd got past it," Devon insisted, squeezing his hands together harder as he fought to maintain his control. "Thought it was behind me. Went back to women, got married. Got divorced. Got married again. Going to wind up divorced again." The ghost of a smile tugged at his lips. "And then I met you two. And it's been so bloody good, so much more than I ever… and I thought maybe I could wear these again, that it would be safe." He shook his head bitterly. "I fucked up then, so badly, when it didn't even matter. If I fuck things up now, with you...."

Jonathan gently pulled Devon's twisting hands apart and held them in his own. "Devon," he commanded, putting a hint of King Arthur's steel in his voice. "Devon, you're not going to fuck up. You're not going to hurt us. We trust you, we—" He bit back the admission of love, realizing he could only speak for himself, at least in that regard. "We aren't going to let anything from the past come between us. In fact," he said, looking to Kit for confirmation, "I think it's time we gave you some new memories to go with these leathers."

Nodding, Kit reached for their joined hands, closing his own over them as well. He scooted closer to Devon's side, pressing against him. "What do you say, Dev? Can we make love to you while you're wearing these sexy clothes? You won't regret it. I promise." He punctuated his request with teasing kisses to the side of Devon's neck.

Jonathan bent forward to run his tongue down the wedge of skin between the supple leather lapels of Devon's jacket. "This bit has been tempting me all morning," he admitted, opening his mouth to suck at the tender flesh.

Devon's head fell back against the sofa cushions as he gave himself over to his lovers' attentions. "Fuck yes," he groaned as Jonathan's teeth tugged at the hairs sprinkled down the exposed skin of his chest.

Kit smiled and reached down to cup the unapologetic bulge pushing at the front of the leather pants. "This is what's been tempting me." Without waiting for permission, he began undoing the fastenings on the trousers, pulling the plackets apart so he could get his hand inside, around Devon's erection.

Jonathan reached for the jacket zipper and inched it down slowly, following the trail of skin that was revealed with his lips. "You are so fucking sexy like this, Devon," he rasped between kisses and love bites. "I nearly ran off the road watching you in the mirror on the way here, thinking about tasting you this way."

Kit agreed completely with Jonathan's sentiment and with the idea of telling Devon. "I got hard as soon as I got a glimpse of you," he murmured, starting to work his hand on Devon's cock. "Just seeing the way the leather clung to you had me wanting to touch you."

Devon arched his back, offering himself completely to his lovers' touch. He wanted to tell them that he was theirs, but Kit's hand and

Jonathan's mouth were rapidly taking away his power of coherent speech. He threaded one hand into Jonathan's sandy-brown hair, guiding his head lower as he reached with the other hand to pull Kit toward him for a kiss.

Kit moved in eagerly. He had started this relationship because of his interest in Jonathan, but his attraction to Devon had grown nearly as strong, and he relished the opportunity to make that clear to him. He slid his tongue between Devon's lips, eager for another taste. He set up a steady rhythm, pumping Devon's erection with deliberate firmness.

Jonathan could feel Devon trembling beneath him as he kissed his way down his toned abdomen. He paused to tease at the dip of Devon's navel, lapping at the depression before closing his teeth around the circumference and sucking hard enough to leave a mark. "Look at you," he murmured, glancing back up Devon's body, where his chest glistened with Jonathan's saliva. Devon's hips pushed into Kit's palm as they shared a heated kiss. "You look so beautiful like this, letting us love you...."

Devon rocked into Kit's fist, moaning against his mouth at Jonathan's words and that incredibly sinful voice. He pushed his tongue deeper into Kit's mouth and tugged at Jonathan's hair, trying to urge him to join the kiss. Jonathan was taking his time, though, thoroughly laving every bit of skin along the way. When he latched on to a nipple and suckled it, the pleasure was so intense Devon shuddered between them.

Kit gave Devon possession of his mouth, not even trying to pull away to voice his own words of appreciation. Words hadn't worked, so he'd let his actions express his feelings. When he felt Devon shake beneath him, he knew their gestures were meeting with his approval. He intensified the movement of his hand, trying to push Devon toward the edge, to let a surfeit of pleasure wash away the unpleasant memories.

Jonathan smiled to himself as he felt Devon tremble against them. His own erection was pressing uncomfortably inside his jeans, but he tried to ignore it as he licked his way across Devon's chest toward his other nipple. "That's right, Devon," he husked between kisses. "Show us how good it feels; show us we're giving you pleasure." He bit down on the pink nub and tugged hard before releasing it. "Let us watch you come...."

Devon writhed beneath Kit's hand. He was so close, so fucking close. All he needed was a little more, a little harder, a little faster.... Then

Jonathan bit his nipple and urged him to come, and Devon lost it, crying out into Kit's kiss, pulsing a stream of hot come over his stomach.

As soon as he felt Devon tense beneath them, Jonathan slid down to lap up the creamy fluid from Devon's cock and Kit's hand. He licked Devon's stomach as he shuddered through waves of aftershocks. When he had cleaned Devon thoroughly, he slid back up to join his mouth to Devon's and Kit's, letting them share the taste of Devon's release.

Kit snaked his tongue into Jonathan's mouth to savor the essence he had helped unleash, continuing to caress Devon's softening cock, gently now, hoping to draw out the pleasure for as long as possible. He ignored his own arousal still painfully encased in tight jeans. This moment was for Devon. "Feeling better?" he asked softly when he finally lifted his head.

The release of tension, both physical and emotional, left Devon feeling deliciously boneless. "Much better," he murmured languidly, moving back and forth between Jonathan's lips and Kit's. "We could spend the rest of the weekend right here."

"No, we can't," Jonathan countered, sliding a hand inside the butter-soft jacket to circle Devon's back. "As incredible as you look in these leathers, we need to get you out of them, because Kit and I have more plans for you, and it would be a shame to stain them."

"That's right," Kit agreed with a grin. "We're not done with you by a long shot. I want to play with your toys."

CHAPTER 10
PLEASURE BOUND

"IF WE'RE going to open the toy box, we should probably move into the bedroom," Jonathan suggested. Rising to his feet, he drew Devon with him, pausing to slide the jacket off him completely and press an appreciative kiss to the curve of his lover's shoulder before leading them into the bedroom.

Kit grabbed Devon's gym bag as he followed them out of the living room. He almost opened the bag himself but decided at the last minute he should probably let Devon do that. He handed it to its owner and waited for him to take out the toys.

Devon rummaged through the contents of his duffel bag until his hand closed around the toy box. He pulled it out slowly and offered the box to Kit. He was still too content from his release to do more than follow Jonathan's lead as he sat down on the bed.

Kit was a little surprised that Devon relinquished control of the box so readily, but he was not about to complain. He opened it eagerly, rummaging through its contents, looking at the collection of toys: anal beads, dildos, blindfolds. With a grin he pulled out a rather large dildo. "This looks like fun." He rifled a little more and pulled out a short thick butt plug. "That looks… interesting." He wasn't sure quite how he felt about the large piece of latex. It looked like it might be a little too big. Then he found the handcuffs. "And just who did you think you'd be using these on?" He winked over his shoulder at Devon.

Devon met the teasing gaze seriously. "I'm hoping you'll use them on me."

Jonathan glanced up from unbuttoning his shirt, looking at Devon with concern. "Are you sure?" He turned Devon's head with a callused palm to his cheek so he could gauge his expression. "Is that really what you want?"

It might not have been what he'd had in mind when he packed them, Devon realized, but it was what he needed now. The closer he moved to real dominance, the greater the risk he'd fall back into old behaviors. He couldn't risk that now, not after the way he'd snapped at Kit in the car. It would be safer to give up that control, and a part of him was honest enough to admit that he craved it as well. "I'm sure," he answered, leaning into Jonathan's caress. "I trust you to give me what I need."

Kit looked down at the cuffs in his hand, then back up at his lover, broad chest bare, tight leather pants unlaced but not lowered. He was such a strong man, such a dominant man, that the thought of having him helpless to their whim was more arousing than it surely should have been, but the effect was undeniable. Devon's words indicated his willingness, and when Kit studied his face, he could see no doubt, only pure trust shining in the green eyes. "Lie down," he requested.

Devon eased back onto the pillows, stretching his hands over his head to allow Kit to secure them to the headboard. Jonathan could understand the allure of relinquishing control, if only temporarily, and was moved that Devon trusted them enough to grant them that power over him. He ran a hand down the broad plane of Devon's chest, reassuring rather than arousing—at least for the moment. "If it gets to be too much, use your safeword," he said, as much to remind himself and Kit as to reassure Devon that they would respect his limits.

Kit startled at Jonathan's words. It hadn't occurred to him that Devon might need or want to use his safeword. His only desire was to ease Devon's memories and add to his pleasure. He glanced at Devon again to make sure this was what he wanted, but Devon's hands were extended willingly above his head, his face a picture of trusting contentment and desire. Making his decision, Kit snapped a cuff around one wrist, threading the other one through the posts of the headboard before attaching it to Devon's other wrist. "Now that we have you at our mercy, what shall we do to you?" Kit asked teasingly.

Devon knew there was no way Jonathan—much less Kit—could do anything that would force him to safeword. Just the fact that he was concerned enough to think of it proved how very different he was from the man who'd introduced Devon to this world. "Whatever you wish," he answered, his cock hardening at the prospect of what his two inventive lovers might do to him.

Jonathan knelt beside Devon on the wide mattress, reaching for the open waistband of the tight leather pants. He slid them down carefully, letting one hand linger over the smooth globes of his lover's buttocks as he used the other to push the leather down the strong thighs. Unable to resist, he bent down to nuzzle into the nest of blond hair around the base of Devon's resurgent erection, breathing in the scent of his previous release and his current arousal.

The golden flesh revealed by Jonathan's slow stripping of their bound lover made Kit's mouth water. He leaned down to nip sharply at a pert nipple, knowing how much Devon enjoyed a bit of rough handling, then pushed himself up to survey the scene. He settled one hand on Devon's thigh, the other on Jonathan's shoulder as he bent again to meet Jonathan's lips where they pressed against Devon's skin.

Devon's muscles tensed in anticipation at the slow glide of Jonathan's hands, pushing the leathers down his legs. He spread them slightly, freeing his ankles from the entanglement, freezing when Jonathan began to nibble alluringly at the base of his cock. The firm tug of Kit's teeth on his nipple made him arch upward, easing the pressure at the same time his body was crying out for more.

At the touch of Kit's hand to his shoulder, Jonathan turned his head toward his younger lover. Their lips met without breaking the contact with Devon's skin. This was something Jonathan had come to savor in the time the three of them had been together—the taste of both his lovers mingling on his lips. Leaning forward, he raised a hand to Kit's shoulder for stability as he deepened the kiss, exploring the recesses of his partner's mouth.

Devon's moan had Kit looking up at the dark green eyes of their bound lover. The lust glittering there surprised him a little given that Devon had just come a few minutes earlier. Then Jonathan drew him back into their kiss, and Kit lost himself in it until Devon's restless movements caught his attention again. A thought struck him. "Do you like watching us together?"

A tremble of need shuddered through Devon. Despite the loss of contact with his own flesh, watching the desire build between his two lovers whetted something deep inside him. Another moan escaped him as he stirred uneasily beneath them, his bollocks tightening into hard, throbbing knots. Kit's question made his cock jump and leak against his thigh. "Aye," he whispered thickly, his accent betraying the primacy of his emotions.

Jonathan recognized the desire in Devon's voice, the need smoldering in the depths of his eyes. Knowing they had brought Devon to release once already, he didn't hesitate to let that need build now. It would only add to the intensity when they finally slaked it.

"Watch us, Devon," he whispered hoarsely, kneeling up to pull Kit against him over Devon's restrained body. Kissing Kit deeply, Jonathan let his hands wander freely over the smooth torso, stroking and kneading the honeyed flesh.

Jonathan's words had as much of an effect on Kit as they did on Devon, playing perfectly into Kit's exhibitionist streak. He knew Jonathan wanted to add to Devon's pleasure—Kit did too—but he was certainly not averse to taking his own pleasure in the meantime. Especially not when it felt as good as Jonathan's hands currently caressing him. Wanting to make Jonathan feel as good as he was making him feel, Kit slid his arms over Jonathan's hips to his back, running his hands up the strong deltoids.

Devon stirred fitfully as his lovers' passion flared above him, heating his own blood as they explored each other's bodies. He could almost feel the touches on his own skin. He flicked his tongue to moisten his mouth and dragged it across his lower lip, imagining it was one of his lovers tasting him. The thought sent a flare of lust shooting through his groin, and he parted his legs restlessly, a low groan rumbling in his chest.

Seeing that their attentions were affecting Devon as much as they were each other, Jonathan threaded a hand in Kit's dark hair. He dropped the other hand to Devon's thigh, nudging it closer to him to widen the triangle of space between Devon's legs. Pulling his lips reluctantly from Kit's, he climbed carefully between Devon's spread legs. He slid his feet beneath Devon's raised knee and stared intently at the beautiful young man before him. "I want to make love to you, Kit," he rasped. "And I want Devon to watch us do it."

"Fuck yes," Kit agreed, climbing over Devon's leg onto Jonathan's lap. Devon raised his other knee to support Kit's back. Kit turned his head sideways and flashed Devon a grateful smile before reaching between his and Jonathan's bodies and closing his hand around both their cocks, making sure to lean back enough that Devon could see them. After all, if Devon couldn't see them, he wouldn't get the full effect. Kit gasped at the sensation of their firm flesh rubbing together in his tight grip, adding a double layer of pleasure. He recalled suddenly Devon's comment about taking two cocks and wondered what it would be like to rub against one of his lovers in much tighter surrounds.

Spreading his legs even wider did nothing to relieve the ache building in Devon's groin. He arched his back instinctively, wishing he could run a hand over his cock, cup his bollocks to relieve the throbbing he felt with every pulsebeat. Just the press of Kit's foot against his calf as he straddled Jonathan sent a spasm of heat jolting up Devon's leg and made his cock jump. When Kit circled both his and Jonathan's shafts, dragging his hand over them slowly, Devon could almost feel the touch himself. "Fuck," he breathed, his voice lost in the low moan coaxed from Jonathan's throat.

Jonathan wasn't sure which was arousing him more, Kit's hand gliding over his cock and pressing it against his own, or the hunger glittering in Devon's eyes as he watched them touching each other. He let his lips wander down the delectable curve of Kit's neck, the slight saltiness of Kit's sweat whetting his appetite for more. Pulling Kit closer, he slid an arm around him for support and bent him backward, enough to let his lips reach the flat brown disks of his nipples.

Kit arched his back, offering himself willingly to Jonathan's questing lips. He gasped when they closed around first one nipple then the other. He reached back to brace himself, his hand coming to rest on Devon's thigh. He squeezed the hard muscle beneath his palm, wanting to include Devon as much as possible in his interaction with Jonathan.

With his free hand, Jonathan scrabbled over the rumpled bedsheets until he found the tube of lube he'd pulled from the toy box while Kit was restraining Devon. Flicking it open without raising his head from suckling Kit's nipple, he squeezed a dollop onto his fingers and reached behind his lover, teasing up and down the younger man's crease, knowing Devon was following every movement.

Kit moaned when Jonathan started teasing his cleft. He was already on edge from making Devon come and from knowing he was watching them. Jonathan's touch was almost more than he could bear. "Don't make me beg," he pleaded, ignoring that he was doing just that.

Devon's own nipples tightened as he watched Jonathan's mouth tug at Kit's pebbled nubs. He couldn't remember the last time he'd ached this badly, needed this badly. When Kit's hand landed on his thigh and squeezed, he groaned, a dribble of precome leaking down his cock to pool against his quivering abdomen. And when Jonathan slid a lube-slick finger into Kit's arse, his own cry blended with Kit's, his hole clenching as if the finger had breached him.

"Not gonna make you beg, kitten," Jonathan rasped, adding a second finger to the tight heat of Kit's channel, scissoring them until they moved easily.

The new nickname registered in Kit's mind only enough to send another curl of desire through his stomach. Usually he hated nicknames, but somehow the way Jonathan said it took any insult out of the name, making him feel cherished instead.

"Gonna make you feel good," Jonathan promised, curving his fingers forward to caress the tiny bump of nerves, "so good." He added a third finger, twisting them sinuously as Kit moaned and rocked against his hand. "Want to fuck you," he said huskily, the words as much for Devon's benefit as they were for Kit and himself. "Want to bury myself inside you, so hard, so deep...."

"Then do it," Kit urged, pushing back against Jonathan's fingers, his words as arousing as anything Jonathan was doing with his hands. "Come deep inside me. Make me feel like I've never felt before." Knowing Devon was watching, Kit grabbed the lube and made a production of coating Jonathan's cock. "Now."

Devon's cock was a dripping rod of steel against his stomach, his asshole pulsing with every thrust of Kit's hips, every rasp of Jonathan's voice. "Please," he moaned, not caring that he wasn't even begging for his own pleasure. "Please...."

Jonathan's fingers dug into Kit's hips, lifting him enough to push the head of his cock against the glistening opening. "Watch us, Devon," he groaned as his slick tip pushed past Kit's tight ring of muscle. Kit's heat closed around him, embracing him, welcoming him, and he pushed into it slowly, his panting breaths mingling with Kit's and echoed by Devon, shackled to the headboard.

Kit keened his pleasure at being filled, his head dropping forward onto Jonathan's shoulder as he pushed down against the invading length. The sound of Devon's cries intermingled with his own and Jonathan's was as arousing as anything Jonathan was doing to him. Jonathan had just gotten inside him and already his control was teetering. He clamped his fingers around the base of his cock, trying to stave off climax a little longer. He might have succeeded if Devon hadn't chosen right then to squeeze his knees lightly, the subtle embrace including him physically in the moment.

Even that fragile connection was enough to set Devon rocking with each movement of Jonathan's and Kit's bodies, a low, constant moan escaping with each shuddering breath.

Jonathan wanted to draw this out, for Devon's pleasure as well as Kit's and his own, but it was too much, Kit squeezing around him and Devon's eyes devouring them. Pumping his hips in short, hard thrusts, he pulled Kit's hand away from his cock and closed his own palm around it, dragging up and down roughly. "Come for me," he gasped, his voice ragged as his control splintered. "Oh fuck, Kit, come with me…."

Kit whimpered, unable to hold back. "Yes," he hissed, his release spattering onto Jonathan's chest.

Jonathan cried out as Kit's come sprayed between them. Still stroking the pulsing shaft, he dragged his other hand through the pearly fluid, raising it to his lips. The salty taste was the final straw to push him over the edge. Biting down on his fist, he stiffened against Kit, pumping his seed deep into his lover's body.

Watching his lovers collapse against each other as they found their release did nothing to ease the fire burning through Devon's veins. He lay trembling, his legs spread wide, clutching at the chain of the handcuffs, making it rattle against the headboard. His breath was a rough, uneven pant of need. "Please," he repeated, a chant of pure desperation. "Please, please…."

Kit lifted his head from where it had fallen against Jonathan's shoulder to look at Devon, lying spread-eagled on the bed. Running a soothing hand along Devon's leg, he looked back at Jonathan, remembering another time with the three of them together when he was the one desperate for release. "I think we need to take care of Devon," he said with a grin, quoting Devon's words back to him.

CHAPTER 11
TOY STORY

JONATHAN FOUGHT to refocus from the haze of pleasure he'd been momentarily lost in. He knew Devon needed them, but he couldn't resist claiming Kit's mouth in a final, lingering kiss before reluctantly slipping from his lover's warmth. Still kneeling between Devon's widespread legs, Jonathan turned to Devon and leaned forward to kiss his other lover just as thoroughly, silencing his almost breathless pleas while Kit rolled to the side to make room for him. "What do you want, Devon?" he asked gently. "How do you want us to please you?"

Devon shook his head, racked with need but too far lost to put any request into words. He flicked his tongue out over lips dry from panting, prompting Jonathan to lean in and kiss him again. Devon moaned into the kiss, tangling his tongue with Jonathan's, wrapping his legs around the other man's hips.

Seeing his lovers entwined, seeing especially how mindless Devon was in his need, Kit took the initiative, sitting up and rummaging in the toy box again until he found the dildo he had seen earlier. He nudged Jonathan to one side, amused when Devon's legs fell back open in invitation. Jonathan rolled so he lay next to Devon without ever releasing his mouth. With a shake of his head, Kit ran the latex toy down Devon's cock and over his bollocks, playing it lightly against his entrance.

Devon shuddered as Kit teased the dildo against his bollocks and arse. He was so aroused that any touch was welcome, though if he had allowed himself a choice, he'd prefer to feel one of his lovers against him rather than a toy. But today he wasn't in control; he'd given himself over to anything his lovers wanted to do to him. He raised his hips as Kit pressed the phallus lightly over his hole, opening himself even more to the teasing touch.

Jonathan raised his head when he felt Devon tremble against him, turning to see Kit stroking over Devon playfully with the large dildo he'd pulled from the toy box earlier. "Is that all right with you, Devon?" he asked, concerned by their lover's uncharacteristic passivity. This was a side of Devon he'd never seen before, so different from his usual self-assurance that he couldn't help but worry a little. "Is that what you want?"

Kit paused in what he was doing, waiting for Devon's answer. As much as he liked the idea of teasing Devon with the toy, he didn't want to do anything the other man didn't want. He remembered all too well what that felt like.

The care in Jonathan's voice wrapped itself around Devon's heart. He wished he could raise his hands to Jonathan's face to draw him into another kiss, but all he could do was shake his head and hope Jonathan could read his emotions in his eyes. "Anything," he whispered, his voice hoarse with longing. "Anything you want."

Kit looked to Jonathan now for direction, ceding control to him.

Jonathan nodded slowly, his eyes drawn back to Devon's. He wanted to watch them as Kit used the toy, needed to be sure it was indeed giving Devon pleasure. He shifted so he could reach both hands to Devon's chest, ghosting his fingertips through the fine dusting of curls there. "Let us please you," he murmured, tweaking the furled pink nipples gently. "Let us make you feel good this time."

"Just relax and feel." Kit added his words to Jonathan's, meeting Devon's eyes as he searched for the lube among the rumpled covers of the bed. Finding it, he squirted some on the flexible shaft before trailing it along Devon's cleft again.

Devon hissed at the pull of the dildo over his crease, the tug of Jonathan's fingers on his nipples. His back arched upward, his body wordlessly asking for what his voice could not.

Knowing the dildo was too large to use on Devon without preparing him first, Kit coated his fingers in the lube already on his arse and worked the first one into Devon's hole.

Jonathan flinched at Devon's hiss, but the need apparent in the gaze meeting his convinced him the sound was not one of pain. Giving in to his lover's unspoken request, he bent closer to Devon's chest, taking a tight peak between his teeth and biting with the firm pressure the other man loved.

Devon pushed up against the finger easing its way inside. He moaned when Jonathan's teeth worried his nipple with just the right amount of pressure. His lovers knew him so well, knew exactly how to touch to make him mindless with pleasure.

Smiling at Devon's eagerness, Kit added a second finger, stretching him for the dildo. "Can you take a third?" he asked.

Devon moaned again, clenching against the invading fullness. "Aye," he gasped, twisting his torso to encourage Jonathan to transfer his attentions to the other side of his chest.

Jonathan bit his way lightly across Devon's broad chest, his teeth teasing the firm pecs and pulling at the curled hairs before latching around the other nipple, bringing it to the same state of distension. Slowly he trailed a series of love bites down the firm planes of Devon's torso. He paused to suck harder at a spot just beside Devon's navel, hard enough to leave a faint mark coloring the golden flesh.

At Devon's reply Kit added a third finger, scissoring them slightly to prepare Devon's opening for the thick phallus. Deeming him ready, Kit removed his fingers and added more lube to the dildo, pressing the tip against Devon's body. The delicate pucker flexed in eager anticipation, bringing a smile to Kit's face. Looking up at Devon's expression, he pushed the toy inside the first inch.

Devon's breath hitched as the dildo breached him. Thicker than the fingers it replaced, the stretch was painful but not unbearable. The bite of Jonathan's teeth into his abdomen at the same moment the head of the dildo pushed its way inside wrung a hoarse cry from deep in Devon's chest. His hips stuttered upward, seeking more contact from both the teeth and the toy.

At Devon's ardent cry, Jonathan twisted to see what Kit was doing, without releasing the skin gripped firmly between his teeth. The sight of the thick latex shaft breaching Devon's body made Jonathan's gut clench with renewed lust. After releasing the bruised flesh with a final moist kiss, he slid lower, letting one hand cover Kit's on the base of the dildo.

Kit let Jonathan guide the rhythm of his hand, the two of them working together now to give Devon the utmost pleasure. It only added to Kit's enjoyment to know that Jonathan was a part of it as well.

Devon stirred restlessly, and Jonathan could almost taste the need seeping from his pores as he licked and bit his way closer to Devon's cock. Sweat and precome whetted his own desire to taste more, and the needy motions of Devon's hips, the strangled little sounds he tried to hold back, were as arousing as hell. He wanted to coax more of those sounds from Devon's lips, to make him lose the tight control he was holding himself in check with. Reaching the base of his lover's purpled erection, Jonathan licked a broad swath through the golden curls but avoided touching the shaft itself with his lips.

"Does he taste as good as he looks, Jon?" Kit rasped, watching with heated eyes as Jonathan lapped at Devon's cock. "He looks like he's hard enough to split me in two." As he spoke, he pushed the dildo the rest of the way inside Devon, twisting it to rub the tip against Devon's prostate.

At Kit's words, a sudden vision flashed through Jonathan's mind of the younger man sinking onto Devon's long, hard shaft, riding him the way he'd already ridden Jonathan. Lifting his head, he caught Devon's passion-glazed gaze. "Do you want that, Devon?" he asked. "Want to fuck Kit too? He's already open for you. Aren't you, kitten?" He ran one hand down Devon's trembling thigh and the other over Kit's smooth flank.

Kit moaned. "Wide open," he replied. "Jonathan stretched me for you, Devon, made me open and aching to be filled again. Shall I? Shall I sink down on you and ride you while Jonathan plays with the toy? Would that drive you wild?"

An aching groan rumbled through Devon's frame at the erotic image his two lovers' voices conjured. "Aye," he gasped, unable to prevent himself from thrusting up as the dildo twisted inside him. "Want it… want you both…."

Moving immediately when he heard Devon's words, Kit released his grip on the toy and scooted forward to straddle Devon. Reaching behind himself, he coated Devon's erection with the lube already on his hand and positioned the cock at his entrance. With a deep, heartfelt groan, he pushed down, taking Devon into himself in one smooth slide.

Jonathan watched as Kit sank onto Devon's rigid cock, his own erection stirring as he imagined the tightness Devon was feeling. Determined to push their lover to the limits of pleasure, he slipped into the space between Devon's wide-flung legs. Bending lower, he slipped his free hand beneath Devon's ass, lifting upward to make it easier to reach with his tongue. Still twisting the dildo gently, he lapped wetly over Devon's sac and farther down his perineum until he reached the place where the dildo entered Devon's body. His breath quickening, he licked around the widely stretched pucker, the musk and sweat and lube mingling on his tongue. He slid the dildo out until just the head remained inside, then pushed it in again slowly, trying to wedge his tongue inside along with it.

Devon felt his control fragmenting as Kit engulfed his cock in his hot, wet channel. Knowing it was Jonathan's come that let him slide in so easily was incredibly arousing, another way of binding all three of them together. The image of both his lovers penetrating him at once flashed through his mind again, but then he felt Jonathan's tongue on his bollocks and any ability to think coherently was lost. He strained up wildly at Jonathan's touch, pushing even deeper into Kit as Jonathan drove his arousal to feverous heights.

"Fuck, Devon," Kit groaned as Devon's cock split him. He knew Jonathan was behind him between Devon's legs, could feel the occasional brush of shaggy hair against his arse, and the thought that Jonathan must be tonguing Devon on top of everything else was an added aphrodisiac. Not that he needed anything more than Devon's erection hitting his prostate with every pass. He clenched his sphincter, trying to add to Devon's pleasure, wondering if he could come again so soon.

Jonathan thrust his tongue harder into Devon, tasting and touching as much of his lover as he could. Kit was swearing and rocking above his head, and Jonathan burrowed deeper, his own hips undulating against the bedsheets in an attempt to gain some friction against his resurgent arousal. Twisting the dildo as far in as it could go, he wrapped his free hand around Kit's hips, joining himself to the rhythm of their coupling, desperate to feel the connection when both his lovers came.

Devon wrenched against the handcuffs as his back arched completely off the bed. A deep, keening wail tore from his throat as the sensory overload of Kit squeezing around him and Jonathan fucking him with tongue and dildo became too much for him to endure. His body locked in a fierce spasm of ecstasy, and his come spurted out to fill Kit and mingle with Jonathan's seed.

Jonathan groaned as Devon froze against him, and raising his head, he suckled the base of the Devon's cock and Kit's entrance, hungry for every taste of both his lovers' pleasure.

Kit's release came in a rush when Jonathan's mouth brushed his hole, sucking and licking at the place where he and Devon joined. A harsh, wordless shout escaped his lips as his cock emptied its load all over Devon's chest, completely untouched, that stimulation unneeded in the wake of the ecstasy he was already experiencing.

Hearing Kit's cry of completion, a sudden need to see his lovers' faces gripped Jonathan's heart. Pulling himself to his knees, he reached a trembling hand to touch first Kit's flushed cheek, then tenderly brush Devon's clenched jaw. He fisted his erection with his other hand, tantalizing himself with the sensation, sending tiny tremors through his groin and down his back.

Jonathan's touch to his cheek drew Kit out of his haze of satiated bliss. Seeing him tugging on his own cock, Kit pushed Jonathan's hand aside and replaced it with his own. "Let me," he urged.

"God, yes," Jonathan breathed, leaning into Kit's touch and pulling Kit into his embrace, kissing him hungrily. He didn't think he was close to coming again, but only a few tugs of Kit's hand sent him spiraling out of control, his release dribbling over Kit's fingers and dripping onto Devon's sweaty skin.

Kit returned the kiss eagerly, continuing to stroke up and down Jonathan's subsiding erection, his hips still rocking gently against Devon, wanting to extend the pleasure as long as possible. Eventually, though, Devon's sated shaft slipped from his passage, and Kit relinquished his hold on Jonathan. Reaching forward, he pressed the releases on the handcuffs, freeing Devon's arms and running his hands down the upturned muscles. He slid back and eased the toy from Devon's body, tossing it to the side to worry about later. He turned to look at Jonathan, who sat there still in a bit of a daze, and with a smile, Kit tipped Jonathan over to lie on one side of Devon while he settled on the other. A huge yawn escaped him as he shifted to get comfortable. "You've worn me out already," Kit joked. "I need a nap."

Jonathan let Kit push him down on his side, feeling too boneless after two orgasms in quick succession to do any more than curl against Devon's warmth. He flung an arm over the sweaty torso between them to clasp Kit's hip on Devon's other side, keeping the connection between all three of them alive. He nuzzled the damp tendrils at the base of Devon's skull, too weary to even raise himself enough to find his lips. "Are you all right, Devon?" he murmured, still wondering at the depth of the other man's surrender to them. "Is that what you needed?"

Still floating on a cloud of endorphins, Devon cleared his throat, reaching to pull both his lovers closer. He still found it hard to speak, knowing he'd need some time to escape the subspace he'd lost himself in and process everything he'd felt. Words trembled on his lips, but he swallowed them back, not yet trusting his control over himself. "Aye," he settled on saying, his voice as rough as if he'd screamed out his release. Letting his eyes flutter closed, he gave himself over to mindlessness again, the dull ache of his muscles and the lingering glow of satiation lulling him to sleep.

CHAPTER 12
SEX ON THE BEACH

KIT STIRRED restlessly when the warm body beside him moved. He opened his eyes slowly, needing a moment to remember where they were and what had happened. The smile that graced his features as memory came flooding back was dazzling… until he realized Devon had left the bed.

"Devon?" he asked huskily. "Everything okay?"

Devon pulled the T-shirt over his head and looked back at the bed where his two lovers still sprawled among the tangled sheets. Kit had pushed up on one elbow, regarding him with vague concern in his still sleep-heavy brown eyes. Jonathan's head was buried in a pillow, his arm thrown around Kit's hip, keeping the connection even at rest.

"I'm good," Devon said after taking enough of an internal inventory to decide it was the truth. "Just need to walk for a while. Clear m'head. Think I'll watch the sun rise on the beach."

Kit nodded and let his head drop back to the pillows, sliding his arm around Jonathan's back, sleep chasing him again.

Jonathan stirred groggily, too pleasantly lethargic to pry his eyes open just yet. In that cloudy half state between wakefulness and sleep, he registered his arm draped over a warm, smooth hip—Kit, then, his arm pressed against Jonathan's back. He stretched out his free hand, needing to touch his other lover, but encountered only cool linen. He cracked an eye open to confirm someone was missing from the bed. "Devon?" he asked, his voice still thick with muzziness.

Jonathan's voice roused Kit. "He went for a walk," he replied once the words registered. "Said he wanted to clear his head." He yawned widely and stretched against Jonathan's side, bodies rubbing together invitingly.

No matter how sleepy he was, the press of Kit's body molding to his was something Jonathan couldn't ignore. He lowered his head to find Kit's lips, not demanding, just enjoying the gift of waking up with him like this. "Kitten." He nestled his head back in the pillows, adjusting to cradle Kit against his shoulder. "I could get used to waking up this way," he admitted, not quite conscious enough to censor himself.

"So could I." Kit thrilled to the core at hearing such an admission. Perhaps Jonathan did feel as strongly for him as Kit felt for his two lovers. "So what's with 'kitten'?" he inquired, the nickname striking the same chord now, in the clear light of day, that it had the night before in the midst of their passion.

Jonathan stroked a hand through Kit's hair, smiling when the younger man hummed at the touch and squirmed closer, a leg settling possessively over his knees. "Just seems to fit," he said with a smile in his voice. "The way you purr when I touch you, and those little kitten licks when you're trying to drive me out of my head." Which was just about any time Kit touched him, Jonathan had to admit, at least to himself.

Kit smiled and let out one of the purrs that had earned him the nickname. "Just be careful not to use it where anyone else can hear it. The Orkneys would give me hell for it."

The actors cast as the Orkney brothers Agravain, Gaheris, Gareth, and Gawain—Colm Murray, Rhodri Hughes, Warwick Greene, and Bevan Campbell—were jokesters enough without giving them that kind of ammunition. "It's strictly between the three of us," Jonathan agreed with another soft kiss. That brought Jonathan's thoughts back to Devon, breaking him out of his languid mood when he remembered their missing lover's behavior the previous day. "Did Devon seem… different… to you yesterday?" he asked Kit hesitantly. This was still so new to him that he wasn't sure if Devon's passivity was all part of the game, but it felt *wrong* to him somehow, and he'd learned over the years to listen to his instincts.

"Yeah, touchy," Kit said after a moment's consideration. "Almost defensive at first, and then it's like he just collapsed." He thought back over the previous day. "He's never been so docile before. Usually he's orchestrating everything we do, however gently."

"I wasn't sure," Jonathan agreed, "but it seemed like more than just playing a game to me." He focused his gaze out the window, but he couldn't see Devon on the small strip of beach visible from the bed. "I'm worried about him, Kit."

Kit nodded his agreement. "I think there's more to his past than he's telling us. Not that he has to tell us everything," he hastened to add, "but I think there are some demons he hasn't dealt with."

Jonathan could understand that—there were things in his own past he'd prefer to keep private, at least for now—but the thought of anything hurting Devon enough to cause his friend to withdraw into himself the way he had made Jonathan's gut clench in anger. Regretfully he pushed away from Kit's tempting warmth to sit on the edge of the bed. "I need to find him. Be sure he's okay." He ran a hand through his hair and looked around the room for something he could pull on. The beach was pretty isolated, but he wasn't sure it was safe to wander out there naked.

"Give me a minute and I'll go with you," Kit offered, worried now about both his lovers. "Our bags are still in the living room. We didn't bring them in here last night." He went into the other room and came back, carrying both duffels. He rummaged through his to pull out a T-shirt and pair of shorts. When he was dressed, he went to Jonathan's side. "He'll be all right," he said earnestly. "We'll make sure of it."

Jonathan pulled out the first pair of ragged cutoffs he touched, slid into them, and buttoned them quickly, not even wanting to take the time to hunt for a T-shirt. He smiled at Kit and leaned in for another fast kiss before heading for the door that led to the beach. "I must love that bastard if he can get me outside before I've had my coffee," he muttered to himself.

Kit followed Jonathan out of the house, looking up and down the beach. He didn't see Devon, but there was only one set of footsteps, leading down across the dunes to their left. "It looks like he went that way." He pointed, heading in the direction the path led.

Jonathan wished he'd thought to grab his camera before leaving the cottage. The frail line of footprints heading over the dune, already disappearing under the prevailing wind, struck him as powerfully evocative. Then he remembered they were Devon's footprints, and the thought of trading on his friend's emotions that way smothered any artistic impulses. Cresting the dune, he was relieved to see their quarry sitting in the sand a short way ahead, his knees drawn to his chest, his arms circling them as he gazed over the water. The pose was an uncharacteristic one for Devon, and it made Jonathan feel surprisingly protective.

Kit climbed the dune a moment after Jonathan. "There he is," he said unnecessarily. "Go get him and let's take him home. I'm hungry."

Devon rubbed a hand over the rough stubble on his cheek, wondering if Lancelot's beard needed a trim. *Sod it. I don't have to do a fucking thing I don't want to this weekend.* Pulling his knees to his chest on the cool sand, he stretched his arms over his head, arching his back until the vertebrae crackled. The twinge of residual soreness reminded him of the marvelous gift his lovers had given him yesterday. Did they had any idea how much it had meant to him, to let himself be so vulnerable, knowing he could trust them completely? *Of course they don't, you git. You haven't told them.* He wondered if he would ever find that much strength.

Lost in his memories, Devon slowly realized he wasn't alone. Somehow, without his hearing it, Jonathan had settled into the sand next to him, mirroring his pose. How long had he been sitting there? One of the things he appreciated most about Jonathan was that he never pushed; he seemed to know instinctively when Devon was ready to talk and when he needed quiet.

Jonathan felt Devon's gaze and turned from his own contemplation of the horizon to meet the intense green eyes, relieved that they contained none of the uncertainty that had clouded them yesterday. "Hey," he said, smiling with relief. "You okay? We were… a little worried about you. I'm supposed to be the moody, brooding one in this relationship."

Devon laughed, reaching to grasp Jonathan's knee. "Worried that I'm going to steal your gig?" He chuckled. "I'm good, mate." Unspoken thanks thickened his voice as he squeezed and then let his hand fall back to his side. He knew Jonathan understood. "I'm impressed you could tear yourself away from Percival long enough to come looking for me," he added, lightening the mood.

Seeing that they weren't immediately getting up to return to the house, Kit slid down the dune and flopped down beside them. "What's this about Percival?" he asked, hearing his other nickname.

"Just surprised you left him enough energy to make the hike," Devon teased. "After all, he's not as young as the rest of us."

Relieved that Devon seemed to be himself again, Kit grinned. "Yeah, well, he's a stubborn old man when he wants to be."

Jonathan elbowed Devon in the ribs, rising to his knees to hover threateningly over the laughing blond. "Old, am I? You're only four months younger. I think Lancelot needs to show proper respect for his king." He pushed a hand against the planes of Devon's chest.

Deciding wrestling with his lovers looked like great fun—and the perfect solution to his hunger—Kit added his weight to Jonathan's, pushing Devon down into the sand.

"Do you yield?" Jonathan growled, slipping seamlessly into Arthur's commanding voice as he found the ticklish spot at the base of Devon's ribs.

"Thought I'd… done that… yesterday," Devon gasped between gusts of laughter as he fought to escape two sets of probing hands.

"You thought once would be enough?" Kit teased. "Now we've got a taste of it, you'll find we're near insatiable."

Devon's words brought Jonathan up short, and he sat back on his heels, relinquishing his grasp on Devon's chest. "About yesterday," he began, not exactly sure what his question should be.

Seeing Jonathan's change in mood, Kit stopped his teasing as well. "You're not usually like that," Kit added uneasily. "Did we do something?"

"You did exactly what I needed you to do," Devon insisted, hating the thought that his demons had threatened Kit's usually unshakable self-confidence. Pushing up on one elbow, he cupped his free hand around the back of Kit's skull, the dark curls tickling his palm as he brought them together in a kiss of reassurance that quickly turned heated. Devon swore he could taste the desire in Kit's kiss.

Devon's kiss caught Kit by surprise, but he wasn't about to complain, not when the prickle of Devon's beard sent tingles along his nerves and the taste of his mouth had arousal shooting straight to his cock. He moaned into the kiss, reaching for Devon blindly to pull their bodies into closer contact.

Jonathan's cock, always unruly first thing in the morning, stirred to life beneath the buttons of his cutoffs as he watched Devon kissing Kit. They needed to talk, he knew, but fuck if right now he wanted to do anything other than get a piece of what his two lovers were sharing. Crawling forward until they were both within reach, he raised a hand to their faces, touching a fingertip to the spot where their lips fused together.

The feel of Jonathan's touch where his lips joined Devon's reminded Kit that they were three, not two. He snaked out an arm for Jonathan, urging him closer and into the kiss.

Devon settled on his back in the sand, freeing his other hand to reach for Jonathan. The movement broke his connection to Kit, and

Devon pulled him downward, Kit landing on top of him with a thump that forced the air from Devon's lungs.

Feeling both his lovers tug him forward, Jonathan didn't need any more encouragement. He flopped onto the sand on his side next to Devon and pressed wet kisses to cheeks, chins, anything he could reach. He ran his hands under both men's shirts, seeking and stroking over the warm skin of their torsos.

Not even hesitating, Kit stripped his T-shirt off before grabbing the hem of Devon's to help Jonathan remove it as well.

Devon hummed with satisfaction as his lovers stripped off his shirt and settled back against him, feeling the light coat of hair on Jonathan's chest rub pleasurably against him on one side, Kit's smoothness against the other. Turning his head, he pulled Jonathan into a hard, deep kiss, challenging the other man to meet him, ravage him.

Jonathan groaned into Devon's kiss, thrusting his tongue deep into the seductive moistness. He groped until first one, then the other hand found the circles of sensitive skin he'd been seeking, one on Kit's chest, one on Devon's. His thumbs rasped over the raised flesh already goose-bumped by the cool ocean breeze, memorizing the differences in shape by touch alone.

Kit's back arched as Jonathan teased his nipple. He was so sensitive there, a fact his lovers took advantage of regularly, and to have Jonathan touch him there now sent what little rationality Kit still had sailing out to sea. Only one thought remained: making love.

Jonathan's hand on his chest as his tongue plundered his mouth set Devon on fire. He needed this, needed more, and he didn't want to wait. He twisted against Jonathan's fingers, willing his lover to realize he wanted a harder touch, while he moved his hand from the back of Jonathan's head to plunge below the waistband of his shorts. Giving thanks to the gods that Jonathan seldom bothered with boxers, he closed around the tight globe of Jonathan's arse, pressing him against his own surging arousal.

"Fuck, Devon," Jonathan gasped, tearing his mouth away to drag in a panting breath. "What you do to me." He slid a hand beneath Devon's back, lifting him enough to let him latch his teeth over the pebbled nub he'd raised, biting it firmly as he rubbed his demanding erection against Devon's groin.

"What about me?" Kit protested, feeling left out of the passionate clinch. He ran a hand down Devon's side to slide between his lovers' bodies, massaging one hard cock, then the other.

"C'mere, sunshine," Devon rumbled, pulling Kit toward him. "Just don't stop what you're doing." He raised his head to lap at the flat disk of Kit's nipple, pressing his other hand against the bulge in the front of Kit's shorts.

"Wasn't planning on it." Kit moaned as he was pulled into Devon's embrace and the erotic tableau on the sand. Devon was hitting all his hot spots. Trying to reciprocate, he flexed his fingers so they added to the stimulation on Devon's erection.

Jonathan lifted his head from Devon's chest to appreciate the sight of his two lovers pleasuring each other. Not that he hadn't appreciated Kit's hand on his cock, but right now he had a different pleasure in mind. "Want to taste you," he rasped to Devon, sliding down to open the zipper and free Devon's thick, swollen shaft. He licked up the creamy ooze of precome that seeped from its tip, moaning as the salty flavor tantalized him. He flicked his tongue over his lips, slid them over the rosy head, and swallowed as much of the length as he could.

"Bloody hell, Jon!" Devon shouted as the other man's mouth engulfed him. He wanted to come, but not this fast, not without bringing his lovers with him. "Easy, okay, love?" He slid his fingers in Jonathan's tangled locks, coaxing him to draw back.

Kit moaned at the sight. Damn, but Jonathan had a gorgeous mouth, especially when wrapped around Devon's cock. He threaded his fingers in Jonathan's hair alongside Devon's.

With two hands pulling at him gently, Jonathan got the message to slow down. Reluctantly letting Devon's length slip from his mouth, he settled for painting long sweeps from base to tip with his tongue, with occasional detours to suck gently at the tight balls at its base. "Better?" he muttered thickly, not wanting to lose contact with the delicious feel of Devon's cock against his lips.

"Damn near perfect," Devon groaned. Now that he didn't have to focus all his energy on trying not to come, he could redirect some of it toward their other lover. He released his grip on Jonathan's hair and wrapped both hands around Kit's hips, pulling him upward. "Straddle me," he instructed as he made short work of the fastenings of Kit's shorts. "And lose these while you're about it."

Kit didn't hesitate, not with that offer on the table. He stripped his shorts off and turned back to Devon. "Which way do you want me?"

"Look at Jonathan," Devon directed. "Look at the lovely, obscene things he's doing with that mouth of his." He gasped as Jonathan gave a very convincing demonstration of exactly how talented his mouth could be. "Yeah, like that, bastard," he growled, taking Kit in hand as soon as he swung a leg over him. This position had the added advantage of giving him a perfect view of Kit's creamy cheeks. Giving in to temptation, he licked a stripe down the shadowy cleft between the smooth globes as he slid his fist over Kit's cock.

"Shit, fuck, Devon!" Kit shouted as Devon teased his arse. He tried to do what Devon said and focus on Jonathan, but it was hard when he was being expertly rimmed. Not to mention the knowing hand that circled his cock. He leaned forward a little, bracing himself on Devon's hip to give him easier access, but it wasn't enough for him to reach Jonathan. Catching his breath between swipes of Devon's tongue, he said, "Turn around this way, Jon, so I can get my hands on you."

Jonathan looked up from his self-appointed task of driving Devon crazy, finding himself staring directly into Kit's coffee-colored eyes. He blinked, taking in the wider picture of Devon tonguing their lover's ass while he worked Kit with his hand. His own balls tightened in response to the sensual image, and when Kit coaxed him to move within reach, he didn't have to be asked twice. Never losing contact with Devon's cock, he scrambled around until he was against Devon's side, his knees brushing Kit's leg where he straddled Devon's chest.

Kit's hips were rocking steadily into Devon's face between the probing of his tongue and the squeezing of his hand, but he forced himself to concentrate long enough to open Jonathan's shorts and push them down, enfolding Jonathan's cock in a firm grasp, stroking in time with Devon's movements.

Whatever Kit was doing to Jonathan, it was making him moan happily around Devon's bollocks, adding another layer of sensation to the hot waves already pulsing through him. When Jonathan worked his hand down the back of Devon's shorts to trace over his crease, Devon cursed against Kit's backside, and his hand tightened involuntarily around the younger man's cock, losing the rhythm of his strokes.

Kit's hand on Jonathan's cock felt so damn good, Devon was writhing and cursing beneath his lips, and Jonathan didn't think he'd ever get enough of either one of them. He pushed harder against Kit's fist, his breath shortening as he sucked Devon back into his mouth and pressed at the entrance that clenched against his circling fingers.

Kit shivered in delight and desire, so close to coming that he didn't know if he could hold back. Wanting to speed things along for his lovers, he slid his free hand down to play along the base of Devon's cock against Jonathan's lips. With the other hand, he gripped Jonathan's shaft more firmly, working it with every bit of experience he possessed.

Devon played his tongue against Kit's hole, moaning steadily as Jonathan increased the suction on his cock and played teasing fingers against his arse. When Kit's hand wrapped around the base of his shaft, it was more than Devon could bear. He stabbed his tongue inside Kit, his hand faltering as his orgasm flared through him, pulsing out into the heat of Jonathan's hungry mouth.

Jonathan swallowed around Devon's twitching shaft, trying to wring as much sensation as he could from his shuddering lover while his own climax neared. He pushed just the tip of his finger inside Devon's puckered entrance, pulsing it in time with Devon's bucking hips.

Waves of aftershocks racked Devon as Jonathan pressed his finger inside him, continuing to suck until Devon was sure his bollocks were drained. At each shuddering wave, he thrust his tongue deeper inside Kit, trying to bring him to the same state of blissful release Jonathan had reduced him to.

Giving up control and hoping Jonathan was close enough to come, Kit spilled his seed all over Devon's chest, long ropes of creamy fluid shooting from his twitching cock as he came. He tried to remember to keep his hand moving on Jonathan's cock, but he had no real idea if he had succeeded.

As Devon's shudders eased and his own increased, Jonathan let the softening cock slide from his mouth and drew a gasping breath. Kit's hand stuttered and then clutched at his shaft, and Jonathan watched as a look of ecstasy transformed Kit's already beautiful face. Pumping into his lover's tightened fist, Jonathan gave in and let his own pleasure take him.

Trembling through the aftermath of his release, Kit rolled to Devon's side, away from Jonathan, struggling to catch his breath. In the back of his mind was the thought that they should at least put their shorts back on in case someone wandered by, but another thought, one that had been growing since yesterday, was taking precedence. He waited to speak, though, wanting to give the other two time to recover as well.

When Kit drew back from his cock, Jonathan pushed himself up enough to bend over Devon's chest and lap up the traces of Kit's come. When he'd cleaned away the last creamy drops, he rested his head, listening to Devon's steadying heartbeat. "That was good," he murmured in contentment.

"That was fucking brilliant," Devon agreed, threading a hand through Jonathan's sandy hair and reaching for Kit with the other.

"Everything we do together is fucking brilliant," Kit chimed in, moving into Devon's embrace. "That's why I think you need to banish some bad memories." He took a deep breath and looked directly into Devon's eyes. "That's why you need to be a Dom again, with us this time."

CHAPTER 13
PLUGGING IN

THE WOOD chafed lightly against Kit's stomach as he waited to see what Devon had in store for him. He was still not quite sure how he'd ended up naked on their back porch, cock ring around his straining erection, butt in the air, hands firmly holding his ankles as he leaned over the porch railing, the afternoon sun warm against his bare skin.

It had taken some convincing on Kit's part to bring Devon around. His initial reaction to Kit's suggestion that Devon act as their Dom had been outright refusal, but that had only added to Kit's determination. Devon needed to get past this and learn to trust himself again. And honestly, Kit needed it too, needed to see that even at his most dominant, Devon would never hurt him the way Devon himself had been hurt. Kit hadn't mentioned the second part, though he knew it would have guaranteed Devon's cooperation. He wanted Devon to do this for himself.

Jonathan hadn't been as sure as Kit that this was what Devon needed, but he was willing to go along with anything that would keep Devon from sliding back into the passivity that had worried him so much the day before. If giving explicit control of their intimacies over to Devon would help, he'd gladly play along—after all, he'd been tacitly following Devon's direction from the first night the three of them had come together, and the results had been pretty fantastic so far.

Consciously taking on a dominant role again wasn't something Devon could do lightly. "I know I directed much of our early interaction," he admitted, "but that was because everything was new to Jonathan and you're just so bloody *young* that taking charge felt natural." He glanced at Kit apologetically as he spoke. "And anyway, that was all suggestions, not commands. You could say no at any time. If I agree with what you're asking now, you'll no longer have that choice."

Devon hadn't said it, but Kit had learned to read his lover well enough already to realize Devon still didn't trust himself again with that much power.

"We have safewords," Kit reminded Devon. "You say I have to trust you, and I do, but you also have to trust me to use my out if I need it. Isn't that why we agreed on them in the first place?"

In the end, it was Jonathan who'd convinced him after listening to both their arguments. "I trust you, Devon," he murmured, resting their foreheads together and rubbing Devon's tense shoulders. "I trusted you to bring me into this relationship, and I trust you to teach me about this. I think you have to remember how to trust yourself."

Determined to dispel the tense atmosphere between them, Devon insisted they spend the morning in nonsexual activities. After dressing, they walked to the small village a mile or so down the road, finding a cafe to eat breakfast and then exploring the shops that lined the single main street. They picked out fruit and vegetables from the market, meat from the butcher, and loaves of crusty bread fresh from the bakery before heading back to the house, Devon promising they could drive to a larger town later to stock up on groceries for the rest of the long weekend.

Kit was eager to get started with the scene as soon as they returned, but the morning was half gone, and Devon had declared they would wait until after lunch so they'd have a longer stretch of uninterrupted time. Jonathan suggested swimming, so they spent the rest of the morning playing in the refreshingly cool surf, though Kit wasn't sure he'd consider it nonsexual activity, given the way Jonathan's cutoffs clung to his arse and Devon's muscles flexed as he moved through the water. Judging by the heated glances he saw between—and received from—his two lovers, they were just as appreciative as he was.

That sensual awareness, never completely gone, built slowly as they returned to the house, showered, and prepared lunch, all of them quieter than usual. Leaving Kit and Jonathan to clean up after they ate, Devon disappeared into the bedroom and returned wearing his sexy leather pants, which delighted Kit immensely. Ordering Kit and Jonathan to wait in the living room, Devon returned to the bedroom, to rummage through the toy box from the sounds of it, though Kit had no idea what Devon was selecting. He wasn't overly concerned, though. He'd gone through the box himself the night before and had seen nothing to upset him. A few moments later, Devon returned and asked both of them if they had brought their cock rings. Kit blushed, but he retrieved it from his bag obediently on Devon's command. With a sheepish grin, Jonathan retrieved his as well.

Devon padded around the beach house like a stalking panther, deciding on the best setting for the plans he was formulating. Ordering both men outside, he assumed a lounging pose on the glider at one side of the wide, shaded porch that faced the beach. "Strip," he growled, his voice allowing no question of disobedience.

Kit almost hesitated. Almost. Then he remembered why they were there. How could he ask Devon to trust himself if he didn't show Devon that same trust? He dropped his T-shirt to the deck, his shorts following close behind. And he realized with a jolt that he was already hard, just from Devon's commanding tone. Jonathan hadn't been wearing anything but his frayed cutoffs anyway, and they quickly joined the pile of Kit's clothes on the wooden deck.

Devon nodded and crossed one bare foot over the other, knowing it emphasized the long, sleek lines of the tight leathers, pleased that both his lovers had obeyed without question. "Put on the rings," he ordered, sliding one hand blatantly over his bulging crotch.

Kit fumbled a little as he moved to obey, a mixture of nerves and desire making his hands tremble, the predatory look in Devon's eyes only adding to his turmoil. Finally, though, he had the ring positioned around the base of his cock. Just realizing he had given up control of his orgasms ratcheted his lust up another notch.

Watching Devon slowly stroke himself, Jonathan adjusted the ring over his own thickening erection. "Fuck, but you look amazingly hot like that."

Kit had to agree. Devon sprawled out lazily on the glider, the powerful muscles of his bare chest flexing with each languid move of his hand. The desire to taste that chest, to slide the leathers off those long legs and devour him, nearly overwhelmed Kit. He swallowed hard and dropped his hands to his side.

As the tense silence lengthened, Kit tried to see himself and Jonathan through Devon's eyes. Jonathan was standing in a relaxed slouch, hands loose at his sides, but his eyes followed Devon's every movement. Kit, on the other hand, was practically vibrating in his eagerness. Whatever he saw, it was enough for Devon to make a decision, sitting forward and catching Jonathan's avid gaze. "Find something to bind him with," he said, nodding his head casually toward Kit. "There's rope in my duffel bag."

Jonathan headed inside, returning a moment later with a coil of smooth braided cord, a pair of scissors, and a few kitchen towels. "I thought maybe these would keep the rope from cutting into him," he said, presenting the items to Devon.

The squeak that escaped Kit could have been a sign of fear or delight, and he himself couldn't say which one it was. He forced himself to stand quiescently, excitement barely under control, waiting to see where and how Devon would bind him.

Devon locked eyes with Jonathan for a long minute, gaze cool and unemotional. When Jonathan's Adam's apple bobbed uneasily for a third time, Devon said quietly, "When I want something from you, I'll tell you. You will do what I tell you, and *only* what I tell you. Do you understand?"

Jonathan nodded, unnerved by this new attitude. "I understand."

"'Yes, Sir' will be sufficient," Devon purred, his voice low and dangerous.

Jonathan's cock, already half-hard, twitched against his thigh. "Yes, Sir," he agreed, placing an emphasis on the honorific.

"You will always address me as Sir." Devon smiled and pointed to the floor next to him. "Kneel. Here."

Jonathan's cock jumped at the command, mute testament to his arousal. He sunk to his knees, sitting back on his heels and resting his hands on his thighs.

Yes, Sir. The words echoed in Kit's mind. *Yes, Sir.* That was what Devon expected from him too, though he hadn't said it. Something in Devon's demeanor made Kit eager to gain his approval. It wasn't something he'd thought about previously. He'd been blithely confident that his simple presence was enough to gain it. Now, though, he would have to earn it. Seeing Jonathan sink to his knees at Devon's command, Kit knew he would do whatever it took too, if only because he didn't want to do less than his lovers.

Dropping the cord onto the porch floor, Devon turned his gaze to Kit and nodded. "Bend over the railing, Kit. Spread your legs and grab your ankles through the rails."

Kit moved slowly but without hesitation to the railing nearest Devon and Jonathan. Taking a deep breath to calm his rapidly pounding heart, he leaned against the smooth wood and bent double, glad for the stretches he did every day for his back that let him do so gracefully. He could only imagine the sight he presented to his lovers, bare arse upturned and open to them. The thought sent a fresh surge of arousal through him, and he could feel his cock starting to leak. And that was how he ended up over the railing, waiting to see what Devon would do next.

The artist in Jonathan appreciated the sensual image Devon had created, Kit's willowy limbs doubled over the faded wooden porch rail. His own arousal grew, suffusing him with heat despite the cool breeze off the ocean. He drew a calming breath, finding himself hoping Devon would command him to do something. *Anything.*

"You like that, Jonathan?" Devon asked, hiding the grin that wanted to spread over his face at Jonathan's hungry expression.

"Yes, Sir," Jonathan answered, remembering the script.

"Open him," Devon ordered, waving a languid hand to give Jonathan permission to move. Not sure if he should rise without permission, Jonathan crawled the short distance forward to kneel before Kit.

"Oh," Devon added as Jonathan reached to cup Kit's cheeks, "and don't use your hands."

Another wave of heat made Jonathan shiver at Devon's command. Leaning forward, his breath ghosting over the smooth globes before him, he dragged his tongue up the shadowy crease.

Kit wriggled in anticipation when he heard Devon's command— he loved being rimmed, as his lovers well knew—but the feeling of Jonathan's tongue was different this time… more intense somehow, and that sent a frisson down Kit's spine. Would it all be this way? Would every touch, every sensation be more, somehow, than it usually was? He moaned, low and long, at the thought.

Kit's moan and the tremble that shook Jonathan's back made Devon glad he'd ordered them to put on their cock rings. As aroused as he was getting just watching them, he wondered if he ought to have put on his own as well. He slid his hand away from his cock and sat forward, giving himself a better view of Jonathan's head moving between Kit's legs. "That's right," he prompted, "open him up good. He's going to need to be good and stretched for what comes next."

Devon's words only added to Kit's arousal. "What… what are you going… to do… to me?" he gasped between strokes of Jonathan's tongue.

At Kit's question, Devon rose to stand beside him, sharply smacking the enticingly displayed bottom. "Some Doms get very angry at a sub speaking without permission, especially one daring to ask questions. I'm not quite that rigid," he added with a smirk, since at least one part of him was very rigid indeed. "But you aren't to speak unless I address you."

Kit yelped when he felt the blow to his backside. It hurt, but only for a second, leaving a bloom of warmth behind. Even as he struggled with that realization, he tried to assimilate Devon's command. "Yes, Sir," he replied after a moment, wanting to do as Devon required.

Devon swatted Kit again lightly, his hand lingering to caress the reddened marks left by his palm. "That really didn't require an answer," he noted, "but I might not have been clear enough. You will not speak unless I ask you a direct question. Do you understand?"

"Yes, Sir," Kit answered, his voice a breathy whisper, his head starting to spin from all the different sensations, physical and mental: Jonathan's tongue, Devon's hand, his own willing obedience, and his growing desire for more. Not to mention his upside-down position over the railing.

Pretty sure he shouldn't stop what he was doing, Jonathan tried to look up enough to catch a glimpse of Devon's face, unsure if he was expected to respond as well. Deciding he had not been addressed directly, he stayed silent, instead using his tongue to tease around the puckered folds of Kit's entrance, pressing in a little more deeply with each pass. Angling his head so he could move even closer, he thrust with a steady rhythm, matching the pulse that throbbed against the constriction of his cock ring. He spread his knees farther apart, trying to relieve the ache in his groin, and focused on stretching Kit as wide-open as he could.

Devon watched Jonathan's increasingly avid probing of Kit's arse a moment longer, then turned back to the glider and retrieved the plug he'd taken from his toy box earlier. He dangled the squat piece of latex casually before his two lovers, leaning back against the porch pillar to gauge their reaction. "Do you think you need lube, Kit?" he asked. "Or does Jonathan's mouth have you wet enough to take this?"

Kit warred with his answer. He wanted Jonathan's mouth to be enough. He *was* wet and open, but he remembered his early experiments with dildos, remembered how, in his ignorance, he had tried to insert the phallus with no lube, and how much *that* had hurt. He'd been fucked dry after a rimming since then, except that it wasn't really dry, not with

precome coating his lover's cock. The plug in Devon's hand was more
like that dildo, and he was afraid to take it dry. "Lube," he whispered.
Realizing Devon didn't have to ask or to listen to his request once made,
he added, "Please."

Devon frowned at Kit's answer. Kit couldn't see it, bent over the
rail as he was, but Jonathan could. He stilled his movements, words
trembling on his lips, words he knew would earn him a punishment of
some sort for breaking the rules, but if they'd deflect Devon's attention
from Kit's transgression…. He pulled back, about to speak, when he saw
the tube of lube in their lover's hand.

"I didn't tell you to stop," Devon growled at Jonathan, threading
a hand into his hair and pulling his head upward to meet his eyes. He
held Jonathan's uneasy gaze for a moment. "Since you did, though, go
back over by the glider and wait for me." Confident of being obeyed, he
didn't watch to see if Jonathan did as he was told. Instead he focused on
Kit, squeezing a generous dollop of lube onto his fingers. "Let's see how
well Jonathan did his job," he said, pushing deep into Kit's hole with his
fingers.

Kit moaned at the heavenly feeling of Devon's fingers inside
him. He wanted to beg for more, for a third finger or Devon's cock,
but he hadn't been addressed, and Devon had said not to speak unless
asked a question. In lieu of words, he pushed back against the questing
hand as best he could in his awkward position, hoping Devon would
take the hint.

"There's a lot that goes into being a Dom," Devon said conversationally
as he worked his fingers, avoiding Kit's sweet spot, "but the most important
thing is knowing your sub, usually better than he knows himself. Knowing
what he needs and knowing how far you can go with him." He brushed a
fingertip lightly over Kit's prostate, smiling at the groan of pleasure this
wrung from his boy. "Pushing your limits is part of the scene, but you have
to believe that I'll never do more to you than you can take. You said you
trusted me. Now it's time to act like it."

Kneeling silently and feeling forgotten, Jonathan dropped his
head in shame. He'd told Devon he trusted him, and then he'd failed
the very first test of proving that trust. He wanted to speak, to apologize
and ask Devon for a second chance, but he knew that talking out of turn
would only make his failure worse. He hoped he'd get a chance to regain
Devon's approval.

Deciding Kit was open enough, Devon withdrew his fingers and coated the head of the plug with lube. He glanced at Jonathan, who was kneeling with his head hung down despondently. Devon knew he couldn't let the other man's action go unchallenged, but he also knew he couldn't—*wouldn't*—be the hard-arsed bastard he'd been trained to be either. *Never again*, he vowed. When Jonathan looked up, Devon motioned for him to move closer.

"You did a good job of opening him up," Devon acknowledged, warming at the flush of pleasure that colored Jonathan's cheeks. "I was going to let you tie him to the pillar as your reward, but your misbehavior has forfeited that. Now you'll just have to watch me do it and think about the fact that it could have been your hands on him instead of mine."

Turning his attention back to Kit, Devon ran a gentle hand over the rosy cheeks presented so enticingly. Once he'd separated them enough to position the plug, he slid it into the glistening channel with one firm twist. "Stand up, Kit."

The shock of feeling the plug inside him combined with Devon's order caught Kit by surprise. It took him a moment to react. When he did, the sudden rush of blood out of his head left him feeling dizzy. He took a step back to balance himself as he grabbed the railing, and he gasped as his movement rubbed the plug firmly over his prostate.

When Kit staggered, Jonathan had to fight the urge to jump to his feet and steady him. *Trust Devon*, he told himself firmly. *Devon knows what he's doing. He won't let Kit get hurt.* Clenching his fists on his thighs, Jonathan bit his lip and waited, wondering what Devon would do next once he had Kit where he wanted him.

Devon gave Kit a moment to adjust to standing upright again. The gasp that escaped when his lover's arse brushed the railing told him the plug was having the desired effect. "Over here," he ordered after a moment, moving away from the pillar he'd been leaning against. "Face Jonathan and wrap your hands around the pillar, behind your back."

Still a little unsteady on his feet, Kit took the three steps to the place Devon had indicated, the plug stimulating him with every movement. He leaned back gratefully against the pillar, positioning his hands as Devon had indicated. The posture left him feeling incredibly exposed, his chest pushed forward as his arms reached back, his ringed cock on prominent display. And through it all, the constant awareness of the plug danced along his nerves, firing them with arousal.

Moving with practiced ease, Devon twisted the rope around Kit's wrists, making sure he left enough slack to prevent the cord from cutting into skin. He debated binding his ankles as well, but he wanted Kit free to move at his command. "Spread your legs wider," he instructed, knowing the movement would stir the plug, stimulating Kit's arousal and feeding his own.

The rope felt odd to Kit. He moved his arms a little to test the knots. The bindings didn't hurt, but he was well and truly bound. He'd be standing against that pillar until Devon released him. Hearing the command, he shifted his feet, moaning when the plug pushed against his prostate once again. His cock twitched eagerly, as if asking for attention.

"Jonathan," Devon called, pointing to Kit's feet. "Here." When the other man knelt beside him, he ran a hand down Kit's smooth torso, tweaking the flat brown nipples, fingering the dark curls that surrounded the base of his cock. "Doesn't he look beautiful like this," he asked casually, "tied up for our pleasure, ready for anything we choose to do to him?"

Jonathan licked his dry lips, his pulse pounding as he stared up at Kit. He did look beautiful, like a statue of some Greek god come to life before them, and so desirable that the breath caught in his throat. "Yes, Sir," he whispered, his voice a hoarse rasp of need.

Devon slid a finger along the length of Kit's straining erection, circling the smooth head just visible beneath his foreskin. "What do you want to do to him, Jonathan?" he asked. "If I let you touch him now, what would you do?"

Jonathan's moan was echoed by an answering one from Kit. He hesitated, unsure what answer Devon wanted to hear, before deciding that honesty was the only choice. "Suck him," he pleaded. "Please, Sir, let me suck him."

Kit barely managed to stop the echoing plea that jumped to his lips. He nodded eagerly instead, shifting a little to tilt his groin outward, pushing his cock toward Jonathan's lips.

Sliding his hand down to stroke his own arousal once again, Devon nodded his approval. "Go ahead, then," he agreed. "Show me how good you can make him feel."

Jonathan leaned forward eagerly, circling his tongue around the darkened tip of Kit's cock, pushing back the foreskin with his lips to reach more of the smooth head. Kit tasted salty from sweat and the sea air, and his cock twitched in Jonathan's mouth as he suckled it. With a groan, he took more of it inside, sliding down until his teeth bumped against the tight ring circling its base. Sucking firmly, Jonathan rocked forward, his own cock rubbing against his stomach as he devoured Kit's.

Instinctively, Kit moved his hands to bury his fingers in Jonathan's hair, but the ropes around his wrists brought him up short. Before he could stop himself, words babbled from his lips. "Feels so good," he gasped. "Just… like that." As soon as he spoke, he realized what he had done, eyes flying up to meet Devon's, embarrassment and shame heating his cheeks.

Devon shook his head, fighting not to let his laughter bubble free. "Kit," he muttered reproachfully, "am I going to have to gag you to keep you quiet?" Stalking to stand behind Jonathan, he reached up to pinch Kit's nipples, just hard enough to be painful. When Kit groaned and arched up into the touch, Devon did laugh.

"Like that, do yeh?" he rumbled, his accent thickening as he let himself react to his own growing need. "I have a set of nipple clamps at home that will look so fuckin' good on you. You'd enjoy that, wouldn't you, sunshine?"

Kit shivered at the touch of Devon's hand. Yes, it was painful, but much like the smacks on his arse earlier, the pain faded quickly, leaving only arousal. His body followed the retreating hand automatically, seeking more of the novel touch. Devon's question penetrated the fog of lust clouding his brain. Nipple clamps… constant pressure on his sensitive nubs. The thought alone had him trembling. "Yes, Sir," he managed weakly, sagging against the pillar, glad now for its support since Jonathan's mouth hadn't stopped its work either, and every bob of his head pressed the plug against his prostate again. Kit could feel his release pushing against the cock ring. The band was winning, but Kit was close now.

The sensuous rasp of Devon's voice and the mental image of nipple clamps adorning Kit's smooth chest made Jonathan groan around the shaft filling his mouth. He wanted to take Kit's balls in his hand, to reach up and feel where the plug entered his body, but Devon hadn't given him permission to touch, and he wouldn't do anything to risk displeasing him again. He tried to relax his throat muscles and take Kit still deeper, rocking with even more urgency as his own arousal grew like a fever inside him, until he was so close that he'd be coming, completely untouched, if it weren't for the ring holding it back.

Watching the erotic scene playing out before him was fraying the limits of Devon's own control, and it was clear both his lovers were close enough to come any minute. When Jonathan moved his hand toward Kit and quickly drew back, he realized he'd never retracted his command against touching. Surprised and pleased Jonathan had remembered that, he decided the other man deserved a reward.

"You're doing so well, Jonathan," he praised, stroking the silky hair beneath his hand. "Do you want to make Kit come now? To suck him until his bollocks are dry?"

Jonathan couldn't hold back the whimper that rose in his throat at Devon's words. Letting Kit's cock slide from his swollen lips, he nodded, his eyes meeting Devon's, proud at having pleased him. "Yes, Sir," he moaned. "Oh fuck yes, please."

Kit remembered not to speak this time, but he turned pleading eyes on Devon as a whimper escaped him. He was so painfully close. He needed to come, and he couldn't think of any place better right now than down Jonathan's throat.

Devon recognized the effort Kit was making to hold back his words and knew the boy had earned his release. "If I let you come now, will you be able to come again?" he asked, even though he knew Kit would likely agree to anything at the moment to win his orgasm. "I expect to feel you coming around my cock when I fuck you later."

"Yes, Sir, oh please, God, yes," Kit babbled, the cool breeze off the ocean on his wet skin adding to his desperation. His recovery time was usually pretty good anyway, and with Devon fucking him, he didn't think he'd have any problem keeping his promise.

With an indulgent smile, Devon leaned over Jonathan to remove the ring, fingers trailing over Kit's saliva-slick cock. "Make him come, Jonathan," he ordered.

Swallowing Kit's length again hungrily, Jonathan sucked and stroked it with his teeth and tongue, doing everything he could to speed his lover's climax.

With the cock ring removed and Devon's order for him to come echoing in his ears, Kit gave up any attempt to control himself. He thrust forward as much as his bindings would allow, trying to get deeper into Jonathan's mouth. After only a few strokes of Jonathan's talented tongue, he let loose a hoarse shout and climaxed hard.

Devon and Jonathan both caught their breath at the sight of Kit's face in the moment he peaked—eyes hazy and unfocused, skin flushed, lips parted in a blissful cry. *And Niall thought he was handsome as a chaste knight.* Devon chuckled. *He should see him like this.* Or maybe better not—Percival might wind up with more screen time than Arthur. Glancing at their king, still caught in rapt admiration of the vision bound before him, Devon considered his next steps. Jonathan wasn't barely out of his teens like Kit. It wasn't as reasonable to expect him to come twice in quick succession. And while Jonathan had earned his relief as much as Kit had, Devon had other plans for that luscious arse.

As the tension eased from Kit's frame and he sagged back against the pillar, Devon slid to his knees and took Jonathan's cock in his hand, rubbing his thumb over the leather strap that still bound its base. "I think I'll show you something different," he mused, drawing the heavy shaft through the channel of his fingers. Jonathan tried his best not to squirm under the touch, the constriction of the ring adding an awareness of how little it would take to make him come once it was removed. As if reading his thoughts, Devon purred, "You can come even when you're wearing a cock ring, you know. It may not be quite as forceful, but that will just make it all the more powerful when I let you come without it." Jonathan shivered, and Devon increased the speed of his strokes, sliding his other hand between Jonathan's cheeks to glide over the sensitive skin of his perineum. "Let go," he whispered huskily. "Trust me."

Those words, even more than the tantalizing touch of Devon's fingers, sent a wave of heat flaring through Jonathan's senses. His cock jerked against the leather strap binding it, only a dribble of cloudy fluid seeping from the tip, but his nerves sang as if he had filled Devon's hand with his seed. He turned his head in wonder to meet Devon's gaze. The orgasm didn't feel any less forceful; in fact, his cock felt more sensitive than ever, leaving him shuddering with aftershocks at each gentling pass of Devon's hand over the still-rigid shaft.

"Very good," Devon murmured, his free hand sliding from between Jonathan's buttocks to rub soothingly up his back, easing him through the new sensation. "And just think how much better it will feel when you come with the ring off."

Light-headed from the intensity of his climax, Jonathan wasn't sure he could feel much better than he did right now. "Thank you, Sir," he murmured, still floating on the high of having earned Devon's praise.

Devon rose to his feet, looking with satisfaction at his two satiated lovers. He'd seen to both their needs; now it was time to take care of his own. Stepping around the pillar, he quickly untied the ropes that bound Kit, running a palm over each wrist to check its condition. Pleased that they were only reddened and not chafed, he stepped back, giving Kit room to move. "Ready to feel something better than that plug up your arse?" he growled.

Kit shook his arms a little to restore the circulation when Devon freed them. Hearing his lover's question, he nodded quickly. "Yes!" he replied fervently. "I want your cock." He paused, then remembered. "Sir."

"Back over the railing, then," Devon ordered. "Show me that beautiful arse of yours, and I'll give you m'cock, all right." When Kit had resumed his position bent double over the railing, Devon grasped the handle of the plug, giving it a final twist before pulling it slowly out. "Do you know the difference between a dildo and a plug?" he asked as he tossed the toy to the porch floor to deal with later. "A dildo is to give you pleasure. A plug is to remind you who you belong to."

Kit grabbed his ankles tightly, steadying himself as Devon withdrew the plug, sending fresh arousal surging through him. "Yes," he whimpered mindlessly, hearing Devon's words. He hadn't thought about it, hadn't pondered the difference, but when his Dom pointed it out, he knew it was true. In this moment, Devon owned him body and soul. "All yours."

"Mine," Devon confirmed as he pushed the tight leathers down his hips and quickly slicked himself with lube. "All mine," he repeated, thrusting into Kit's well-prepared channel with a single long stroke.

Still kneeling before the empty pillar, Jonathan watched as Devon filled Kit, claiming him. A bitter taste of jealousy rose in his throat, but he swallowed it back, knowing it was unwarranted. Kit had done so well; despite his few mistakes, he had taken everything Devon had demanded of him. He deserved everything Devon was giving him now.

Kit's hips rocked forward against the railing as Devon claimed him. A moan tore from his throat at the sensation and the thought. He wanted to reach for his resurgent erection, but he dared not move without permission lest Devon stop what he was doing.

Devon wanted nothing more than to slake his need by fucking Kit senseless, but a low moan from behind them made him pause and turn his head. Jonathan still knelt where he had left him, watching them with an empty hunger in his eyes. Stretching a hand out, Devon beckoned him to join them. "C'mere, Jon," he invited, his voice unsteady as he rocked back against Kit. "Come here and touch me."

At Devon's request, Jonathan scrambled across the rough floor, kneeling behind the two men bent over the railing. He hadn't been given permission to speak, but he didn't know what Devon wanted from him, so he risked talking out of turn. "Sir—" He hesitated. "—please, Sir, what do you want me to do?"

Too close to his own climax to care, Devon rasped, "Anything you bloody want," as he fought to hold off just a little bit longer.

Since Devon's ass was pumping in his face, Jonathan grasped the strong hips and pressed his face into it, probing at Devon's hole as he had at Kit's. Devon tasted stronger, darker, and Jonathan sucked and thrust greedily, needing to make Devon feel him to add to the pleasure being buried balls-deep in Kit had to bring.

Devon groaned as the heat of Jonathan tonguing him threatened to push him over the edge. He slowed his thrusts into Kit, pushing back against Jonathan's mouth. "Good," he moaned. "Ah fuck, Jon, so fuckin' good."

Kit whined in protest at the slowed movements. He could feel a second climax building, but he needed a thorough reaming to reach it.

The needy sound escaping from Kit broke the last of Devon's restraint. Clutching the slender hips hard enough to bruise them, he pounded into Kit unmercifully, the strength of his climax building until it roared out of him with the power of a storm wave crashing over the seafront.

This was what Kit craved, the hard fucking Devon was giving him. When Devon's release filled him, he shuddered and came.

Jonathan felt the shudders as Devon came buried deep inside Kit, felt the answering tremors as Kit must have come again beneath him. He pulled back when Devon went lax against his mouth, his own arousal still hard and insistent. He hadn't been given permission to touch himself, but he was past caring any longer. Tearing off the cock ring and wrapping his fist around his cock, he jacked off quickly, groaning as he spilled hotly over his quivering thighs.

His arousal sated, Kit felt the blood pooling in his head and the wooden railing pressed hard against his stomach with Devon's weight on top of him. He waited a minute to see if Devon would give another order, but when none was forthcoming, he asked, "Are we done? Because if we are, I'd like to stand up."

A bit flustered at having let himself drift enough to forget about his partners, Devon rose, offering a hand to help Kit up from his awkward position. "You okay, lad?" he asked, concerned by how roughly he had pounded into him at the end. "I wasn't too hard on your back?"

Thankful for the steadying hand, Kit grinned widely. "It was bloody brilliant! We should definitely try this again sometime."

Turning to Jonathan once Kit was steady on his feet, Devon was surprised to see the other man sitting back on his heels, wiping his hand on his thigh, the ring off his softening cock. He raised an eyebrow and Jonathan shrugged. "I couldn't wait," Jonathan said, his voice quiet but level.

"I ought by rights to punish you for that," Devon said with a grin. "I had other plans for you, and when you're subbing, your orgasms belong to me. But Kit hasn't left me the energy at the moment. I'll take it out on your arse the next time. For now, let's clean up and then get dinner started. In fact, you can pick up out here first as part of your punishment. Come join us in the shower when you're done."

Kit was torn between staying with Jonathan and going inside with Devon. He understood what Devon was saying about them obeying him—they'd agreed to that before they started—but he didn't feel right about just walking off and leaving Jonathan either, not when Devon hadn't actually told him not to come. He glanced back and forth between the two men but eventually decided that rocking the boat wasn't worth it at this point. They could talk about it later, when they weren't all on a high from the scene.

Jonathan shook his head as Kit and Devon disappeared into the house, trying to escape the last of the headspace he'd entered during the game. He was going to need to find a little time alone to process everything that had just happened. Maybe later he'd take a walk along the beach.

CHAPTER 14
LIP SERVICE

KIT ROLLED over, slowly brought to wakefulness by the cold against his back where Jonathan had been during the night. He lay there for a minute, listening to the water running in the bathroom, figuring that was why Jonathan was up so early. The water shut off after a few minutes, but Jonathan didn't reappear. Heaving a sigh, Kit sat up, looking down at Devon still asleep next to him. The evening had been a little awkward after their scene. Jonathan had been subdued, not really responding to Kit's teasing, but Devon had drawn him aside, telling him to give Jonathan time, that for some people it took a while to let go of their headspace after an intense session. Kit certainly didn't have the experience to argue with that, but it was morning now, and Jonathan was still acting strange. He nudged Devon until his eyes opened. "Jonathan took a page out of your book and disappeared. I don't think I like my lovers leaving in the morning without so much as a kiss."

Yawning and running a hand through his hair, Devon pushed up on one elbow to peer over Kit's shoulder, as if to confirm that Jonathan was really gone from the bed. He still felt a bit guilty about having lost himself so much in his own pleasure at the end of their session the night before that he'd left Jonathan to find his own release. They'd all been too tired after dinner to do more than nestle together and share a few kisses before falling asleep, but it hadn't escaped Devon's attention that Jonathan had taken the side of the bed facing the wall. He'd hoped a good night's sleep would provide enough distance to make it easier to discuss how things had gone during the scene—what had worked and what hadn't—but that would be hard to do with Jonathan missing.

"Probably took his camera and went looking for something to shoot. He mentioned wanting to do that yesterday," Devon said, hoping it was nothing more than that.

"You're probably right," Kit agreed, bending down and kissing him. "Feeling better this morning?"

Deepening the kiss felt so good that Devon pulled Kit closer, cupping the firm buttocks in his palms to mold their bodies together until they both began to stir again in response. "Feeling bloody wonderful," he admitted. "What about you? Back still feeling all right? I did work you pretty hard for a first time."

Kit rubbed against Devon like a cat in heat. "My back's fine," he assured his lover. "And I promise I'll tell you if it bothers me, regardless of the circumstances." His desire building again, Kit felt Jonathan's absence keenly. "Let's see if we can find our king," he suggested. "I wouldn't want to start anything fun without him."

Nodding in agreement, Devon let Kit pull out of his arms. His conscience was pricking him for not having clearly ended the previous day's scene before they left the porch. He'd been so buzzed at having controlled a session again that he'd forgotten one of the simplest rules: make sure to give your sub plenty of aftercare. Especially when the sub was as new and inexperienced as Jonathan. Devon only hoped Jonathan wasn't suffering for his mistake now.

"He's out on the beach somewhere," Kit added when Devon didn't reply. "I heard the door close when he left. Why don't we split up and see how quickly we can find him?"

"The wind has already blown away his footprints," Devon observed when they made it outside a few moments later, having tarried only long enough to pull on a minimum of clothes. "You go left and I'll go right. The first one to find him, give a yell."

"Okay," Kit replied. He couldn't quite shake the feeling that something was wrong. Why else would Jonathan have left their bed so early without telling them where he was going? "We didn't scare him off with that scene on the porch yesterday, did we?" he asked, needing that last bit of reassurance before they went searching.

Devon frowned at the confirmation that Kit had felt the same concerning vibe from their lover. "I have a feeling not much scares our king, for all this is all new to him," he replied, hoping he was right. "But if something is bothering him, we should talk about it and not let him brood on it by himself."

Kit nodded. "You're right, on both counts. Let's find him and bring him back where he belongs so we can enjoy the rest of our break."

Devon headed down the beach, his stride turning into a lope as he saw no sign of Jonathan. Despite his calm words to Kit, Devon was growing more and more concerned the longer he thought about it. He'd forgotten one of the prime responsibilities of being a Dom and let his own pleasure make him neglect his sub. Granted, he'd never been a Dom to two partners at once before, but that didn't excuse his lapse. Devon wondered if he'd been wrong to let Kit and Jonathan talk him into this. He couldn't—wouldn't—make the same mistakes again, especially as much as he was coming to care about the two of them. He'd rather have a vanilla relationship than risk losing them—or harming them—because he could no longer handle a D/s dynamic.

Kit started off in the opposite direction, thoughts wandering back over the scene on the porch. He had been so lost in his own passion, in what Devon was doing to him, that he hadn't really considered Jonathan in the whole process. He hadn't been in a position to influence matters, given that he'd been tied to the post and then bent over the railing, but he hadn't made an effort to pay extra attention to Jonathan after the session ended. His thoughts were interrupted by the sight of their errant lover hunched over his knees on the beach, a pose eerily reminiscent of the way they had found Devon the previous morning.

Jonathan stared vacantly at the horizon, letting his thoughts flow as freely as the tide that washed and receded over the sand. He'd already accepted that his surge of jealousy when Devon claimed Kit as his—only his—was not a momentary reaction to the arousal of the moment. The question was what he wanted to do about it. His own feelings were equally strong for both his lovers, but if they didn't feel the same—if Devon and Kit had connected in a way that made him extraneous.... He wanted that connection too, wanted it so badly his gut churned at the thought of giving it up, but if it wasn't what they wanted, he'd step aside.

"Jonathan?" Kit called, approaching slowly so as not to startle him. "What are you doing sitting out here alone when you have two lovers waiting for you back at the beach house?"

Hearing his name, Jonathan looked up to see Kit approaching over the rise of the dunes. Damn, but he was beautiful, and his spirit was as expansive as his body was desirable. No wonder Devon would want him all for himself. "Took some pictures," he answered, gesturing to the camera that was his excuse for wandering off. "Thought the two of you might have wanted some privacy," he couldn't stop himself from adding quietly.

"Privacy?" Kit repeated, stunned that such a thought might have crossed Jonathan's mind. "Why in the world would you think we wanted privacy from you? Privacy for the three of us from the rest of the cast, absolutely, but from you?"

The sincerity of Kit's response gave Jonathan hope that perhaps the situation wasn't as dire as he'd begun to think it. "You seemed pretty—involved," he offered, not sure exactly how to refer to what he'd seen, or thought he'd seen, between Kit and Devon. "I thought you might have wanted some time to talk things over."

Realizing this was not going to be a short conversation, Kit sat down on the sand next to Jonathan. "Of course I was involved," he said. "Devon was fucking me over the railing of the beach house after you had tortured me with your mouth for God only knows how long. How could I not be involved? And Devon and I did talk about where you disappeared to, but I don't think that's what you meant. What's going on in that overactive brain of yours?"

The image of Devon driving into Kit flashed before Jonathan again, bringing with it the same wave of jealousy he'd felt when watching it happen. "You said you were his," he admitted, before he could think how much this would reveal. His voice was raw as he continued, so softly Kit could barely hear him. "Only his."

Kit froze. Had he really said that? Of course he had. He would have said anything Devon wanted if it meant more of the glorious pounding. "They were words of passion," he said slowly. "In that moment, I was his, but that doesn't mean I want you less. If you had been standing where he was, claiming me the way he was, I would have said the same thing to you." Not sure he was helping his case, he changed tacks. "If I belong to anyone, it's to both of you, equally. How do I convince you of that?"

At Kit's words, a little of the constriction eased around Jonathan's heart. He'd spoken only of want, of belonging in a physical sense, but right now Jonathan would take that and be glad for it. Before he could formulate an answer to Kit's question, a shout from over the ridge brought his head up again.

"Oi!" Devon called, seeing Kit hunched beside Jonathan on the damp sand, the surge of relief so strong he instinctively hid it with humor. "I thought you were going to call me if you found him! Trying to keep the king all to yourself, you treacherous knight?"

Kit flinched at Devon's words, not because they were right, but because they were so in line, jokingly, with the very real path of Jonathan's thoughts. "Come join us," he called, not wanting to shout Jonathan's concerns back across the sand.

Something in the tone of Kit's voice and in Jonathan's body language as he hunkered into himself told Devon this was not a moment for continued teasing. Reaching his two lovers, he crossed around them to drop at Jonathan's other side, looking up searchingly at Kit as he did. "Everything all right?" he asked, raising a hand to rest on Jonathan's knee. "Jon?"

Jonathan looked up at his other lover, noticing abstractedly how the sun formed a halo around his tousled golden hair. He hesitated, a lingering reminder of their earlier roles leaving him unsure how to voice his fears.

"He's going to be fine," Kit answered for the other man, "but we gave him a scare, however unintentionally. He thought we didn't want him anymore. Or at least, not as much as we wanted each other."

Jonathan flinched at hearing his insecurity laid bare so bluntly, but he owed it to both the others to be honest with them. "When you… claimed… Kit," he said, forcing himself to meet Devon's gaze, "I wanted it to be me." He swallowed, realizing he needed to explain more clearly. "I wanted it to be me you were claiming that way."

Devon shook his head, anger at himself warring with guilt over his failure to make sure that he'd cared for both his partners' needs. Maybe he *had* been wrong to try to step back into that role after all, if all it did was lead to hurting Jonathan this way. "Jon, I—"

"I know it was only part of the game," Jonathan went on, before Devon could say something he didn't want to hear. "But I… I hope you'll be able to say that to me one day. I want to be able to give that to you… to both of you," he added, looking to Kit in turn.

"So do I," Kit interjected before Devon could reply. "I want to lay claim to you and have you do the same to me, just as Devon did. The fact that our game worked out the way it did yesterday is coincidental." He picked up Jonathan's hand. "Remember something the next time you doubt how much we want you. Devon and I are here together because we both wanted you so much that we took each other on as part of the bargain."

"And now I can't imagine not wanting both of you. You've both come to—to mean a lot to me," Devon finished awkwardly. He'd never been good at expressing his emotions, no matter how deeply felt— probably one reason why he had two failed marriages. "I'm sorry I made you feel excluded in any way, my king," he added, trying to lighten the mood. "Tell me how I can make it up to you, and it will be done."

Jonathan drew a deep breath, so aroused by the images his mind was conjuring that he found himself trembling. "Take me that way," he asked, then hesitated, realizing it sounded too much like a demand. "Or any way you want. I want to give myself to you, however you want me. To both of you."

Jonathan's words slammed into Devon like a tidal wave, bringing him instantly to full, aching arousal. Jonathan still trusted him that much, after the way he'd failed him? He raised his hand to Jonathan's hair, pulling him closer to rest their foreheads together, blinking back a sudden sting of tears. "It will be my privilege," he vowed, "and a very great pleasure for both of us. All three of us," he corrected himself, hoping Kit understood the importance of what Jonathan had just asked.

Kit trembled, hearing Jonathan's words. The image he created sent such desire rushing through him that he was glad to be sitting. He heard Devon's words, then the correction, and leaned in so his forehead touched theirs. "For all three of us," he echoed, needing them both to know that he wanted this too.

Devon rose to his feet, offering his hands to help both his lovers up from the sand. "Let's get back to the house before I forget myself and take both of you right here," he rumbled, only half joking.

Kit laughed, thinking of their encounter on the beach the previous morning. "I wouldn't complain about a repeat of yesterday." He paused when he realized how much that could refer to. "Any of it," he added with leering grin.

Kit's laughter was always contagious, and Jonathan couldn't help but smile in response to it. "I think we've already been lucky not to get sand in some places where sand was never meant to go," he teased. Excited—exhilarated—at the thought of what was to come, he threw back his head and laughed. "Last one back to the house has to bottom!"

Not about to be outdone, Kit sprang to his feet and sprinted toward the house. He certainly didn't mind bottoming, especially not with

Jonathan and Devon as lovers, but he'd done that already this weekend. Now he wanted to top.

Devon pushed himself to sprint past both Jonathan and Kit to reach the porch steps first. After all, he was supposed to be the Dom in this relationship—he could hardly let either of his subs best him. Collapsing onto the bottom step, he grinned up at them both. "What took you so long?"

Arriving at the steps of the porch mere seconds before Jonathan, Kit turned back to him. "You should know better than to challenge two younger men to a race," he teased. "You set yourself up to lose."

Taking a deep breath, Jonathan tried to slow the racing of his heart—racing that wasn't only due to the distance they'd just run. Sinking slowly to his knees in the loose sand, he bowed his head. "You're right," he agreed. "I lost. I will serve your pleasure, however you wish."

Kit's gaze darted to Devon's face. He had gotten there first, so he was the one who would control what happened next. "You beat us both," he said softly, though he didn't drop to his knees. This needed to be first and foremost about Jonathan. "Tell us what to do."

His blood pulsing with desire, Devon nodded toward the spot on the porch they'd occupied earlier the day before. "Get naked," he growled, rising to his feet to head inside and gather the things he'd need. "Kneel there and wait for me. And don't touch each other—that's my privilege alone."

Kit scrambled onto the porch, shedding clothes as quickly as he could. He had no idea what Devon had in store for them, but if yesterday's session was any indication, the pleasure would be mind-blowing. And he didn't want to give Devon any reason to leave him out of it.

Jonathan stepped out of his shorts and tossed them on the glider, then pulled his T-shirt over his head and disposed of it the same way. For a moment he drank in the beauty of Kit's sleek, slender body as he quickly stripped. Then, glancing back toward the screen door, he sank to his knees on the cool wooden planking, resting his hands on his thighs and trying to regulate his breathing. He wasn't sure why he found this so arousing, but he was already hard just in anticipation of what was to come.

Devon pushed the door open with his shoulder and stalked back onto the porch, dropping an armful of supplies onto the glider as the screen slammed behind him. Tossing the cock rings at both men, he smirked. "You know what to do with those. Neither of you are coming until it pleases me to let you."

Kit fastened his ring around his cock quickly, then watched Jonathan doing the same, and rocked back on his heels to see what came next.

There was already precome leaking from the tip of his cock as Jonathan tightened the ring around its base. Giving himself over completely to his role, he wet his lips, anxious to earn the right to be granted pleasure at his lovers' wills.

Knowing that anticipation was its own powerful aphrodisiac, Devon stood silent for a long moment, eyeing the two men kneeling at his feet who trusted him to see that all three of them got what they needed. Kit was as eager to please as a pup, his eyes shining with expectation as he knelt back on his heels. Jonathan's posture was much quieter, his eyes closed as he breathed in and out evenly, almost as if he were lost in mediation, but a nearly imperceptible quiver revealed that he wasn't as calm as he appeared.

"Jonathan!" Devon snapped, his voice loud in the early morning silence. "On your feet."

Jonathan stood, his stomach roiling as he waited anxiously for Devon's next order.

"Bend over and hold the railing," Devon instructed, picking up the plug and a tube of lube from the glider. He didn't miss the flash that lit his lover's eyes when he saw what Devon held.

"Do you remember what I told Kit yesterday?" Devon asked as he coated the plug liberally with the slick gel. "About the difference between a dildo and a plug?"

"Yes, Sir," Jonathan answered softly, watching Devon over his shoulder with a frisson of anticipation.

Seeing Jonathan bent over, hands on the railing, Kit had an idea of what he must have looked like the previous day. The vision before him was unbelievably arousing. And then to hear Devon mention the plug, the sense of being *claimed* rushed through him again, even though Jonathan was the one who would soon be stretched that way.

"Do you want this, Jonathan?" Devon asked, holding the plug so Jonathan could see it as he worked a lube-slick finger into Jonathan's tight entrance, followed quickly by another. As much as he wanted to see Jonathan stretched by the thick latex, he wasn't going to hurt him by shoving it in without preparing him first.

"Yes, Sir," Jonathan gasped as Devon's fingers eased into him, stretching him, preparing him. The plug was thicker than a dildo, thicker than either of his lovers, but he wanted to feel it inside him, wanted what it represented. "Want to belong to you," he added, moaning as Devon twisted three fingers inside his tight passage.

Devon withdrew his fingers without warning and thrust in the plug, turning it until it was seated firmly. "You do," he insisted, threading his fingers into Jonathan's wind-blown hair and guiding him back to his knees, knowing the contact would press the plug even deeper inside. "You're mine, and you're going to do whatever I tell you to do, aren't you?"

"Yes, Sir," Jonathan rasped, biting back a gasp as the plug moved inside him. He tried to relax his muscles around the intrusion, knowing the greater width would leave him stretched and ready for whenever Devon was pleased to claim him.

Hearing Devon's words, seeing the plug slide into Jonathan's body, the feeling of being claimed came back to Kit as strongly as it had when he was the one stretched wide-open. He imagined for a moment he could still feel the plug moving inside him, stimulating his prostate, opening him for Devon to take him.

Devon circled Jonathan slowly, considering what type of service would best suit what Jonathan needed to feel. "I don't think I want to bind you," he mused. "You did so well yesterday not using your hands. Hold on to your ankles and don't let go until I tell you to."

Jonathan clasped his ankles obediently, looking up at his lover with a gaze of quiet trust that Devon found humbling. "How would you like to serve me?" Devon asked, wondering if Jonathan would be able to give him a preference. "To serve us," he corrected, glancing apologetically at Kit.

Kit caught the slip and the correction. He was beginning to understand why Jonathan might have felt neglected during their earlier scene. With Devon having to tell them what to do, it was harder for them both to have his attention. Still, he could be patient when necessary, and it was Jonathan's turn now to be the center of Devon's concentration. He smiled at his lover, letting him know all was well with him.

Jonathan shook his head at Devon's question. *Anything*, he thought, *just tell me and I'll do anything you want.* It already felt difficult to put his thoughts into words, though. He shook his head again, hoping Devon would understand.

Squatting on the ground before Jonathan, Devon lifted his chin, forcing him to meet his eyes. "Jonathan," he said, "tell me why you want to do this. I want to understand, so I know how to give you what you need."

He wasn't sure he understood it himself, but Devon had asked, so Jonathan forced himself to try to put his chaotic thoughts into words. "I... usually, I'm the one in charge, the one who has to set the direction—at home with my son Josh, here on the set. Letting someone else—letting *you*—tell me what to do, to have to obey without thinking... feels good. Feels right. I trust you, Devon. I can let go and know you won't let me hurt, that you'll make it good for both of us. For all of us." He drew a quavering breath. "Sir."

Devon met Jonathan's gaze, humbled by the honesty of the response. He wondered if Jonathan understood the magnitude of the gift he was offering by his submission. His voice thickened with emotion as he brushed his thumb gently against Jonathan's cheek. "I hope I will always deserve that trust." Devon pushed back to his feet. "Kit," he called, motioning the younger man to join him. "Jonathan wants to serve us both. What should we ask him to do?"

Kit froze, caught off guard by the question. He had expected to follow orders, not give them. Mind scrambling to come up with a response, he seized on his second favorite use of Jonathan's mouth aside from kissing. "Have him suck us," he suggested timidly, rising to his feet and moving to Devon's side.

Devon nodded, knowing from experience how talented Jonathan had proven to be at using his mouth. He moved his hand to the top of Jonathan's head, guiding it gently toward Kit's already straining hard-on. "Go ahead, Jonathan," he instructed. "Suck him."

Keeping his eyes on Devon, Jonathan flicked his tongue over the head of Kit's cock, pushing into the slit before circling the silky surface. Leaning forward, he slid his lips around the bulbous head, pausing to suckle it, scraping his teeth lightly over the smooth skin, trying whatever he thought might feel good to his lover.

Kit started to reach for Jonathan, to caress his hair and urge him on, but Devon hadn't given him permission to touch, and he distinctly remembered that not being allowed the day before. He wanted to ask, but Devon had demanded silence except when addressed. Contenting himself with rocking his hips against Jonathan's lips, Kit let a long moan escape to show his enjoyment of Jonathan's attentions.

Encouraged by Kit's moan and by Devon's hand on his head gently caressing his hair, Jonathan took Kit deeper into his mouth. Swirling his tongue around the slender shaft, he sucked harder, rocking in time with the thrusting motions of Kit's hips.

Shivering, Kit clenched his hands on the muscles of his thighs, trying desperately to keep himself from reaching out to touch. "Please," he whispered finally, unsure whether he was asking for permission to touch or for more from Jonathan or both.

A sharp smack on the buttocks was Devon's reaction to Kit's plea. "I'm definitely going to have to gag you." Devon sighed. "You just can't seem to keep that mouth shut, can you?" A soft moan drew his attention back to Jonathan's mouth, stretched sinfully around Kit's shaft, and to Jonathan's eyes meeting his imploringly.

Kit winced a little as he rocked forward into Jonathan's mouth, caught off guard by the blow, but Jonathan's moan sent vibrations quivering around his cock, drawing an answering moan from his throat. He bit his lip to stop himself from begging for more.

Devon's blow pushed Kit deeper into Jonathan's mouth, bumping him against the back of Jonathan's throat. He fought not to disgrace himself by gagging, conscious to relax his muscles and take in more of the silky length. The thrust rocked him back on his heels, pushing the plug harder inside the tight walls of his channel, wringing a small moan from his throat. He tried to hold Devon's eyes, silently pleading with him to overlook Kit's lapse, to focus on him instead.

The heat in his own body grew as Devon watched Jonathan devour Kit's cock. He moved his hand toward his own insistently throbbing shaft, but he paused when Jonathan held his gaze, when he heard the moans wrenched from both their throats. Shite, he wanted to feel that for himself. And Jonathan *had* said he wanted to serve both of them….

Still stroking Jonathan's hair, Devon moved closer until his hip brushed against Kit's, raising Devon's own level of arousal even higher. "You're doing so well, Jon," he praised, tracing the corner of Jonathan's mouth where it curved around the base of Kit's shaft with his other hand. "You're making Kit feel so good." He slid his thumb inside the moist cavern, next to the tongue that worked against the satiny flesh. "Can you take more? Can you take both of us?"

Jonathan groaned at the image of both his lovers' long, hard cocks filling his mouth. He nodded, dragging his tongue over Devon's thumb, wishing he could reach for Devon's cock to guide it to his lips, wishing he could tell him how much he wanted both of them inside him.

Kit whimpered again, increasing the pressure on his lip to stop himself from begging Devon to do that. Already the hot wetness of Jonathan's mouth felt heavenly. To see those luscious lips stretched wide around not only his cock, but Devon's as well, to feel the added sensation of Devon next to him, rubbing against him.... The thought alone probably would have made him come had it not been for the cock ring.

Devon raised the head of his cock to Jonathan's lips, his breath hissing as Jonathan opened wider to take him inside. The warmth of Jonathan's mouth closing around him, the moist flutter of tongue, the friction as he slid against Kit, all were so intense that he tightened his grip on Jonathan's hair, holding his head still until he could adjust to the sensations.

Jonathan couldn't hold back another moan as Devon's cock nudged against his lips and slowly slipped inside. The stretch hurt a little, but the feel of both of them filling his mouth was such a heady pleasure it was easy to ignore the discomfort. Devon clutched at his hair, keeping him from moving his head, so he slid his tongue around the thickness filling him, savoring each man's taste, trying to lave as much of each shaft as he could.

Kit shivered at the surfeit of sensation. Between Devon's cock rubbing against his and Jonathan's talented tongue teasing them both, his nerves were sizzling with desire. He wanted to thrust so badly, but he was afraid of hurting Jonathan now that they were both in his mouth, so he forced himself to stillness, his nails biting into his flesh to keep himself under control.

When Devon regained enough mastery to trust himself not to come immediately, he relaxed his grip on Jonathan's hair, moving his hand to cup his lover's cheek. "Jon," he murmured hoarsely, "my God, Jon, what you make me feel." Flexing his hips, he carefully pushed deeper, encouraging Jonathan to start moving again.

As stretched as he was, Jonathan couldn't move as freely as he had with only Kit in his mouth. He wrapped his lips over his teeth to be sure he wouldn't cut into the delicate flesh and began to suck gently, pulling back slowly until only the two mushroomed tips remained in his mouth. He circled the base of each head with his tongue, flicking over the sensitive flaps of skin, and then he pushed forward again, taking the lengths into his mouth as far as he could, doing everything he knew how to give both his lovers pleasure.

It worked. Kit was mindless with it, pulling back when Devon thrust forward and vice versa, so that his cock slid against Devon's even as it rubbed against Jonathan's tongue. Knowing he was probably going to get smacked again for talking, he begged anyway. "Please, Devon. Need to come."

The things Jonathan was doing were rapidly shredding the little control Devon had left. When Kit begged him to come, he knew he should reprimand him for speaking without permission, but in the lad's place, he'd be pleading the same way. He couldn't even stop his own hips from moving in time with the seductive pull of Jonathan's mouth. "Would you like that, Jonathan?" he rasped, as his cock dragged wetly against Kit's. "Both of us, coming down your throat?"

Jonathan groaned, as much at the ragged husk of Devon's voice as at the words themselves. Seeing the state he was reducing his lovers to gave him a sense of pride and power he hadn't expected to feel. He nodded in avid agreement, every rocking movement pushing him back against the plug that filled his ass the way their cocks filled his mouth, every sound coming from his lovers fanning the flames of his own fierce arousal.

"Fuck yes," Kit begged, the thought of his fluid mixing with Devon's in Jonathan's mouth enough to set him trembling. He was going to have bruises on his legs from gripping them so hard, but if he couldn't control his mouth, he would at least control his hands.

Reaching down, Devon cupped Kit's swollen sac in his palm before grasping the ring encircling the base of his cock. "Pull back, then," he ordered, releasing the catch and letting the ring drop to the porch floor.

Jonathan gasped at the momentary sense of loss when Kit slipped out of his mouth, even just long enough to let Devon remove the cock ring. As soon as the slender length filled him again, he rocked faster, sucking harder, pressing his tongue against any skin it could reach. His cock aching with his own unfulfilled need, he clenched harder around the plug that rived him with each pulse of his mouth, desperate now to bring his lovers release in the hope of earning his own.

Kit trembled at the rush of feeling once the cock ring was removed. He struggled to control himself long enough to slide his length back inside Jonathan's mouth. "Close," he warned, though who he was warning, Jonathan or Devon, he couldn't say.

"Jon," Devon gasped as their lover's efforts became more intense. "Fuck, Jon, bloody fuck, you feel so good." Cradling the back of the tawny head, he abandoned the last of his self-control and pumped into the lascivious heat, seeking the release only Jonathan's mouth could give him. "Take me," he groaned. "Take us, fuck yeah, Jon, take it, fuck!"

Kit rocked in counterpoint to Devon's thrusts, his own control long gone. His only concern was not hurting Jonathan, and he hoped the opposite rhythm he and Devon had fallen into would keep them from choking him. He knew how it felt to have a cock forced down his throat by an inconsiderate lover, though Devon and Jonathan had both been careful not to do that to him. He didn't want to do it to Jonathan either.

Once both Devon and Kit began thrusting into his mouth, Jonathan gave up any effort at retaining control. Relaxing his throat muscles as much as he could, he braced himself and let them fuck his mouth, all his focus narrowing down to the sensations of being filled, of being stretched wide at both ends, of his own primal need to come. He trembled and clenched and cried out as two bodies stiffened against him and the hot, wet spill of their release filled his mouth. He swallowed as best he could around the pulsing lengths, trying to keep any drops of the creamy fluid from escaping his numbed lips.

Feeling his release fill Jonathan's mouth, Kit collapsed backward, barely catching himself on his hands, his entire body shuddering with the force of his climax. Every orgasm had been spectacular since he hooked up with Jonathan and Devon, but the ones this weekend had been the best, as if giving up control had somehow heightened the pleasure he gained from the entire experience.

Devon let out a long, low groan as he shot into Jonathan's mouth, the heat of his and Kit's come swirling around him as Jonathan swallowed it down. He leaned into Jonathan's kneeling form, his legs almost too weak to hold himself up after the power of his climax. Pulling away from Jonathan's lips as Kit collapsed beside him, Devon dropped to his knees, retrieving the cock ring he'd taken off Kit and fastening it around the base of his own shaft before he could start to soften. Then he dragged

Jonathan's head to his, claiming him in a fierce kiss, drinking in the salty taste of their ejaculate as he ravaged Jonathan's mouth.

Feeling empty when both his lovers pulled out of his mouth, Jonathan was shocked when Devon knelt to kiss him. His lips were almost too swollen to bear the pressure of Devon's mouth, but he returned the kiss as fiercely as he could, his body racked with tremors as waves of heat flared from his bound cock and his stretched hole. Moaning, he followed Devon's head as he began to pull away, trying to hold the plundering lips to his.

Watching his lovers kiss, seeing the still-swollen length of Jonathan's cock, Kit's desire stirred anew, though he doubted he could get hard again right away. He hoped, though, that Devon would let him help get Jonathan off, whatever that entailed. It was odd, seeing his cock ring around Devon's cock, and it made him wonder exactly what Devon had planned now. "How are you going to take care of Jonathan?" he asked softly.

"We'll both take care of Jonathan," Devon promised, placing a final, gentler kiss on their lover's glistening lips before helping him rise to his feet. "But he has to finish taking care of us first."

CHAPTER 15
RAISING THE BAR

SITTING BACK on his heels, Kit decided that Devon was a genius, an absolute genius. There in the middle of the porch was probably the most delicious thing he had seen in a year, maybe even longer. Jonathan's body was stretched to its full length, his hands pulled over his head and secured to one of the beams that supported the roof. His feet were separated by a thin metal bar, heavy straps surrounding his ankles to hold it in place. His cock, still encircled by the leather ring, jutted forward proudly, making Kit want to shuffle forward and lick it, and the handle of the butt plug peeked out from between his arsecheeks, tempting Kit to play with it. It was a good thing Devon had gotten his own cock ring to put on Kit, or Kit would be coming again simply from the vision Jonathan presented.

Jonathan was used to his body being on display, or at least he'd thought he was. But even the total nudity required in several of his films had never affected him the way this did. These were his lovers, the two men he trusted more than any others. They'd both seen him undressed more times than he could count since filming started, and in some pretty erotic situations since becoming a threesome. But he had never felt this *naked* before, this vulnerable.

He wiggled his jaw a little, his lips bruised and swollen from stretching around both Devon's and Kit's cocks. He'd been so desperately hard after bringing them both off, hoping his efforts had pleased them enough to let him come. Kit had wanted to let him, he knew. And then Devon had answered, "*He has to finish taking care of us first.*"

Devon had been gentle but implacable as he'd ordered Jonathan to rest, instructing Kit to hold him—a command Kit had shown no hesitation in following. Devon brought out a bottle of water for each of them and smoothed some lip balm onto Jonathan's lips, ruffling his hair and praising him again before disappearing back into the cottage.

Kit gulped part of his water before setting the bottle aside and stroking his hands over Jonathan's skin, trying to be as soothing as possible. When Jonathan didn't immediately pick up his own bottle of water, Kit opened it for him and pressed it to his lips. "Drink," he said gently. "You're amazing. You looked so sexy on your knees serving us. I don't know what else Devon has planned, but I'm sure he'll make it good for you since he's making you wait for it."

Jonathan remembered Devon telling him something similar yesterday when he'd brought him to climax through the cock ring, promising his orgasm would be even more intense when he came without it. Jonathan hadn't felt it at the time, but he hadn't waited for Devon to take care of him again, and bringing himself off by his own hand was never as powerful as coming with Devon or Kit. He could only trust that Devon was right and hope this time he would earn the privilege to come from the attentions of his lovers.

He wasn't sure how long he rested in Kit's embrace until the tenseness humming along his nerves eased somewhat, though his cock still throbbed almost painfully against the constrictive leather strap. However long it was, the minute Devon reappeared to drop an armful of supplies on the glider, the tension was back full force, leaving him trembling with anticipation in Kit's arms.

Devon sat down beside them and wrapped an arm around Jonathan, then directed Kit to retrieve some lube and the third cock ring from the glider. He still wore Kit's ring, his cock hard and hot where it pressed against Jonathan's hip. "Hands and knees," he ordered when he returned, putting Kit onto the floor in front of them and handing the lube to Jonathan. "Kit's recovery time is likely shorter than ours, but even so he'll need some help to get hard again this soon. A little direct prostate stimulation should do the trick."

Kit moved quickly into position, not about to pass up the chance to have their hands on him. He doubted, honestly, that he'd need much more stimulation than the sight of whatever Devon ultimately decided to do to Jonathan, but he wasn't about to miss the opportunity to have one or both of his lovers playing with his prostate.

Nudged forward by Devon, Jonathan slicked his fingers and eased one into Kit, nerves flaring at the heat and constriction. Refusing to let himself think about what that would feel like squeezing around his cock, he moved the pad of his finger in small circles until Kit's shout confirmed he'd found his sweet spot. Jonathan massaged it with short, firm strokes, clenching around the plug reaming him in a futile attempt to feel a bit of the pleasure he was giving Kit. Devon stroked a palm down his back but slid it to his flank before it reached the plug's handle, leaving Jonathan aching to feel his hand on it. Working a second digit into Kit, Jonathan tried to transfer his frustration into making Kit as needy as he was. Judging by the eager way Kit thrust back, he'd succeeded. When Kit was hard again and all but fucking himself on Jonathan's fingers, Devon snapped the cock ring into place around Kit's shaft, then helped Jonathan to his feet.

Devon directed Kit to bring the rope from the glider and knotted it carefully around Jonathan's wrists, testing the slack before tossing the cord over the exposed ceiling beams of the porch and pulling him upright. Devon was good at this, Jonathan admitted—he could still touch his feet to the porch floor, but only by keeping his arms and spine perfectly straight. Devon ran a possessive hand down his back but stopped when he reached the first swell of his ass. Jonathan almost spoke then, hoping his lover was going to take the plug out—but Devon only told Kit to kneel at Jonathan's feet and stalked back over to the glider. When he returned, he held something Jonathan had never seen before.

"Spread his legs apart," Devon ordered. Kit looked up at Jonathan with an expression that was apologetic and eager at the same time. Devon buckled the leather straps around Jonathan's ankles, adjusting the metal bar so it held his feet shoulder-width apart. Jonathan's erection, which despite the cock ring had wilted some while Devon was stringing him up, began to stiffen again at the predatory look in Devon's eyes as he examined his handiwork.

"Fuck, but you look beautiful like that," Devon rasped, and Jonathan swelled to rock hardness at the words of praise. Devon had promised they'd see to him—they'd both see to him—after he'd pleased them again first. Trying to hold himself still and wait on Devon's orders, Jonathan shivered, wondering what he meant to do next.

Kit tracked every movement Devon made, noticed every twitch of Jonathan's body. Finally Devon had Jonathan positioned, leaving Kit wondering what Devon intended. Bound as he was, Jonathan wouldn't be able to do anything but accept whatever he and Devon did. Whatever Devon told him to do, he corrected himself. Though not bound by any ropes this time, Kit was as bound by Devon's will as

Jonathan was. And while that was still a curious feeling, one he hadn't had time to get used to, it wasn't a bad feeling. In fact, the anticipation had him buzzing with lust.

Devon watched both his lovers thoughtfully as he finished adjusting the spreader bar to just the right distance. He wanted Jonathan to feel stretched and exposed, but not in pain. Judging from Jonathan's pliant demeanor and his rampant erection, he was in just the headspace Devon wanted him. Kit was still obviously high with anticipation, but he had managed to obey Devon's orders so far without speaking. He hoped Kit would be able to follow his lead, because it was important to Jonathan that both of them were a part of what was to come.

"Fuck, but you look beautiful," Devon repeated, sliding a hand around his own resurgent erection. He hoped he'd be able to hold off long enough to give Jonathan what he needed, but the man was enough to tempt a statue to life. "Isn't he beautiful on display for us like this, Kit?"

"Fuck yes," Kit replied, fingers twitching. "I just want to touch him." He slanted his eyes up at Devon. "Let me touch him." It took him a moment, but he remembered to add, "Sir."

Fuck yes, Jonathan echoed silently, barely managing to bite back the words. *Let him put his hands on me—I need to feel his hands on me.*

Devon shook his head, placing a finger over Kit's lips, and Jonathan's heart fell. "You can't seem to keep from running this pretty mouth. Let's see you put it to better use—on him."

Eagerly, Kit moved forward, hands sliding over Jonathan's skin as he attached his lips to the odd script of the tattoo on Jonathan's hip. He always intended to ask Jonathan about it when they weren't having sex, but he never managed to remember. Maybe this time. He sucked forcefully, knowing the other man enjoyed the added pressure. He could smell the precome leaking from the tip of Jonathan's cock despite the cock ring, and the scent only heightened his desire.

Jonathan arched forward into Kit's touch, the movement straining his already taut arms, but it was worth the pain to feel the hot suction of his lover's mouth against his skin. He undulated his hips, trying wordlessly to urge him to increase the pressure of the kiss.

"I didn't give you permission to touch," Devon pointed out, his tone all the more powerful for being quiet. "Keep your hands at your sides until I tell you to move them." He nodded as Kit was quick to obey. The lad always seemed to try to stretch the limits. He'd need to find a way to deal with that, but not today. Today they both needed to focus on Jonathan.

"Use your teeth," he ordered instead. "You know he likes it rough."

Kit quickly dropped his hands to his sides, embarrassed at being caught in an act of disobedience, however unintentional. He knew he was only supposed to do what Devon said, but he kept forgetting, so caught up in the moment that he didn't think before he acted. He almost raised his head to apologize, but there hadn't been a question in Devon's words. There had been a command. Parting his lips, he sucked harder on Jonathan's skin, pulling it between his sharp teeth and biting down more firmly than he would have dared with anyone else.

A shudder of pleasure shook Jonathan when Kit nipped his skin. The bite was firm enough to tease, but he was already so aroused that he needed more. He tensed his hips, trying to push into the delicious pain, when the plug he had almost grown accustomed to twisted abruptly, drawing an involuntary gasp from him.

"Like that, do you?" Devon purred, turning the plug again. "We're going to make you want us so badly, Kit and I," he promised. "Kit's going to bite you until you're ready to scream, and every time he does, I'm going to turn this until you're wide open and ready for us to take you. And we are going to take you, Jonathan. Both of us. Because that's what you want, isn't it?"

"Yes," Jonathan moaned, rocking back onto the thick silicone shaft in Devon's hands. Another tremor of need shook him, his cock straining so hard against the ring it felt as if it would burst. "Fuck yes, please, Sir. Want you to fuck me."

Kit reared up on his knees, trembling at Devon's words, imagining the plug turning inside him like it turned inside Jonathan. He scooted around so he could reach Jonathan's nipples, taking one in his teeth and biting down as hard as he dared.

Jonathan bucked against the twin agonies of Kit's teeth on his nipple and the twisting fullness in his channel, the two together almost more than he could bear. He tried to shift his feet to an easier position, but the bar held his legs fast, preventing him from any movement except squirming against his lovers.

Devon could see the effect their attentions were having, but he wanted Jonathan mindless with passion before they claimed him, knowing that building his need would make the release all the more powerful when he finally granted it. "Harder," he barked at Kit, pressing the plug in deeply enough to graze over Jonathan's prostate. "Make him feel it."

Kit wanted to do as Devon asked, but he couldn't make himself inflict pain on his lover, even knowing Jonathan craved it the way Kit craved a gentler caress. It was too reminiscent of them biting him beyond his limits. Perhaps if Devon hadn't pushed him, he'd have been able to continue, but the thought of biting Jonathan any harder turned his stomach. "I can't," he said softly, falling back to sit on his heels. "I'm sorry." His gaze switched between Jonathan's face and Devon's, knowing he was letting them both down but unable to do otherwise, not when he could already see the light bruise he had raised on Jonathan's hip and the way the nipple he had been biting was swollen.

Crying out softly at losing the delicious sting of Kit's teeth, Jonathan dropped his head to look down to where Kit knelt disconsolate before him. The forlorn expression on Kit's face hurt more than anything he'd done to Jonathan's body. "Kit," he whispered quietly, "no, don't, it's okay."

Seeing Kit's stricken face and hearing Jonathan's urgent words, Devon rose to stand before them. His former master would have come down hard on them both for refusing a command and for speaking out of turn. But Devon was realizing that Robert's training no longer dictated his actions. Bending on one knee before his lovers, he touched Kit's shoulder and Jonathan's hip, where a bruise was already darkening over the outline of the kanji characters.

"You tried, lad," he acknowledged. "You did your best, and I willna' fault you for that." He ran his hand up Jonathan's chest, smiling wolfishly as the muscles fluttered beneath his touch. Ghosting his fingers over the abused nipple, he gave it a sharp tweak, wringing a startled gasp from Jonathan's lips. "Take care of the plug," he ordered Kit, "and let me see to our king's pleasure."

Feeling some of his worry dissipate when Devon didn't punish him, Kit moved around behind Jonathan, one hand caressing the smooth skin of Jonathan's arse while the other reached for the handle of the plug, turning it firmly in the tight sheath. He might not be able to bite hard enough to please his lovers, but he knew he could handle this to their satisfaction.

Jonathan longed for his arms to be free so he could bury his hands in Devon's thick hair, pull Devon up to his mouth, and kiss him until they were both senseless. "Thank you, Sir," he whispered instead, knowing he'd gladly bear whatever punishment he earned for speaking without permission.

He cried out in ecstasy when Devon latched on to his other nipple, biting down almost hard enough to draw blood. Kit worked the stiff latex shaft inside him in concert with the pull of Devon's teeth until Jonathan's entire body stiffened, waves of heat igniting inside him, his cock pulsing as strongly as if he'd come, though the ring held back anything more than a dribble of fluid from leaking from its engorged tip.

Devon raised his head when he felt Jonathan tense beneath him, watching hungrily as a look of pure bliss transfigured his lover's face. "So damn responsive," he praised, raising a hand to brush Jonathan's cheek. "Do you have any idea what it does to me to make you feel this way?"

Jonathan turned his head, trying to catch Devon's hand with his lips. "Only you," he rasped, his voice shaking with the power of the sensations overwhelming him. "Only you two."

Trembling as he felt the muscles in Jonathan's arse contract under his hands, Kit wished he could see Jonathan's face, for he loved the sight of it contorted with passion. He rested his cheek against Jonathan's skin, breathing in the dark scents of his body, struggling to stay where Devon had ordered him rather than standing up and plunging into Jonathan like he wanted to.

Almost there, Devon thought, hearing the tremor in Jonathan's voice and feeling his body quiver beneath his touch. *Almost where I want you, love, but if you can still talk, you can take just a little more.* Giving in a bit to his own tightly reined desires, he circled Jonathan rapaciously, inflicting a livid trail of love bites in the spots that tempted him most— the crease between abdomen and hip, the base of a rib, just below the hollow that pulsed wildly in Jonathan's throat—all spots that would be hidden beneath his costume but would remind his lover of this moment every time he moved for the next few days.

A sheen of sweat broke out over Jonathan's body despite the cool snap of the ocean breeze. Beads of moisture trickled down his chest and mingled with the saliva Devon left behind wherever his teeth cut into skin. His own teeth dug into his bruised lower lip, holding himself back from pleading without shame for Devon to put his mouth on his cock, for

Kit to rip the damn plug out of his ass and just please fuck him already, he was so fucking close to coming…. He moaned, low and deep, when Devon bit into the flesh just over his pubic bone, sucking and grinding until Jonathan writhed underneath him, his struggles only prompting Kit to corkscrew the butt plug that reamed his ass without mercy.

Kit knew Jonathan had to be going out of his mind between the movements of the plug and Devon's mouth. Knowing he was probably overstepping his bounds but wanting to add to Jonathan's pleasure, he nibbled lightly at the lower curve of Jonathan's arse, layering one more sensation onto the others that already surged through the quivering body. As his teeth closed over that tempting bit of flesh, he pushed the plug in as deep as he could, his fingers sliding inside with it as he twisted it in Jonathan's passage, hoping to wring another cry of pleasure from their lover's lips.

A wail of surrender escaped Jonathan's throat when Kit's teeth joined Devon's in tormenting his overstimulated flesh. His cock jumped and throbbed against his belly, his balls so hard and full of juice they ached. The stretch of Kit's fingers moving inside him, adding to the plug's unyielding friction, was suddenly more than he could bear. His head sagging to his chest, he closed his eyes and begged for the release his body screamed for. "Please, Sir, no more," he panted, twisting uselessly against the restraints that held him immobile for his lovers' pleasure. He didn't even know which one of them he was pleading with anymore. "Take me, please, need you to take me, please…."

Devon's own arousal was an insistent ache in his loins, but he gritted his teeth and willed himself under control. Jonathan needed to feel claimed by both of them—and he was selfish enough to want to be the one who took him last. Letting the swollen nipple slide from his lips, he sat back on his heels and drank in the vision of Jonathan splayed before him, begging to be taken.

"Kit," he commanded, his voice hoarse with lust. "Take off your ring. You're going to fuck Jonathan."

Kit didn't need to be told twice. He stripped the ring off as expeditiously as possible, rising to his feet. Looking around Jonathan to see where Devon had left the supplies, he grabbed the lube and slicked his erection before pulling the plug from Jonathan's hole. "Are you ready for me?" he asked, lining himself up at the stretched aperture.

"So fucking ready," Jonathan rasped, unable to stop himself from shaking as Kit pressed against his back, his cock nudging at his wide-open entrance. After squeezing around the plug for so long, he felt empty, desperate for Kit to fill him, hard and deep. He twisted his head as far as he could to try to see his lover's face as he was taken. "Please, Kit, make me yours...."

Devon might have given Kit permission to fuck Jonathan first, but that didn't mean he planned to sit idle while it happened. While Kit tore off his cock ring and slicked up with lube, Devon leaned forward, resting his weight on his palms, admiring the beauty of Jonathan's bound body and waiting for the instant Kit slid inside.

Unsure he had the right to touch, Kit clenched his hands into fists as he pushed home, sliding into the loosened passage, expecting to encounter some resistance still, but there was none. The plug had stretched Jonathan well. Grinding his hips against Jonathan's arse, Kit nuzzled the back of his neck, finding a spot beneath the fall of hair where no marks would show to bite down.

The moment Kit breached Jonathan, Devon flicked his tongue over the swollen head of Jonathan's cock, licking up the single drop of precome that trembled on its tip. Jonathan was shaking so badly that Devon didn't have to move his head to lap and nip at every part of the still-confined erection, careful to use his teeth gently this time. His only goal now was to add to the amalgam of sensations Jonathan was feeling and hold his own need in check until Kit was finished with him.

"Oh God," Jonathan groaned, the rasp of Devon's tongue and teeth on his cock and Kit's slippery glide into his clenching passage setting his nerves on fire. His hands clutched into fists around empty air, his feet scrabbling for purchase on the worn floorboards—he felt as if he was going to burst out of his body at the intensity of stimulation consuming him. "Fuck, Devon, please.... Kit... can't... can't...."

Kit couldn't either. He slammed forward with all his strength, driving relentlessly into Jonathan's body. He aimed for his lover's prostate, hoping Jonathan was as close to the edge as he was. Then he remembered the cock ring and knew it wouldn't matter. He fought his release, wanting to wait for Devon to give permission, but he didn't know how long he would be successful.

Rocking back on his heels, Devon watched Kit pound into Jonathan with a ferocity all the more impressive as the lad had remembered not to use his hands. Jonathan was straining to take him deeper, his head thrown back, his chest heaving with every moaning breath. Suddenly Devon needed to be the one thrusting into Jonathan that way, the one making Jonathan cry out in ecstasy. "Kit," he ordered, "touch him. Let yourself come."

Kit's hands replaced Devon's mouth, wrapping around Jonathan's body and providing just the angle to slam into his prostate with every thrust. Jonathan's hips bucked in a broken rhythm as he fought for the release his cock ring kept just beyond his reach. "Kit," he moaned, "yours, please... need...."

"Mine," Kit agreed, his hold on Jonathan's cock letting him find the leverage he needed to go just that little bit deeper. He could feel Jonathan's body contracting around him, trying to climax, and it was enough to trigger his own orgasm. He pounded into Jonathan's passage one last time, coming with a ferocity that stunned him, leaving him leaning on Jonathan as he tried to keep his balance. When he could control his limbs, he sank to his knees, head resting against Jonathan's thighs. "Mine," he murmured one more time.

Jonathan cried out as Kit tensed and then collapsed against him, the warm rush of Kit's release filling his channel. He was so close, and he couldn't stop shuddering, couldn't seem to draw enough breath into his lungs. His heart was pounding against his ribs, the blood pulsing in his veins like liquid fire, each beat making his cock jump in Kit's slackened grip. When Kit slid down his back to the floor, Jonathan's knees buckled and he sagged into the restraints holding him upright, beyond feeling pain at the ropes cutting into his wrists.

Devon's hands shot out to catch Jonathan's hips, holding him steady as he wavered on his feet. Jonathan's body glistened with sweat, his breath rasped raggedly from his throat, and Devon had never wanted anyone more in his life. "Gonna take you now, Jonathan," he crooned, his lips gentling as he circled behind his lover, kissing a path across his collarbone, over his shoulder, and down the trembling planes of his back.

"Kit." He nudged the replete young man with his knee. "Move and kneel in front of Jonathan."

Devon's words penetrated Kit's satiated brain slowly, and he realized his Dom had given him an order. Of course Devon wanted him to move. He should have thought of it himself. There was no way Devon could take Jonathan with Kit in the way. Moving much more slowly than was his wont, he shifted so he knelt in front of Jonathan, lifting his eyes to see what he had wished for earlier: Jonathan's face contorted with passion. Without any conscious decision on his part, he reached out to touch, hands sliding up Jonathan's thighs, caressing gently. He didn't want to intrude, but he needed to be a part of the erotic tableau in front of him.

Pressing against Jonathan from chest to toes, Devon ground his cock against Jonathan's taut arse, sliding into his crease and pulling Jonathan's hips hard into his. "You're mine, Jon," he growled, releasing his ring and sheathing himself in one smooth thrust, his lover so open from the plug and wet with Kit's come that he entered him easily.

Jonathan let himself lean back against the strong body behind him, only the rope and Devon's hands on his hips keeping him on his feet. Kit had left him so near the edge, and when Devon slid inside him, finally rasping the words he had needed from both his lovers, something inside him soared. He could feel it swelling inside him, the thin rind of his skin barely containing it, about to shatter into pieces beneath its power. His back bowing to mold himself to Devon, he gasped out words, no longer able to stop their flow. "Yours, Devon. Now, please… yours… please, need you… need… please…."

Devon dropped his forehead to Jonathan's shoulder, holding the trembling, sweaty body to his, fighting to retain his quickly waning control. *Might as well try to hold on to the tide*, he realized—buried in Jonathan's tight heat, his lover's desperate words urging him on, he could only cling to Jonathan and let their need take them both. "Now," he groaned, his own voice shaking. "Yeah, gonna… now…." Drawing a heaving breath, he held them both still. "Kit, take off Jonathan's ring."

Kit obeyed with alacrity, closing his hands over Jonathan's straining erection to release the leather strap. Even after the ring fell from his grip, he lingered, not able to make himself let go. He knew this was Devon's time—he wanted to give his two lovers this moment together—but his hands weren't listening.

Jonathan's entire body tensed when the agonizing grip of the ring eased at last. His muscles clenched down on Devon buried inside him, the only contact he could control. "Devon," he moaned, "Kit… yours… now, please."

Devon lifted a shaking hand to turn Jonathan's head, enough to reach his lips with his own. He closed his other hand over Kit's on their lover's cock. Taking Jonathan's mouth in a breathless kiss, he pumped his hips once, twice, and then he could no longer hold back and his orgasm slammed through him. He crushed Jonathan's head to his, pistoning his hips and his hand as he tried to carry Jonathan with him in this tidal wave of pleasure.

Kit had frozen when he felt Devon's hand close over his, afraid he'd been caught in disobedience, but Devon simply took up his rhythm, their rhythm, as he surged forward with the all the force of the sea. Kit heard the groan that surely indicated Devon's climax, but his hand never slowed as he continued to push Jonathan on.

Jonathan gave himself over to Devon's kiss, the blissful slide of his hardness inside him, of both his lovers caressing his cock. He thought he'd come as soon as the ring was removed, but he kept soaring higher and higher, impossibly high, until he thought he couldn't endure an instant more of the exquisite stimulation. Then Devon crushed their bodies together, flooding Jonathan again with warmth, and his overloaded nerves snapped. He spasmed between his two lovers, shuddering uncontrollably as wave upon wave of ecstasy engulfed him, filled him, overflowed him, and swept him away. If not for Devon's mouth on his, he would have forgotten to breathe.

When Jonathan's release coated his hand, Kit leaned forward and licked at the hot fluid, starting with Devon's fingers. One at a time, he sucked them into his mouth, lapping up every drop. When he finished with Devon's hand, he turned his attention to Jonathan's softening shaft, cleaning it as carefully as he had the other man's hand. Finally done, he turned his attention to his own fingers, not wanting to miss a single bit of Jonathan's flavor.

Devon was drifting somewhere in a blissful haze where all that existed was Jonathan's mouth joined with his. Kit's lips carefully cleaning his hand recalled him to the reality of the world around them. As wonderful as it felt to be buried in Jonathan's warmth, he needed to give his lover back his freedom. "Unbuckle his legs, lad," he instructed, holding Jonathan steady while Kit removed the restrictive spreader bar.

As soon as Kit tossed the device aside, Devon reached up, still holding Jonathan to him with one arm, and released the knots that held his arms secured. Once the rope slid over the ceiling beam, he lowered himself and Jonathan to the porch floor, removing the cord from Jonathan's wrists, pressing his lips to the reddened grooves left behind.

Kit moved closer to his two lovers, needing to maintain that contact with them. His head was spinning, and he was sure Jonathan had to be completely overwhelmed. He hoped being surrounded on both sides would help steady him.

Jonathan's eyes fluttered open slowly as he regained enough strength for even that much motion. He was on the floor, cradled in Devon's arms, Kit pressed against his side. For a moment longer he simply let himself lie there and absorb their presence, searching for some way to express everything they'd given him. Finally he gave up, knowing anything he said would be only words. He took a hand in each of his, Devon's and Kit's, and simply held them. "Thank you," he murmured.

Squeezing Jonathan's hand gently, Kit lifted his head, meeting Devon's eyes over their lover's chest. He saw the same surprise, the same incredulity he felt at Jonathan's words reflected back in Devon's gaze. If anyone needed to be saying thank you, it was them, not Jonathan. Lowering his head back to Jonathan's shoulder, he kissed the strong muscle gently as he pondered ways to thank Jonathan without saying the words.

Devon bent to kiss Jonathan's other shoulder, mirroring Kit's action. "Don't thank us," he muttered, wishing he could use words the way Jonathan could to explain what the scene had made him feel. "That was incredible. You were incredible."

Still enough in his headspace to welcome Devon's praise, Jonathan smiled. He had been claimed. He belonged to both his lovers now. He knew that to them, the words were only part of the game, but for him, they were true. His heart was theirs.

CHAPTER 16
BEACH BUMS

TWO DAYS later, their last full day of vacation, Kit looked at the bottle of sunscreen on the shelf in the bathroom, trying to decide whether to take it outside with him. He started to reach for it when his eyes landed on a bottle of baby oil right next to it. He had no idea where the oil had come from—it might have been left by a previous renter at the beach house—but it certainly gave him ideas. Oil-slick bodies sliding against one another, writhing together in rising passion…. His cock twitched in his swim trunks, and he grabbed the bottle on impulse. He'd see if he couldn't use it to catch his lovers' attention.

Outside, he paused on the steps to look at the two men lying on large towels on the sand. He really was lucky to have two such incredibly beautiful lovers, and even more so to have been able to steal these few days away with them. He deliberately avoided thinking about having to leave the hothouse isolation of the beach early tomorrow morning in time to make it back for their calls tomorrow night. Settling on his own towel, he grabbed the bottle of baby oil and poured some of the liquid into his palm, spreading it over his legs, feeling it cover his skin and get caught in the fine hairs on his shins. He watched out of the corner of his eye to see if Jonathan and Devon had noticed him yet.

Devon pushed up on his elbows as he heard Kit settle back on the sand, his attention instantly caught by the enticing display before him. Kit was coating himself with oil, his palms gliding over his smooth thighs, leaving them glistening in the warm afternoon sun. Even before the conversation that led to their agreeing to seduce Jonathan together, Devon had been impressed by the younger man's attractiveness in character, but Kit's allure was even stronger out of costume. In fact, the fewer clothes he had on, the more alluring Devon found him, if the way his cock was hardening against the warm sand beneath his towel was any indicator.

Jonathan had been half dozing in the sunlight, but a muffled sound from the man beside him made him open his eyes, curious as to what had caught Devon's attention. Devon was lying on his stomach, leaning up on his elbows, staring at Kit. *And no wonder*, Jonathan thought, watching as Kit poured a handful of baby oil onto his palm and stroked it over his chest. That sight was enough to make his cock stir inside his cutoffs, and as his gaze shifted to Kit's face, he realized Kit knew exactly what effect he was having on them both.

Knowing he had both his lovers' attention, Kit trailed his hands across his chest slowly, letting his fingers linger where he was most sensitive. He toyed absently with his nipples, keeping his gaze studiously fixed on the horizon as if he had not a thought in his head beyond relaxing on the beach. Only the tent in his swim trunks belied his casual attitude.

When he had spent all the time he could justify on his front, Kit rolled onto his stomach. "Would one of you put some of this on my back?" he asked lightly.

Devon and Jonathan both jumped to their feet at the invitation, reaching Kit's towel at the same time.

Looking up at them, Kit batted his eyelashes teasingly. Adopting a falsetto, he asked, "Are you going to fight over me?"

"Yield to your king," Jonathan demanded in Arthur's most regal tones, while struggling to hold back a most unkingly burst of laughter.

"I see no king here," Devon retorted. "This prize should belong to one with the strength to seize it." As he spoke, he made a grab for the bottle of oil in Kit's hand.

Kit tried, most unsuccessfully, to smother the chuckles their exchange brought to the surface. This was exactly what they needed: a little playfulness to counteract the thought of leaving in the morning. Continuing in his falsetto, he urged them on. "Oh, sirs, surely I am not worth fighting over."

Devon plucked the bottle of oil from Kit's hand with a flourish. "Allow me, my beauty," he said, bowing over the slippery hand with all the grace of a courtly lover.

Kit simpered with delight. "It would be my pleasure, good sir," he replied, reclining again on his towel.

Jonathan took advantage of Devon's action to snatch the bottle of oil from his slackened grip. He grinned widely as he waved the bottle over his head, feeling as carefree as if he were a boy again, teasing his younger brothers. "Careless, Devon!" he taunted. "You have to be able to hold on to what you claim!"

Devon lunged for the bottle, missing Jonathan's hand but pulling on his arm with enough force to overbalance the other man and land them both on the sand. The two tussled in mock battle, possession of the bottle changing hands several times, until with a sudden move, Devon flipped Jonathan onto his back and straddled his hips, pinning him and reclaiming the prize with a cry of triumph.

Kit pouted prettily as they struggled, pretending annoyance that their attention was diverted from him. "My back?" he demanded haughtily, keeping the falsetto in place.

After dropping a kiss onto Jonathan's mock scowl to show there were no hard feelings, Devon climbed off one lover and onto the other, his thighs spanning Kit's arse as he popped open the cap and poured some oil onto his palm. "My apologies," he said, rubbing the oil onto both hands before stroking them down Kit's shoulders. "Just a minor distraction that had to be dealt with. Now, let me tend to you, my lovely one."

Kit purred in very real contentment as Devon's hands moved over his back. Though he had told Devon repeatedly that their earlier scene hadn't bothered his back, he was feeling the effects of their rather athletic sex over the past few days, and the gentle massage was not at all amiss. "You are too kind, good sir."

Having spread a coating of oil over all of Kit's exposed skin, Devon massaged it in lightly, his touch gentle over the scar that extended below the waistband of his lover's trunks. He let one hand trace along the raised skin, sliding beneath the thin nylon to teasingly caress the hidden curves of Kit's buttocks.

Kit twitched on the towel when Devon's hands made their way into his shorts. Glancing over to where Jonathan watched the two of them with hungry eyes, he suggested, "You could oil my legs."

"If Devon will share," Jonathan rasped, moving to kneel at Kit's feet. "After all, he does have his hands full with other things."

Devon grinned and tossed the bottle to Jonathan, taking the opportunity to lean back and glide his free hand below Kit's shorts and cup both cheeks. "I'd say my hands are exactly where I want them."

Kit hummed with pleasure. "Exactly where I want them too."

Jonathan coated both his hands with the slippery liquid, then clasped Kit's ankles and rubbed his feet, his touch firm but lingering. He'd always found having his own feet massaged surprisingly erogenous, and he hoped it would have the same effect on Kit. He pressed his thumbs in circles over the arched instep of each foot before gliding his fingers to grasp and coat each individual toe with oil.

Kit sighed with the pleasure of the double massage, Devon's hands on his back and buttocks and Jonathan's hands on his feet. He flexed his toes, encouraging the sensual contact.

Devon turned his head to wink at Jonathan over his shoulder when Kit sighed beneath their dual ministrations. Since the younger man was lying facedown on the towel, he couldn't see the wicked glance Jonathan flashed in return. Two pairs of hands began a sensual assault, Devon working his long fingers between the rounded cheeks as Jonathan's strong grip kneaded a tantalizing path up the firm legs.

Kit shivered under the combined assault, giving himself over completely to their care. And when they were done with him, he would make sure he and Jonathan took care of Devon. It was the least they could do after Devon had taken such good care of them while they'd been at the beach. Since the morning Devon had strung Jonathan up on the porch, they'd returned to less scripted lovemaking, but Devon's natural dominance had come to the fore more than once as he guided rather than ordered them into some delicious variations.

Jonathan drizzled an abstract design on the back of Kit's thighs with the quickly depleting bottle of oil, using a lighter touch to smooth it into the nubile flesh. His strokes turned into caresses, skimming over the short, soft hairs, inching slowly beneath the hem of the colorful bathing trunks until his hands met Devon's. He pinched at a firm cheek before returning to tease down Kit's legs again.

"Why, good sirs," Kit gasped, "if I did not know better, I would think you were trying to seduce me."

"If you only think it, we're not making our intentions clear enough," Devon retorted. With a wordless lift of his eyebrows, he held out a hand to Jonathan, who poured a healthy dollop of oil onto his fingers. Devon shifted to straddle Kit's waist and give him better access to his goal, immediately demonstrating to Kit exactly what his lovers had in mind. Sliding his hand below the waistband of Kit's trunks, he rubbed the oil-slicked fingers enticingly down the cleft of his arse in unmistakable invitation.

"My back," Kit said immediately, having been warned more than once about the danger of too much weight directly on the rod that straightened his spine.

"I won't put any pressure on it," Devon promised. True to his word, Devon braced most of his weight on his knees so Kit felt only the warmth of his skin and the unmistakable bulge of arousal. "Relax and let us clarify those intentions for you."

"I… begin to… understand," Kit choked out as Devon's finger kept the man's promise, stroking him intimately. "But you might… want to be… even clearer."

This time it was Jonathan's turn to catch Devon's eyes. With a saucy wink, he moved forward, nudging one knee between Kit's thighs and straddling one of them, giving Kit a good idea of his own state of arousal in the process and making it easier for his hands to meet Devon's from the opposite direction. His sword-callused fingers joined his partner's in the teasing touches, gathering up more oil before sliding inside to assist in the mutual seduction.

Feeling the second finger join the first, knowing Devon and Jonathan were both inside him, Kit trembled, suddenly fighting his climax. Dropping the teasing, he mumbled, "If you don't stop, I'm going to come."

"And that's a problem why?" Devon asked, looking up at Jonathan. Finding his face conveniently close, Devon leaned forward the fraction it took to touch Jonathan's lips with his own. It felt so good to slide his tongue into Jonathan's mouth as their fingers reduced their young lover to moans and whimpers.

Jonathan met Devon's tongue eagerly, sucking at it as his free hand burrowed deeper into Kit's trunks. Cupping Kit's silken sac in his palm, he squeezed it gently as his finger rubbed in tandem with Devon's inside Kit's tightly clenching channel.

Giving up any semblance of resistance, Kit bucked into his lovers' hands, fucking himself on their fingers with abandon. When Jonathan's hand closed over his bollocks, he lost it, coming in his shorts like a randy teenager.

Devon felt a laugh building in his chest as Kit came undone beneath their hands. Pulling his mouth away from Jonathan's, not without a groan of protest, he gave Kit's trembling buttocks a loving pat. Stretching out on one side of Kit, he pressed close, rubbing against the slick skin, transferring some of the oil to his own chest and legs. Jonathan followed his lead, lying down against Kit's other side. They lay there peacefully for a few minutes until Devon lifted his head.

"Why Jonathan, I do believe we've overwhelmed our young friend here. Whatever should we do about it?"

Deciding the time had come to take back some control over the situation, Kit rolled to his back, pushing Jonathan and Devon into the sand. "I think you should take me into the water and clean me up," he declared.

"An excellent suggestion," Jonathan agreed, sliding his hands from Kit's trunks and under his shoulders and hips. With a shout of pure joy, he lifted the lithe body into his arms and took off toward the waves, Devon following a few steps behind. Splashing into the surf until it lapped at his waist, he dumped Kit into the water, cackling with uninhibited laughter.

Devon waded into the ocean behind his lovers, his own spirits soaring at seeing Jonathan relaxed enough to let his sometimes unhinged sense of humor loose. They'd been working under a crushing film schedule for weeks, and this kind of release was exactly what they all needed. Especially after the intensity of the sessions when they'd first arrived. Stepping back into a Dom role hadn't been as difficult as Devon had feared—how could it be with such responsive subs as Jonathan and Kit?—but being in charge all the time wasn't healthy either. They needed the relaxation, the freedom of making love without the constraint of a scene, for the pure joy of it. When Jonathan dumped Kit into the water, Devon dove for Jonathan's knees, tackling him and bearing him underneath the surging waves.

Kit came up spluttering and immediately looked around to see which of his lovers was closest. Spying them wrestling in the surf, he joined them, ganging up on Devon. His hands, still slippery from the baby oil, slid harmlessly off Devon's leg where Kit tried to grab hold.

Jonathan's arousal had flagged with its first contact with the cool water, but wrestling with Devon began to revive it, and watching Kit rise out of the waves with beads of water glinting against the slick sheen of oil that covered his skin brought it back to full attention. He sidestepped a feint from Devon and wrapped his arms around him instead, pulling Devon firmly against the hard column filling the front of his cutoffs.

Seeing Jonathan had Devon pinned, Kit came up behind him, sandwiching Devon between them. "Now that we've caught him," he asked Jonathan in what he hoped was a wicked-sounding voice, "what shall we do to him?"

"I'd say turnabout is fair play," Jonathan answered, hooking his thumbs below the waist of Devon's trunks and pulling them down to bare skin usually hidden from the sun. He dipped his head to nip at a slightly reddened shoulder, the taste of seawater adding to the tang of Devon's sweat. "What do you say, Devon?" he rumbled, passion as well as humor deepening his voice. "Shall we take you, right here?"

Not waiting for Devon's reply, Kit nodded effusively. "That sounds like a splendid idea to me." He pushed the trunks lower and slid his slippery hand into the crease of Devon's arse, the gentle waves lapping around his waist.

Devon wasn't about to protest, not when Jonathan's lips were wandering down his chest, his tongue dancing over tightened nipples. Not when Kit's hands were suddenly everywhere, squeezing and stroking in payback for earlier teasing. "Fuck yeah," Devon groaned, not sure what he was agreeing to but willing to go along with anything his lovers wanted.

"Let us take care of you," Kit requested, dropping his own trunks so he could rub his resurgent erection against Devon's arse.

Jonathan nibbled at the pink pearls of Devon's nipples just hard enough to leave them aching for more. He moved lower, following the path of golden, oil-glistening skin that led below the water's surface, when Devon grasped his shoulders and pulled him back up. Firm lips pressed to his, a forceful tongue pushed its way inside his mouth, and greedy hands slid his own shorts down his legs and pulled him demandingly against his lover's hard, hot body.

The warmth of the sun on his shoulders matched the heat flaring inside him as Devon pressed back into Kit's embrace and pulled Jonathan against him. He sought Jonathan's mouth hungrily, the force of their kisses and the steely press of Jonathan's cock against his own arousal as Kit slid wetly against him from behind so exactly what he needed that he couldn't get enough.

Kit pressed firmly against Devon's backside, rubbing against him urgently. Eventually he changed angles a little so his hand could move between them, down into Devon's cleft. Hoping his fingers were still oily enough, he probed gently at the tightly furled portal. "Let me in," he husked.

Breaking away from Jonathan's lips long enough to pull in a lungful of air, Devon gasped. Despite the coolness of the water, Kit's fingers set flames dancing where they pressed against him. "Do it," he growled, clenching around them even as he arched back for more. "Fuck yeah, want to feel you." His hands burrowed into the wet tangle of Jonathan's hair, pulling him back into another fiercely demanding kiss.

Devon's command was all the encouragement Kit needed to push his finger inside, shunting it back and forth a few times to coat the entrance as well as he could. When Devon uttered no protest, he added a second finger, searching for Devon's prostate, wanting to lavish as much pleasure on Devon as Devon had lavished on him earlier.

Jonathan couldn't believe how close to the edge he was already, just from the hard glide of Devon's cock against his and the heat of Devon's tongue invading his mouth. He wrapped his hands around Devon's hips, trying to pull him even closer, bringing them both nearer to the fierce pleasure that danced just out of reach.

Supported, surrounded by his two lovers, Devon let himself rock between them, Kit's fingers filling him, stroking him, Jonathan's strength rubbing against him, the crystalline waters doing nothing to cool the heat that intensified with each rock of their hips.

"Come for us," Kit rasped, his fingers dancing persistently over Devon's prostate.

Suddenly it was too much—Kit's fingers pressing against him from the inside, Jonathan's cock sliding slickly against his. With a muffled cry, Devon threw back his head as he shook with the force of his release, Jonathan following him only a moment later.

"Wanna fuck you," Kit murmured against Devon's neck as he felt his lovers climax. "Can I?"

"Mmmnn," Devon moaned, grateful that Jonathan had enough strength to hold them both up. "After that, you can do anything you bloody want." He turned his head, seeking the moistness of Kit's lips as he pushed back in invitation. "Now, yeah?"

Kit offered Devon his mouth as he shifted his hips to replace his fingers with his cock. "Tell me if I hurt you," he requested as he started to push inside slowly.

"Won't hurt me," Devon insisted, pressing back to force Kit deeper inside. "Ready for you... want you," he growled, leaning into Jonathan for stability, knowing his other lover would always be there to support him, to support them both.

Jonathan slid his hands up to cup Kit's buttocks, merging the three of them into a single embrace, rocking along with Devon to each thrust of Kit's hips. "Feels so good," he moaned as aftershocks continued to shake through him with each glide of their bodies.

Kit couldn't make his brain work enough to voice his agreement, but Jonathan was right. It felt amazing. Devon was hot and tight around him, the remnants of his orgasm making his muscles clench strongly around Kit's cock. He gasped for breath as he teetered on the edge of release, the tingling building in his groin and lower back. "Close," he gasped.

This couldn't be happening, Devon thought. He'd just come, but Kit rubbing over his sweet spot with every stroke and Jonathan rubbing against his cock felt so bloody good, and the feeling was building inside him again with the insistence of the waves crashing against the shore, and fuck if he wasn't going to come again.

Kit mimicked Jonathan's posture, closing his hands over Jonathan's arse, pulling him against Devon and providing Kit the leverage he needed to thrust just enough deeper to push him into release. His hips stuttered roughly against Devon's as his seed spooled out of him to coat his lover's insides.

"Love"—Kit bit back the next word before it escaped, brain rushing frantically for something he could say—"the way you make me feel," he finished lamely, cursing inwardly for letting his emotions get so close to the surface.

"Yeah," Devon agreed, shuddering in his lovers' arms as Kit filled him with warmth and Jonathan wrapped him in a tight embrace. "Love the way you make me feel too. Both of you."

Jonathan pressed a slow kiss to Devon's lips, then leaned forward to claim Kit's in turn. "Guess it's unanimous, then," he murmured, the warmth of his feelings stronger than the rays of the sun that caressed their entwined bodies. "Love all the ways we love each other."

CHAPTER 17
COLD COMFORT

DECIDING THE swim trunks around his ankles had to go, Kit lifted a foot, trying to pull it free of the clinging fabric. He hadn't counted on the effect of his lovers' weight on his balance, though, and as soon as his foot left the seabed, his equilibrium deserted him, sending him flailing backward into the water, taking the other two men with him. Pushing back above the surface of the gentle waves, he shook the salt water from his eyes and pulled the offending shorts to the surface. "Damn swimsuit," he muttered, balling it up and throwing it to the shore.

"Oi!" Devon protested, torn between pulling up his own trunks and following Kit's example. "This isn't a nude beach, you know!"

Jonathan quirked an eyebrow at his lover's misplaced modesty. "We just fucked in the middle of the ocean, Devon. It's a little late to be getting shy now, isn't it?"

Kit grinned. "And before that, the two of you had your fingers up my arse on the towels over there. If we haven't scandalized anyone yet, we're not going to," he added, starting toward shore. "Come on, Devon, where's that vaunted Northern courage?"

Knowing he was being manipulated but feeling too good to care, Devon pulled his own trunks off his ankles and rose to his feet. He wasn't surprised that he was already halfway to being hard again, just from his lovers' comments and the idea that someone might have seen them. He was to the point he was surprised when he *wasn't* hard around these two.

Jonathan had already pulled off his cutoffs and was making his way back to the beach. Kit followed immediately, flopping down on his towel. "It doesn't look like we took very good care of you there, Jonathan," he teased, eyeing Jonathan's half-aroused cock. "You did come, didn't you?"

A glance at Devon revealed, to his surprise, that the other man was half-hard as well. He knew Devon had come—twice!

Jonathan shrugged. "Yeah," he answered, stretching out on his own towel and shading his eyes from the sun with a raised hand. "Need a little more recovery time, though. I'm not as young as you anymore."

"Oh, I bet I could get you interested again," Kit postulated, pushing up on one elbow and leaning toward Jonathan with every intention of sucking him until he was hard again.

Giving up on blocking the sun while on his back, Jonathan rolled onto his stomach, pillowing his head on his forearms, only to find Kit leaning toward him with an unmistakable look of lust on his face. Chuckling, Jonathan reached up to pinch the pouting lower lip between his thumb and forefinger. "Believe me, I'm flattered, but at the moment I don't think I'm up to anything more energetic than soaking up some rays."

"Then I'll just go suck Devon for a while," Kit mock-sulked. "He's up for it. Aren't you, Devon?"

"Ahh, youth," Devon sighed, lying on his side where he could ogle both Jonathan's and Kit's nude forms. "I could be, but where's the rush? Jon's right. Let's just relax and enjoy the sun for a bit. We'll be back to cold and cloudy England before we know it, and the scenery won't be near as impressive as it is right now."

Jonathan snorted. "You could be?" he echoed, arching an eyebrow. "Seems to me you and Kit both came twice already this morning, and you're not that much younger than I am."

"Having multiple orgasms is a state of mind as much as a state of body," Devon countered with a smug grin. "Once you know you can come more than once, it gets easier to do it again."

"I think I can, I think I can," Jonathan chanted, breaking into a fit of laughter as Devon flicked him with the end of his spare towel.

Kit laughed along with them without the slightest idea what to say to that. He had to admit he was intrigued, but he didn't want to press too much. His eyes landed on the Celtic scrollwork across the small of Jonathan's back. "When did you get the tattoo done?" he asked, running his fingers across the dark ink.

Jonathan hummed his pleasure at the touch. "I got that one to celebrate my first film role. I figured I'd put it somewhere it wouldn't be likely to be seen on-screen."

"That worked out well," Devon commented with a sardonic grin. They'd joked about how many of Jonathan's films had managed to include a shot of his naked backside. "Let's see, *The Janus Affair,*

Justice, Tender Persuasion—not that I can fault the directors. After all, it is your best feature."

"Oh, I don't know," Kit disagreed. "I've gotten pretty fond of another one of his features. So are all your tats related to filming, then?"

"Not this one." Jonathan rolled on his side, running his fingers lightly over the tattoo on his hip. "I got this one when Josh was born. I was in Japan filming *Tomoshibi Shan* when Jean was pregnant with him, so when he was born, I had his initials done in kanji."

"What about you, Devon?" Kit asked, turning to face him. "You've got the one for Man U, obviously, but I'd always heard tattoos were addictive. Have you ever thought about getting another one?"

A shadow flickered over Devon's face so quickly Kit wasn't sure he hadn't imagined it. "There's not much beside the Devils I love enough to mark this perfect body for," he answered, waggling his brows as Kit shifted into a comfortable position on his towel. "You've never been tempted yourself?"

Kit shrugged. "I'm a little like you. I don't want to get one just for the sake of having one since I want to have a career as an actor. I'm not opposed to getting one if I had something worth commemorating, like Jon has Josh. I'm just not at that point in my life yet, I guess."

"If I had kids, I'd have their names on my other arm," Devon admitted. The twist in his smile was too pronounced to go unnoticed this time. "Course, the way things worked out, it's probably for the best I don't. It would be hell to drag a child through the shitstorm this divorce has turned into. My unlamented ex-wife is fighting me over everything. I can't imagine how much worse it would be with a kid in the middle."

Jonathan reached over to clasp Devon's shoulder in sympathy. "I have to give my ex a lot of credit. No matter how bad things got between us at times, Jean and I always managed to put Josh's welfare first. Sounds like you're not as lucky."

"There's a reason she's going to be my ex-wife as soon as the lawyers can manage it." Devon turned onto his stomach and closed his eyes. "Enough of that. Shite, I'll miss this sun when we're back on set!" He let the warmth seep under his skin, easing the tension that built whenever he thought of Marcy and her exorbitant demands.

"I'll miss having you both naked whenever I feel like it," Kit joked, taking his cue from his lovers and relaxing onto the towel. They had the rest of the day still to spend however they pleased, and they could enjoy being together even if they weren't making love.

Easing back onto his towel, Jonathan turned his head to keep both Kit and Devon in sight. He sometimes found it hard to just relax, his thoughts even at the end of a long day's shoot looking ahead to the next day's scenes or the next role. He'd seldom taken the time to just lie back and do nothing, and he was surprised to find how much he'd needed it. And how much it meant to share the time with the two men at his side. Wondering again how he'd gotten lucky enough to have both of them in his life, he closed his eyes and drifted into sleep beneath the warm sun.

A SHADOW falling over his face woke Jonathan sometime later; judging by how far the sun had moved across the cloudless sky, at least a few hours had passed. Devon's towel was empty—it must have been his getting up that woke Jonathan. He twisted his neck to stretch it and spotted Devon a little farther up the beach, next to the ice chest Jonathan had dragged from the cottage. A cool beer would hit the spot perfectly just about now. "Hey, toss me one, will you, babe?" he called to Devon.

The sound of their voices roused Kit to an unpleasantly dry throat as well. Seeing where Devon was standing, he shot his lover a smile. "Damn, a beer sounds good. Is there anything good in that cooler?"

"I got an assortment of whatever they had at the local grocery," Jonathan admitted. "So there's a little bit of everything. Whatever you grab's fine for me; you already know I'm easy."

"When it comes to beer, maybe," Devon drawled, picking a bottle at random and lobbing it toward Jonathan with a laugh. "In other ways you're damn obtuse, or it wouldn't have taken the lad and me so long to lure you into our bed, now would it?"

"I'd just about given up," Kit agreed, walking over to dig in the ice chest for his own beer. "If Devon hadn't come up with the idea of doing this together, I probably would have chalked you up as a lost cause."

"I couldn't see what was right in front of me," Jonathan admitted, pushing his hair back from his forehead and dragging the beer bottle over the heated skin. "Fuck, that feels almost as good as drinking it will." He sighed, twisting the cap off and taking a long swig of the icy liquid.

Devon watched the muscles in Jonathan's throat as he swallowed, the warmth of the air around him suddenly pooling in his groin. He reached blindly for a beer himself, wrenched off the cap, and took a long swallow, nearly spitting it out when he realized what he'd grabbed.

"Who the fuck did you buy this swill for?" he complained. "Even the damned Orkneys don't drink light beer."

Laughing out loud at Devon's predicament, Kit fished a Guinness out of the cooler. "Here, lover, try this," he suggested. He switched the bottles out of Devon's hand, dumping the light beer into the sand beyond his towel. He looked back in time to see both men raise their drinks to their lips and gulp some down. He would have sworn he was sexed out, what with the scenes they'd played this week, all the times they'd made love, and his two climaxes already that morning, but watching their lips around the rims of the bottles, watching their throats work, Kit felt himself reacting again. He grabbed his own beer and took a deep swig, trying to dispel the building heat.

"Prima donna," Jonathan groused, walking over to the cooler to see what else he'd bought that might offend Devon's delicate tastes. The ice surrounding the sweating bottles looked so refreshing that he picked up a cube and rubbed it over his neck, letting the melting water run in cooling rivulets down his chest.

Kit's eyes followed the rills of water, watching the way Jonathan's nipples puckered from the cold. He stuck his hand in the cooler and grabbed a cube of ice, going to Jonathan's side. With a devilish grin, he swiped the cold chip directly across Jonathan's nipple.

Jonathan's sudden intake of breath drew Devon's attention to his two lovers and the sensuous scene they were playing out before him. Stopping his return to his towel, Devon paced over to the cooler and picked up another chunk of ice to rub over the other side of Jonathan's chest. He met Jonathan's smoldering gaze challengingly. Dragging the ice lower, he traced it slowly around the kanji characters low on his lover's hip.

Jonathan's cock jutted from its nest of tangled curls, damp with a fluid that had nothing to do with ice. *Or maybe it did*, he thought, as Devon slid the ice even lower and Kit crouched down to pick up a fresh cube, drawing a tantalizing trail up the outside of Jonathan's thigh. "Mmmnn," Jonathan hummed, letting his head fall back and closing his eyes against the warmth of the sun on his face. "Mmmnn, yeah, feels good."

Kit met Devon's eyes and grinned, images of all the places they could rub ice running through his head. Most of them would be much easier if Jonathan wasn't standing. "Lie back down," he instructed, "and we'll make it feel even better."

After draining the last of his beer, Jonathan dropped the bottle onto the sand and returned to his towel. Sprawled on his back, he let himself relax under the warm sun and the teasing coldness of his lovers' caresses. This was a different way of giving in, of giving up control, but the trust and love he felt for the two men beside him were still the same, only growing stronger every time they came together.

Devon pulled the cooler closer to retrieve another frosty cube and painted a line of ice water up Jonathan's leg from ankle to knee to hip. He followed the crease where the long limb connected with Jonathan's groin, realizing suddenly that the man had no tan lines—his skin had the same warm glow across his entire body. "Been tanning in the nude before this, haven't you, Jon?" he asked, watching the skin tighten as he ran the melting chunk of ice over his lover's lightly furred bollocks.

Jonathan couldn't restrain a hiss of shock as the cold cube slid over his balls. "Sorry I didn't make a public announcement," he answered hoarsely, his sac tightening under the cold touch. "Next time"—his voice cracked as Kit slid a cube up the length of his already-dripping shaft—"next time, I'll be sure to invite you both to join me."

"You'd better," Kit agreed, circling the head of Jonathan's cock with the ice. He was sure the cold had to be almost painful, yet Jonathan's hips pushed up into his hand. Pulling back, he bent his head and licked the chilled skin, tasting the salt from the sea and Jonathan's own essence.

Jonathan's gasp of discomfort turned into a moan of pleasure as Kit's warm tongue replaced the coldness of the ice. At the same instant, Devon slid his cube beyond Jonathan's balls, freezing the sensitive skin of his perineum. Jonathan bit back a wail, bucking his hips in a vain attempt to escape the frigid torment. "Christ, Devon," he stammered, "that's—that's—"

Devon might have taken pity on Jonathan's cry of protest if the way his cock was leaking didn't tell a different story. He worked the ice over the smooth flesh behind his bollocks until it melted between his fingertips. After scrabbling in the ice chest for another cube, he returned to the same patch of skin before circling even farther to skate the ice over Jonathan's puckered entrance. Devon kept the touch light, watching Jonathan's face for any sign of real discomfort.

Jonathan's toes clenched in the sand, the muscles in his thighs tensing as his hips strained upward. The conflicting sensations of Kit's warm mouth sliding over the slick head of his cock and the iciness of Devon's teasing around his hole were starting to short-circuit any conscious reactions. All he could do was rock between the two extremes as his lovers alternately tormented and soothed him.

Feeling Jonathan beginning to thrust into his mouth, Kit increased the suction, dropping the sliver of ice that remained in his hand and wrapping his cold fingers around the base of Jonathan's cock to guide and encourage him. Jonathan's hissing sounds of pleasure urged him on.

"Kit," Jonathan moaned as the cold fingers encircled him, "don't... stop... so good."

Convinced that Jonathan's gasps and moans didn't contain any objections, Devon circled the tight rosette a little more firmly, bathing it in icy liquid. Once the edges of the cube had melted into smoothness, he eased the tip of the cube inside, pulling it back when Jonathan's entire body bucked.

"Too much?" Devon asked, rubbing his other hand over Jonathan's shoulder. "Do you want us to stop, Jon?"

Kit pulled back as well, waiting for the reply. He didn't want to overwhelm Jonathan, just drive him almost crazy with desire.

"N-no... fuck no," Jonathan gasped. "Feels... feels...." His mind refused to come up with words to describe the things his two lovers were making him feel.

Devon leaned forward to cover Jonathan's mouth with his own, the kiss quickly turning into a hungry duel of lips and tongues. He was throbbing with arousal, but he could wait, channeling his own desire into stoking Jonathan's passion even higher. Breaking away from the kiss, he touched Jonathan's shoulder, encouraging him to roll onto his side.

Kit shifted to allow Jonathan's movement, reaching into the ice chest to grab another cube. Settling himself on his back, he urged Jonathan to move up over him so he could return his mouth to his erection. He closed his fist around the ice, letting it cool his skin so it would contrast sharply with the heat of his mouth when he wrapped it around Jonathan's shaft.

Kneeling, Jonathan automatically moved his hands to Kit's shoulders to steady himself. His entire body felt hypersensitive, every touch, each perception of cold or warmth stronger and more arousing than the last.

Devon paused to take a long draught of his beer as his lovers repositioned themselves, the cool burst on his palate giving him a wicked idea. Grabbing another handful of ice, he knelt behind them and spread Jonathan's cheeks apart. He rubbed a cube down Jonathan's crease and around the wet hole while he popped another cube into his mouth.

The slow pressure of Kit's mouth as he took him back inside made Jonathan's back arch in pleasure, the coolness of Kit's hand a sharp but stimulating contrast that kept him teetering on the edge of control. The sudden shock of the ice Devon ran down his ass forced a surprised yelp from him and made him buck so fiercely he shoved his cock deep into Kit's throat.

Kit almost gagged when Jonathan's arousal drove hard into his mouth, but he made himself relax and let his lover move at will. He couldn't see what Devon had done to inspire such an energetic reaction, but he was certainly going to ask about it later. In the meantime, he was going to do his part to add to the sensations swamping Jonathan. He reached blindly around the towel for the ice cube he had dropped, lifting it over his head to run it randomly over Jonathan's chest.

Jonathan gasped when the ice in Kit's hand dragged over his nipples, hardening them to steely points. He wanted to feel Kit's mouth on them, sucking away the chill to replace it with a different kind of ache—but then he'd have to stop what he was doing to Jonathan's cock, and that felt so fucking amazing that he couldn't help but moan in pure wantonness.

Devon grinned widely at the reaction he'd caused. Taking the cube of ice in his mouth between his teeth, he leaned forward and retraced the same path, circling the cube around Jonathan's entrance as he clenched against the coldness. Dropping the other cube and grasping Jonathan's hips with both hands, he pressed the icy wedge into Jonathan's opening, using his tongue to push it as far inside as he could.

"Fuck, Devon!" Jonathan shouted, his entire body shaking at the icy invasion. Devon merely tightened his grip and continued to ream Jonathan's musky channel with his tongue. He was going to make bloody sure the only discomfort Jonathan felt was because he hadn't come yet.

Feeling Jonathan push back against Devon, Kit pulled off Jonathan's hard cock. As much as he enjoyed sucking Jonathan, he really, really wanted his lover inside him. Sliding up the towel, he paused to lick at the peaked flesh he had so recently teased with the ice cube, pulling first one, then the other nipple into this mouth and biting at it lightly. Releasing it, he slid up farther and licked at Jonathan's lips. "I want you to fuck me," he whispered firmly.

"Oh God," Jonathan moaned, forcing his mouth against Kit's. "Want that too. Want to come inside you." Trying to keep from losing it right then from Kit's words and Devon's wicked tongue, he reached an unsteady hand toward Kit, hoping he could wait long enough to prepare him first.

Devon's bollocks throbbed heavily at Kit's words. He loved rimming Jonathan, loved the dark, sultry taste on his tongue, but he wanted to feel that heat squeezing around his cock when he came. He pulled away from Jonathan just long enough to find the bottle of baby oil, then pressed it into Kit's palm and reached for another shard of ice.

Kit poured some of the oil from the bottle into his palm and stroked it over Jonathan's straining shaft. He didn't even bother with his entrance. Jonathan and Devon had stretched him earlier with their fingers. That would be enough. He was too desperate to have Jonathan inside him to wait any longer. Spreading his legs, he urged Jonathan to move between them and claim him.

Jonathan didn't need much urging. He needed to bury himself inside Kit's heat, to counteract the chill of the breeze drying the icy wetness from his skin and to satisfy the aching need only his lovers could assuage. Lowering himself onto the inviting body beneath him, he sank his tongue into Kit's mouth and his cock into Kit's channel, making Kit his in every way he could.

Kit gave Jonathan his mouth willingly, his hips bucking as he was filled. A moan escaped him as he was claimed.

Watching Jonathan enter Kit, hearing their moans of pleasure, Devon couldn't wait any longer. He trailed the dripping cube of ice up and down Jonathan's crease, tracing a similar path with his tongue up Jonathan's neck until he reached his ear. "Want you," he husked, running his free hand down the broad planes of Jonathan's back. "Will you let me take you?"

"Always," Jonathan groaned, torn between pushing deeper into Kit's warmth and pushing back against the seductive press of Devon's frigid fingers. "Always want you, any way—" He gasped as Devon plunged the second cube inside him. "—any way I can have you."

Jonathan's words set a tendril of heat spiraling in Devon's belly to rival the sun's rays against his back. He grabbed the bottle of oil Kit had dropped and coated his cock with feverish hands, then squeezed more oil over Jonathan's crease. Jonathan was already dripping wet from the ice and Devon's tongue, but Devon wasn't taking any chances. Spreading his legs wide around Jonathan's, he clutched his lover's hips and filled him with one long, smooth glide. He could feel the coolness of the melting ice quickly dissipate as he matched his strokes to Jonathan's, their three bodies moving in a single dance beneath the sun's golden haze.

Kit moaned as Devon's weight was added to Jonathan's, Devon's power to Jonathan's already moving inside him. He loved every configuration of the three of them together, but there was an extra intimacy to being joined this way, one to another to the third, all three of them moving as one to achieve their mutual pleasure. That it was more than simple pleasure was written indelibly on his heart, but he dared not speak of that yet. Not until he knew his lovers felt the same. "Fuck," he hissed. "Feels so fucking good."

They'd made love this way several times before, but for the first time, Jonathan knew the term was literally true. He felt so full of love enclosed in Kit's tight embrace, each drag of his cock sending waves of delicious friction pulsing through them both and wringing cries of pleasure from Kit's throat, while Devon's chest pressed against his back, Devon's thickness stroking his sweet spot with every slow, deep thrust. If he'd had enough breath left to speak, he might have told them both, but all he could do was moan with each ragged breath as he neared his climax, fighting to hold off long enough to take both his lovers with him.

Of all the ways they made love, this was Devon's favorite—feeling both his lovers moving beneath him, hearing the sounds of pleasure from two pairs of lips, made him feel as if he was loving both of them at the same time, and there was no feeling in the world better than that. He reached for Kit's hip with one hand while he kept the other on Jonathan's lean flank. Stroking the warm skin below his palms, Kit's slick with oil and Jonathan's with sweat, made Devon's cock surge inside Jonathan's constricting embrace. When the answering quiver transmitted to both the bodies beneath him, he felt Kit tense beneath Jonathan and Jonathan in turn clench around him, Devon's orgasm blindsided him, making him seize up against Jonathan's back and clutch his lovers' hips hard enough to leave bruises. Throwing back his head, he cried out in ecstasy as he filled Jonathan with pulse after pulse of his release.

That extra little thrust as Devon found his release, or maybe the tenor of his cry as he came or the clasp of his hand on Kit's hip… whatever it was, it set fire to Kit, his climax rushing over him, streaking his stomach and Jonathan's, leaving him trembling with the soul-stirring power of the sensations.

The hot splash against his stomach as Kit came and Devon's climax filling him with warmth were what Jonathan had been waiting for. With a final deep moan, he let the waves break over him, flooding him with such fierce pleasure that he shook with it as he emptied himself deep inside Kit. He locked his elbows to keep from collapsing on Kit, letting his head drop to lick at Kit's lips while he struggled to catch his breath.

Kit returned the kisses mindlessly, unable to do more than tangle his tongue with Jonathan's, overwhelmed still by the force of his release and the sensation of Jonathan's warmth filling him.

Finally Jonathan's trembling limbs refused to support Devon's weight against his back any longer, and they collapsed in a tangle of arms and legs against the crumpled towels. Devon rolled to the side to keep from crushing the others, resting his head on Kit's stomach and pulling Jonathan into the circle of his arms. "That was bloody amazing," he groaned, pressing a lazy kiss to the curve of Jonathan's shoulder. "I don't think I can move for the next few hours."

Kit's gaze slid down Devon's body to rest on his lily-white arse. Said arse wasn't quite so white anymore. In fact, it was turning a vivid shade of pink. "That might not be such a good idea," he murmured. "Unless you want to explain to Niall why you've got a sunburned bum."

Devon craned his neck, trying to see whether Kit was just taking the piss with him. Reaching back to touch the area in question, he discovered that even the pressure of his fingers was already painful. "Shite, I hope there are no bloody riding scenes when we get back," he complained. "Where the fuck did my trunks wind up, anyway?"

Jonathan pushed up on one elbow and surveyed the damage with a grin. "I should definitely have asked you sunbathing with me before this," he agreed. "Don't worry, Devon, there's still plenty of ice left."

Kit's grin grew at the suggestion, but he had another of his own to add. "If that doesn't help, I could show you all the things I can do with a bottle of aloe vera. You can have the back seat on the way home tomorrow too. That way you can stretch out and keep your weight off your poor sunburned arse."

Chuckling, Devon retrieved his trunks and pulled them gingerly over his backside while eyeing his lovers. Their vacation wasn't over yet. "I won't be the only one leaving with a tender arse tomorrow," he murmured.

Jonathan smiled, thinking how much had changed in the past few days. He wouldn't hazard a bet what Devon had in store for their asses, but he was pretty sure that whatever it was would be mind-blowing. If Kit agreed—and Jonathan was certain he would—they'd have to be sure Devon continued to stretch their limits even after they returned to the routine of filming.

Chapter 18
Out of the Bag

KIT LOUNGED on the couch in the trailer Bevan Campbell shared with the other three actors who, along with him, portrayed the Orkney brothers in the *Camelot* miniseries. The group, including Kit as Percival, had become as close as brothers themselves, and now Kit waited for Bevan to finish getting out of costume. The others had gone on to their favorite pub to prepare everything for Bevan's surprise party. Kit's job was to make sure Bevan arrived at the opportune moment. He'd already prepared a list of reasons why they couldn't go straight to the pub, but apparently they weren't going to be necessary because Bevan sat down on the couch next to him, his face serious.

"We haven't seen nearly as much of you over the past month," Bevan said, his Scot accent strong. "Is everything all right?"

"Everything's fine," Kit hastened to reply, thinking of everything that had happened since he and Devon had first seduced Jonathan. "It's been a busy month, that's all."

"Not busy enough to keep you from spending more time with Jonathan and Devon than you have with us," Bevan observed. "Colm's worried we've done something to upset you, Warwick thinks you're just tired of all the juvenile jokes and looking for some more mature companionship, and Rhodri—well, maybe best you don't know what Rhodri suggested."

Kit was pretty sure whatever Rhodri suggested couldn't be any more far-fetched than reality. "What does Rhodri think?"

"That you and Devon have gotten together."

Kit had always been open about his sexual orientation, and Devon's bisexuality was enough of an open secret, at least in the acting community, that the idea wasn't outside the realm of possibility "He's not entirely wrong," Kit admitted, thinking that of the four Orkneys, Bevan would be least likely to scoff at the truth. "You have to admit, he's a sexy bastard."

"Both your trailer mates are dead sexy blokes," Bevan agreed. "I have to say, I'm glad I won't need to compete with Devon for the lasses' attentions. Not that Jonathan isn't competition enough. A poor knight like me wouldn't have a chance if he decided to have a go at Blythe or Elsinore."

Kit's pride swelled at the thought that he and Devon had succeeded where Blythe Thompson or Elsinore Clarke, the actresses portraying Guinevere and Morgaine le Fay, would have failed. "I think you're safe," he blurted out, realizing too late how much he might be revealing by his comment.

"I've never heard of him getting involved in an offscreen romance before, but there's always a first time." Bevan shook his head. "Women can't resist that kind of a challenge. Ellie was telling Addison just yesterday that she thought his accent when he wasn't in character was positively sinful."

And isn't that the truth, Kit thought ruefully. "As far as I know, Jon isn't interested in any of the birds," he assured Bevan. "He has to be careful about things like that because of his son and all. It wouldn't do for Josh to get the wrong idea about things."

"So, you and Devon, hmmn?" Bevan grinned. "Does he live up to his reputation?"

"More than," Kit replied immediately, sure he must have a shit-eating grin on his face as he thought back to the long weekend at the beach. "They both do."

"Both?" The look on Bevan's face as he moved from confusion to comprehension was priceless. "Both? You're taking the piss, aren't you?" Kit raised an eyebrow, making Bevan splutter. "You lucky sod, you're shagging both of them?"

"Um...." Kit hesitated, not quite sure how to interpret his friend's reaction or how to explain the complexities of his relationship with Jonathan and Devon. "Yes?"

"Rhodri's going to shit a brick." Bevan chuckled. "He and Colm had a bet on which one of them would bag someone from on set first. You've topped them both without even trying."

"Not them!" Kit exclaimed without thinking, his skin heating immediately as he realized what he'd just revealed. "I'll stick with Jon and Devon, thank you very much."

Bevan broke into laughter. "I think Colm and Rhodri would be even more shocked than you at that idea. Though they'll be so relieved you're not really snarked at us, you might get at least a snog out of them." He clapped Kit on the shoulder. "C'mon, after a bombshell like that, I need a drink."

Kit shook his head again. "No, I'll pass. I get enough snogs from Jon and Devon. You're not... I don't know, scandalized?"

"Hell, Kit, we've known all along you were gay, and Devon's always had the reputation for going both ways. Jonathan's the only real surprise, since he's never been rumored to be anything but straight."

"He wasn't," Kit admitted, "or at least he'd never acted on it. I didn't figure you'd be bothered if I told you I was with one of them, but even people who are good with two gay guys might not know how to react to three of us. Even I didn't know how to react to the idea when Devon first suggested it."

"Besides being jealous as hell?" Bevan shrugged. "Once they get past the surprise, I doubt anyone on the set will have any problems with it. What's that old Hollywood saying? As long as it doesn't frighten the horses...."

Kit laughed. "I guess we're good, then. You know how much the horses love Jon." Surreptitiously, he glanced at his watch. "Okay, enough of the heart-to-heart. I'm thirsty. Let's head to the pub."

"Speaking of snogs, maybe I can get a few from the girls." Bevan grinned. "Today's my birthday, you know."

"Yeah, I seem to remember hearing something to that effect," Kit agreed. "I'll buy you a pint when we get to the pub."

"YOU WANKER!" Bevan rounded on Kit when they entered the pub to shouts of "Surprise!" and "Happy Birthday!" from the assembled cast and crew. "You're becoming a right pro at keeping secrets, aren't you?"

"I had a good teacher," Kit murmured, thinking about all the secrets in Devon's past as Bevan was swallowed by the crowd. He spotted Devon at the bar, lounging against it with the same loose-limbed grace he'd demonstrated so regularly at their beach retreat. The trousers and shirt Devon wore weren't as revealing as his leathers, but Kit didn't need to see the line of muscle to know what Devon looked like beneath his clothes. The image was permanently imprinted on his brain. Devon's fair head tipped sideways, leaning close to Jonathan's darker one, the contrast making Kit smile as he crossed the room to join them.

"Damn, we're a couple of lucky bastards, aren't we?" Devon murmured in Jonathan's ear as he watched Kit walk toward them.

Jonathan's gaze lingered on Kit as he made his way across the crowded pub. Kit was dressed as outrageously as usual, his jeans low and loose, his short, tight T-shirt leaving a swath of fawn-colored skin visible along with a hint of his treasure trail as he moved. Out of costume, he'd let loose his dark hair so that it bounced around his face in windblown—or sex-tousled—glory.

"That we are," Jonathan agreed, turning to bump foreheads with Devon, his voice low enough that only Devon could hear him. "I hit the jackpot with the two of you."

Kit wended his way through the morass of actors to join his two lovers at the bar, insinuating himself in between their larger bodies. He was tempted to tilt his head up for a kiss from one or both of them, but they hadn't talked about how they were going to explain their relationship to the rest of the cast, and he thought they might want to think about it first. He'd need to tell them about his conversation with Bevan too, but that would have to wait until they had more privacy. "Hi," he said instead, letting his hands brush their thighs discreetly. "Did you order me a drink?"

"A Busted Cherry, with extra fruit." Devon nodded, his eyes sparkling.

Kit scowled, though Devon was hardly the first to give him a hard time about his preference in drinks. "What? Just because I like a sweet drink sometimes is a reason to take the piss?"

"Devon just can't remember ever having a cherry," Jonathan retorted, giving Devon a mock punch in the shoulder. "Don't let him get under your skin, Kit-Kat." Though Jonathan had definite plans for getting under Kit later in the evening—or over him, or both. He wasn't particular, as long as it involved Kit and Devon naked in a bed.

"Speak for yourself. I've had many a cherry and remember every one of them." Devon squeezed Kit's shoulder with a wink. "I have to admit a special fondness for the most recent one I claimed." *And the last,* Devon added silently.

"Kit-Kat?" Rhodri parroted. The Welsh actor jabbed Kit in the stomach with his elbow as he followed him to the bar. "If I didn't know our king had better taste, I'd think what Bevan just told me was true."

Kit glared silently at his friend, willing him to silence. Rhodri wasn't discreet in the best of circumstances, though, and the kind of gossip he now had in his possession hardly qualified. "You should know better than to believe everything Bevan tells you."

"Is it true?" Rhodri asked, oblivious to Kit's glare as he took in the two older actors. "All three of you, together?"

"And if it is?" Devon's eyes darkened as they held Rhodri's. "Why would it matter to you?"

"Because it means Colm owes me twenty quid," he answered with a grin.

"No," Kit insisted with a smirk, "you only figured out about Devon and me. You missed Jonathan entirely, so he only owes you ten." Realizing the cat was out of the bag, he looked back and forth between his lovers. "I sort of told Bevan about us while I was delaying him getting here, and well, what one Orkney knows, they all know."

"For sure." Rhodri nodded emphatically. "Just like the brothers we play on-screen."

Jonathan frowned. He should have expected someone to have found out about them before now—it was next to impossible to keep a secret for long on a movie set—but he'd been so caught up in the emotions of their relationship that he'd been living in the moment, not thinking about the larger implications. It wasn't that he was ashamed of being with Kit and Devon by any means, but he wasn't especially fond of being the object of gossip. "I don't mind the cast knowing, but I'd rather not see us splashed across the tabloids," he said softly.

"It won't go beyond us, though I think you could trust the rest of the cast and crew too," Rhodri asserted. "What happens on location...."

"Stays on location," Warwick added, coming up with Colm to join the group at the bar.

"Thanks, mates," Kit said. "It'll be good not to have to keep what I'm doing a secret anymore."

"Don't think that means we want to hear about it!" Warwick, the most straight-laced of the Orkneys, said quickly. "We don't care who you shag, but we don't need details!"

Kit grinned back at him. "You sure, Warwick?" he teased. "I could tell you some things that would make your hair curl as pretty as Colm's there." Even as he threatened it, though, he knew he wouldn't. Some things were simply too precious, too private to share.

"I want to hear!" Colm chimed in. "I'll just pretend it's two birds. Maybe I'll pick up some ideas for when I lure Ellie and Blythe into bed."

"At least your dreams are big, little man," Rhodri said, ruffling Colm's curls with brotherly affection. "But they'd be missing some necessary equipment to emulate these two."

"Some very significant equipment," Devon purred, the sultry tone itself enough to stir said equipment to life under Kit's jeans.

"I'm a resourceful bloke. I'd improvise," Colm countered with a grin.

"How about this?" Kit laughed. "When you get Morgaine and Guinevere in your bed, I'll give you the benefit of my advice and experience. Until then, I think I'll keep it to myself." He figured Colm had about as much chance with either of the girls as he did and none with both of them. Blythe and Ellie were a lot of fun, and he'd hit it off with Blythe in particular because of their implied roles as rivals for Arthur's affection, but neither of them were the kind to mess around on set. Then again, Jonathan hadn't been either, so he supposed he ought to be a little careful what he agreed to.

"Did I hear my name bandied about?" Having given Bevan his birthday kiss, Blythe glided toward the laughing group at the bar. "Show some respect for your queen, and someone get me a drink, by your mercy!"

"Allow me, my Guinevere," Jonathan answered in Arthur's regal tone, stepping closer to Kit to make room for her at the bar. The move bumped their hips together, Jonathan's jeans brushing over Kit's burgeoning arousal and surprising a hiss of breath from him. Their eyes met for a moment of unspoken promise before Devon snaked an arm around Kit's waist, pulling him back and allowing enough room for Jonathan to turn and gesture for the barman—and for Devon to rub his own crotch against Kit's buttocks.

"Later for that, sunshine," he murmured into Kit's ear. "I know just talking about this makes you hot, but I think this group's had enough to assimilate for one night. Besides, the focus is meant to be on Bevan, not us."

Kit bit back a moan at the unbelievable sensation of being sandwiched, however innocently, between his two lovers even as he nodded. "I didn't mean to steal his thunder, but he cornered me in the trailer while I was delaying him, and once he knew, there wasn't any stopping him from telling the others. I hope you don't mind."

Devon shrugged. "I've had worse said about me than that I'm shagging two incredibly hot men."

Having claimed their drinks from the harried bartender and put in an order for Blythe, Jonathan turned back from the bar. "Someone was bound to figure it out sooner or later," he said, offering Devon and Kit their glasses. "I just hope it doesn't leak out beyond the cast. You don't need that complication to deal with in your divorce proceedings." Even though his own split from his ex-wife had been wholly amicable, Jonathan could empathize with what Devon was going through.

"Let's not mar the evening with that rot," Devon growled, lifting his glass. "To Bevan's birthday!"

"To Bevan!" the rest of the cast echoed, lifting their glasses in reply.

AT DEVON'S place a few hours later, Kit sighed in repletion and snuggled up between his lovers. They'd sandwiched him between them like at the bar and driven him out of his mind with pleasure, reassuring him that he hadn't messed anything up by telling Bevan—and by extension the others—the truth about their relationship. "I don't think the Orkneys will tell anyone intentionally, but they aren't always as discreet as they should be. Is it going to be a problem if Niall finds out?"

"He cast you and Addison knowing you're openly gay," Jonathan mused, referring to Addison Nichols, the classically trained actor Niall had chosen to play Merlin. "Given that, I'd hope it won't be an issue, unless he has a policy against castmates of any gender getting together. Some directors do, but they'll generally make a point of letting everyone know up front if that's the case." He slid his hand from Kit's hip to glide over Devon's back. "You sure it won't be a problem if Marcy finds out?"

"We were separated before filming started, so she can't claim the two of you had anything to do with breaking up our marriage." Devon shrugged, the muscles that had tensed at the mention of his not-soon-enough-ex-wife relaxing under Jonathan's soothing touch. "Lord knows there are enough other examples of my less-than-sterling character she's already trotted out." Not that Devon didn't have ample evidence of her own cheating to counter with. At least he had waited until it was clear the marriage was over and they'd formally separated before letting his eyes rove. "What about you, Jon? Marcy knew I was bi before we got together. This will come as a shock to your son, won't it?"

"We raised Josh to be pretty open-minded." Jonathan smiled as he thought of his son. "Actually, he's been a fan since he saw Kit in *Around Every Corner*. Josh will be so excited at the chance to meet 'Davey' that the rest may not even register with him."

"I'd love to meet him," Kit said, "because he's your son first, of course, but it's always fun for me to meet fans. I'm fully aware I wouldn't have a career if it weren't for them."

"Jean and I have been talking about sending him over to visit during his next school break," Jonathan said with pride. "I'd like both of you to meet him. He's the best thing to happen in my life." *Though getting together with both of you is a close second*, Jonathan admitted to himself, even if he wasn't ready to confess the depth of his feelings to his lovers. Coming into the open about their relationship was a big enough step for the moment.

"That would be fantastic," Kit enthused. "We can take him into London, see all the touristy things there, and then get him out into the country and show him the real England. When are his holidays? If we plan it right, maybe we can talk Niall into giving us a couple of days off so we can do it up right for him."

"The semester ends in a few weeks. He has a week's break, but I can talk to Jean about letting him miss a bit of school so he could stay longer. If we take him to a museum or two, he'd be able to make the case that it's an educational visit."

"Sounds like a plan, then," Devon said sleepily, throwing an arm over Kit and Jonathan. Though he'd never been tempted to have a child of his own, he found himself looking forward to meeting Jonathan's son.

CHAPTER 19
JUST DESSERTS

JONATHAN JUGGLED the box from the pastry shop in one hand as he struggled to unlock the front door. He was sure Devon and Kit hadn't noticed, but today was a month since the night the two of them had seduced him. A month that had turned his world upside down, introduced him to sensual pleasures he'd never dreamed of—a month that had reawakened emotions he hadn't really expected to feel again. Call him romantic, but he wanted to mark it somehow, even if it was only with a fancy dessert.

The sound of voices through the open window caught Jonathan's attention as he dropped his burdens onto the kitchen table. He wasn't surprised to see Devon and Kit on the porch, and he grinned when he noticed they had each brought something too. "Were you two planning on staying on the porch all night?" He held the door open for his lovers. "We won't have nearly the privacy here that we did at the beach cottage."

Kit flushed at the insinuation, despite his enjoyment of all that had transpired during their weekend away. "N-no," he stuttered. "We were just discussing Devon's dessert. He got a little touchy when I suggested it was flan instead of scotch trifle." As he said the last two words, he imitated Devon's accent teasingly. "Apparently," he added, going back to his usual voice, "they're quite different."

"O'course they're different!" Devon insisted, a trifle belligerently. "For one thing, scotch trifle has scotch in it!" He brandished the bottle, which already had a healthy portion of its contents missing. "Damn good scotch, too, if I do say so m'self."

"Looks like you've already started sampling it." Jonathan winked at Kit as the two trooped inside. "I hope you plan to let us catch up with you."

"Well, I had to make sure it was good enough for the trifle, didn't I?" Devon said as he set the dessert down with care. "Fetch us some glasses, and we can drink a toast all 'round."

"Sounds good to me," Kit agreed. "I have the perfect toast too."

Jonathan pulled three tumblers down from a shelf and handed them around. "I wasn't sure either of you would remember what today was."

Devon uncapped the scotch and poured several fingers' worth into each glass with a flourish. "I only make m'mother's trifle on special occasions." He grinned. "And they don't come more special than this."

"I was standing outside the door worrying you'd think I was foolish for caring what today was," Kit replied honestly. "I... well, this just feels different than any other relationship I've been in, and I want to celebrate every step, however small. I guess I shouldn't have worried, yeah?"

Jonathan smiled and shook his head. "I brought home dessert too," he confessed. "Chocolate mousse. I just wanted something special to celebrate our first month together."

"Raspberry fool," Kit said, opening his bakery box. "The stunt guys all raved about one of the bakeries in town."

"Looks good," Devon agreed, swiping a finger into the creamy confection and popping it into his mouth. "Mmmnn, it's no scotch trifle, but it's not half bad."

Jonathan watched Devon lick a trace of the fool from his lip, making him hungry for his own taste. Swallowing down the surge of lust for the moment, he raised his glass to his two lovers. "A toast," he began, searching for words that could express what they had both come to mean to him in just a few short weeks.

"To another month as wonderful as this one has been," Kit chimed in when Jonathan hesitated. Though he spoke only of the present, he yearned for a lifetime of such months, a relationship that would endure the test of time and provide the love and support he craved.

"And another month after that," Devon added, raising the glass to his lips. Given his abysmal track record with relationships, it was probably foolish to hope for anything lasting from this unconventional threesome, but he'd be thankful for every day he had with his lovers.

"And another after that," Jonathan agreed, draining his glass. It was a good thing he'd hesitated, he thought. The other two were only talking about a few months of pleasure. They didn't need to know he'd been hoping for something more.

Months. Kit knew he had been the one to specify that time frame, but a part of him had hoped his comment would spur one of his lovers to ask for more. They had, in a way, and he was glad to know they hoped to see the relationship continue, but his heart quailed at the thought that those months would run out, and that someday he might not have them in his life. He suppressed a sigh at the thought. After all, they were supposed to be celebrating.

And another, and another, Devon thought. If they could just string together enough of those months…. Shaking his head to dispel the morose thoughts, he poured another round of shots, emptying the bottle. This was supposed to be a celebration, after all. "That's the last of the scotch, so drink up," he said. "If you want any more after this, you'll have to eat the trifle."

Kit sipped his scotch and smiled. "Are you sure we're good enough for your mother's scotch trifle?"

"Well, now." Devon waggled his eyebrows. "That all depends on what you have to offer in return, doesn't it?"

"You've already swiped a taste of my fool," Kit replied. "What more do you want?"

"How about a taste of mousse?" Jonathan drawled, the increasingly innuendo-laced banter having an undeniable effect on him. He ran a finger through the rich chocolate, holding the sweet-laden digit to Devon's lips. "Try this."

Devon lapped at the creamy treat, lingering over Jonathan's skin before pulling the finger into his mouth. Hunger gnawed at him, and it wasn't for any of the desserts, at least not unless he could taste his lovers along with them.

Jonathan pulled his finger from Devon's mouth and covered the warm lips with his own, tasting the mousse mixed with scotch, whipped cream, and Devon's own spicy flavor. "Not bad." He licked his lips as he pulled away. "Of course, I'll have to taste the others too, just to be fair."

Kit stuck his finger in his own dessert. "My turn," he declared, licking the digit clean.

"No, no, sunshine," Devon protested, covering Kit's hand with his own and smearing them both with the creamy puree. "You do it like this." He proceeded to wipe the sweet over Jonathan's face.

Jonathan yelped at the unexpected attack, rubbing at his face before swiping a handful of filling from the trifle dish, which he lost no time pushing into Devon's laughing mouth.

Not wanting to be left out of the fun, Kit dipped his hand in the mousse and added it to Devon's face. "Like this?"

Devon's and Jonathan's eyes met, both glancing at the so-far pristine Percival. With a wink, Devon launched a tackle to pin the lithe body against the table, pull off Kit's shirt, and bare his chest to Jonathan, who proceeded to coat it with swirls of dark chocolate.

"No fair," Kit protested even as he arched into Jonathan's touch. "You're ganging up on me!"

"You've never complained about it before." Jonathan leaned forward to lick the confection from one side of Kit's smooth chest as Devon did the same to the opposite half.

With their lips on his skin, Kit decided they were right. "When you put it that way," he gasped, burrowing his fingers into their hair to keep their heads in place.

Devon reached blindly across the table, no longer caring which dessert he found. His fingers hit the trifle bowl, and he scooped up a handful of the moist custard. He tore open Jonathan's shirt with the other hand, wiped his fingers on the light mat of hair, and then pulled Jonathan forward to nuzzle at him hungrily.

"Shit, Devon!" Jonathan jumped when the cold mess hit his skin, his exclamation morphing into a low moan as Devon latched on to his chest. He scrabbled for a hold on the table, his hand landing squarely in the center of the fool Kit had bought. He swiped the handful of goo over Kit's chest as he cradled the back of Devon's skull with his other hand, directing his attentions toward a suddenly aching nipple.

Kit ignored the mess dripping down his chest in favor of the mess on Jonathan's. Leaning up and nudging Devon aside, he licked delicately at the trifle, then closed his lips over the sticky nipple, sucking it into his mouth as he tried to clean it of every trace of dessert.

Feeling hot and overdressed, Devon pulled his sweatshirt over his head and tossed it in a corner, then started to clean the smeared whipped cream and fruit from Kit's chest.

Kit's lips closing around his nipple sent a flare of raw need lancing through Jonathan. He wanted to fuck Kit. He wanted to fuck Devon. He wanted either of them to fuck him. He didn't care as long as long as the three of them were together. Twisting closer to Kit and pulling Devon's head up to his with a groan, he plunged his tongue into the other man's mouth, kissing him until they were both panting raggedly. "Help me get Kit-Kat naked," he growled.

Kit leaned back on the table, lifting his legs to facilitate his disrobing. He was not about to complain about a plan that included him being naked, especially if his lovers were naked too.

Fighting for breath after having Jonathan's tongue halfway down his throat, Devon grinned. "Glad to help, my king," he agreed, working at Kit's zipper, "as long as I get to strip you off after him."

"I'll help with that!" Kit gasped.

As soon as Devon had the fastenings undone, Jonathan pulled Kit's jeans off his narrow hips, dropped them to the floor, and reached for the column of rosy flesh he'd bared. "This definitely looks good enough to eat," he murmured, licking at the smooth head.

Devon scooped up a dollop of mousse and nudged Jonathan's mouth away long enough to spread it around the head of Kit's cock. "That should make it taste even better." He laughed as he started work on removing Jonathan's jeans. "Too bad we don't have a cherry for on top."

"I haven't had a cherry for quite a few years," Kit reminded them. He pushed up on his elbows and helped Devon work Jonathan's jeans down.

After lapping away the last of the chocolate, Jonathan kicked the jeans off his ankles and knelt long enough to get Devon as naked as the rest of them. From that vantage point, he couldn't resist taking a nip of Devon's firm ass, smoothing over the reddened mark with his tongue. "Not quite as sweet back here."

Kit stuck his hand in the raspberry fool and smeared it over Devon's backside. "Try it now," he suggested with a leer. "That ought to make things a little sweeter."

The cool confection actually felt good on his abused arse, Devon thought, and Jonathan's tongue felt even better as he cleaned away the fruity treat. Devon held Jonathan's head down when he would have pulled away, inviting more of his attentions as he offered Kit a kiss in thanks.

Kit relaxed into the kiss, letting it slide from a quick peck of gratitude into an expression of all the bottled emotions that had led him to buy the dessert in the first place. He slid his tongue out to caress Devon's lower lip, teasing gently along the seam until the lush lips parted. He was tempted to see if he could wrest control of the kiss from Devon, but he decided on seduction instead, his darting tongue beckoning to Devon's, asking him to claim Kit's mouth. Devon kissing him this way always helped soothe the lingering worry that the other man desired him less than he desired Jonathan. He knew his own feelings on the matter, but he still sometimes wondered how Devon felt.

Devon had meant the kiss as just a teasing thanks, but Kit's response encouraged him to linger. The lad tasted of fine scotch and dark chocolate and berries, but the flavors weren't half as sweet or intoxicating as Kit's soft lips. With a muffled groan, Devon followed the beckoning tongue into the decadent heat of Kit's mouth, sticky hands cradling his lover's head as he feasted.

As Kit captured Devon's attention, Jonathan took advantage of the distraction to do some feasting of his own on Devon's taut buttocks. Nibbling across the pale globes until he reached their juncture, Jonathan licked up and down the shadowed cleft, the darker flavor as delicious to him as the sweetness of the desserts.

When Jonathan's tongue slid between his cheeks, Devon's cock jumped, pulsing against Kit's smooth thigh. He drew away instinctively from the kiss, arching into the hot, wet caress, but Kit tangled sugary hands in his hair, pulling him back roughly.

"I'm not done with you yet," Kit declared. In truth, he hoped never to be done with his two lovers. He seized control of the kiss, invading Devon's mouth as his had been so recently invaded. He loved the way Devon tasted, and the scotch and desserts only added to that. He flexed his thigh against Devon's engorged arousal, wanting to add to his pleasure.

Kit's insistent response made Jonathan grin to himself. Something about Kit giving orders to Devon made his heart swell with love for them both. Still holding Devon's hip with one hand, he stretched enough to claim another handful of mousse. After painting a swipe down Devon's crease—it *was* his favorite dessert, after all—he slicked the rest over Devon's thick cock.

"Bet this stuff makes good lube," Jonathan murmured, urging Devon forward before bending to enjoy his own treat.

"There's only one way to find out," Kit replied, lifting his head from Devon's mouth enough to speak. He slid his hand between them to encircle Devon's chocolate-covered erection. "Well, lover," he teased, "I'm game if you are."

Devon hissed as first Jonathan's hand and then Kit's coasted over his cock, the dessert's coolness doing nothing to lessen the heat of his arousal. He lifted Kit fully onto the table and nudged his thighs apart until his lover was open before him. After dipping his fingers into the mousse to coat them, he eased a creamy digit inside the tight passage, stretching it to receive him.

Kit braced his heels on the edge of the table, spreading himself wide for Devon's touch. It was as powerful, when it came, as ever, and love swelled through Kit along with his desire. Consciously he relaxed his muscles, wanting Devon inside him as quickly as possible. "Another one," he pleaded, using the leverage of his feet to rock against Devon's hand.

The thrust of Kit's hips pushed Devon back against Jonathan, and Jonathan took advantage of the moment to work his tongue into Devon's tight entrance. At Devon's appreciative yelp, Jonathan grinned and reached around until his hand plopped into something cold. Not until he slid the coated finger alongside his questing tongue did he discover that he'd dipped into the trifle. *Wonder if his mother would approve?* Jonathan chuckled to himself as he enjoyed the mingled flavors of scotch and Devon.

"Another one," Devon agreed hoarsely, urging Jonathan as much as he was answering Kit. Being caught between them like this, giving and receiving pleasure in equal measure, made him feel like the luckiest bastard in the world—for as long as it lasted. Well then, he'd just have to do his damnedest to make it last as long as he could, wouldn't he? Twisting his fingers inside the eager clench of Kit's muscles, he arched into Jonathan's touch, moaning his approval as he leaned forward to crush his mouth to Kit's.

Kit opened his mouth to Devon's kiss as his sphincter opened to the man's fingers. He was eager to be filled, every orifice, every inch of him aching with emptiness as Devon pulled his fingers back before sliding them inside him again, tongue teasing Kit's lips before surging inside to claim him. Kit wasn't sure what was different this time, for Devon wasn't doing anything he hadn't done before, but he felt every touch more keenly, every caress more intensely until he was shivering with his pent-up emotions, making him hope Devon had come to care for him in his own right rather than as a partner in seducing Jonathan. Lust and love mingled in his heart and in his loins, pushing him closer and closer to his release with every pass of his lover's talented fingers, every stroke of his lover's clever tongue.

As much as Jonathan was enjoying Devon's reaction to his slickened fingers and tongue, watching Devon preparing Kit was turning him on even more. He couldn't see Devon's face, but if Kit's blissful expression was anything to go by, they were both more than ready. With a final smack of his lips, he sat back on his heels, wrapping his hands around Devon's hips and urging him forward. "Go on, Devon," he coaxed, his voice a low rumble of lust. "Can't you see how much he wants you? Love him—let me watch you take him."

Though he couldn't hold back a moan of loss when Jonathan pulled away from him, the sensuous growl only confirmed what Devon already knew. He couldn't wait any longer to lose himself in Kit's hot, slick embrace. He'd never dreamed, only a month ago when he had half-teasingly suggested "sharing" Jonathan with Kit, how quickly the lad would burrow his own way into Devon's heart. With a growl of acceptance, he removed his fingers and eased the sticky head of his cock in their place. "Aye," he panted, "let me in—let me love you, sunshine."

"Yes," Kit pleaded. "Love me." He pushed up with his hips, impaling himself as best he could on Devon's erection.

Jonathan couldn't hold back a moan of arousal as he watched Devon's cock glide into Kit's enveloping heat. Still holding Devon's hips, he pressed a cheek to his backside, instinctively rocking in time with his movements.

"Jon," Devon gasped, fighting not to simply lose control and slam into Kit's velvety sheath. "You too. Please, need you inside me," he panted, trying to reach the other man and pull him toward them.

Jonathan didn't need to be asked twice. The connection between the three of them was never stronger than when he sank into one of his lovers as the other two loved each other. He coated himself quickly with a smear of mousse—the stuff really did work as lube!—wrapped his arms around the two men he loved, and joined himself to them both.

The shivers of delight already coursing through Kit increased when he felt the added power of Jonathan's thrusts into Devon's body. He had never imagined, before Devon made his unusual proposition, what it might be like to have two lovers. One had been enough for him, but now… now he could not imagine going back. The puissant connection between the three of them far surpassed anything he had ever known, especially when they were joined like this, all three of them striving as one for completion, for one another's pleasure even more than their own. "Close," he groaned, tossing his head back and forth as Devon's cock pummeled him relentlessly.

Jonathan's cock stretched Devon, filled him, completed him. Devon let the thrust of Jonathan's hips push him deeper into Kit, let the love he felt for both of them flow through him like a conduit, returning redoubled from both directions. With a strangled groan, he dug one hand into Kit's hip and one into Jonathan's, bearing down as his orgasm shook through him in wave after wave of fierce pleasure.

The sensation of Devon's seed spooling out inside him was all it took to trigger Kit's climax. With a hoarse shout, he pushed up against Devon's groin, taking the spurting shaft deeper inside him as his own cock twitched and discharged its load all over his sticky stomach and chest.

Jonathan was already achingly close to coming even before he'd slid inside Devon. The undulating clench of pressure around him as Devon climaxed and Kit's cry of ecstasy at his own release pulled Jonathan over the edge too. With a muffled groan, he molded himself to Devon's broad back as he lost himself in the power of his orgasm, his hips pumping again and again into the slick channel until the aftershocks finally faded.

As content as he was cocooned between his two lovers, Devon could already feel the lingering stickiness of the desserts pulling on the hair and skin in his most sensitive areas. "We made a right mess, didn't we?" He snickered, looking at the smears of custard, chocolate, and cream that adorned all three of them. "We'd better shower this off before we're stuck together permanently!"

"I could think of worse fates." Jonathan chuckled, pulling away reluctantly. "But I suppose you're right. This would ruin the nice clean sheets I put on the bed just for the occasion."

Kit grinned. "I'll buy you a new set of sheets, Jon," he teased, eyes flashing with good humor and love. "I was hoping for a second helping in bed."

CHAPTER 20
TIED UP IN KNOTS

"DAMN, NIALL'S good," Kit murmured as Rhodri turned off Colm's TV as casually as if it were his own. They'd all spent so much time in one another's pockets that they'd done away with most boundaries some time ago. Kit had joined the four actors playing the Orkney knights to watch the first episode of *Camelot* being broadcast. He'd hoped to watch the premiere with Jonathan and Devon, but the two men had been called by Niall for some urgent last-minute reshoots. "He's got me perfectly willing to believe Arthur's looking to play the field, even knowing they're going to make him marry Guinevere before too long."

"Just wait until you and Lancelot show up." Colm grinned at Kit. "Jonathan may have been following Niall's direction to work in some ambiguity about Arthur's interests, but when you're on camera together, it's going to come across loud and clear."

"We'd heard Jonathan was a method actor, but who'd have expected him to go to the lengths he has to be sure he's getting it right?" Warwick teased. "The man's a credit to his craft, I'll give him that."

"Sod off, Warwick," Kit snapped. "He isn't with Devon and me because it's implied in the script. Give him—and us—some credit for having morals. He doesn't make a habit of sleeping with costars just because his character has sex with their character."

"He'd be a busy boy if he did." Rhodri smirked.

"Enough," Bevan said as Kit's temper rose. "You know they're just taking the piss, Kit. Everybody thinks the world of Jonathan. Why don't we get online and see if we can find some reactions to the episode? That'll give us something constructive to do." A glare at the younger, more excitable Orkneys accompanied the last statement.

Mollified, Kit nodded. "Sure. We can share any reviews with everyone tomorrow on set."

Colm opened up his laptop and passed it to Kit. "See what you can find."

Kit typed in a search for "*Camelot* miniseries" and grinned as hundreds of hits popped up. He skipped the first few because they were the show's official site, the IMDB listing, and other informational sites. About halfway down the first page, though, he found a fanboard listing. Deciding that could provide some interesting comments, he clicked on it and grinned as he skimmed down the posts. "Well, they like it," he told the others. "I can almost hear them squealing through the computer."

"Let me see," Rhodri demanded, elbowing his way in next to Kit. "Arthur's a hot stud—we knew that. Niall's a brilliant director—old news. Arthur's boffing Sir Kay."

"Not in this lifetime!" Kit scowled. "Besides, they're like brothers."

"That seems to be part of the appeal," Rhodri joked, reading down the rest of the comments. "One way or another, though, Niall's got the girls all in a tizzy over the possibility that Arthur might be willing to mess around with the boys."

"Oh, look at that!" Colm pointed out, skimming down a few more posts. "It seems speculating about the characters isn't enough. They're going to speculate about the actors too!"

"What do you expect when half the cast is openly gay?" Bevan replied.

"Not half," Kit amended. "Addison and I don't count as half. You all know about Jon and Devon, but they aren't out." He wasn't entirely sure how Jonathan would feel about speculation concerning the actors' personal lives. He doubted it would bother Jonathan what they were saying about Arthur—Niall had made no secret on set of wanting exactly the kind of speculation they were getting. Their private lives were different, though. At least they were supposed to be.

"Devon may not have said anything publicly, but I don't think it's any real secret he's bi," Rhodri insisted. "And don't forget Glynn and Éamon. I know they aren't here yet full-time, but our adult Bors and Kay aren't just out. They're partners and have been for at least three years."

Kit shook his head. "I keep forgetting about them since they haven't gotten here yet, other than the one day Éamon was here to film the coronation scene, but that still isn't half the cast."

"It's enough to make the fangirls squeal to high heaven, apparently." Bevan laughed. "Don't worry, Kit. Once you and Devon make it on-screen, they'll forget about pairing Arthur with anyone but Percival and

Lancelot. I've watched you three together, and the chemistry lights up the screen."

"Us?" Kit teased. "You should see the four of you. They'll be screaming incest."

Warwick's face tightened into a scowl, but Rhodri crowed in laughter. "Yeah, but you know the fan sites eat that up. Look at all the stuff about the brothers on *Supernatural*."

"I think Niall will give the fans all the homoerotic undertones they can ask for," Bevan agreed.

KIT GRINNED all the way home at the reactions to the first episode on the fan sites. He hoped Devon and Jonathan had made it to his house. They'd called as he was leaving Colm's to say they had finished refilming the two critical scenes between Arthur and Lancelot that had gotten damaged during editing. Niall had needed them to reshoot the scenes immediately so the episode would be ready on time.

He pulled in the driveway and saw Jonathan and Devon sitting on his porch steps, beers in hand. "Rough shoot?" he asked, getting out of the car.

"Not really," Jonathan answered, setting his bottle on the step and standing as Kit approached. "Just bad timing that we had to miss the get-together." He wrapped an arm around Kit and pulled him in for a quick kiss as soon as he moved within reach.

"What did you think of the first episode?" Devon claimed his own kiss as soon as Jonathan released Kit. "Did the transition from young Arthur to our king here work as well as it looked in the dailies?"

"It worked amazingly well," Kit enthused, opening the door and gesturing for his lovers to go inside. "Everything looked incredible. And we found a fan site when we were surfing for viewer reactions. They're already totally convinced Arthur was scoping out his knights."

"Not in the first episode," Jonathan protested.

"Of course not—neither of us has arrived at Camelot yet," Devon added with a grin at Kit.

"Come on, I emailed myself the link to the site so I could keep checking it," Kit said. "I'll show it to you." He went into his room and settled on his bed, popping open his laptop while he waited for his lovers to join him. Pulling up the site, he tipped the screen so they could see it more easily. "There. See?" He scrolled down until he found one of the more memorable quotes. "She says, 'I swear, Arthur was checking out Kay's arse through the whole coronation'. So, Jonathan, something you want to tell us?"

"Éamon wasn't around long enough for anything to happen," Jonathan answered with a straight face, though his blue eyes sparkled with humor. "He was only able to get a short break from the film he's finishing up to let Niall show the grown-up Kay with Arthur in the 'sword-from-the-stone' and coronation scenes." He glanced at the laptop again, shaking his head. "Can't say that I remember his ass in particular. In fact, if I remember the day we were filming the coronation, I was more concerned with the way my own ass was feeling."

"That's right, it was the first week after we'd gotten together, wasn't it?" Devon's expression was smugly satisfied. "I can see that you might have been a bit… sensitive."

"And I sure as fuck wasn't checking out anyone else," Jonathan asserted. "I could barely believe I was lucky enough to be with the two of you at all."

"We're the lucky ones," Kit said with a lascivious grin, running his hand down Jonathan's chest. "But this isn't about you anyway. It's about Arthur. No reason Arthur shouldn't have been checking Kay out. After all, he wasn't married or even engaged at that point, and Kay is a fine-looking man. Not as fine as Percival and Lancelot, maybe, but if I hadn't met you—and if Éamon weren't so totally married to Glynn—I wouldn't have kicked him out of bed."

"I guess I should consider myself fortunate that you saw me first, then," Jonathan countered. "Anyway, Kay is Arthur's foster brother—even if Niall plans to play up the idea that Arthur is attracted to one or two of his knights"—he caught Kit's wandering hand and dropped a kiss on the palm, then reached across to where Devon half-reclined on Kit's other side to squeeze Devon's thigh—"Kay wouldn't be one of them."

"I wouldn't put anything past Niall if he thinks it would draw viewers," Devon responded. He leaned over Kit to pull Jonathan toward him and capture his lips in a short, hard kiss. "But Éamon would have to get past me and Kit first if he thought he could make a move on you."

"Damn straight," Kit agreed, leaning up and nuzzling their cheeks until he could join the kiss. It was as awkward and messy as only a kiss between three men could be, and far more perfect than any kiss with any past lover.

"What else do they have to say?" Devon asked when the three of them broke apart to catch their breath. "Do the fans find our king as irresistible as we do?"

"Pretty much," Kit said, scrolling down to some of the later comments. "Look at this one. '*Sigh* Jonathan Braedon is just dreamy. I wonder if he's seeing anyone.' Or this one. 'Jonathan Braedon is the hottest thing on two legs!'"

"That's only because they haven't seen you and Devon yet." Jonathan shook his head. He had his fans, but he didn't consider himself a sex symbol. "Once the episodes with you two air, the fans will be going wild for you."

"Don't sell yourself short—we're only the first to give you the appreciation you deserve." Devon grinned. "Though I think whoever wrote that first comment might be surprised if she knew who you're really 'seeing.'"

"She might be," Kit agreed, not sure he wanted to bring up the rest of what he'd read at Colm's, but Jonathan and Devon had a right to know so they could be prepared. "But I don't know that they all would be. There was already some speculation about what might be going on behind the scenes, given the number of gay actors Niall cast."

Jonathan frowned. "Some people don't seem to understand that it's acting," he said. "I can't tell you the number of times I've read that I must be seeing whatever actress I was starring with in one movie or another. It's one reason I had a rule never to get involved with a costar— until the two of you were too damn seductive to resist."

"I've stopped paying attention to anything written about me," Devon retorted. "Lord knows I'm no saint, but I couldn't possibly have shagged everyone I've been paired up with in the press."

Kit chuckled. "They may've been right a time or two where I was concerned, but with the exception of the fact that I have two lovers instead of one, the idea that I'm shagging you two isn't any big deal for my reputation. Everybody already knows I'm gay."

"And I don't give a rat's arse what they say about me." Devon glanced at Jonathan, who was gazing at the computer screen with an unfocused expression. "What about you, Jon?" he asked in a less assertive tone. After all, they hadn't really talked about anyone outside the relatively closed production set finding out about their relationship. "Will it be a problem if people start speculating about you personally, not just about Arthur as a character?"

Jonathan didn't answer immediately. It wasn't that he hadn't considered the effect that being identified as gay, or at least bi, might have on his career before this. But that wasn't the main reason he'd decided against acting on his attraction to men until now. Having his preteen son living with him as much as he could when he wasn't filming on location somewhere was a much bigger factor. But now that he'd relinquished that self-imposed limitation, he'd have to deal with the repercussions, both with Josh and with the media. He had a feeling that breaking the news to his son would be by far the easier of the two.

"I think given the homoerotic undertones Niall is weaving into the series, there would be speculation even if this hadn't happened between us," he said finally. "And I don't think I need to validate speculation with a reaction, whether it's true or not." He'd have to talk to Josh, and soon; he owed that to his son. But no one else, other than possibly his ex-wife, Jean, had any need to know what was going on in his personal life. His feelings for Devon and Kit were too new and precious to him to want to see them reduced to crude tabloid fodder.

"So no, it's not going to be a problem," Jonathan concluded. He looked at first Devon, then Kit. "Let the fans speculate all they want. It doesn't matter what they imagine, as long as we know the truth."

"Speaking of homoerotic undertones," Kit drawled, running his hand up Jonathan's thigh, his relief at hearing that what he'd read on the fan site wouldn't cause problems between himself and his lovers palpable.

"What undertones are those?" Devon moved closer to Kit so he could reach across him to caress Jonathan as well. Jonathan shivered beneath the dual caresses with a rumble that sounded suspiciously like a purr at the touches that didn't go quite far enough.

"The ones that have Arthur, Percival, and Lancelot drooling over each other." Kit leaned in closer to nuzzle Jonathan's neck. "The ones that have them unable to keep their hands off each other whenever the other knights aren't looking. The ones that—"

"The ones that haven't aired yet," Jonathan reminded Kit, arching his neck to give greater access to his throat.

"And just imagine the posts once they do," Devon said with a leer.

Kit wasn't sure he wanted to imagine them, honestly, but he'd worry about that later. For now, he had two gorgeous men in his life… and a plan. "Keep Jon warm." He stood and put his laptop aside on his dresser. "I need to get something from the bathroom."

Devon murmured his agreement before nudging Jonathan down to recline against the pillows. Kicking off his shoes, he straddled Jonathan's hips, aligning their lower bodies and bending forward until their shoulders touched. "Warm enough?"

"Getting there." Jonathan threaded a hand into Devon's hair, pulling his mouth within reach. He slid his other hand under the hem of Devon's sweater, skimming the waist of his slacks before slipping lower and palming a firm buttock. "Plenty warm in here." He broke away with a squeeze and a grin.

"It's about to get even warmer," Kit replied, returning from the bathroom with his prize hidden behind his back. "Are you feeling adventurous tonight, Jon?" He hoped the answer was yes because he really wanted to use his hidden toy on Jonathan, but if he said no, Kit figured he could talk Devon into using it on him. He wasn't sure enough to suggest using it on Devon.

"As long as it doesn't end up on a fan site somewhere." Despite the teasing answer, Jonathan didn't try to hide his anticipation. It was usually Devon introducing the toys in their intimacy, so couldn't wait to see what Kit had behind his back. Judging from the gleam in Kit's eyes, Jonathan was pretty sure he'd enjoy it, whatever it was. Not that there'd been anything he hadn't loved yet with either of them.

"Been shopping on your own, sunshine?" Devon asked, his eyes darkening to a shadowed emerald.

Kit shook his head. "I've had these for a while, but we haven't been over here much and I kept forgetting to drop them in my bag." He tossed the string of anal beads on the bed. "I told you about them when we were discussing safewords, remember?"

Jonathan picked up the knotted string from the bed, trying to remember the specifics of the conversation. Most of his attention at the time had been focused on ensuring he'd never again make assumptions like the ones that had led to his using Kit much too roughly. "Beads?"

"Anal beads," Devon clarified, flicking the bottommost ball with a long finger and setting them swinging. "Who were you planning on using them on?"

"I was hoping Jon would be game since he's the one everyone was lusting over tonight, but if not, you can use them on me," Kit offered, not ready to give orders the way Devon had at the beach. He didn't think Jonathan would refuse if he did, but he wasn't ready for that kind of responsibility. He'd rather have it be a mutual decision.

"How do I put them in?" Jonathan asked, blue eyes darkening with arousal.

Kit shook his head. "You don't. You lie back and let me tease you with them while Devon drives you wild with his mouth."

Jonathan promptly dropped onto his back, spreading his arms wide. "Have at me!"

"Might be easier if you lose these first." Devon trailed his fingers up the inside of Jonathan's jeans. Jonathan gripped the duvet cover as Devon coasted over his hardening length through the denim, never lingering long enough in any one spot.

"It's called a zipper," Jonathan rasped. "You grab the little metal part and pull down, dammit."

"He knows what it is," Kit joked. "He also knows the value of anticipation." He picked up the beads and trailed them up the center of Jonathan's chest.

Swallowing hard, Jonathan seriously considered begging, but Devon had proven to him how much holding back could intensify his pleasure once he was finally allowed release. Instead he decided that if he had to wait, there was no reason he had to suffer alone. "If you're not going to use those on me," he murmured in his most sultry voice, "why don't you give me a demonstration, kitten?"

Devon had to bite back a grin at Jonathan's ploy. They'd both had ample evidence of how much Kit got off on being watched. Biding his time, he continued his meandering exploration of Jonathan's groin, knowing just where to touch and when to ease off to gradually stoke his arousal.

"I'll demonstrate," Kit promised, brushing the beads across Jonathan's lips. "On your tight arse, just as soon as Devon and I get you stretched out enough. The last few beads are pretty big." To demonstrate, he turned the string in the opposite direction so he was holding the smallest bead. "Open wide." The largest ball barely fit between Jonathan's lips.

Jonathan swiped his tongue over the bead's cool, smooth surface, moistening it before taking it into his mouth. Kit's eyes were on him as he worked the bead as if it were one of his lover's balls, swirling his tongue around the circumference, letting it slide partway out before sucking it in again. He could tell Kit was making the connection, his dark eyes kindling as Jonathan pushed the now-slick bead out of his mouth, wetting his lips.

"Fuck, Jon," Kit groaned. "I thought I was supposed to be teasing you!"

"I'll stop when you do," Jonathan countered, looking down at Devon, who was still driving him crazy with maddening strokes up and down his thighs. "What about you, Devon? If Kit uses those beads the way he said he would, I'm going to need something else to put in my mouth."

"Remind me to show you someday what happens to pushy bottoms." Devon chuckled, but he wasn't immune to imagining what Jonathan's mouth would feel like on his bollocks. He ran his thumbs up the defined ridge of flesh straining the front of Jonathan's jeans, flicked up the zipper's tab, and pulled it downward, so slowly Jonathan could feel each individual tooth as it slid through the catch.

Kit caught Jonathan's hands as they reached impatiently for his shirt. "You sure you want to do that?" he asked. "Devon already warned you about pushy bottoms. I've got a couple of ties in the closet that would make sure you couldn't do anything but lie here and take what we decide to do to you."

"Just remember that what goes around comes around," Jonathan warned as he settled back onto the duvet. Though he still itched to get his hands on his lovers in turn, Devon had finally eased his zipper down far enough to set his cock free from the constriction of its denim prison. He shifted his hips, the drag of the damp cotton sufficient to make him catch his breath.

Devon leaned close enough for Jonathan to feel the warmth of his breath against his insistent erection. "That's assuming we let you come at all, isn't it?"

"You wouldn't." Jonathan couldn't quite keep the statement from sounding like a question. Kit might tease him, but he wouldn't take it that far. After their weekend at the beach, he wasn't quite so sure about Devon.

"Maybe you should get those ties anyway," Devon suggested to Kit. He wasn't planning to make Jonathan suffer, but a little tension to get his blood heating wouldn't hurt.

Kit considered for a moment, then shook his head. "Jon can be good, can't you?" When Jonathan nodded, Kit held out his hand. "Arms," he demanded, catching the wrists Jonathan extended in a tight grip. He moved one to the post of his headboard, guiding Jonathan to wrap his hand around the wooden rod. "Hold that and don't let go." He repeated the action with his other hand on the opposite side of the headboard. "Now," he purred, opening the buttons on Jonathan's shirt, "we play."

"Might be hard to get off this way." Jonathan wriggled his arms without loosening his grip on the headboard.

"You're never hard to get off," Devon countered, working a hand into the open placket of Jonathan's jeans. Jonathan's cock jumped beneath his boxers, and Devon grinned. "I rest my case."

"I don't have to take your shirt off to drive you wild," Kit assured Jonathan, smirking at Devon as he trailed his fingers over Jonathan's nipples. "All I have to do is get it open. Now are you going to quit trying to run things and let us make love to you?"

Jonathan cocked an eyebrow, about to make a teasing comeback, but Kit's words made him pause. Here he didn't have to try to run things. He could trust these men—his lovers—to make him fly, if he'd just lie back and let them. Releasing a tension he hadn't realized he was holding, he focused on the sensation of Kit's hand on his chest, of Devon's easing inside his jeans. "Yes," he murmured, the word turning into a soft moan as Kit's fingernail grazed a tightened nub. "Let you do whatever you want."

Devon felt the moment Jonathan gave in. God in heaven, there was nothing that made him harder than a strong man willingly submitting to him. To them, he amended, meeting Kit's gaze across the breadth of Jonathan's chest. Between the two of them, they could drive Jonathan wild. Still tracing over the increasingly damp front of Jonathan's boxers, he slid the other hand beneath his waist. "Lift up," he instructed, tugging at the loop of Jonathan's jeans.

Eager to comply with anything that got him naked faster, Jonathan canted his hips, the movement pressing his chest more firmly into Kit's touch.

While Devon stripped Jonathan from the waist down, Kit turned his attention back to Jonathan's upper body. He lowered his head to nip at the expanse of skin, perhaps not as hard as Devon would have done, but hard enough to wring a groan from Jonathan nonetheless. Deciding he liked the sound, he shifted to better keep his balance and proceeded to trace the lines of Jonathan's muscles with his teeth and tongue.

Though he pulled Jonathan's jeans and boxers off quickly enough, Devon took his time on the way back up. Starting at his lover's toes, he searched out every sensitive spot, licking until Jonathan started to squirm, and biting just hard enough to win a gasp of pleasure. Using a forearm to hold Jonathan down when he tried to arch up, he worked his way upward until the crown of his head was bumping into Kit's from the opposite direction.

The heavy press of Devon's arm across his hips brought Jonathan out of the sensual haze his lovers' attentions had wrapped him in— though he'd defy anyone to keep their head with both Kit's and Devon's mouths roaming over every inch of skin they could reach. He thought about asking Kit when he was planning to use the beads but decided that might sound like he was trying to run things again. He settled for spreading his legs a little wider, hoping at least one of his lovers would take the hint.

"I think someone's in a hurry," Kit drawled, Jonathan's restless movement drawing his attention. He reached in the drawer and grabbed the tube of lube. "Switch places with me, Devon, so I can introduce our king to his new lover."

Rising to his feet, Devon stripped off his own clothes and moved to the head of the bed, settling with his back to the headboard and a knee on each side of Jonathan's shoulders. He wanted to watch Kit tantalize Jonathan with those beads. A warm swipe over his bollocks snapped his gaze back to the man beneath him.

"You can't expect me to resist temptation when you dangle it right in my face." Jonathan drew his tongue over the crinkled skin again with an unrepentant smile.

"I think we've created a monster," Kit quipped as he slicked his forefinger with lube and trailed it over Jonathan's bollocks. He worked the tip inside the ring of muscle, coating Jonathan's entrance well. When it relaxed around his finger, he withdrew and drizzled a generous amount of lube over the strand of beads. "I've tried to warm them up, but this may be a little cold at first," he warned Jonathan as he pressed the first bead against his arse.

Jonathan wasn't sure whether his shiver was from the coolness of the bead or the unaccustomed pressure. Though it certainly wasn't the largest thing he'd taken inside him—the plug Devon used at the beach house was significantly bigger—there were at least a half dozen beads on the cord, each one wider than the last. Willing himself to relax, he let Kit press the first bead inside, gasping at the stretch and release of muscle.

Seeing the bead pop inside, seeing Jonathan consciously give in to the pressure and the novelty of the toy, Kit stroked his hand up Jonathan's thigh at the same time he bent his head and licked a long stripe along the underside of his weeping cock. "Do you have any idea what it does to me to watch you give in like you do?"

"I like letting you watch," Jonathan admitted, glancing up to include Devon. "Like knowing I'm in your hands." His gaze returned to Kit, who still hadn't removed any of his clothes. "I'd like watching you, too, undressing for me. Knowing I'd be able to feel your skin against mine, the way I can feel Devon."

His pride and his arousal swelling at Jonathan's admission, Devon leaned forward to run his hands down the strong chest. When Kit scooted back on the bed to start pulling off his shirt, Devon slid to one side so he wouldn't block Jonathan's view. Not that he'd object to watching Kit's delectable striptease himself. Tracing one finger over the hint of stubble on Jonathan's chin, he wrapped the other hand around his own erect cock, rubbing circles over the sensitive tip with his thumb.

Feeling both his lovers' eyes on him, Kit took his time unbuttoning his shirt, finally letting it fall from his arms. He unsnapped his jeans and shimmied to get them over his hips, exaggerating the movement suggestively. "All of it?" he teased, toying with the waistband of his boxers as he stepped out of his jeans.

"Fuck yes, all of it," Devon rasped before Jonathan could answer.

Kit grinned and lowered the elastic slowly, deliberately keeping the head of his cock inside the cloth as he revealed more and more of his treasure trail. Finally, though, the shaft popped free, and he kicked the boxers off his feet, more interested in getting his hands on Jonathan again than in continuing to provoke him. "Ready for the next bead?" he asked, tugging on the cord just enough to pull the first bead so it stretched

Jonathan's entrance again. He couldn't stop the groan that escaped at the sight of the silver ball in his lover's body.

"Do it," Jonathan answered hoarsely, fingers tightening around the wooden posts of the headboard.

Recognizing the effort Jonathan was making to relax as Kit worked in the next bead, Devon leaned forward to nip at Jonathan's pebbled nipples. "You're doing fine, love. Making us proud."

"So proud," Kit echoed as he pressed the first bead back inside and added the second. It stretched the crinkled skin wider than the first had, but not as wide as Kit's or Devon's cock would. The motion was different from any other kind of fucking, the beads moving independently, bumping against each other, hitting in different places at unpredictable times. "You're the most incredible thing I've ever seen."

"Feels... good. More?" Jonathan's request was meant for Kit and Devon both. The erotic stretch of Kit's beads and the nips and tugs of Devon's mouth moving over his chest were both delicious but not enough to sate his growing hunger to feel, offer, give all of himself to both his lovers.

Devon glanced up at Kit, raising an eyebrow in silent question. Though they hadn't planned any of this ahead of time, Kit had taken the lead so far, and Devon was willing to let him continue to direct the action.

"Arthur won't have any shirtless scenes for a few days," Kit mused aloud with a nod toward Devon. "I think you should decorate our king since he likes the feel of your teeth so much."

Convinced by Jonathan's sudden hiss of inhaled breath that he liked that idea—not that he needed any more evidence to know exactly how much Jonathan liked it when things got a bit rough—Devon nuzzled though the wedge of soft hair coating Jonathan's chest. Latching on to a spot a few inches below the notch of his throat—low enough not to be seen but high enough that the rub of his costume would remind Jonathan of this night for the next few days—Devon bit down, sucking on the skin between his teeth until the blood rose to the surface. Jonathan groaned, and Devon lapped over the purpled mark, then moved lower, to a spot just below the dip of Jonathan's bottom rib.

"Fuck, Devon." Jonathan's voice was rough with desire. "Fuck yeah. Want your marks on me."

Kit smiled at the harsh edge to Jonathan's voice. Deciding he wanted to add to it, he worked the third bead, this one significantly wider than the first two, into Jonathan's passage, bending his head and licking around the stretched entrance as he did. He could taste the salt of Jonathan's sweat and smell the musk of his arousal, the combination serving to fire his own need. Lifting his head a little, he closed his mouth around the tip of Jonathan's cock, sucking it clean.

"God, Kit...." Jonathan's words morphed into an incoherent moan. He clenched around the beads filling him, the motion enough to shift them against his prostate. Light flared behind his closed eyelids, spreading through his nerves in jolts of sensual energy. "Not gonna... last if you... do that."

"Who says we want you to last?" Devon moved down to the loose flesh where Jon's hip met his thigh. Head brushing against Kit's, he turned and swiped his tongue quickly over the place where Kit's lips stretched around the crown of Jonathan's cock, gleaning a taste of both his lovers before lowering his head and raising another love bite in the crease of skin.

Kit stirred the beads in Jonathan's passage, popping the third one in and out of his tight entrance to tantalize him more. When Jonathan squirmed harder, Kit straddled one firm thigh to help hold Jonathan in place and pushed the fourth bead inside along with the others. Releasing Jonathan's cock long enough to speak, he peered up at his lover. "That's the middle bead. The others get bigger. Tell me if they get too big."

"You've had a plug in that's bigger than that," Devon observed, not seeing any sign that Jonathan was in distress. In fact, judging by the slightly unfocused look of his blue eyes, their lover was sinking further into subspace. Sliding a hand under the thigh Kit wasn't kneeling on, Devon pulled it outward, widening the space between Jonathan's legs. Besides giving him better access to Jonathan's body, the move was enough to set the beads shifting inside.

"Mmn-hmmn," Jonathan hummed in agreement, finding speech more difficult as the fullness within him grew. The wider diameter burned when Kit inserted it, but the pain quickly turned into a heat that spread through his body every time the beads moved inside him. "Want more. Want it all."

Kit hoped Jonathan wouldn't change his tune when the bigger beads went in. The one already inside him was about the thickness of

Kit's cock with the last one being nearly half again that size. Still, he had to trust both his lovers to know their own limits. Sucking Jonathan's cock back into his mouth, he popped the fifth bead past the guardian ring and into Jonathan's body, feeling the telltale tensing and then the deep sigh as Jonathan breathed past the inevitable pain and found the pleasure to be had in the stretch.

The pain was more intense this time, enough to tamp down Jonathan's impending need to come, but once the first pangs eased, he found himself loving the stretch, the heaviness, even the burn. Being breached at his lovers' hands, because they wanted him to accept it and he wanted to please them, only added to the intensity. He wondered how far he could let them stretch him, if the feelings would continue to grow more powerful. "More," he pleaded. "Let me take them all."

Kit debated trying to distract Jonathan from the initial burn, but after a moment, he decided it was better for his lover to be fully aware of what he was doing. To that end, he lifted his head and nudged Devon's shoulder, motioning for him to pause a moment as Kit pressed the penultimate bead against Jonathan's entrance. "Take a deep breath," he urged.

Jonathan filled his lungs, holding the breath as Kit eased the cool silver globe inside. He released the air slowly, in little huffing exhalations as he let the pain wash over him, through him, until he was floating on top of it.

"Sweet God, you're so hot like this, Jon," Devon growled, gliding a hand across the reddened entrance to cup their lover's heavy sac in his palm. "Giving yourself to us completely. Trusting us completely."

"Know you'll... take care of me." Jonathan wished he could use his hands so he could touch his lovers, to reinforce the connection that linked the three of them so intimately, but he wouldn't disobey the command Kit had given him. He'd have to rely on his voice to convey the depth of his emotions. "Always, since the first time."

"Every time," Kit promised, the desire to kiss Jonathan nearly overwhelming. Devon was blocking his access, however. He poked Devon's hip with one finger. "You're in my way. I want to kiss Jonathan."

"When did you get so bossy?" Devon grumbled, though he could understand the need behind Kit's request. He paused to claim his own quick taste of their lover's lips before sitting up to watch Kit kiss Jonathan.

Ignoring Devon's comment, Kit swatted him on the shoulder for taking liberties before leaning up to kiss Jonathan deeply. Their tongues twined together in an intimate, soulful kiss that left Kit's head spinning and Jonathan panting for breath. "Ready for the last one?" Kit asked. "Once it's in, the pain's over, and all that's left is pleasure."

"'S always pleasure." Jonathan's words were slurring, the rush of Kit's lips opening against his, Kit's body covering him, intoxicating him. "Re-ready," he panted, letting the tension seep from him with the words. "Please."

Kit nodded and sat back on his heels, adding more lube to the already slippery strand, not wanting there to be any friction as the last bead popped in. He nudged it against Jonathan's distended entrance, but the muscle didn't give right away, and he had to push harder to get it inside. It finally went past Jonathan's sphincter with an audible pop. Kit winced in sympathy, but a glance at Jonathan's face revealed only bliss.

Devon's cock was heavy against his belly as he watched Jonathan ride through the strain of accepting the final bead. It might not have been the widest he'd ever been stretched, but even a plug wasn't as heavy and filling as the full length of beads. Judging by the sigh as Jonathan's lids fluttered closed, he was enjoying the sensation as much as Devon was enjoying it vicariously. He had to hand it to Kit; the lad had the makings of a fine Dom in him. Devon froze for an instant as the thought stirred old memories to life, but he pushed them away, focusing on the man beside him instead. Deciding Jonathan deserved a reward, he leaned forward, dragging his tongue over the dilated muscle before opening his lips around the heavy bollocks and taking them into his mouth.

"You're blocking my view, bastard," Kit groused affectionately, rapping Devon on the head. "How'm I supposed to drive Jonathan wild when I can't see what I'm doing?"

"Bitch, bitch." Devon caught Kit's hand and nipped at the palm lightly enough to just catch the skin already toughened from the sword practice all their roles required. "Keep hittin' me with this and you'll draw back a stump." He pressed a kiss into the same spot as proof he was only teasing and then returned to nuzzle the smooth skin under

Jonathan's bollocks. "Remind me to blindfold you sometime to prove how much you can feel when you can't see."

The teasing exchange between the two barely registered in Jonathan's consciousness. All he knew was that he missed the feel of their hands and lips on his body and that he desperately needed to come. He tried to reclaim their attention, but all that came out was a needy-sounding whimper.

"I think Jonathan likes us fighting over him," Kit joked, sliding his hand back between Jonathan's thighs to find the end of the string of beads. He tugged lightly on it, pulling the beads back toward him before switching direction and pushing inside with his fingers, driving the balls deeper into Jonathan with each bit of pressure he applied.

The whimper morphed into a smothered wail, making Devon's lips twitch in sympathy. "Maybe so, but I expect he'd like to come even more." He slid forward until he was level with Jonathan's face, cupping Jonathan's stubbled chin with one hand while continuing the intimate caress with the other. "Am I right, Jonathan? Do you want us to let you come?"

Jonathan had to drag in two gasping breaths before he could speak. "Fu-fuck yes," he stuttered as he tried to find his voice. "Please. Make me come."

"Only if you promise to make us come when you're done," Kit bargained. He didn't know what they could use as a safeguard to make sure Jonathan kept his word, but honestly, Kit wasn't worried. He and Devon had been finding ways to share Jonathan since the first time.

"Promise," Jonathan agreed immediately. He'd have agreed to anything in that instant to earn his release, though what Kit was asking was hardly a penalty. Seeing to his lovers' pleasure only guaranteed extending his own.

"Did you honestly think he'd say no?" Devon grinned at Kit and then bent down to claim Jonathan's mouth in a fierce kiss, hard enough for his teeth to bruise the parted lips. Once he pulled away and moved down the bed again, though, he curled his lips over his teeth before taking Jonathan's leaking cock deep into his mouth.

Kit had expected exactly the response he got, but he wasn't going to tell Jonathan that. Then again, neither Jonathan nor Devon seemed particularly interested in continuing the conversation. Kit set about adding his own layer of sensation over Devon's sucking, playing with the beads in earnest, bumping them together as he fucked Jonathan with them.

The unyielding wood of Kit's headboard dug into Jonathan's palms as he grasped the posts like a lifeline. The implicit restraint and Kit and Devon leaning over his thighs as they teased and tantalized him were all that was keeping him tethered to the bed. The dual sensations of Devon's mouth on his cock and Kit's fingers sliding in and out of him, each pass nudging one of the beads against his sweet spot, had him soaring. His brain had disengaged from his body, overloaded by the jolts of pleasure that zinged in ever-faster waves across his synapses, electrifying every atom of his being. Words were beyond him, a low keen like the hum of a power line the only sound he seemed capable of making.

Devon knew the instant they'd pressed Jonathan to his breaking point. The muscles of his abdomen tensed, freezing in a fleeting instant of agonized anticipation. Then Jonathan cried out hoarsely, his cock surging in Devon's mouth. Devon swirled his tongue over the pulsing crown, adding to the tremors of orgasm shaking Jonathan's body.

The contractions of Jonathan's guardian muscle around the tips of Kit's fingers made him wish another, more sensitive appendage was feeling that massage, but there would be time for that later. Instead he stroked his hand over Jonathan's inner thighs soothingly, helping him to come down from the powerful orgasm.

When Jonathan's shaft stopped twitching in his mouth, Devon lifted his head and leaned forward, tipping Kit's chin toward his. Capturing Kit's lips, he pushed his tongue inside, sharing the salty taste of Jonathan's release.

Kit sucked the flavor from Devon's tongue, surging forward to catch every last droplet, his hand resting tenderly on Jonathan's thigh even as he all but attacked Devon's mouth. When he could taste nothing but Devon, he broke the kiss and smiled at their lover, still obediently clutching the headboard. "You all right up there, Jonathan?"

"Wondered when you'd remember about me," Jonathan rasped, still tingling with the aftershocks of a fiercely powerful climax. Needing to return at least a portion of the pleasure he had received, he wiggled his arms, even that motion enough to set the beads still filling him moving and triggering another wave of pleasure. "Can I let go of these now so I can see about keeping my promise?"

"Aren't you forgetting something, stud?" Devon asked, reaching down to twist the cord dangling down Jonathan's crease. He glanced back at Kit, still willing to cede the dominant role. After all, Kit had been doing just fine so far. "Or did you have something else in mind before we set him free?"

"Just taking these out," Kit said, his hand joining Devon's on the string. "I don't want him moving unexpectedly and hurting himself." He glanced up at Jonathan. "They'll hurt more coming out than going in because you're not desperate for them now like you were then," he warned. "Just try to relax and let them go."

"I'm not sure I can get any more relaxed," Jonathan answered. Though the movement of the beads made him instinctively want to clamp down around them, he willed himself to lie still, reminding himself the sooner the beads were gone, the sooner one of his lovers could fill him in their place. "The two of you set me off like fireworks on the Fourth of July. I'm wiped out."

"I'd bet we can wring another pop or two out of you," Devon countered, pushing up to claim Jonathan's lips again, a lazier joining this time, intended to take his mind off Kit easing out the largest of the beads.

Seeing Devon doing his best to distract Jonathan, Kit tugged on the cord, popping the biggest bead out quickly, stroking Jonathan's thigh as his muscles twitched in response to the sudden stretch of his sphincter. "Easy," he soothed. "That's the hardest one. Each one gets smaller now."

"Might be easier just to yank them out all at once," Jonathan suggested when Devon let him up for air. "Like pulling off a bandage— just get it over with." He grinned at Devon and raised his head to resume the kiss, imagining he could still taste a hint of Kit—and of himself—on Devon's tongue.

"If that's what you want," Kit agreed, waiting until Jonathan was lost in the kiss again to pull the remaining beads free. Jonathan's body jerked hard, then subsided. Kit leaned down and kissed his belly tenderly.

"You're amazing, you know that?" He wanted to say more, but he didn't know if he could say the words.

"Me?" Jonathan wished more than ever for the use of his hands so he could pull both the men who'd just brought him such pleasure into his arms. "All I did was lie here. You two are the amazing ones."

Devon wasn't sure he could make Jonathan understand how rare it was to find someone who gave himself as fully and unconditionally as Jonathan did. "Trusting us, making yourself vulnerable to us the way you did, giving us complete control of your pleasure—you have no idea how arousing that is."

"Why wouldn't I trust you? I know you'd never push me too far— even if I thought for a few minutes there that I couldn't take any more, it just made it that much more powerful in the end."

Kit couldn't stop a bit of a snicker at the image Jonathan's final words evoked, but he had other more important things to address. "But that's just it," Kit said. "You thought you couldn't take any more, but instead of calling a halt, you went with it, went through it because we wanted you to. That's a serious turn-on. And speaking of turn-ons...." He leaned up and claimed Jonathan's lips, then dropped a quick kiss on each wrist. "You can let go now. I've got something else powerful for your end."

Devon raised an eyebrow at Kit's assumption that Jonathan's end was his, but after all, Kit had been in charge and had well earned the prize. Devon slid an arm under Jonathan's shoulders to help him sit up as he flexed his stiffened fingers, then tweaked the tempting upper curve of buttocks with his other hand. "And while Kit's laying claim to this, I seem to remember you offering me your mouth."

"How do you want me?" Jonathan answered eagerly, working out the kinks in his wrists.

"Hands and knees," Kit said immediately, wanting to watch Jonathan being fucked from both ends. He reached for the lube and coated his cock, knowing he wouldn't be able to resist the temptation of Jonathan's upturned arse for more than the few seconds it took him to get in position. "That way I can see what Devon's doing to you while I pound you into the mattress."

"More like what Jonathan's going to be doing to me," Devon replied, kneeling up so he could lean back against the headboard. When he rested his hands on Jonathan's broad shoulders, his erection was at the perfect level for Jonathan's mouth.

Jonathan didn't wait to be asked, leaning forward to swipe his tongue over the reddened head of Devon's shaft. "Mmmnn." He licked his lips and met Devon's passionate stare. "Love the way you taste, babe."

"Good thing, since you'll be tasting it all." Devon resisted the urge to push his hips forward and force his way into Jonathan's mouth. Jonathan had proven to be as skilled at sucking cock as he was at everything else he set his mind to learn.

The moment Jonathan was settled on his hands and knees, Kit reached for his hips, steadying Jonathan for his inward plunge. He wouldn't have dared to thrust as hard or as deep if he hadn't spent the past half an hour stretching Jonathan with the beads, but as it was, he didn't feel any need to constrain himself. He groaned deeply with the pleasure of being enclosed in the slick heat, a little looser than usual because of the beads but still snug enough for him to feel it along every millimeter of his cock. "So hot," he said, bending to kiss Jonathan's back. "So fucking hot, letting us fuck you from both ends."

His lips wrapped around the crown of Devon's cock, Jonathan couldn't tell Kit that it was just as hot to be in the middle of two such incredible lovers. He'd just have to demonstrate instead. Clenching his muscles around the thickness of Kit's shaft, which was rubbing him in just the right spots in a way the randomness of the beads couldn't match, he tried to give back some of the same delicious sensations. Pleasuring Devon was even easier—all he had to do was take him deeper into his mouth, until Devon's wiry pubic hair was tickling his nose and the blunt head of his cock was nudging the back of his throat. Remembering something he'd read, he tried to relax the muscle there, letting Devon push deeper until he could swallow around the invasive shaft.

"Ah fuck, Jonathan, when'd you learn to do that?" Devon gasped when Jonathan deep-throated him like a pro. Jonathan smirked at him, lips stretched around Devon's cock as he let him slip back just long enough to swirl his tongue up and down his length before swallowing him again.

Kit wasn't going to last long after the provocation of fucking Jonathan with the anal beads and now being squeezed by his inner muscles. He wished he'd thought to put on his cock ring, but it was too late for that now. He wasn't about to pull out to go searching for it. He'd just have to hope being sandwiched between them was enough to get Jonathan ready again. He slipped a hand around Jonathan's waist and sought his lengthening shaft. Stroking it rapidly, he used every trick he'd ever learned about giving a lover a hand job to get Jonathan hot and bothered all over again.

Jonathan would have sworn he was past the age of being able to come twice in the space of minutes, but neither of his lovers seemed to have gotten that memo. His cock was as hard beneath Kit's palm as when he was pleading with them both to let him come the first time. Nor was the tightness in his balls any less intense than the first time—in fact, having Kit and Devon filling him rather than a cold length of beads was even more arousing. Feeling another climax bearing down on him, he focused on bringing his lovers with him, squeezing around Kit behind him and Devon before him, wanting to bring them both off before he lost himself again.

The increased suction of Jonathan's mouth was quickly bringing Devon close to losing control. He met Kit's eyes over Jonathan's back, the wide brown pupils hinting that the younger man's climax was nearly as imminent. He stretched a hand forward to clasp a muscular buttock, letting the force of Kit's thrusts push Jonathan forward on his straining erection. "Fuck, close," he warned.

"Come," Kit ordered. "Both of you. I want to feel it."

Jonathan's entire body clenched at Kit's command, his convulsive swallow around Devon's cock the trigger Devon needed. Throwing his head back with a shout, Devon pulsed down Jonathan's throat as Jonathan struggled not to lose a drop of the thick cream.

That, on top of Kit's commanding him to come, was all the spark Jonathan needed to go up in flames. The dominant tone seemed to come naturally to Devon, and it never failed to press Jonathan's buttons, but hearing it from Kit was an unexpected stimulation. Even Devon wasn't immune to it, if the way he'd come down Jonathan's throat was anything to go by. Then Kit's cock pressed directly against his prostate and Kit's grip tightened around his cock and Jonathan was coming again himself, splattering Kit's hand with his release.

Kit wished he could taste Devon's come in Jonathan's mouth the way he'd tasted Jonathan's on Devon's tongue, but the geometry of their situation made that impossible. He'd have to settle for the hot rush of fluid over his hand and the spasms of Jonathan's passage around his cock. It cindered his control, his orgasm tearing through him with all the force of a firestorm. His grip on Jonathan's hips tightened, his fingers digging in enough to bruise as he thrust deep one last time, panting against Jonathan's neck as he came and came and came in seemingly endless waves. He needed to move to keep from crushing Jonathan into the wet spot on the bed, but his muscles simply refused to obey him.

Jonathan's bliss-racked muscles couldn't withstand Kit's weight collapsing against his back. His joints buckled, and he dropped to the mattress, panting roughly, fortunately letting Devon's cock slide from his mouth first. Devon slipped beside them, turning Jonathan gently onto his side and pushing the tousled hair out of his eyes.

"Bloody amazing," Devon murmured, dropping a kiss to Jonathan's shoulder and levering up on an elbow long enough to press another to Kit's. Kit nestled immediately against Jonathan's warmth, and Devon eased back down, molding himself to Jonathan's side and curling a leg over both of his lovers', the three of them forming a sweaty, sated knot.

"HEY, KIT," Bevan called, coming to sit next to Kit in the catering tent on set. "I haven't seen you since the first episode aired. Getting too good to hang out with us?"

"Of course not," Kit protested. "The filming schedule has been crazy. That's all."

Bevan nodded sagely. "And what free time you do have, you've been spending with your lovers. I get that. We miss you, though. So where are the king and his champion anyway?"

"They were talking with Niall about a scene for this afternoon," Kit said. "Niall had something he wanted to try. It didn't involve Percival, and I couldn't think of a reason to hang around."

Bevan nodded again. "Yeah, you want to be careful. You probably don't want Niall finding out."

"What don't you want me finding out about?" Niall walked into the tent along with Jonathan and Devon. The stern expression on his face as he glanced at Kit was softened by the twinkle in his eyes.

"Um." Kit hesitated, eyes flying to Jonathan and Devon for guidance. "Well, you see, you didn't say it wasn't allowed and...."

"We're, uh... that is, Devon and Kit—well, they—we—" Jonathan stammered, uncharacteristically tongue-tied.

"What they're trying to say is that we're... seeing each other," Devon put in, though he couldn't force himself to state it more bluntly. He told himself it was out of respect for their director's dignity. "The three of us."

"Of course you're seeing each other. You're on set together all the time. What's that got to do with Kit not wanting me to find out about something?"

"He means they're sleeping together," Bevan tossed out helpfully. "All three of them."

He yelped when Kit kicked him underneath the table.

"Tell me something I don't know," Niall said with an indulgent shake of his head. "I know they're good actors, but nobody's that good. I have eyes even when they're looking through a camera lens."

"And it doesn't bother you?" Jonathan asked in relief and some disbelief. He'd never allowed his personal life to disrupt a film, but he'd never been in a situation anything like this before. Most directors he'd worked with frowned on relationships even between costars of the opposite sex. He'd half expected Niall to go ballistic when confronted with their ménage.

"Why would it?" Niall asked. "It's done wonders for your performances. In fact, I was thinking about refilming some scenes we did soon after you arrived because the difference in chemistry on film is startling. I also had a few thoughts for some shots I want to add while we're on location next month. Now that you aren't trying to hide, I can use your relationship to play up the suspicions I want to cast."

Kit looked back and forth between the director and his lovers. "Wait. You're asking us to mess around on set?"

"Within reason," Niall cautioned. "I was thinking some long, soulful looks, maybe a pair of entwined silhouettes on the wall of Arthur's tent. That sort of thing. If you agree, of course, since none of that was in the original script you read or the contracts you signed."

"Oh, I think we could force ourselves to go along with that." Devon grinned like a kid in a candy store. The real problem was going to be not getting carried away by their newfound freedom.

CHAPTER 21
CABIN FEVER

LIGHTNING FLASHED overhead as the car inched along the narrow track that pretended to be a road. The headlights barely penetrated the driving rain more than a foot or two, but Devon and Kit had no other choice. Mudslides had closed the main highway in both directions, and this was the only side road they'd seen. If they were in luck, they'd find a place to weather the storm. If they weren't, they would be spending the night trapped in Devon's car. "There!" Kit said urgently, pointing to the right. "I see a house. Maybe we can wait out the storm there."

Devon struggled to hold the car on the road's slick surface, his shoulder muscles tense with the strain of trying to keep the vehicle under control in the treacherous conditions. "Can't be soon enough for me." He scowled. "Never thought I'd hate anything worse than flying, but driving in this muck is coming close." The hours they'd spent in the close confines of the car were setting his nerves on edge almost as much as being trapped in an airplane did. He fishtailed the car down the unpaved drive, the normally hard-packed ground a swamp of slippery mud, before bringing it to a sliding halt near the building's front porch. A wave of relief washed over him at being able to escape the car's stifling atmosphere, even if it meant getting drenched in exchange. "Let's make a run for it."

Kit nodded, knowing all about Devon's claustrophobia. That was why they were in a car fighting this storm rather than taking a plane with the rest of the crew to start location filming on the Isle of Skye. As soon as the car stopped, he threw open the door and raced through the soaking rain toward the porch. He could hear—barely—Devon's footsteps splashing right behind him. It couldn't have taken them more than thirty seconds to reach the shelter of the covered terrace, but they were both soaked to the skin. "We look a mess," he commented, turning back to Devon. "I hope whoever lives here will take pity on us rather than running us off."

"They'd have to be more heartless than my ex-wife's solicitors to turn us away in a storm like this," Devon answered, shaking the water from his hair. He knocked heavily on the door, reasoning that the steady lash of the rain might make it difficult for anyone inside to hear them. When several moments passed with no response, he pounded even harder. "Looks like no one's home." He frowned, trying the doorknob to confirm it was locked. "We may have to do some breaking and entering."

"Before we break anything," Kit said reasonably, "let's look around for a spare key. Some people leave one under the mat or a flowerpot or something." He trailed off, feeling ridiculously young all of a sudden. It had seemed like a good idea when it occurred to him, but hearing it out loud, it sounded foolish.

"Worth a try," Devon agreed, crouching down to lift the small mat in front of the door. Sure enough, there was a key swimming in a puddle of muddy water. "Brilliant deduction, sunshine." Devon grinned, fitting the key in the lock and opening the door. "Let's get in and get dry."

Immensely relieved that Devon hadn't dismissed his notion out of hand, Kit preceded Devon inside, searching the wall for a light switch. He found one, but when he flipped it, nothing happened. "Bloody hell!" he muttered. "Electricity's out. Do you have a torch in your car? Because it's a long time 'til morning with nothing to see by."

"You expect me to run back outside for a torch in that?" Devon gestured at the torrential rain that made it almost impossible to see out the windows. "I'm not even sure I have one in the boot, and if I do, chances are the batteries will be dead. Let's see if the owners have some candles before we decide whether one of us needs to go back to the car, shall we?"

"I would have got it," Kit replied defensively, wishing Jonathan were there with them. He told himself that was ridiculous, that even before they'd started their threesome he and Devon had been friendly, maybe even friends. It didn't change his nervousness, especially after listening to Devon curse and rant as they fought the worsening weather. "I just wanted to know if you had one before I got wet again." He felt along the wall, hoping to find a fireplace. People kept candles on mantels, after all.

Devon waved his arms in the air ahead of him, managing to trip over only a piece or two of furniture before walking into something large and unyielding. Squinting in the almost nonexistent light, he was able to make out that it was some type of cabinet. He pulled open a drawer and rummaged through it blindly, shouting in triumph when his fingers closed around a familiar shape. "If they have candles, at least we can light them," he called, flicking the wheel of the lighter to spark it.

"Let the flame burn for a minute," Kit suggested. "So we can see if there're candles in the room."

Devon held the igniter down as long as he could, cursing when the flame burned his fingertips. Popping his thumb into his mouth, he lit it again with his other hand, holding it aloft. "Hurry up and find something before I burn m'fingers off," he growled.

In the dim light, Kit saw what he was searching for. On the mantelpiece sat four fat tapers. He grabbed two of them and made his way back toward Devon. "Here," he said. "Light these."

It took just a minute to find the wicks and send a flickering glow throughout the room. The area was small and stuffy but tidy, the furnishings sturdy and unpretentious. "Looks like it's maybe a weekend cottage," Devon conjectured. "Judging by the dust, I'd say no one's been here for at least several weeks." The unusual darkness outside the windows made the small room's walls feel as if they were closing in on him. He tried to swallow down his growing discomfort, hoping the dim candlelight would keep Kit from noticing his distress until he could get it under control.

"That's good for us," Kit declared, taking one of the candles. "Shall we try to find some towels?" He started toward the interior door of the room. "And we should try to call Jonathan. It's too late to call Niall, but we obviously won't be making it to filming tomorrow as planned."

"You find towels; I'll call Jonathan," Devon agreed, pulling out his cell phone. Hearing Jonathan's quiet, husky voice was just what he needed to calm his nerves and distract him from this bloody cabin fever. Devon pressed a speed dial button and held the phone to his ear, frowning and staring at the display when he didn't hear anything. "No signal," he complained. "How about yours, Kit?"

Kit's frown mimicked Devon's. He took out his phone and tapped it awake, but the familiar bars didn't appear. "Nothing." He grimaced. "I guess we won't be calling Jonathan after all." He disappeared down the hall and came back with an armload of towels. "We can get dry, at least."

Devon took a towel and dropped onto the couch with a sigh, rubbing it over his dripping hair. "Jonathan'll be pacing the floor until we call to let him know we made it," he muttered. He pulled his sopping shirt over his head and let it fall to the floor, toweling the moisture from his chest. "Damn it, I hate to think of him worrying about us." He frowned as he thought of their other lover, forced to stay behind to finish filming rather than leaving Glastonbury early for the long drive with them to the Isle of Skye, where they would film a series of scenes with Arthur and the knights on campaign.

They'd been looking forward to making this drive together for a lot of reasons, but especially as a way to distract Jonathan from the departure of his son, Josh. The youngster had come to visit from the States a little over two weeks ago, delighting everyone with his sense of fun and his unending curiosity about everything to do with filming. Jonathan hadn't wanted to put the boy back on a plane to fly home, but school was starting back up, and though the school had agreed to let him miss the first few days of classes, Josh finally had to leave. Jonathan had been quiet and withdrawn since his departure three days ago. And then Niall had changed the filming schedule, and Jonathan had to stay in Glastonbury another day before he could leave for the Isle of Skye, which would have made all of them late for filming if Jonathan drove with them.

"I know," Kit agreed, caught by the sight of the pale gold skin appearing in the candlelight. "I wish there was something we could do, but it'll have to wait until the storm passes for sure. Maybe then we'll be able to get a signal." Devon was trying hard to hide his uneasiness, but Kit had been watching closely for the signs. What Devon needed was a distraction, he decided, moving to his lover's side and pulling the towel from his hands. He had no idea how things would work between them without Jonathan there. They'd fucked and sucked and done all kinds of other things to each other, but only with Jonathan a part of it. That was beside the point now. Devon needed this and Jonathan wasn't here, which left Kit to take care of his antsy lover.

"In the meantime, let me help you relax," he purred, his voice deepening as he ran the towel over Devon's strong back.

A hum of pleasure rumbled through Devon's chest at the feel of Kit rubbing the towel over his chilled back. A pleasant ache started building lower down as Kit slid the towel around his ribs to drink up the dampness from his bare chest, relieving some of the tightness and making it easier for him to draw a steadying breath. Devon turned enough to catch the hem of Kit's damp T-shirt and pull it up over his companion's head. "Need to get your head dry before you catch cold," he teased, rubbing the shirt over the long dark strands before dropping it to the floor. "Can't have Percival fighting the sniffles."

"Lancelot either," Kit countered, leaning into Devon's warmth and rubbing the towel over his back. He hadn't realized how cold he was until he felt the other man's heat. Deciding he needed to feel even more of it, he reached for the button on Devon's pants. "We'll be warmer if we get out of these wet clothes."

Devon ran his hands down the smooth planes of Kit's chest, slicking away the moisture with his palms and then returning to linger over the lad's chocolate-drop nipples. *The lad*, Devon laughed to himself. Thinking of him that way was more habit than anything else— he'd realized Kit wasn't a lad the very first night, when they'd agreed to seduce Jonathan together. His palms coasted over the tightened disks, the evidence of Kit's arousal making his own cock thicken in response. Devon tried to remember exactly when he'd stopped seeing Kit as a rival for Jonathan's attention and realized he wanted Kit too. He found it hard to imagine now that he'd ever looked at the younger man without wanting to love him.

Kit moaned with pleasure at the attention paid to his nipples. His lovers had learned quickly that they could drive him out of his head with desire just by playing with him that way. His back arched as he pushed his chest against Devon's hand. A part of him felt awkward without Jonathan there too, but Devon's touch was distracting, demanding, and Kit relaxed into it, savoring being the sole focus of his lover's attention this once. He and Devon had come together because they both wanted to be with Jonathan, but trembling under Devon's touch, Kit could honestly say he wanted Devon as much as he had ever wanted Jonathan. Struggling for some semblance of coherency and grace, he pushed Devon's pants down, then fought with the buttons on his own jeans.

Kicking his slacks off his ankles, Devon covered Kit's hand with one of his own, popped open the button of his jeans, and slid the denim down the narrow hips. "Not bothering with underwear again?" he growled, his other hand dropping to curve over the swell of Kit's buttocks. "Jonathan's teaching you all kinds of bad habits."

"Are you complaining?" Kit asked on a gasp as Devon gripped his arse. "It's one less layer to get out of the way!" He loved those strong hands. Devon touched him with such authority, such possessiveness, that Kit just wanted to surrender to them and their magic.

"Can't argue with that," Devon agreed distractedly, cupping his palms around the chilled globes and pulling Kit's body flush against his. The heat of Kit's cock sliding against his quickly spread, and he hitched his hips forward, repeating the inflammatory friction.

"Bed!" Kit insisted, knees trembling as heat spread through him from every point of contact with Devon's warming skin. Even so, he knew his lover had to be as chilled as he was. "Surely there's a bed somewhere in this cabin."

"If our king was here, he'd have found it already." Devon chuckled. He turned Kit in his arms, facing him in the direction of the nearest doorway—which had the happy side effect of aligning his cock with the crease of Kit's arse. "Surely Percival's keen senses can track so simple a thing as a bed?" He nudged his hips, urging Kit forward and slipping into the warmly beckoning cleft.

Kit's head fell back on Devon's shoulder as he focused on making his feet work enough to carry him out of the room and into the hallway, not an easy task with the ample erection nudging his crease. "Percival's keen senses have been hijacked by Lancelot's cock," he retorted, reaching behind him to grab Devon's arse and keep him close as they searched for a bed. At this point Kit would just about take any horizontal surface. A flash of lightning illuminated the first room they entered, enough that they could see a large four-poster bed against one wall. "Found it," Kit pointed out redundantly.

"Cheeky lad," Devon grumbled, adding an extra push to seat himself even closer between said cheeks. The bedroom was even smaller than the parlor, but Devon barely noticed as Kit pushed back against him seductively. Kit's arse squeezing around the length of his cock felt so damned good he was tempted to take him just like this, pushed up against the bedpost, until he remembered something they were unlikely to find as easily as they had the bed—lube. Without it, as much as he wanted to sink himself into Kit's tight heat, he'd have to find another way to be sure his lover was ready for him first. With a sudden move, he lifted Kit into his arms and tossed him onto the bed.

Kit let out a shout of surprised indignation when he was summarily thrown onto the mattress. He might have protested more, but Devon followed him down onto the bed, spreading his legs and bending to lick a wet stripe up the underside of his cock. That silenced everything but a groan of heated pleasure. Even that sound strangled in his throat when the talented tongue slid lower , and Kit spread his legs even farther. "Oh fuck!"

Devon lifted Kit's hips and draped the long legs over his shoulders, opening his lover to him completely. With a possessive growl, he lowered his head, spreading the creamy cheeks apart to lick wetly over the delicate skin. He could taste traces of his own precome mixed with Kit's musky essence, and the flavors fed his hunger for more. Once he'd coated the entire crease with his saliva, he teasingly circled the wrinkled entrance, pressing around it and over it with the lightest of touches.

Kit writhed on the bed, tossing his head back and forth as Devon tantalized him. Devon knew what that particular caress did to Kit, knew that he would come apart in no time. "Please!" he begged. "Devon, fuck me!"

Kit's pleas were making Devon's cock granite-hard, but as badly as he wanted to give him what he was begging for, he was going to guarantee Kit was as well prepared as he could make him first. Holding Kit down with a large palm against his abdomen, Devon started to work his tongue inside the quavering channel. The first breach of the tight ring sent Kit's cock bouncing against the back of his hand. Devon curled his palm around it and stroked, pressing his tongue deeper until they were cheek to cheek. He might not be Jonathan, but he knew how to make Kit howl. He stroked the leaking cock at a demanding pace, trying to coax every bit of sensation he could out of his increasingly vocal lover.

"Oh shit," Kit cursed as Devon stimulated him inside and out. He'd thought he knew how good his lovers could make him feel, but this was different somehow. He was the undivided center of Devon's attention, and Devon was his only concern. He reached down and wrapped his hand around the other man's, helping Devon lavish pleasure on his aching erection.

Devon slid his tongue from the well-slicked channel and carefully slipped a thick finger in its place, putting pressure on Kit's prostate as he lapped over his tightening bollocks. He was so on edge himself that just the touch of Kit's hand covering his was nearly enough to shake his control. "Let go, kitten." The nickname felt natural to him for the first time. He couldn't see Kit's face in the dim candlelight from the other room, but he could imagine his flushed cheeks, his wide eyes, his mouth gasping with pleasure. "Come for me, Kit, only for me."

With you, Kit wanted to protest, but his body was no longer under his control. It reacted instinctively to Devon's command, to the combination of tenderness and passion he heard in the rich voice, and his cock twitched before spilling its load over his stomach and their entwined hands.

Devon slicked himself with the creamy fluid that flowed over his hand and pressed the head of his cock into Kit's still-trembling entrance. "Now," he groaned as he slowly pushed into the tight embrace he longed for. "Fuck, Kit, need—ah fuck!"

"Me too," Kit groaned as Devon's thick shaft split him open. It burned a little, but he was relaxed from his orgasm and stretched from Devon's tongue, and his body adjusted quickly to the now-familiar girth. He shifted, trying to get the angle right so Devon would hit his sweet spot.

All Devon's instincts screamed at him to push for his own release, but the unquenched hunger in Kit's voice drove him to hold on until he could take his lover with him. Sitting back on his heels, he wrapped his hands under Kit's back, careful to support his weight so the movement wouldn't put undue pressure on the rod that straightened his spine, and pulled Kit up against his chest. The change in position sheathed him even deeper in Kit's insistent heat. Biting his lip with the effort to hold back his climax, he palmed Kit's shaft and rocked his hips in short, jabbing thrusts. "S'good," he moaned. "So fuckin' good."

Kit shifted to get comfortable in the new position, pulling his knees up under him so he could react more readily to Devon's movements. The constant stimulation on his prostate along with Devon's hand on his cock had his desire stirring again almost immediately. He canted his hips a little more, picking up the pace as he rode Devon.

"Fuck yeah," Devon panted, letting Kit take control of their movements, his fist keeping pace with the changing tempo. His other hand cradled Kit's skull, holding it steady enough for him to take Kit's mouth, claiming it with all the power of his unsatisfied need.

Devon's mouth had always been Kit's undoing, and now, with Devon's unique flavor mingled with what had to be Kit's own taste, it was enough to set Kit's senses spinning out of control. He leaned into the kiss, trying to climb inside Devon. Anything to get closer to his lover… his love. Suddenly the mudslide, the weather, even Jonathan's absence faded into nothingness in the perfection of this moment, and he focused on the beauty of the present, of Devon's lips on his, Devon's hands on his body, Devon's cock inside him. He pushed down faster, nearly wild with the need to come again.

Devon groaned against Kit's mouth, the muscles in his neck cording with the effort to wait until he could bring Kit off a second time. Despite the coolness of the room, a sheen of sweat broke out over his skin, adding to the slickness where their bodies slid together. He could feel his orgasm threatening, his bollocks swelling with seed as he shook with his need for release. Tearing his mouth from Kit's, he cried out hoarsely, his fist flying over Kit's cock. "Now," he groaned, "God, Kit, now—can't—can't—"

The desperation in Devon's voice called to something within Kit, and a second climax built quickly. He tried to give voice to it, tried to tell Devon he didn't have to wait any longer, but the words wouldn't come, lost in a hoarse shout as his body convulsed in a second orgasm. He bore down on the cock inside him, hoping it was enough to trigger Devon's release as well.

The hot splash of Kit's come on his fist set off his own climax, pumping out of him in what felt like an endless wave of ecstasy. He bent his head to capture Kit's mouth again, more gently this time, as the tremors of their pleasure shook them both. Being trapped in this cabin no longer seemed so terrible. As long as Kit was with him, somehow it would be all right.

Leaning into the tender kiss, Kit let his breathing slow and his heartbeat settle, taking comfort in the familiar feeling of Devon's arms around him, hoping Devon would take comfort from his embrace. He had succeeded in a temporary distraction, but they could well be here for days. Kit smiled. He was up to the task.

CHAPTER 22
COMING WHEN CALLED

MORE OUT of habit than out of any real expectation of having a signal, Kit switched on his phone as he came back in from getting his and Devon's bags from the car the next morning. To his surprise, he had two little bars. "Devon!" he called excitedly. "I've got a signal. We can call Jonathan."

Devon walked into the living room from the small shower, one towel wrapped around his hips, the other rubbing at his damp hair. He peered out the window at the sodden scene. The rain had eased up from the torrential downpour of the night before, but fat drops still fell and splattered thickly in the mud-slicked drive. "Doesn't look like we'll be going anywhere for a while, until things dry out," he muttered. "At least we'll be able to let Jonathan know we're all right."

"I checked the kitchen, and it's well stocked," Kit told him, "so we're okay there. We just need to let Niall know where we are at this point, and Jonathan." He didn't feel a bit guilty about trying to reach their lover before calling their director. Smiling with anticipation, he pressed Jonathan's number on speed dial.

Jonathan stirred groggily from his awkward position on the... on the couch? It took him a disoriented moment to realize where he was. He must have fallen asleep there last night, waiting to hear that Devon and Kit were safe. It took him a moment longer to realize what had awakened him—a vibrating hum from under his left hip. His cell phone must have dropped from his hand when he fell asleep, after what felt like days of trying both his lovers' numbers over and over again. He fumbled for the phone and raised it to his ear. "H'lo?" he mumbled anxiously.

"Jonathan?" Kit asked when he heard the sleepy voice on the other end of the line. Feeling silly, he told himself that of course it was Jonathan. "It's Kit. Devon and I are stuck in a cabin halfway to the Isle of Skye. There were mudslides on the road in both directions, so we pulled over to wait out the storm."

Jonathan shut his eyes and let the warm honey tone of Kit's voice soak into his soul. The specific words didn't register, but that didn't matter. They were safe—they were both safe. Rationally he had known they were probably not in any real danger, but he hadn't been feeling very rational last night when he hadn't been able to get an answer on either of their phones for hours and the news of mudslides in Scotland had come across the TV. He offered a silent prayer of thanks to whatever deity might be listening, then realized Kit had stopped speaking and was probably waiting for some response. Since he had no real idea what his lover had said, he just murmured, "I'm glad you're both safe. I was—I got a bit worried when I couldn't reach you."

"We tried calling last night," Kit told him, "but we couldn't get a signal through the storm. This morning, though, I turned on my phone and there it was. I called as soon as I realized." He felt bad for having spent the night tucked safely in Devon's arms while Jonathan was back in Glastonbury alone and worried. "How are you holding up?" He didn't want to mention Josh by name and bring back Jonathan's blues.

"I'm okay now that I've heard from you." Jonathan stretched to crack the stiff joints in his back. "Where are you, anyway?"

"Middle of fucking nowhere," Kit replied with a laugh. "The road was blocked, so we turned back, only to find out that another mudslide had blocked the road behind us. We saw a turnoff and took it and found a little cabin. Nobody's here, so we let ourselves in."

"Breaking and entering? Let's hope I won't have to come bail you out of jail," Jonathan teased, relieved that they'd found a place to take shelter for the night. He knew Devon would have had a hard time if they'd had to spend the night confined in the cramped space of the car. "How's Devon doing?"

Kit looked over at Devon, leaning against the countertop. "He's wearing a towel and looking sexy as hell," Kit joked. "Seriously, though, he's doing okay. We had some bad minutes in the car, but we took care of each other."

Devon watched Kit's changing expressions as he responded to Jonathan's side of the conversation: joy, concern, mischief. A swell of tenderness for Kit warmed him. He could feel a flush of color staining his cheeks, and out of habit he hid his discomfort behind teasing. "I'll say we took care of each other," he growled loudly enough for Jonathan to hear.

"Am I to understand that Mister Aldridge used the fact that he had you alone, without me there to chaperone, to take advantage of you?" Jonathan responded in mock-outrage. He could imagine how his two lovers would have taken care of each other. Just the thought was enough to stir his cock to semihardness.

Kit grinned and blew Devon a kiss. "He took terrible advantage of me without you to make him behave," he protested. "He... he... made me come... without him!"

"Sounds like you both came without me," Jonathan groused, shifting position to ease the growing ache in his groin. He didn't really begrudge them the time together, but dammit, he missed them already! *Is this what it will be like when filming is over and we go our separate ways?* he wondered sadly. Pushing the depressing reflection from his thoughts, he turned back to his two randy lovers. "And I suppose you were too shocked by his behavior to do anything about it?"

"I was absolutely horrified," Kit insisted with another grin for Devon, beckoning him closer. "But I got my revenge. I held him down and rode him until I got what I wanted."

Jonathan's cock pressed insistently against the zipper of his jeans at the positively sinful image Kit's words conjured. He could picture them both so vividly—Devon's strong body sprawled across the bed, Kit crouched over him, sliding onto the other man's beautiful thick cock, his dark head thrown back in ecstasy as he pushed down, taking it all inside him in one slow glide. "Fuck," Jonathan whispered, easing down his zipper to give himself some relief from the painful pressure.

The change in Jonathan's tone sent lust pulsing through Kit too. He had been teasing when he started the conversation, but all of a sudden, the teasing was gone. "I want—" he replied in the same low, desperate tone. "I want to push you back on the bed and slide over you, feel you slide inside me."

"Fuck, Kit," Jonathan moaned, wedging the phone against his shoulder so he could free both hands to push his jeans open. "What would you do to me? What did you do to Devon? Tell me."

Kit's eyes closed as he brought back his memories of the night before. "I'd straddle you," Kit said softly, "after you stretched me with your tongue so I was empty and aching for you. And then I'd scoop the come off my stomach and smear it on your cock as lube. When you were all slick, I'd sit down hard on your cock, feeling it split me open, and then I'd ride you until we both came."

"You know sod-all about building anticipation, do you, lad?" Devon laughed at Kit's blunt description. Even so, his own arousal was starting to tent his towel as he dropped onto the couch next to his lover. "Ye're supposed to make phone sex slow and seductive, not 'wham bam and thanks for calling'!"

"Fine," Kit replied. "You talk to him." He handed Devon the phone with a leer. "Show me how it's done."

Devon took the phone with an answering leer and leaned back comfortably into the sofa cushions. "We were wet," he purred without preamble, his voice deep and husky with promise. "Dripping wet, water trailing down over both our bodies. We couldn't wait to get naked." He let his hand drift down to his shaft, which his own words had caused to stiffen even further. "Are you naked, Jonathan?"

Kit decided it didn't matter if Jonathan was naked or not. Devon was almost there, only the towel in the way, and Kit's still-damp T-shirt and jeans that he'd thrown on to go outside were suddenly uncomfortable. Standing so he was in Devon's line of sight, he stripped.

"Give me a minute," Jonathan gasped, switching the phone to speaker before he pulled his shirt over his head and kicked his jeans to the floor. Devon's voice could make him hard just ordering drinks in a bar—when he set out to sound provocative, he could make a statue come. "Naked," Jonathan admitted, playing in the light hairs of his abdomen. "You too, Devon?"

Unknotting the towel, Devon stroked his hand over his erection, smearing the droplets of fluid that had already seeped from the tip at just the thought of Jonathan naked for him. "Fuck yeah," Devon growled, motioning for Kit to sit back beside him. "Naked for you—hard for you." He raised his fingers to his lips, licking them with a quiet hum of pleasure. "Wet for you."

"We both are." Kit sat next to Devon and snagged the phone from his hand. After turning on the speaker, he set it on the table in front of them.

"Dammit, Devon," Jonathan groaned, his cock twitching against his belly at the decadent words. It would feel good to take it in his palm, but it was too soon for that. He trailed his fingers up his torso instead, teasing at a hard nipple. "Wish I was there with you—with you both," he added as Kit's words made his shaft jump again.

"We didn't have any lube," Devon continued, reaching forward to run a teasing finger over Kit's bare chest, circling one of the flat brown nipples without touching it. "It was too fucking dark and wet to go outside to get any from our bags. So we had to… improvise." He hissed as Kit pulled the teasing finger to his mouth and bit down on it, hard enough to distract him from the phone and Jonathan for the moment.

Kit grinned when he heard the sound that escaped Devon. Feeling creative, he lowered his head and bit one of the puckered nipples that beckoned him so temptingly. He didn't hold back, knowing Devon wouldn't mind if he was rough.

Jonathan grinned at the hoarse exclamation that escaped from Devon. "What did Percival do to you?" he asked, knowing his lover's playful side all too well.

"He bit m'bleeding nipple!" Devon complained, grabbing Kit's head with his free hand and pulling it closer. "The only way he's getting away with it is if he bites the other one too."

Kit didn't hesitate. He bit down hard on the other pebbled nub. "I didn't bite you hard enough to make you bleed, you Northern bastard."

Jonathan pinched and pulled at his tightened nubs, imagining—wishing—it was his lover's mouth, either one of them, teasing him that way. "I'd bite you too, Devon," he promised, pulling on his aching flesh. "Good and hard, the way you like it."

Devon pulled Kit into a deep kiss. "There was no biting last night," he continued after he'd released Kit's mouth and resumed exploration of his smooth olive skin. "I had to get him ready for me, since he was begging me so nicely to fuck him into the mattress."

"Begging you?" Kit retorted. "Try distracting you!"

"And just who was begging 'Please, Devon, fuck me'?" Devon countered, stroking his palm downward to circle Kit's slender shaft. "I tell you, Jonathan, he was beggin' for m'cock. I had to rim him just to shut him up."

Kit had no coherent response to that, not with Devon's wicked hand fisting his cock. He opened his mouth to reply, but all that came out was a strangled moan.

The image of Devon's fair head buried between Kit's thighs was almost enough to push Jonathan into losing control. He raised a hand to his lips and closed them over two of his fingers, wetting them thoroughly with his saliva before reaching behind his swollen balls. He coasted them over the crinkled skin, dampening the rippled entrance with a light touch. "Tell me," he husked, pressing a fingertip inside. "Tell me what it was like, Devon."

"I threw him on the bed." Devon moved his hand over Kit's shaft as Kit arched up into his touch. "I put his legs over my shoulders, and I licked him, licked him until he was dripping and moaning—and then I put my tongue in him and fucked him with it, as deep as I could go." Jonathan's ragged breath came from the other end of the line, and Devon imagined him touching himself, fingering himself. "Are you doing it, Jonathan? Fucking yourself on your fingers?"

"Shit yeah, Devon," Jonathan gasped, pushing a second finger inside. It felt good, but fuck, Devon would feel better. "I'm imagining it's you, opening me up, making me ready for you."

Kit reached into the bag he had retrieved from the car while Devon was showering and pulled out the tube of lube he'd stashed there. Coating his fingers, he urged Devon to part his legs. He would simply do to Devon whatever Devon told Jonathan to do.

Devon sprawled deeper into the couch cushions, draping one leg over the back and dropping the other to the floor to give Kit better access to his body. He groaned as Kit's lube-slick fingers skated around his entrance. "Bloody hell, that's good," he rasped, his praise meant for both Kit and Jonathan. "Want your fingers—inside—stretching—"

"Devon." Jonathan hissed at the yearning tone in his lover's voice, twisting his fingers deeper inside himself as he imagined what was happening on the other side of the call. "Are you—is he—"

Kit added a second finger, stretching as Devon asked, twisting and scissoring his fingers. He dropped his other hand to his own erection, stroking it slowly as he prepared Devon. He closed his eyes and pictured Jonathan in his house in Glastonbury, fingers penetrating his own arse.

"Yeah," Devon agreed, his back arching up to urge Kit's fingers even deeper. "He is—he's got his fingers in me, and fuck, does it feel sweet!" Kit's fingertip pressed against his prostate, eliciting a heartfelt groan. "Fuck," he panted, squeezing his hand around the base of his cock. "Sweet Jesus, Kit, do that again!"

Kit hastened to do as Devon asked, dragging his fingers across his lover's prostate repeatedly. "Talk to Jonathan," he urged, the sound of Devon's voice arousing him as much as the sight of his fingers disappearing into the man's body. "Tell him what I'm doing to you. Tell him what you want him to do to himself."

Jonathan licked his lips and started to stroke his cock slowly, closing his eyes and imagining his lovers' hands touching him, stretching him, loving him.

Even across the staticky connection, hearing Jonathan's panting breaths and quiet moans was arousing Devon as much as the licentious curl of Kit's fingers. "Open yourself up, Jonathan," he husked, his voice deep with his own growing need. "Do you feel Kit's fingers? Touch—touch your cock, fist it—that's my hand, Jonathan, my hand stroking you, rubbing over the tip, stretching open the slit, making you drip for me, so fuckin' wet for me you ache."

Kit moved his hand from his cock and wrapped it around Devon's, brushing away the other man's fingers so that his palm connected with Devon's skin. He swiped his thumb over the leaking tip, using the fluid to smooth his progress up and down the thick flesh.

"Oh God, Devon," Jonathan panted, rubbing his thumb over the tip of his cock, coaxing more precome from the slit at Devon's instruction. He curled his fingers until they found his pleasure center, the touch sending a flush of heat throughout his body. "Kit," he moaned, "so good, so fuckin' close."

When Kit batted his hand away from his cock, Devon leaned forward enough to wrap his palm around Kit's shaft instead, stroking him in time with Kit's motions. "Let go, Jonathan," he urged his distant lover as the heat of his own impending climax began to flare out of his control. "Let it happen. Let us hear you come undone for us."

Kit fought his release when Devon fisted his cock. He could come from that touch alone, but he wanted more. He wanted to be inside Devon when he gave in to his orgasm.

Jonathan writhed in a broken rhythm, back onto Kit's fingers, forward into Devon's fist. "Devon," he cried out, "talk to me, please. So close—need you, please."

"Jonathan," Devon moaned, Kit's touch and Jonathan's hungry voice driving him close to his own limits, "we're here, we're with you, we—" He bit back the words his heart was aching to say, the words he knew for himself at least were true—*we love you*. He'd wait until they were face-to-face again to say them aloud, but his heart echoed them now. "Come for us, Jonathan. Christ, Kit, now!"

Hearing Devon's plea, Kit pulled his fingers from his lover's body and ran his hand down his cock, slicking it up enough that he could push inside the tight passage. "Now," he echoed, the heat of Devon's body and the clenching of his muscles enough to shatter what little restraint he had left.

Devon crying Kit's name gave Jonathan the connection with his lovers he needed to succumb to a shattering, shuddering orgasm. His fingers slid from his body, his fist continuing to stroke through the aftershocks as on the other end of the phone, Kit and Devon were finding their own pleasure with each other. He was a little surprised that he didn't feel jealous or left out. It was right that they should love each other as much as he loved them.

Devon heard Jonathan's shout and knew he had brought himself to completion just as Kit's long, hard cock filled Devon's channel. He wrapped his hands around Kit's hips and pushed onto the spearing length, needing only a few thrusts to explode into his own climax.

Kit thrust wildly into Devon's channel, the walls massaging his cock as Devon came. With a deep, heartfelt groan, Kit gave up and gave in, his release pouring out of him, flooding Devon with the evidence of his pleasure and his yet-unspoken love.

When the sounds of passion from the phone had quieted, Jonathan wiped his hands on his rumpled shirt and cleared his throat. "So, I guess I know how the two of you will be spending the next few days," he commented wryly. "Hope you packed enough lube to last."

Devon held Kit close when he tried to sit back, cradling him against his chest. "Have you heard a weather forecast? Any idea how soon we can get out of here?"

"The rain should let up by tonight, but it sounds like another day or so to get the roads cleared," Jonathan said ruefully. "Niall can probably shuffle the location shooting schedule to try to work around the two of you until you can get there, but maybe we'll all have some downtime for the next few days."

Kit laughed. "A vacation! Now if you were just here to share it with us, everything would be perfect." He sobered. "We missed you last night, Jonathan. Don't ever doubt that."

"I know," Jonathan answered. "And I'll miss you both until we're back together." He laughed suddenly. "Or at least I will if your cell phones go dead!"

Feigning horror, though Jonathan couldn't see it, Kit gasped, "Oh no! I forgot my charger! Whatever are we going to do?"

"Wanker!" Devon and Jonathan chorused in unison, dissolving into laughter.

"I'll call Niall and let him know I heard from you," Jonathan said once he'd caught his breath. "I'll tell him your phone is nearly dead and you'll need a little time to let it recharge before you can call him." He snickered again softly. "Not that you won't need to work things out with Niall, but he isn't going to be able to do much of anything to get you out of there until the rain clears completely. And that will let you conserve your power for more important things."

Devon nudged Kit as he sat upright, swinging his legs back to the floor. "We can let it recharge while we make some breakfast," he suggested. "That way we'll all have plenty of power for round two!"

"Is ten minutes enough?" Jonathan replied. "Because that's about as long as I can wait."

They all laughed as Jonathan rang off, leaving Kit and Devon alone in the cabin again. "You need another shower," Kit teased, his confidence restored by their lovemaking the night before, a good night's sleep, and Jonathan's acceptance of the current situation. "I'd join you, but I don't think we'd have breakfast anytime soon if I did."

"And this would be a problem?" Devon countered, eyeing Kit as he bent to retrieve his shirt and jeans from where he'd dropped them on the floor. He wondered when being exiled in this tiny, isolated cabin had changed from something he'd have to endure to something he was actually looking forward to. If he was honest with himself, he knew when—the minute he realized that having Kit with him in exile would make it bearable.

"I don't know," Kit replied, wrapping his arms around Devon's waist. He'd worried, even as he was falling asleep last night, that he might not be enough, by himself, to keep Devon from going stir-crazy for whatever time they were confined to the cabin, but Devon wasn't acting antsy. He wasn't acting like being stuck here without Jonathan was a hardship. He was acting like he was thrilled to have Kit there with him, giving Kit hope that Devon might eventually see him for himself, not merely as a partner in seducing Jonathan. "It depends on how hungry you are and for what."

"As if you need to ask," Devon retorted, covering Kit's hand with his own and lowering it to his resurgent erection. He could feel Kit's cock hardening against his crease and shifted his stance, letting the shaft nudge between his cheeks. He'd wondered, in the early days after he'd first proposed sharing Jonathan between them, whether Kit was simply putting up with him as a means to the end he really wanted—Jonathan. Alone like this, though, it was easier to believe that Kit's desire for him, Devon, was real. Like Niall had said, none of them could feign passion this well.

"Well, I did hear your stomach rumbling earlier," Kit joked, rubbing against Devon provocatively. He slipped a hand between them to finger Devon's dripping hole. "And I've fucked you once already this morning, so I figured you might be satisfied with that." He pushed two fingers in deeper, aiming for Devon's prostate. "It was satisfactory, wasn't it?"

"More than satisfactory, and you bloody well know it." Kit's probing fingers sent stars shooting behind Devon's lids, but as amazing as it felt, he wanted to give Kit back some of that pleasure. Twisting in their embrace, he let Kit's hand slide free and captured his lips in a deep, hard kiss. If it wasn't quite as hard as he might have kissed Jonathan, it was imbued with every bit as much emotion. When Kit's mouth opened to him in welcome, Devon wrapped his hands around Kit's hips and hoisted him to sit on the kitchen table, never breaking the seal of their lips.

Kit surrendered to Devon's kiss as completely as he'd ever surrendered to Jonathan's, putting his mouth, his body, and his heart into Devon's capable hands. He knew how high Devon could take him when he fucked Kit over a railing or drove him out of his mind with a toy, but he wondered what it would be like simply to make love with Devon. No toys, no hurry, no distraction. Just making love.

Devon stepped closer until he was up against the table between Kit's legs. He braced an arm against his lover's spine so he could lean him backward, freeing some space between them to tweak at a pearled nipple. "Is this okay on your back?"

Pleased at the care Devon was showing, Kit nodded and wrapped his legs around Devon's waist, knees spreading wider in an invitation Devon was eager to accept. Devon worked his way down Kit's smooth torso, dropping kisses and tender nips to the line of Kit's collarbone, the hollow of his throat, the plane of his sternum.

Kit whimpered as Devon caressed him tenderly. He knew this side of his lover existed, but he so often saw the kinkier side that it was easy to forget how carefully Devon had loved Jonathan their first night together. To be touched that way now, like he was the most precious—no, like he was the only thing in the world—sent his heart soaring. Wanting to share some of the joy he was feeling, he stroked Devon's golden hair, still wet from his morning shower, carding his fingers through the long strands as he massaged his skull. It wouldn't be fair to Jonathan to say "I love you" to Devon first when he loved them both, but he hoped his fingers said it for him as he did his best to convey his emotions in silence.

There was nothing especially erotic about Kit's hand in his hair, but it sent a surge of warmth through Devon. He wanted to believe that this was more than just passion to Kit, that he wasn't alone in the feelings that had been growing in him in equal measure for both his lovers. With the breakup of his marriage, though it had been over in all but name long before the divorce proceedings started, Devon was emotionally vulnerable. He'd proposed seducing Jonathan to Kit thinking it would be a fling, a physical release that, if he was lucky, would last until filming ended. Lord knows he'd never expected to fall in love with not one, but both of his partners. Kit's response gave him hope, but he wasn't ready to put his emotions into words yet—if he'd ever be. His track record with relationships was piss-poor, and he wasn't about to put this one at risk by assuming too much. He'd let his actions speak for him. Laying Kit flat against the table, Devon trailed kisses lower, down the flat stomach before detouring to follow the alluring dip of Kit's pelvic bone.

"Rim me again," Kit begged as soon as Devon's lips neared his groin. If they were making love—and he was pretty damn certain they were—then he wanted it to be so powerful, so overwhelming, that he'd never forget it no matter what happened between them, all of them, later. "Rim me until I can't take it another second. And then rim me some more."

That was a request Devon was more than happy to indulge. "Put your feet up on the table," he suggested, the change in position opening Kit to him fully. He skimmed his palms up the long, lean thighs, inhaling the musk of their earlier lovemaking and the scent that was Kit's alone. He parted the globes of Kit's buttocks with his thumbs, and he nuzzled between them, dragging his tongue over the crinkled skin until Kit was squirming beneath him.

Kit wasn't sure he could be any more open to Devon than he was like this, knees bent and pulled up to his chest, arse on the edge of the table, every inch of him splayed as wide as he and Devon's hands could make him. And that tongue, that wonderful, tickling tongue, was claiming every inch of him as Devon's, anointing his entrance, his perineum in preparation for a long, drawn-out session. At least he hoped it would be long and drawn-out. His body was already tingling again, but he'd come once, and the chance to come down from that first high, a luxury his lovers didn't usually afford him, meant he'd have more control this time. Hopefully enough for a truly thorough rimming, the kind that usually made him come halfway through.

Devon wondered where Kit's impatience had gone. He usually needed to have Kit in a cock ring to be able to spend this much time pleasuring him—not that he was about to complain at the chance to savor the dark, smoky taste of his most intimate flesh. When Kit mewled at a particularly slow pass of Devon's tongue from the root of his cock to his tailbone, Devon rewarded him by curling his tongue and pressing it inside the tight ring of muscle. He liked the sounds that won from Kit so well that he pushed deeper, licking the inside of the tight channel as thoroughly as he had anointed the outside.

Unable to stay still any longer, Kit squirmed on the table, rocking his hips as best he could, trying to get closer to Devon, to get Devon's tongue farther inside him. It felt so damn good. He tried to tell Devon that, to encourage him to keep going, but the sounds that left his lips bore no resemblance to any word ever spoken, a long, keening cry of delight. His eyes rolled back in his head when Devon pulled his hips forward a little more, lifting them slightly to change the angle and allow for a deeper penetration. "Devon!" he wailed, his orgasm taking him completely by surprise, his cock spurting untouched all over his chest, one energetic surge even hitting him in the chin.

"Fuckin' Christ, Kit!" His lover's climax startled him since he hadn't even touched Kit's cock. Devon licked the streaks of white from Kit's skin before claiming his mouth, sharing the mingled flavors in a hungry kiss. "So damn responsive. I love—" He broke off before he could embarrass himself, wiping a spot of come off Kit's chin with his thumb. "—love that I could make you come just from rimming you."

"I think you could make me come from just about anything you did to me," Kit admitted, leaning into the touch like the kitten Devon and

Jonathan so often called him, his heart so full of love that he only barely held back the words. "Let me take care of you now?"

"I can wait." Devon had got such a rush from Kit's spontaneous orgasm that he'd be able to bring himself off in the shower with just a few hard tugs.

Kit shook his head, releasing his hold on one knee to reach for Devon. "Please. I know I won't come again, but I want you to come inside me. I want to feel that and know I made you feel as good as you made me feel."

"Just knowing I made you come like that made me feel fuckin' incredible," Devon admitted, but he was hardly immune to Kit's request. He pressed a kiss to the hand that held him and slid his palms under Kit's arse, guiding him forward. "Lube?" he remembered suddenly, glancing over his shoulder at the couch where they'd left the tube earlier.

"Do you really think we need it after you had your tongue up my arse for that long?" Kit laughed. "Quit stalling, or I'm going to think you don't really want me after all."

"No chance of that, sunshine." Devon lined himself up and eased slowly past the furled ring into the tight channel, the drag of skin slicked only by his saliva adding an extra sensitivity to their joining. "Not hurting you, am I?" he asked, not willing to take his own pleasure while causing Kit any discomfort.

"Not at all," Kit replied breathlessly. He rocked up against Devon, urging him to move as he wished, to take his ease in the heat of Kit's body. "If anything could get me hard again, it would be you filling me like this."

Devon slid forward until he was sheathed to the root. Pausing, he freed a hand to raise Kit's chin, losing himself in the depths of his expressive eyes. Tilting his head, he pressed his lips to Kit's, the kiss as slow and tender as the thrust of his hips, until the emotion of the moment overwhelmed him and he came in long, shuddering waves.

Subsiding back onto the table as Devon came deep and hot inside him, Kit sighed in completion. He might not have come again, but he didn't need to in order to feel the incredible connection forged by the moment. He stroked Devon's hair again as he'd done before, giving him time to recover. "I vote we forget about breakfast and the shower and everything else and go snuggle in bed until the rain stops," he said softly when Devon raised his head again.

"Sounds good to me," Devon murmured, closing his eyes as Kit stroked his hair. Spending the morning with Kit in his arms sounded just about perfect. "We'd better bring the phone with us, though. Wouldn't want to worry Jonathan if he can't get in touch with us again."

CHAPTER 23
EXCEPTIONAL RESTRAINT

JONATHAN ROCKED on his heels as he watched the helicopter settle onto its pad, having to consciously restrain himself from running up to the chopper before its rotors stopped moving. He was normally a patient man, but three days without his lovers, the first spent worried sick about their safety, the last two days missing them more than he would ever have imagined, had stretched his patience to its limits. The instant the big blades stopped rotating, he ran across the tarmac to meet them.

Devon stumbled out of the copter and into Jonathan's strong arms. Mindful of their lack of privacy, he only allowed himself a moment to relax in Jonathan's comforting embrace before pushing him aside with a smile. "Good to see you, Jonathan, but there's something I promised myself I'd do as soon as we landed." With a wide grin, he dropped to his knees and planted an extravagant kiss on the cracked asphalt.

From his seat inside the helicopter, Kit smiled down at Jonathan, chuckling the whole time. "You should have seen him, Jonathan," he recounted, covering his concern for Devon with humor. "For somebody who talks as big as he does, Devon sure is a wimp when it comes to flying."

Devon clasped Jonathan's shoulder as he helped him back to his feet, sharing Kit's laughter. "First class on a 777 is flying," he protested. "A private Lear jet is flying. Bumping knees with Kit on that airborne Cuisinart is *not* flying."

"Poor baby," Jonathan crooned, winking at Kit over Devon's shoulder. "Didn't the stewardess come around often enough with drinks?"

"Apparently not," Kit teased, sliding down from the bird. "He's been complaining since we left the cabin." He embraced Jonathan quickly too. "I think we should take him wherever passes for home around here."

"I wouldn't say no to a nip or two to settle m'stomach after that fun-house ride." Devon draped a companionable arm around each of his lovers. "Home, driver," he decreed as Jonathan led them to his car.

"If I wasn't so glad to see you, I'd make you walk," Jonathan countered. He elbowed Devon and then slid a hand under his jacket for a teasing grope, knowing it wasn't visible to the crew Niall had sent to rescue the two actors after realizing it might take a week or more to clear the roads. "I hope you aren't too worn-out from the rigors of flying. I have some definite plans for the two of you once I get you alone."

Kit met Devon's eyes and grinned. Jonathan wasn't the only one with plans. "Do tell," he asked, not wanting to tip their hand too soon.

"While you two were off in your private love shack, some of us were working," Jonathan pretended to grumble. "I have three days of catching up to do."

"Oh, I think we can take care of that," Devon promised, his lips twitching as he exchanged a glance with Kit, who had done his best to take Devon's mind off his fear of flying by encouraging him to plan what they could do to celebrate once they were reunited with Jonathan again. "After all, we had three days of missing you too."

"And a long, bumpy flight to imagine how we were going to celebrate our reunion," Kit added as they reached the car. He slipped into the back seat, letting Devon join Jonathan in the front. Devon could start the seduction.

"Oh?" Jonathan put the car in gear and pulled out of the small airstrip's parking lot. "And what ideas did the two of you come up with?"

Devon bumped Jonathan's knee with his arm, mimicking the way he had begun their seduction the night they started this adventure. This time, though, he could do more than hint at his interest. He slid his palm lovingly up Jonathan's jean-clad thigh until he could curl it around the package concealed behind the faded button-fly.

"We had all sorts of ideas." Kit leaned forward and draped his arms over the back of the seat. He settled his hands on Jonathan's chest, caressing firmly, unlike their first night together when he hadn't been sure enough of his welcome to be so bold. He tweaked one of Jonathan's nipples, then brushed back and forth across the abused flesh to soothe it.

"And you thought the copter ride was scary?" Jonathan muttered, trying to keep his attention on the road, fortunately empty of traffic during the island's off season, while his lovers teased him with their tantalizing touches. "As much as I appreciate the sentiments, it might be safer to wait until we get to the cabin before you—fuck!" he shouted as Devon's large hand closed around his rapidly hardening cock.

"We certainly weren't planning on fucking you in the car," Kit replied jokingly.

"Absolutely not," Devon agreed, his fingers wandering lower. "I've had enough of small, cramped places. We need plenty of room for what we have in mind."

Jonathan slammed the car into Park in front of the tourist cabin Niall had reserved for the three men, giving silent thanks that he'd been able to get them there in one piece. Not that he minded his lovers' attentions—in fact, it recalled pleasant memories of the first night the two of them had come on to him—but he hadn't been driving at the time!

Kit bounded out of the car, grabbed Jonathan's door, and pulled it open. Glancing around to make sure no one else was around, he leaned in and kissed Jonathan quickly before stepping back and waiting for his lover to join him on the driveway.

The fleeting touch of Kit's lips against his was all it took to break Jonathan out of his reminiscence. Unbuckling his seat belt and firmly, if reluctantly, removing Devon's hand from his crotch, he climbed out of the car and up the steps. As he unlocked the door, he reminded himself he needed to give a key to each of his lovers in case their schedules didn't overlap while they were on the island.

Devon grinned at Kit as they watched Jonathan bound up the front porch steps and into the house. "Ready for phase two, sunshine?" he drawled.

Kit grinned back. "I was born ready," he replied cockily, pushing Devon ahead of him.

The instant the door closed behind them, Jonathan wrapped his arms around them both. "I don't know which one of you to kiss first," he complained. "Fuck, I missed you two!"

Devon turned until he could pull Jonathan fully into his embrace. "Kit's had his kiss. It's my turn now," he demanded, taking Jonathan's mouth and demonstrating exactly how much he'd missed him.

Kit watched them for a few seconds as they attacked each other with lips and tongues, his body reacting to the flagrantly sexual display. His patience didn't last long. "Save some for me," he said, wrapping his arms around both his lovers and nuzzling against their cheeks. "My kiss outside doesn't count as a real kiss."

Pulling away reluctantly from Devon's insistent mouth, Jonathan turned his head to bump noses with Kit. "Oh no? Then why don't you show me what counts as a real kiss?"

Kit grinned. "I thought you'd never ask." He lifted his hands to cradle Jonathan's skull, tipping his head slightly to one side as he leaned forward to brush their lips together. The first pass was just as feathery as the one in the car had been, but Kit didn't stop there. He kept sweeping his lips across Jonathan's until they parted. His tongue darted out to tease the seam, urging Jonathan to open for him more. When he did, Kit surged inside, claiming the cavern again.

Devon watched Kit's wickedly seductive tongue tease at Jonathan's lips, knowing exactly how impossible he was to resist. With a low growl, he joined his mouth to theirs, his tongue flicking between the two to mingle the taste of both his lovers.

Giving up any attempt to control the kiss, Jonathan opened himself to Kit and Devon. When both their tongues surged into his mouth at once, he moaned softly. This was what he had missed, the three of them together, taking from and giving to each other in equal measure.

Kit caressed Devon's tongue with his own in quick welcome, but then he turned his attention back to Jonathan. After all, their plan had been to show their lover exactly how much they had missed *him*. "Let's take this into the bedroom," he suggested, pulling away enough to speak before returning to the kiss.

Jonathan was again teased with memories of their first night together. So much had changed in the few short months since that night, but the thrill of anticipation and desire he felt for the two men embracing him had only grown more powerful. "I'm ready when you are," he answered, echoing his original response.

Devon followed Jonathan into the cabin's spacious master bedroom, letting the growing intensity of his desire drive him. His anticipation had been building ever since they'd learned Niall was sending a helicopter to rescue them. Their discussion on the chopper, which he knew Kit had started simply to distract him, had developed into a plan to show the lover they'd been separated from how keenly they'd felt his absence. Because as much as Devon had enjoyed being the sole focus of Kit's attention, they had both missed Jonathan the way he suspected an amputee would miss a limb, his presence in both their thoughts only making the deprivation more vivid. As soon as they crossed the threshold to the bedroom, he pulled Jonathan back into a demanding kiss, tugging at the buttons of the other man's plaid shirt.

Seeing Devon start to undress Jonathan, Kit moved behind Jonathan and began unbuttoning his jeans. This encounter was all about Jonathan, about how glad they were to be back with him. Pushing the denim lower, he ran his hands over the strong thighs and then up to frame the already stiff cock. "Are you glad to see us?" he asked teasingly.

"Mmmnn-hmmnn." Jonathan moaned his agreement into Devon's mouth as he pushed back against Kit's matching erection. The first time he had found himself in this position, he hadn't known what to expect, much less how to respond. Now he knew exactly how incredible his lovers could make him feel, and more importantly, how to return that pleasure to them. He reached for the hem of Devon's shirt, trying to bare the broad chest to his touch, only to find his hands caught and held in a strong grip. Confused, he pulled his lips away from Devon's as he tried to tug his hands free.

"Want to touch you, Devon," he protested as the grip tightened around his wrists. He could hear Kit chuckling behind him, not pausing in his quest to free Jonathan completely of his clothing as Devon shook his head and smirked.

"Not part of the plan," Devon murmured huskily. Holding Jonathan's hands secured between them, he knelt down and teased at an erect pink nipple, tweaking it to full tightness before biting down, hard enough to draw a gasp of potent pleasure from Jonathan. He wouldn't have dared to be so rough the first time they were together, but he'd learned exactly how to skate the line between pain and pleasure, exactly how to push Jonathan to his limits.

Kit backed toward the bed, drawing Jonathan and Devon with him. They definitely needed to be horizontal for the next part of the plan. When he reached the bed, he released Jonathan long enough to quickly strip his own clothes off.

Devon continued to hold Jonathan still as Kit dropped his clothes on the floor and crawled onto the large bed. He pushed Jonathan forward into Kit's strong embrace before making short work of stripping off his own garments and joining his lovers.

Jonathan had stopped struggling the instant Devon's teeth closed over his nipple. He no longer had to plead for a harder touch. Devon knew exactly the right amount of pressure to drive him mindless with the mingled sensations of pain and pleasure. Jonathan almost growled when the delicious tortured stopped. When Kit released him to remove his clothes and climb into bed, Jonathan stood quietly in Devon's grip, waiting to see what his lovers' "plan" would involve next.

Kit caught Jonathan when Devon pushed him into his arms, pulling Jonathan onto the bed and holding him in place. Jonathan was an incredibly unselfish lover, as he had demonstrated countless times, but he wasn't going to be allowed to follow that tendency tonight. Tonight was all about taking pleasure in Jonathan's pleasure.

Jonathan wasn't about to protest when Kit's arms closed around him. He pressed closer against the warm skin, the simple feel of the hair on his chest and legs rubbing over Kit's smooth flesh sending his arousal surging against Kit's hip. He shifted in his lover's arms, trying to bring them into closer contact as he reached up to hold Kit's head steady for his kiss.

Kit didn't fight the kiss, but he did take control of it, rolling Jonathan onto his side and throwing his leg over him so Jonathan was effectively pinned to the bed. Their tongues tangled together as completely as their arms and legs. Kit captured Jonathan's hands with his, pulling them over their heads as he slid his lips from Jonathan's mouth to his neck.

"No marks," Jonathan teased, though they no longer needed that reminder either. They'd all become expert at knowing exactly what the lines of their costumes would hide.

"Don't tell me that. I'm not the one who likes to bite," Kit retorted playfully, although he had left his share of marks on both his lovers at their request. He nipped playfully at the skin just below the line of Arthur's tunic.

Devon arranged himself at his lovers' sides, leaning up on one elbow, trailing his free hand down the sculpted muscles of Jonathan's back. He'd always found Jonathan's understated musculature sexy as hell, but he could tell how much more prominent their constant sword training had made it over the months they'd been together. Letting his hand drift lower over the curve of lean buttocks, he smiled when Jonathan's hips arched up into the touch. He swatted the creamy globes playfully, leaving a rosy pink outline of his palm on the pale flesh.

"None o' that," he scolded, trailing his fingers down one hard thigh and up the other.

Jonathan winced at the firm smack of Devon's palm against his ass. The blow wasn't really painful. In fact, the way it pushed him more firmly against Kit tempted him to incite Devon to do it again. "Or what?" he taunted, looking over his shoulder. "You'll give me a spanking for being naughty?"

The sound of Devon's palm connecting with Jonathan's arse did unspeakably erotic things to Kit's insides. Devon had swatted him that way more than once, always to a most pleasurable end. He wondered what it would be like to be spanked, not just once but thoroughly. It wasn't something he'd ever considered before, but now…. That wasn't on the agenda for tonight, though. Turning his mind back to the matter at hand, he looked at Devon, waiting for his answer.

Devon eyed Jonathan consideringly, noting in passing the spark of excitement in Kit's eyes at the mention of spanking. That was an interesting development, but Devon filed it away for future reference. Tonight his focus was on Jonathan. He ran the flat of his hand over the reddened mark on Jonathan's arse, his voice an amorous rumble. "No, I think you might enjoy that too much," he countered. "We had something different in mind to keep you from distracting us from the plan." He nodded to Kit, a sly smile spreading across his face.

Kit smiled back, stretching Jonathan's arms closer to the headboard and waiting for Devon to pounce. He ran his tongue along Jonathan's jawline and up to his ear, blowing in it softly.

Jonathan hummed at the warm puff of Kit's breath in his ear, wriggling to increase the delicious contact of skin against skin. "Missed you," he murmured, trying to tug his arms free to return to cradling Kit's head in his palms. He frowned when Kit didn't release the clasp that held his arms over his head.

"Trust us," Kit said as Jonathan struggled. "Just let us love you."

Jonathan's gaze flew to his lover's face at Kit's words, the response he longed to make trembling on his lips. Kit was smiling, his eyes meeting Devon's over his shoulder. Sure they didn't mean the same thing he did, Jonathan said the words anyway, knowing they'd hear only the obvious interpretation. "Always," he answered. "But I need to love you back."

"Too distracting." Devon shook his head, reaching into his suitcase for the few toys he'd thought to toss in before leaving on their ill-fated drive. "We had three days to miss you and think about all the things we wanted to do to you once we were together again." He pulled out a pair of soft suede restraints, gliding the velvety leather up Jonathan's spine, across his shoulders, and up one arm to meet Kit's hands. "This way"—he stretched Jonathan's arm to the nearest bedpost, securing it with practiced expertise—"we can give you our undivided attention."

As soon as Devon had one arm secured, Kit rolled, flipping Jonathan onto his back and stretching their clasped hands toward the other bedpost. "You can love us back next time," he promised as he held Jonathan's hand in place for the second cuff.

The same rush of heat Jonathan had felt at being restrained on the porch at the cottage and in Kit's bed flared inside him as Devon fastened the flexible cuffs around his wrists. The sudden jump of his cock as it surged from the tangle of tawny hair between his legs left little doubt that he had no real objection to the position he found himself in. "I was good last time. Are those really necessary?" he asked, his voice hoarse with desire.

"Yes," Kit replied. "This way you don't have to think about being good. You can just relax and enjoy."

"What do you have in mind this time?" Jonathan asked, certain his two lovers had come up with some inventive new form of loving torture during the copter ride.

The unquestioning, unconditional trust in Jonathan's reply made Devon's heart soar and his cock swell in response. He bent forward to brush his lips against Jonathan's, angling his head to rub their beards together in a gentle abrasion. Something about the position reminded him of their first night together, and his answer unconsciously echoed his words on that earlier evening. "You're going to make love to Kit," he whispered against Jonathan's ear, "and then I'm going to make love to you."

"Remember what we talked about on the phone?" Kit added. "Remember how I promised to ride you until we both came? That's what I want to do to you, lover. Will you let me?"

"Yes," Jonathan answered, trembling in arousal at the images Devon's voice and Kit's words promised him. "God, yes, kitten, I want that so much."

Devon slid forward, giving Kit room to move between Jonathan's legs as he knelt near the head of the bed, his hand straying across the silky hair on Jonathan's chest.

Kit grabbed the lube from the table by the bed and slicked his fingers. Turning so his back was to Jonathan, he slid a finger inside himself, hissing at the stretch. Looking over his shoulder as he moved his finger, he met Jonathan's eyes. "I pictured you doing this," he said in a low, sultry voice, "while we were on the phone." He twisted the digit so it coated the walls of his passage completely. "I imagined you lying in bed, touching yourself, stretching yourself." He added a second finger. "Is this what you were doing, Jonathan? Is this how you were pleasuring yourself?"

"Couch," Jonathan croaked, his eyes burning as he watched Kit's long fingers sliding into himself, stretching himself open. "I was—on the couch—fuck, Kit, hurry, need to feel you!"

Kit smiled, removing his fingers from his arse and turning back to face Jonathan. He scooted up so he could straddle Jonathan's hips and ran a sticky hand over his thick cock. Meeting Devon's eyes for a moment, he quipped, "I think he might have missed us."

"Seems right, as much as we missed him," Devon agreed, finding Jonathan's taut nipples and pulling on them with the pressure the other man loved. "Wasn't the same without you, Jonathan," he husked, swallowing around the tightness in his throat.

"So much," Jonathan admitted, his back bowing as he tried to arch closer into Kit's and Devon's touch. "Both of you—missed you so much—please! Need you—" He was begging, but he didn't care. He was going to shatter into pieces if they didn't love him *now*.

Kit leaned forward and kissed Jonathan deeply, silencing the pleading words. He wanted Jonathan as much as Jonathan wanted him, but he also did not want to rush, not after three days of separation. The insistent movement of Jonathan's hips persuaded him, though, so he sat back up and positioned the thick cock at his entrance, sinking down onto it slowly. "Was this what you imagined?" he asked Jonathan when he had taken in all of the long shaft.

Jonathan hissed with pleasure, as much at the sight of Kit sliding over his rigid arousal as at the tight clench of muscle around his shaft. He fought back the urge to thrust up into the slick channel, trying to accede to his lovers' wishes to let them see to his pleasure, since there was no other way he could see to theirs. "Better," he gasped, the sound transforming to a moan when Devon leaned forward to take a nipple into his mouth while still tugging and twisting the other. "Better... than anything I imagined," he panted.

The first time they'd done this—set out to seduce Jonathan— Devon had held back while Kit initiated their new lover. Jonathan hadn't known what to expect then, and Devon hadn't wanted to overwhelm him. Now, though, he wanted nothing more than to drive Jonathan wild with as much sensation as he and Kit could give him. He tweaked and bit at Jonathan's chest, leaving vivid marks as he worked his way across the muscular expanse, wringing increasingly frantic moans with each nip of his teeth.

Kit rode Jonathan slowly, his hips rising and falling at what was surely a maddening pace, but he wanted this moment to last. He smoothed one hand over Jonathan's abdomen while he tangled the other in Devon's shaggy hair, completing the circle, making them one unified whole again as they strove for Jonathan's pleasure.

Devon slid his hand forward to cover Kit's, lacing their fingers together as he worked his way down Jonathan's torso. He stopped to pay particular attention to the kanji tattooed on Jonathan's hip, worrying the inked skin over the sharp hip bone until Jonathan bucked beneath him. Looking up, he caught Kit's gaze, smiling at the sensuous picture he made as he rocked up and down on their lover.

Jonathan tried to hold himself still as long as he could, but as Devon's mouth moved lower, adding to the tremors Kit's slow but insistent pace wrung from him, he couldn't stop from canting his hips, needing more of the maddening contact. He clutched at the empty air that was all he could touch; his heels dug into the mattress as he pushed upward. "More...." His voice trailed into a moan as Devon bit his hip bone. "So good, please, need more."

Kit obliged, picking up the pace of his hips, trying to add to the pleasure Jonathan was feeling. He gasped when the shifting of Jonathan's hips changed the angle to rub directly across his prostate. Determined to take Jonathan with him when he came, he flexed his sphincter, hoping to drive the other man wild.

Driven by Jonathan's plea and Kit's gasp, Devon's dipped his head lower until his mouth reached the thatch of curls at the root of Jonathan's cock. Grasping Kit's hip with his free hand, he lapped at the place where his two lovers joined, dragging his tongue over the rippled skin that stretched around Jonathan's cock, across the base of the stiff shaft as Kit lifted up, over the younger man's smooth bollocks when he slid back down.

"Bloody hell!" Kit swore explosively at the attentions of Devon's tongue. He grabbed the base of his cock and squeezed hard, trying to hold back his suddenly imminent climax. He wasn't ready for this to be over yet.

A wail of pleasure tore from Jonathan's throat when the moist rasp of Devon's tongue joined the tight clench of Kit's muscles on his throbbing cock. He thrust his hips up wildly, the combined attentions of his two lovers sending him over the precipice of ecstasy. His pelvis locked as he twitched and shuddered, pumping into Kit's enveloping heat while Devon's tongue echoed each pulse of his shaft.

The hot burst of Jonathan's seed inside him left Kit teetering on the brink. He slammed down on the thick cock, driving it just a little bit deeper inside of him, triggering his own climax. He collapsed forward onto Jonathan's chest, reaching up to tear open the restraints. He needed his lover's arms around him, the plan be damned. Devon could tie him back up later or figure out some other way to put Jonathan at his mercy.

Devon pulled back as Kit sank bonelessly against Jonathan, who instinctively wrapped his arms—now free of the restraints—around Kit's sweat-coated back. Resting on one elbow, Devon ignored the insistent ache of his own unslaked need, content for the moment to watch his lovers as they nuzzled breathlessly. The next phase of the plan would need some revision, but he could be flexible. A wide smile spread across his face as an idea began to take shape. *Oh yes, that could be very good*, he thought, chuckling quietly.

The sound of Devon's laughter brought Jonathan out of the sensual haze he'd been floating in. He had felt the power of Kit's release erupting over him, but in their mutual euphoria they'd neglected their other lover. He stretched out a hand in apology, glad he'd been given back the freedom to do so. "Sorry, Devon," he murmured, running his hand down the planes of his broad golden chest.

"Don't be." Devon grinned, capturing Jonathan's hand and holding it still. A gleam of lascivious mischief lit his eyes. "It's my turn next."

CHAPTER 24
DOUBLE BLIND

THE WORDS were teasing, but Devon was using *that* voice—the slow, deep, sinful tone that promised unnamed devilry and made Jonathan's blood race straight to his groin whenever his lover used it. "I wouldn't want you to miss your turn," Jonathan drawled in agreement, stirring to renewed hardness at the promise implicit in Devon's tone while still sheathed in Kit's sated embrace.

Kit grinned at Devon's comment and Jonathan's reaction. With a heartfelt groan, he rolled to Jonathan's far side, leaving him open to Devon's touch. He glanced up at Devon, wondering what delights the other man would suggest this time.

"Since it *is* my turn, I get to pick the accessories," Devon continued, reaching beneath the bed to retrieve his duffel bag. He pursed his lips in consideration as he evaluated the abbreviated contents he had brought with him, selecting a length of silky material and a plain black satin band before returning it to the floor. "I think I want to blindfold you."

"That's it?" Kit asked incredulously. After all the incredibly kinky things they had talked about doing to Jonathan while they were in the helicopter, Devon had settled on *blindfolding* him? Maybe that was all he'd thought to throw in his suitcase before they left home. Either way, it was Devon's turn, so it was his choice.

"For now." Devon flashed a significant glance at Kit before returning his regard to the man who had occupied his thoughts, if not his bed, for the past three days and nights. He planned to do more than make up for that absence now. "Have you ever been blindfolded during sex before?" he asked Jonathan conversationally as he weighed the relative merits of the two pieces of cloth in his hands.

Kit's groin tightened despite the cataclysmic orgasm he had just experienced. He couldn't decide if it was the thought of being blindfolded or simply the thought of sex that did it. He'd learned all kinds of things about himself since taking up with Devon.

"No," Jonathan admitted, a slow, sweet heat growing inside him at the prospect, like warm honey flowing through his veins. "I told you I was pretty vanilla before the two of you." He licked his lips, his gaze moving between the scraps of fabric and Devon's dancing jade eyes. "What do you want me to do?"

"Whatever I tell you, of course," Devon admonished lightly. He hadn't meant to slide into his Dom manner, but apparently just handling the blindfolds was starting to pull him into that mind-set. "The black, I think," he decided, tossing the scarf in Kit's direction with seeming indifference to where it landed. "Strong and elegant, not a lot of unnecessary flash." He adjusted the satin band over Jonathan's eyes, rewarding his acceptance with a slow, thorough kiss. "I'm going to leave off the restraints, as long as you do what I tell you. This is my turn. Remember that—if you start improvising, I'll have to tie you back down."

Kit caught the length of silk Devon tossed him, waiting for his own directions. He recognized that tone of voice from their weekend at the beach and the occasional evening since then. It was definitely to everyone's pleasure to listen when Devon used that tone.

The tremor of pure lust that shook Jonathan when his vision was taken away shocked and surprised him. Not being able to see what was happening around him made him feel vulnerable, bared to Devon and Kit in a way that transcended the fact that they were already naked. He leaned back on his elbows, trying to breathe slowly and evenly and allow his other senses to take more of a role in gauging his surroundings. "Whatever you tell me," he agreed quietly, waiting for Devon's next directions.

Once again, Jonathan's reaction aroused Devon fiercely, while at the same time he felt a surge of tenderness at the trust so freely and completely given. He would do everything in his power to show the other man how much that trust meant to him—how much *Jonathan* meant to him. "Don't move," Devon husked as he knelt at Jonathan's side, leaning forward until his breath ghosted over Jonathan's face. With moist, open lips, he traced the borders of the blindfold, top and bottom, and then slid worshipfully over every plane and line and angle of Jonathan's well-defined features.

Kit twisted the silk in his hands, wondering if he dared join them without Devon's express direction. In the end, the lust and love he felt watching the two of them won out over what little restraint he had without Devon's specific orders. He lifted one of Jonathan's hands to his mouth and sucked avidly on each of the digits in turn.

Jonathan drew a shaky breath, trying to hold himself still beneath the loving attention he was receiving from both his lovers. The touch of Devon's lips on his face, of Kit's mouth on his fingers, felt warmer than before, the moist friction against his skin more sensuous—or maybe he simply noticed it more with his eyes covered. The soft sounds of Devon's breathing and the little noises Kit made as he slid each finger into his mouth shivered along Jonathan's nerve endings, awakening them even more to the tactile sensations.

Tamping down his own reaction at the unsteadiness of Jonathan's breathing, Devon paused over Jonathan's lips, brushing over them lightly, so lightly, again and again until they opened beneath him with a moan. He let his tongue slip out, tracing delicately over the slightly chapped skin. He could feel Jonathan's lips quivering under his touch, knew he was fighting the impulse to meet Devon's tongue with his own. Devon's gut clenched with desire, his cock swelling against his thigh as he recognized Jonathan was holding back because *he* had told him to. He settled his mouth more firmly over Jonathan's for just a moment, sucking the lips inside his, before releasing them and sitting back again.

Kit slid his lips over Jonathan's palm, stopping at the strong wrist, his tongue soothing the marks left by the soft restraints. The skin wasn't abraded, barely even chafed, only slightly reddened, but Kit lavished attention on it nonetheless, for it was proof of Jonathan's cooperation, his willing submission to his lovers. The silk in his hands trailed across Jonathan's arm and shoulder as he nibbled and sucked on the smooth skin.

The sensation of lips gliding over his skin moved from Jonathan's mouth to his wrist along with something else, something soft and teasingly light—probably the silky scarf. Suddenly he couldn't tell if they were Devon's lips or Kit's lips. They felt firm and insistent like Devon's, but something in the way they lingered over the place the restraints had rubbed made him think it might be Kit. He started to call his name, then bit back the sound before it could escape. Devon hadn't told him not to speak, but he hadn't given permission either. Deciding to follow Devon's lead as best he could, Jonathan remained silent, his quickened breathing sounding loud in his ears.

Jonathan's demeanor pleased Devon immensely, the way he lay still and quiet beneath their attentions stirring the desire he always felt to a different level of need. Deciding Jonathan was ready to move to another level as well, Devon leaned forward again, mapping the defined muscles of Jonathan's chest—over his collarbones, down his sternum, across his ribs, through the light mat of enticing curls that covered his lean muscles.

Releasing Jonathan's wrist, Kit trailed his fingers up Jonathan's arm, tracing the curve of muscle until his hands joined Devon's on their lover's chest. The silk in his hand glided behind his fingers, giving him ideas. He let the cloth drag across Jonathan's stomach, watching the skin jump beneath the gentle tickling. He glanced at Devon, waiting to see if he would give some indication of his plans. Devon had helped Kit love Jonathan well. Now Kit wanted to return the favor.

Devon nodded to encourage Kit to continue. He couldn't blame Kit for wanting to join in. Jonathan was bloody irresistible like this. He forced back his own growing need, leaning forward to bite gently at Jonathan's neck while he coasted his fingers over the pink nipples that always seemed to anticipate his touch.

There were definitely two sets of hands touching him now, Jonathan thought, and the erotic glide of silky fabric over his abdomen made him shiver in anticipation of where else it might stray. He focused his attention on the slide of callused fingertips over his skin, the lack of other sensory input heightening his awareness of each caress. Maybe he was imagining it, but he thought he could tell Devon's broader fingers, firmer touch, the rougher texture of his skin, from Kit's more slender hands, smoother skin, teasing gestures. His nerve endings sang at each touch, reactions shooting down his limbs and echoing in his loins. He felt himself hardening and swallowed unsteadily, curling his hands into fists to resist the urge to touch his lovers in turn.

Seeing Devon paying attention to Jonathan's nipples, Kit moved his hands lower over Jonathan's flat stomach, the scarf slipping from his hand. With one hand he traced the outlines of Jonathan's tattoo, so telling of his lover's dedication to his son. He played with the wiry nest of curls around Jonathan's twitching cock with the other. With a grin, he lowered his head and licked the shiny tip.

Jonathan couldn't stop his hips from levering upward when a warm, wet tongue rasped without warning over the head of his cock. He didn't know if it was Devon or Kit, though he suspected Kit—and now, feeling the tug of what had to be Devon's beard against the hair on his chest, he was sure of it. Drawing a hissing breath, he settled back against the bed, hoping the fact that he'd spread his legs a bit farther apart would pass unnoticed.

Grinning at the reaction Kit had wrung from Jonathan and the subtle repositioning he'd tried to hide, Devon decided to see just what it would take to make their lover lose control. After brushing his beard over one peaked nipple, he turned his head suddenly and took it between his teeth, biting down hard enough to leave a bruise that would last for several days. He released the purpled flesh with a final nip and swung to the other side of Jonathan's chest, hovering close enough to ensure his presence was felt. "Don't have to put the cuffs back on you, do I?" he growled, taking the nub between his teeth in warning.

A blast of heat flared in Jonathan's gut at Devon's demand. Did he want Devon to tie him back up? Some part of him surely did, he realized, but he managed to gasp a hoarse "No—no, Sir," stretching his wrists to grasp at the sides of the mattress. "No," he repeated a little more firmly now that he had some way to ground himself.

The moment the word *Sir* crossed Jonathan's lips, Kit felt the change in the body beneath him. His gaze flew back to Devon, waiting to see how he would respond, whether he would take control of the situation as he had at the beach or if he would find some way to defuse it. Either way, Kit needed some sign.

Hearing Jonathan call him *Sir* nearly snapped the last of Devon's control. His body screamed to roll Jonathan over and bury himself inside that tight, hot sheath. He was reaching for Jonathan's shoulder when he realized what his lover had done. Unable to give pleasure to his partners in any physical way, he was giving Devon what he knew Devon wanted. *Damn the man for being so perceptive!* Devon thought with a rueful sigh, cursing himself as well for falling into old, bad habits. Tonight was about him pleasing Jonathan, not the other way around. Drawing a deep breath, he forced himself to calmness, shutting off that primal part of his brain that demanded he take advantage of Jonathan's submission. Instead he touched Jonathan's shoulder gently, meeting Kit's eyes and shaking his head. "Kneel up, Jonathan," he urged, his voice neutral rather than commanding.

Jonathan obeyed immediately, already sliding his legs beneath him before he registered the change in Devon's voice. *Busted*, a tiny voice whispered in his head, not sure whether he felt disappointment or relief at the change in mood.

Kit shifted to allow Jonathan to move. Clearly Devon didn't intend to play as they had at the beach, but Kit still didn't know what he did intend to do.

Once Jonathan was kneeling on the bed, Devon moved behind him. With the change in position, he could reach Jonathan's back and Kit could attend to Jonathan's front at the same time. Winking at Kit, he dipped his head to trail biting kisses over a sharp shoulder blade.

Seeing how Devon positioned himself, Kit grinned. He could deal with having Jonathan's front all to himself while Devon attended to Jonathan's back. He leaned forward and nipped at Jonathan's collarbone, adding to the sensual pleasures Devon was bestowing.

Kneeling back on his heels, Jonathan let his head drop, arching it to one side to allow Kit access where he teased at his collarbone. He was sure now that Kit was in front of him and Devon behind him. Devon's beard brushed over his shoulder blades, moving lower as he followed the curve of Jonathan's spine downward. Biting his lip to hold back a moan of pleasure, Jonathan clutched his thighs and braced himself to endure the sensual torment.

Knowing the dual sensations would excite Jonathan even faster, Devon deliberately kissed a slow trail down his spine, giving each vertebra its share of lips, tongue, and teeth before moving to the next. He wrapped his hands around Jonathan's hips, feeling the growing heat beneath his palms, the quivers as Jonathan fought to hold himself still.

Shifting on the bed, Kit worked his way down Jonathan's chest, nibbling at any patch of skin that caught his fancy—and they were many—his hands resting the whole time on Jonathan's widespread thighs. He couldn't resist stroking the hair-dusted skin, fingers climbing higher and higher until the tips teased the sides of Jonathan's thick cock.

When Kit's fingers reached his cock at the same instant Devon's hot mouth reached the curve of his backside, Jonathan's tenuous control shattered. A whimper of need escaped, and after that he gave up even trying to hold it back. "Please," he gasped, moaning when Devon's fingers parted his cheeks, his wet mouth moving even lower into the sweaty crease between them. "Fuck, Devon, please."

Devon's moan echoed Jonathan's as the sharp, salty tastes of sweat and Kit's come hit his tongue. He burrowed lower, lifting Jonathan's hips until his mouth could reach the puckered opening. Once he'd laved it thoroughly with his saliva, he thrust his tongue as deep inside as it could reach, too close now himself to bother with subtlety any longer. He needed to fuck Jonathan, and he didn't plan to wait much longer to do it.

Jonathan's begging had Kit's insides trembling. Lowering his head, he lapped again at the tip of the heavy cock, sucking on it gently.

Devon slid two fingers inside his mouth to wet them and worked first one, then both around his tongue inside the straining channel. He knew he was being rougher than he usually would, but the needy sounds Jonathan made with each twist of his fingers reassured him that his lover wanted this as much as he did. When Jonathan's passage was stretched as much as his shredded control would allow, Devon drew back and sat back on his heels, pulling Jonathan with him onto his thighs. Taking his leaking cock in hand for the first time, he smeared a coating of lube over its tip and positioned himself at Jonathan's wet portal.

Feeling the head of Devon's stiff shaft nudge his ass, Jonathan arched his back, desperate for Devon to thrust deeper inside him. He'd never been taken in this upright position before, usually preferring to see his lover's face; but the blindfold had removed that option, and he found that sinking onto Devon's hard length while strong arms cradled him and callused fingers tugged at his nipples felt so perfect that he cried out in joy. And when Kit's mouth closed around his cock, his cry grew into a wail of overwhelming pleasure.

Kit adjusted quickly once Devon was inside Jonathan, letting Devon's rhythm dictate the pace of his sucking as each thrust pushed Jonathan's cock a little deeper into his mouth. He swallowed hard each time the tip hit the back of his throat, letting his muscles milk their lover's shaft even as he was sure Jonathan's muscles were milking Devon's cock.

Jonathan was so tight around Devon, pushing back against him so hungrily, that Devon's climax threatened after only a few quick thrusts. Only the knowledge that Jonathan had already come once and would be slower to come a second time helped him hold back as he pumped his hips in short, sharp jabs, every drive pressing the head of his cock over Jonathan's prostate. Holding Jonathan against him with one big hand around his hip, he tugged at his nipples with the other, closing his mouth over the shoulder that heaved and trembled against him. Despite his efforts, his orgasm hit him with the power of an avalanche, and he let it carry him under, biting into Jonathan's skin as he pulsed his release into the clenching sheath that surrounded him.

Rocking back onto Devon's thick cock, his hips bucking up into Kit's eager suction, Jonathan was nearly delirious with sensation. He didn't need to see his lovers; he could hear their ragged breathing and urgent moans, feel their hands still caressing him as they stretched him and swallowed him. The sound rose to a roar of white noise and a flare of unbearable heat, and then he was coming hard down Kit's throat, screaming out rawly as Devon filled him and each hot, slick slide sent aftershocks racing through every nerve in his body. He sagged in exhaustion, only his lovers holding him upright.

Kit swallowed hard, relishing the flavor—different from Devon's, smoother, a little less bitter—relishing being reunited with Jonathan. He dropped a hand to his cock, pulling hard a couple of times until he came again, all over Jonathan's legs.

Devon leaned heavily against Jonathan's back, meeting Kit's eyes over Jonathan's lowered head. Caressing the sweat-tangled hair, he gently removed the blindfold and dropped his own head to rest against his satiated lover's. Entwining his hands with Jonathan's and Kit's, he sighed in perfect satisfaction. "It's good to be home."

"It's good to have you home," Jonathan agreed, quietly thrilled at Devon's choice of words. *Home* wasn't a place anymore but wherever his lovers were. "But next time somebody else gets to be in the middle."

"Devon and I had each other to ourselves for three days. This was about showing you how much we missed you," Kit insisted.

"You'll have your chances with both of us, I'm sure." Devon didn't know yet when he would have fly to LA to deal with his divorce, but the trip was inevitable. Refusing to let that thought taint the time they shared now, he added, "It doesn't matter who's where. No matter how we position our bodies, it's all making love."

Exclusive Excerpt

No Limits

Exploring Limits: Book Two
By Nicki Bennett and Ariel Tachna

For three actors in a committed gay ménage, balancing work, sex, and romance might be their most challenging role yet.

The Dom who taught Devon about BDSM is back to reclaim his sub and break up the trio. He leaves chaos across the set of *Camelot* and Devon reluctant to resume his dominant role with his lovers, Jonathan and Kit.

But facing their pasts and discovering and exploring new kinks might not be the ultimate test of their relationship….

Filming is ending on the miniseries that brought the three of them together, and they're about to go their separate ways, pulled in different directions by family, obligations, and careers. How will they hold onto the love they've built when production wraps?

Each man has a unique idea about how to maintain their relationship, but will promises and memories be enough?

This volume includes newly edited and expanded versions of the novellas:

Breaking Limits
Transcending Limits
No Limits

Coming Soon to
www.dreamspinnerpress.com

HE STRAINED wildly against the restraints, but the metal only cut into his wrists, adding a trickle of blood to the sweat that coated his clammy skin. The blindfold kept him from seeing, the ball gag kept him from crying out, but nothing could keep the walls from pressing down on him, crushing him beneath their relentless weight. He fought for a lungful of air, but he couldn't catch his breath, couldn't stop the trembling that shook him as the dark and the cold and the silence closed around him. He'd buried him here, and he'd never get out, never get away....

A hoarse cry broke the stillness of the late summer night. Devon Aldridge's arms flailed against empty air as he struggled, shivering when the warm breeze wafted over his sweaty skin. His arm struck something and he recoiled violently, pulling away with another raw sound.

Knocked out of a sound sleep by Devon's harsh cry and a glancing blow of his elbow, Kit Webster shook his head, trying to wake up enough for rational speech. "Devon?" he asked softly, not wanting to wake their third lover if Devon's cry had not already done so.

"Devon?" Jonathan Braedon muttered groggily, reaching for where his lover should have been lying curled against him. His eyes fluttered open when his hand met only empty space and cool sheets. "What's wrong, babe?"

Kit sighed. So much for not waking Jonathan. Since they were all awake anyway, he leaned over and switched on the lamp. His eyes widened when he saw Devon huddled in one corner of the bed, knees drawn up to his chest, shivering violently. Pushing back the covers, he knelt up, trying to catch Devon's eye. "What's wrong, luv?" he asked.

Devon blinked as the voices penetrated his nightmare—warm voices, caring voices—his lovers' voices. The sudden snap of the light revealed not the dank crawlspace of his nightmare, but the familiar bedroom of Jonathan's rental house. Kit and Jonathan stared at him with worried expressions.

Jonathan couldn't imagine what might have disturbed Devon so much, but it didn't matter now; he had to do something to ease the panicked look in his lover's eyes. He slid over the sheets, reaching forward slowly to stroke Devon's leg, his touch as gentle as if he were calming Hengroen, the horse he rode in his role as Arthur in the *Camelot* miniseries that had brought them together. When Devon didn't pull away from his hand, he moved closer, drawing the shaking man into a loose embrace. "It's okay, babe," he murmured, his voice low and as soothing as he could make it. "Ssshh, it's okay."

Devon allowed himself half a dozen heartbeats resting in Jonathan's strong arms before swinging his legs off the edge of the bed and sitting up. "Sorry about that," he muttered, trying to force his voice to sound light-hearted. "Probably shouldn't have eaten that leftover curry right before bed—bloody indigestion's giving me the heebie-jeebies!"

Kit frowned, looking to Jonathan for guidance. It seemed an awfully pat answer for what appeared more than just a simple nightmare. He wanted to push, to insist on a better explanation, but he wasn't sure that was the best path to follow.

Shrugging at Kit's questioning gaze, Jonathan returned his attention to the man beside him. He'd dealt with a preteen son long enough to recognize an attempt at distraction when he saw one. Tugging unconsciously at his earlobe, he moved next to Devon, putting an arm around the bigger man's shoulders, relieved that at least they were no longer shaking. He tried to think of a clever response to draw Devon out, but he was too worried to be subtle. "Don't try and bullshit us, Devon. That wasn't something you ate giving you *agita*. What's going on?"

Kit scooted to Devon's other side, his arm going around his fellow countryman's waist, waiting for an answer.

Devon really didn't want to have this discussion, but he knew Jonathan wasn't going to let it drop that easily. Rubbing his hand through his hair, he sighed. "It was just a nightmare, Jon. Maybe a delayed reaction to the bloody helicopter ride or something."

"That was over a week ago, Devon!" Jonathan knew how much Devon hated flying, even when it was the fastest way to rescue him and Kit from the mudslide that had trapped them on their way to location filming, but he couldn't believe that was still bothering him. He traced his hands over Devon's shoulders, feeling the tension in the set of the broad muscles. "At least tell us what the nightmare was about," he urged, kneading the tight deltoids with gentle pressure.

"My mum always said talking about a nightmare took away its power," Kit added. "It always worked for me. It isn't as frightening when you think about it calmly."

Feeling like the world's biggest prat for making the two of them worry, Devon shook his head. He should have been stronger, should have been able to keep his reaction inside, but Robert's call had shaken him even more badly than he'd realized. "It was just… I was trapped. Underground. You might have noticed I don't do small spaces well." He swallowed hard, hoping at least part of the truth would be enough to convince his all-too-perceptive lovers that it was just a random bad dream.

Devon's answer was too calculatedly casual, but Jonathan didn't know what good it would serve to push any further. Obviously, Devon didn't intend to share whatever was troubling him. Trying his best not to feel shut out, Jonathan settled for pulling Devon back down beside him on the wide bed. Holding him close as Kit spooned against their lover's other side after flicking off the light, Jonathan ran his hand through the tousled golden hair. "Go back to sleep, babe," he whispered, too wide awake himself to close his eyes. "We've got an early call."

KIT DIDN'T know what was going on, but Devon had been off his game all day. His takes had gotten a little better as lunchtime neared, Lancelot's persona winning out finally over Devon's fatigue; but then, during lunch, Kit saw Devon on the phone, talking very agitatedly, and it seemed he never had recovered. Concerned, Kit decided to see if he could catch Jonathan alone for a minute. Fortunately Niall was finished with Lancelot, but he wanted to shoot an interaction between Arthur and Percival one more time, giving Kit the opportunity he sought as they walked back to the trailer once the director was finished with them. "Did Devon seem to be acting odd to you?" he asked.

"I thought at first he was just tired," Jonathan agreed, rubbing his beard with the back of his knuckles. "Even after he fell back asleep last night, he was pretty restless. But he's pulled some all-nighters before this and never blown his lines the way he did today. He wasn't Lancelot, and that isn't like Devon at all."

Kit sighed, a mixture of relief and concern. At least he wasn't the only one who'd noticed. "He was doing better right up until he got a call at lunchtime," Kit added, not sure Jonathan had seen Devon on the phone. "Do you suppose it was his ex-wife calling and making problems over the divorce?" They had talked about Devon's divorce on more than one occasion. It was one of the few things that really seemed to tear Devon up.

"Maybe, but usually when he's dealing with Marcy or the lawyers he gets quiet. Today he seemed"—Jonathan searched for the right word—"brittle, maybe, like he was angry but trying to hide it by joking around." He shook his head with a frown. "Whatever it is, he obviously doesn't want to talk about it."

"So you think we should just ignore it?" Kit asked, surprised. "I mean, he seemed really upset. I hate to see him like that." He hesitated, thinking for a moment. "You know what it reminds me of?"

"What?" Jonathan asked. He didn't want to just ignore something that was troubling Devon so deeply, but he wasn't sure what they could do to help if their stubborn lover wouldn't confide in them.

"The day we went to the beach house," Kit replied, "when Devon was in such a mood. You remember, he told us a little about his"—he looked around to make sure no one was within earshot—"past. It reminds me of the mood he was in that day."

Jonathan nodded slowly, considering Kit's insight. Not for the first time, he thought how much the people who only saw Kit's beauty and charm underestimated the younger man. He had a sensitivity to the emotions of others that Jonathan envied. "But once we got him to the beach, he was fine. I thought we'd convinced him we didn't hold his past against him—in fact, I thought we'd made it pretty clear that under the right circumstances, we even enjoyed it." He couldn't hold back a small grin as he remembered just how much they'd all enjoyed Devon's dominance that weekend.

"So what changed?" Kit mused. "Could we have done something that triggered another memory? Or I could be miles off the mark, and it could be something totally different. I really think we should at least ask him." He paused outside the door to their trailer, wanting to be in agreement with Jonathan before they stepped inside and faced Devon.

"You're right," Jonathan agreed, "we have to ask. I'm just not sure that in the mood he's in, he won't think we're ganging up on him."

"Do you want to talk to him alone?" Kit suggested, seeing the sense in Jonathan's concern. "Or I could, if you'd prefer."

"Let's see how he's doing now that filming's done for the day first," Jonathan suggested. Kit's idea made sense, but a part of him didn't want either of them to question Devon alone. As unlikely as it seemed at the beginning, they'd managed to make their unconventional threesome work, and his gut told him whatever the problem was, they needed to solve it together.

Kit nodded and opened the door. Stacy and Carol, their makeup artists, were inside waiting for them, but there was no sign of Devon. Putting on his best face, Kit stepped into the trailer and smiled at the women. "Is Devon finished already?" he asked, playing up his surprise.

"He was here and gone in about fifteen minutes," Stacy confirmed. "He didn't say much, but I got the impression he was in a bit of a hurry."

"Yeah," Carol agreed, "he didn't even tease us about our plans for the night the way he usually does."

Jonathan met Kit's eyes over the pictures of his son that covered one corner of his makeup mirror. The fact that Devon hadn't waited for them worried Jonathan even more than his unusual edginess. Something was definitely wrong, and whether it upset Devon more or not, they needed to find out what it was.

Kit saw the determination on Jonathan's face and nodded slightly. They would finish up here and get home as quickly as possible so they could get to the bottom of this. Pasting on a passable smile, he looked at Carol. "So, what *are* your plans for the evening?"

Jonathan closed his eyes and let his mind drift as Stacy worked, only half listening to Kit's and Carol's chatter. He couldn't help but worry that confronting Devon would only serve to drive their prickly lover further away. They had no choice but to try, though. They'd just have to make Devon see that they weren't trying to pry—their concern for him was based in love. He was startled when Stacy broke him out of his reverie with a nudge of his shoulder. "Go home and get some sleep in your own bed, Jonathan," she teased.

"Who says he'll be anywhere near his own bed?" Kit replied with an impish grin. "Last I heard, the king had plans for the evening."

"My only plans right now involve finding some food." Jonathan laughed, careful to keep his tone teasing. He picked up Excalibur from where it leaned against the side of their wardrobe closet, having gotten in the habit of taking it home with him when they left the set so he could practice his swordplay during their rare free time. "C'mon, Percival, let's see if we can hunt down the king's champion and see if he'll join us."

"I could eat," Kit agreed, levering himself out of his chair and heading toward the door. "See you tomorrow, ladies," he added as he stepped out into the cooling night air, shutting the door behind them when Jonathan joined him.

Inside the trailer, Stacy paused in putting away the cleansing supplies and straightening the counter. She met Carol's eyes speculatively. "You think…?" she asked.

Carol looked at the door, then back at Stacy. "Nah," they said in unison after a moment, returning to their work so they could get on with their own plans for the evening.

AFTER DEVON'S uncharacteristic behavior all day, Jonathan wasn't sure they'd find him at home, but he was relieved to see Devon's car parked in the drive as they pulled up behind it. He cocked an eyebrow at Kit, then shrugged. "Looks like the lion came back to his den after all," he muttered. "Let's see if we can find out what's got him so worked up."

Kit nodded and got out of the car, waiting for Jonathan before walking to the door and inside. They no longer knocked at each other's houses, having long since exchanged keys. Deciding to opt for humor, Kit chirped, "Hi, honey, we're home."

Devon grimaced, draining his tumbler of scotch and giving serious consideration to downing another before facing his lovers. At least they didn't seem to be irritated at him for leaving without a word to them. He knew he should try to think up some plausible excuse, but he was still too shaken by the day's events to think of anything clever. Falling back on his experience that partial honesty was the best policy, he turned to greet them, rubbing the back of his head, which really did ache. "Sorry for leaving like that," he grumbled. "I've had the headache from hell all day, and when Niall cut me loose, all I could think of was getting home and taking something to get rid of it."

Kit crossed to where Devon was sitting on the couch, took the glass from his hand, and set it on the table. "If it's a headache that's bothering you, this isn't the cure. I'm sure Jonathan will get you a glass of water. Close your eyes and let me see if I can help you relax," he suggested, his fingers going to Devon's neck to probe the tense muscles.

After carrying the tumbler and the half-empty bottle into the kitchen, Jonathan returned with a fresh glass of ice water and the bottle of aspirin he'd retrieved from Devon's kitchen cabinet. He set the water on the table, shook out two tablets, and handed them to Devon. With a comforting smile, he knelt at Devon's feet, pulled off his shoes and socks, and set them off to the side. Taking one of the strong, slender feet in his hands, he began to rub it soothingly, alternating long, gentle strokes with firmer pressure at the reflexology points on the instep and the base of the toes. "Just relax and let us take care of you, Devon," he urged, watching his lover's face as both he and Kit continued their ministrations.

Letting his eyelids fall closed, Devon arched his shoulders, trying to let go of his tension beneath the calming touches. *This is what's real*, he told himself. *This is what I need to concentrate on. The hell with what that bastard said.* The pounding ache that had inhabited his skull all day long was finally beginning to ease when the ring of the telephone sounded from the kitchen. His eyes snapping open, Devon jumped to his feet before either of the others could think to answer it.

"What the fuck?" Kit muttered, looking at Jonathan. He got up and started after Devon. He had no idea what was going on in Devon's head, but it was past time they found out.

Jonathan caught Kit's arm, preventing him from following Devon and pulling him back to wrap his arms around Kit's narrow hips. "Let him go, Kit-Kat," he urged, looking up from where he still knelt at the foot of the couch. "We'll find out what's bothering him, but he won't appreciate feeling like we're eavesdropping or spying on him."

"It just eats at me to see him so upset." Kit gestured helplessly toward the kitchen. "There's got to be something we can do for him. Something."

"Let's get him fed and take him to bed," Jonathan answered with a waggle of his eyebrows and a leering smile. "Between the two of us, I think we can find some way to clear up his bad mood." He rested his chin on Kit's hipbone, his expression sobering. "And after that, we'll talk."

His pulse slowing with relief, Devon couldn't help but smile when he walked back into the parlor to see his lovers embracing. "Starting without me again?" he growled playfully, hoping the teasing would distract them from the near-panic with which he'd run for the phone. "That was Niall. He wants me in early tomorrow for some reshoots of my scene with Guinevere with new and improved dialogue."

"We were just waiting for you," Kit replied with a grin, relieved to see the black cloud lifted, at least for the moment. "How does dinner sound? I bet we could convince Jonathan to cook if we asked him nicely."

Jonathan glanced up at Devon with a smile in his eyes. They'd keep it light and playful for now; Devon needed relaxation, not confrontation. "And after that, we'll see what else we can cook up," he drawled, reaching out to invite their lover to rejoin them.

COLD SWEAT trickled down his back as he fought to steady his breathing. He couldn't fail again, that was why he was here in the first place, but he could feel the walls closing in on him with each shuddering breath. He twisted against the cramp in his shoulder blade—he'd wrenched it during his struggles, and the cruel pull of the restraints behind his raw back made it worse. The movement sent a shower of damp earth falling over his face, and he couldn't hold back the moan of terror as his lungs seized and his limbs twitched in a futile need to break free, to claw his way out of here, to escape....

Devon's struggles and his sudden cry woke Jonathan with a start. His arms tightened instinctively around the thrashing limbs, but that only made Devon fight harder, his elbow striking Jonathan in the chest. "Devon!" He let go and raised his hands instead to hold the shaggy blond head still. "Devon, wake up. It's okay. It's me, Jonathan," he murmured, trying to keep his own fear out of his voice.

Jonathan's cry woke Kit as well. *Shite!* he thought. *Here we go again.* He settled his hands on Devon's shoulders, kneading soothingly as he added his own soft murmurs to Jonathan's. He didn't know how to get Devon to open up to them, but this had to stop.

Devon's eyes snapped open to meet Jonathan's, his lover's gaze wide with love and concern in the darkened bedroom. He drew a ragged breath and shook his head, the warmth of Jonathan's hands at his temples and Kit's on his shoulders grounding him from the last remnants of the nightmare's terrors. He raised a palm to scrub at his face, horrified to discover his cheek damp with tears. "Fuck," he whispered, wiping at the other cheek in turn. "Fuck, I'm sorry."

"You don't have anything to apologize for," Jonathan insisted, pulling Devon forward to rest their foreheads together. "But you have to tell us what's doing this to you, babe. Let us help you."

Kit's hands drifted lower over Devon's back. "You're covered in sweat!" he observed, surprised. This wasn't just a bad dream. Devon was having night terrors! "Why don't you go with Jonathan and have a quick shower while I get us all a drink, and then we'll talk."

Still half caught in the submissive mindset of the dream, Devon was unresisting as Jonathan helped him to his feet and led him toward the bathroom, murmuring soothing words and wrapping an arm around his trembling shoulders. "The water will make you feel better," Jonathan promised, his eyes meeting Kit's in concern over Devon's lowered head.

Once Jonathan and Devon disappeared into the bathroom, Kit scampered down the steps in search of the brandy and three glasses. He was putting them all on a tray to take back upstairs when the phone rang. Frowning as he glanced at the clock, he wondered who could be calling at such a late hour. Niall had phoned earlier, so surely it wasn't him. "He picked up the receiver. "Hello?"

Silence stretched on the other end of the line as the caller processed the realization that Devon hadn't answered the phone. *So the big blond isn't spending his nights alone!* This could be even more intriguing than he'd hoped. "Have you worn Devon out?" he rumbled in amusement.

"Who is this?" Kit demanded, not recognizing the voice but taking offense at the insinuating tone.

"Tsk, tsk." The caller chuckled softly. "You haven't earned the right to ask any questions… yet." The voice hardened into a tone of command. "Tell Devon I'll be expecting an introduction." Not bothering to wait for a reply, he severed the connection, his groin tightening in anticipation. *Oh yes, this will be good, very good indeed.*

Kit frowned, looking down at the tray. Tea might well have been a better choice, but especially after that phone call, he needed a brandy. Picking up the platter, he headed back upstairs to see if Jonathan and Devon were finished and to join them if they were not.

Growing up in Chicago, NICKI BENNETT spent every Saturday at the central library, losing herself in the world of books. A voracious reader, she eventually found it difficult to find enough of the kind of stories she liked to read and decided to start writing them herself.

Facebook: www.facebook.com/100011754789784

When ARIEL TACHNA was twelve years old, she discovered two things: the French language and romance novels. Those two loves have defined her ever since. By the time she finished high school, she'd written four novels, none of which anyone would want to read now, featuring a young woman who was—you guessed it—bilingual. That girl was everything Ariel wanted to be at age twelve and wasn't.

She now lives on the outskirts of Houston with her husband (who also speaks French), her kids (who understand French even when they're too lazy to speak it back), and their two dogs (who steadfastly refuse to answer any French commands). The cat pretends they're all beneath her, no matter what language they're speaking.

Visit Ariel:
Website: www.arieltachna.com
Facebook: www.facebook.com/ArielTachna
Email: arieltachna@gmail.com

OUT of
BOUNDS

NICKI BENNETT
AND
ARIEL TACHNA

An Out and About Novel

Out and About: No commitments, just fun.

Liam Gruene and his best friend, Kate Weaver, start Out and About to give LGBTQ singles fun, safe, stress-free events where they can meet other LGBTQ singles. Liam hopes—but doesn't really expect—to meet someone for himself in the process.

Erik Jansen moved to Houston a few months ago after a bad breakup. Since his move, he's thrown himself into work at the expense of a social life. When Liam withdraws funds managed by Erik's firm to finance his new venture, it brings Out and About to his attention and he thinks what the hell. It can't be any worse than trying to meet someone at any of the gay clubs and bars around the city.

Erik and Liam hit it off right away, but Erik can't forget that Liam is a client and Out and About is Liam's job. Erik has an ironclad rule against mixing business and pleasure, and that puts Liam firmly out of bounds.

www.dreamspinnerpress.com

CHECKMATE

Nicki Bennett
and
Ariel Tachna

All for Love: Book One

When sword-for-hire Teodoro Ciéza de Vivar accepts a commission to "rescue" Lord Christian Blackwood from unsuitable influences, he has no idea he's landed himself in the middle of a plot to assassinate King Philip IV of Spain and blame the English ambassador for the deed. Nor does he expect the spoiled child he's sent to retrieve to be a handsome, engaging young man.

As Teodoro and Christian face down enemies at every turn, they fall more and more in love, an emotion they can't safely indulge with the threat of the Inquisition looming over them. It will take all their combined guile and influence to outmaneuver the powerful men who would see them separated… or even killed.

www.dreamspinnerpress.com

ALL FOR ONE

Nicki Bennett
and
Ariel Tachna

All for Love: Book Two

Aristide, Léandre, and Perrin pledge only three loyalties in life: their king, their captain, and their passion for each other. So when the musketeers discover a plan to accuse M. de Tréville of treason, the initial impulse to kill the messenger, Benoît, is tempered by their need to unmask the plotter. But their first two suspects, the English ambassador and Cardinal Richelieu, prove to be innocent, forcing the musketeers to delve deeper into the inner machinations of the French court.

Meanwhile, Aristide finds himself falling in love with the ill-fated messenger, a blacksmith without a home who rouses all of his protective, possessive instincts. Benoît, however, has no interest in any man. Torn between desire and duty, Aristide must find a way to protect the king and clear his captain's name—all while heeding the demands of his heart.

www.dreamspinnerpress.com

www.ingramcontent.com/pod-product-compliance
Lightning Source LLC
Chambersburg PA
CBHW050020070726
47506CB00015B/393